Anne Holt is one of Europe's most popular and respected authors. She has worked as a lawyer, a Minister of Justice, an assistant district attorney, a TV news anchor and a journalist. She lives in Norway.

Praise for *Punishment*:

'A thoughtful, tense novel . . . I look forward to the subsequent ones'

Peter Guttridge, *Observer*

'A genuinely puzzling and deeply unsettling thriller. Anne Holt is the latest crime writer to reveal how truly dark it gets in Scandinavia'

Val McDermid

Also by Anne Holt

Punishment
The Final Murder

DEATH IN OSLO

Anne Holt

Translated by Kari Dickson

SPHERE

First published in Norway in 2006 by Piratforlaget AS
First published in Great Britain as a paperback original in 2009 by Sphere

A CIP catalogue record for this book
is available from the British Library.

ISBN 978-0-7515-3716-1

Papers used by Sphere are natural renewable and recyclable
products sourced from well-managed forests and certified
in accordance with the rules of the Forest Stewardship Council.

Mixed Sources
Product group from well-managed
forests and other controlled sources
www.fsc.org Cert no. SGS-COC-004081
© 1996 Forest Stewardship Council
FSC

Typeset in Caslon by M Rules
Printed and bound in Great Britain by
Clays Ltd, St Ives plc

Sphere
An imprint of
Little, Brown Book Group
100 Victoria Embankment
London EC4Y 0DY

An Hachette UK Company
www.hachette.co.uk

www.littlebrown.co.uk

To Amalie Farmen Holt,
my champion,
the apple of my eye, who is growing up

Thursday 20 January 2005

1

I got away with it.

The thought made her pause a moment. The old man in front of her lowered his eyes. His ravaged face was turning blue in the January cold. Helen Lardahl Bentley took a deep breath and finally echoed the words the man had asked her to repeat:

'I do solemnly swear . . .'

Three generations of deeply religious Lardahls had worn illegible the print in the century-old leather-bound Bible. Well hidden behind the Lutheran façade of success, Helen Lardahl Bentley was in fact a sceptic, and therefore preferred to take the oath with her right hand resting on something she at least could wholeheartedly believe in: her own family history.

'. . . that I will faithfully execute . . .'

She tried to hold his eye. She wanted to stare at the Chief Justice, just as everyone else was staring at her – the enormous crowd that stood shivering in the winter sun. The demonstrators were too far from the podium to be heard, but she knew they were chanting, 'Traitor! Traitor!' over and over, until the words were drowned out by the steel doors of the special armoured vehicles that the police had rolled into position early that morning.

'. . . the office of the President of the United States . . .'

The whole world was watching Helen Lardahl Bentley. They watched her with hate or admiration, with curiosity or suspicion, and perhaps, in the quieter corners of the world, with indifference. For those few seemingly never-ending minutes, she was at the centre of the universe, caught in the crossfire of hundreds of TV cameras, and she must not, *would not* think about it.

Not now, not ever.

She pressed her hand even harder on the Bible and lifted her chin a touch.

'. . . and will, to the best of my ability, preserve, protect and defend the Constitution of the United States.'

The crowd cheered. The demonstrators were removed. The guests on the podium gave her congratulatory smiles, some heartfelt, some reserved. Friends and critics, colleagues, family, and the odd enemy who had never wished her well all mouthed the same word, silently or with loud joy: 'Congratulations!'

Again she felt a flicker of the fear she had repressed for over twenty years. And then, only seconds into her office as the forty-fourth president of the United States of America, Helen Lardahl Bentley straightened her back, ran a determined hand through her hair, and looking out over the crowd, decided once and for all:

I got away with it and it's time I finally forgot.

2

The paintings were certainly not beautiful.

He did not care for one in particular. It made him feel seasick. When he leant in close to the canvas, he saw that the wavy yellow and orange strokes had cracked into an infinite web of tiny fine lines, like camel dung in the baking sun. He was tempted to stroke his fingers over the grotesque, screaming mouth, but he didn't. The painting had already been damaged in transport. The railings to the right of the agonised figure now had a sad fringe of threads that curved out into the room.

Getting someone to repair the large tear was out of the question, as it would require an expert. And the very reason that these paintings were now hanging in one of Abdallah al-Rahman's more modest palaces on the outskirts of Riyadh was that he always avoided experts, whenever possible. He believed in honest handicraft. He had never seen the point in using a motor saw when a simple knife would do. The paintings had been stolen from a poorly secured museum in the Norwegian capital. He had no idea who had stolen them or who had handled them on their journey to this windowless gym. He didn't need to know who these petty criminals were; they would no doubt end up in prison in their respective countries without being able to say anything of any real consequence as to the whereabouts of the paintings.

Abdallah al-Rahman preferred the female figure, though there was something repulsive about her too. Even after more than sixteen years in the West, ten of which he had spent in prestigious schools in England and the US, he was still disgusted by the woman's bare breasts and the vulgar way in which she offered herself up, indifferent and licentious at the same time.

He turned away. All he had on was a pair of wide white shorts. He stepped back up on to the treadmill, barefoot, and picked up the remote control. The belt accelerated. Sound was coming from the speakers on either side of the colossal plasma TV screen on the opposite wall:

'. . . *protect and defend the Constitution of the United States.*'

He simply could not understand it. When Helen Lardahl Bentley had been a senator, he had been impressed by the woman's courage. Having achieved the third highest grades in her year at the prestigious Vassar College, the short-sighted, plump Helen Lardahl had then fast-tracked to a PhD at Harvard. By the time she was forty, she was well married and had been made a partner in the sixth largest law firm in the US, which in itself demonstrated extraordinary competence and a healthy dose of cynicism and intelligence. She was also slim, blonde and without glasses, which was smart too.

But to stand as presidential candidate was downright arrogant.

And now she had been elected, blessed and sworn in.

Abdallah al-Rahman smiled as he increased the speed of the treadmill with one push of a button. The hard skin on the bottom of his feet burned on the rubber belt. He increased the speed again, right up to his pain threshold.

'It's just incredible,' he groaned in perfect American, secure in the knowledge that no one in the whole world would hear him through the metre-thick walls and the triple-insulated door. 'She actually thinks she's got away with it!'

3

'An historic moment,' Johanne Vik said, and folded her hands, as if she felt obliged to say a prayer for the new president of the United States.

The woman in the wheelchair smiled, but said nothing.

'No one can say that that isn't progress,' Johanne continued. 'After forty-three men in succession . . . finally a female president!'

'. . . *the office of the President of the United States . . .*'

'You have to agree that it's quite something,' Johanne insisted, her eyes glued to the TV screen again. 'I actually thought they'd elect an Afro-American before they accepted a woman in office.'

'Next time round it will be Condoleezza Rice,' the other woman said. 'Two birds with one stone.'

Not that that would be much progress, she thought to herself. White, yellow, black or red, man or woman, the post of American president was male, no matter what the pigmentation or sex of the person was.

'It's not Helen Bentley's feminine qualities that have got her to where she is,' she said slowly, bordering on disinterested. 'And definitely not Condoleezza Rice's black heritage. Within four years they cave in. And that's neither minority-friendly nor feminine.'

'That's pretty—'

'What makes those women impressive is not their femininity or their slave heritage. They'll milk it, of course, for all it's worth. But what's really impressive is . . .'

She grimaced and tried to sit up straight in the wheelchair.

'Is something wrong?' Johanne asked.

'No. What is impressive is that . . .'

She braced her arms against the armrests, lifted herself and twisted her body slightly closer to the back of the chair. Then she absent-mindedly smoothed her sweater down over her chest.

'. . . they must have decided bloody early on,' she said finally.

'I don't understand . . .'

'To work so hard. To be so clever. Never to do anything wrong. Never to make mistakes. Never, never to be caught with their trousers down. In fact, it's totally unbelievable.'

'But there's always something . . . some little secret . . . Even the deeply religious George W had—'

The woman in the wheelchair lit up with a sudden smile and turned towards the living room door. A small girl of about eighteen months peeked guiltily round the door. The woman held out her hand.

'Come here, sweetheart. You should be asleep.'

'Does she manage to get out of the cot by herself?' Johanne asked with some concern.

'She goes to sleep in our bed. Come here, Ida!'

The child padded over the floor and let herself be lifted up on to the woman's lap. Her black hair curled over her round cheeks and her eyes were ice blue, with a clear black ring round the iris. The little girl gave the guest a shy smile of recognition and then snuggled down.

'It's strange that she looks so like you,' Johanne said, leaning forward and stroking the girl's soft cheek with the back of her hand.

'Only the eyes,' the other woman replied. 'It's the colour. People are always deceived by the colour. Of the eyes.'

Once again they were silent.

In Washington DC, the people exhaled grey steam in the harsh January light. The Chief Justice was helped down from the podium; from the back he looked like a sorcerer as he was led gently indoors. The newly elected president was bare-headed and smiled broadly as she pulled her pale pink coat closer.

In Oslo, evening was advancing stealthily outside the windows in Krusesgate and the streets were wet and free of snow.

An odd-looking character came into the large living room. She limped, dragging one foot behind her, like the caricature of a villain in an old-fashioned film. Her hair was tired and thin and looked like a bird's nest. Her legs resembled two pencils and went straight down from under her apron into a pair of tartan slippers.

'That girl should've been in her bed ages ago,' she muttered without saying hello. 'Nothin' gets done right in this house. She should sleep in her own bed, I've said it a thousand million times. Come over here, my princess.'

Without waiting for the woman in the wheelchair or the little girl to respond, she scooped the child up on to her difficult hip and limped back the way she had come.

'Wish I had a woman-who-does like her,' Johanne sighed.

'It has its advantages.'

They sat in silence again. CNN switched between various commentators, interspersed with clips from the podium, where the elite gathering of politicians had admitted defeat in the face of the cold and were leaving to prepare themselves for the greatest swearing-in celebrations the US capital had ever seen. The Democrats had achieved their three goals. They had beaten a president who was up for re-election, which was a feat in itself. They had won by a greater margin than they had dared to hope for. And they had won with a woman at the helm. None of these facts were to be underplayed. Pictures of Hollywood stars who had already arrived in town or who were expected in the course of the afternoon flickered on the screen. The entire weekend was to be filled with celebrations and fireworks. Madam President would go from one party to the next, receiving praise and giving endless thanks to her helpers, and would undoubtedly change into an array of outfits along the way. And in between it all, she would reward those worthy of reward with posts and positions, compare campaign efforts and financial donations, assess loyalty and measure ability, disappoint many and please a few, just as forty-three men had done before her in the course of the nation's 230 years of history.

'Do you think you can sleep after something like that?'

'Sorry?'

'Do you think she'll be able to sleep tonight?' Johanne asked.

'You are funny.' The other woman smiled. 'Of course she'll be able to sleep. You don't get to where she is without sleeping. She's a fighter, Johanne. Don't let her neat figure and feminine clothes deceive you.'

When the woman in the wheelchair turned the TV off, they heard a lullaby being sung elsewhere in the flat.

'Ai-ai-ai-ai-ai-BOFF-BOFF.'

Johanne chuckled. 'That would frighten the life out of my children.'

The other woman steered the wheelchair over to a low coffee table and lifted up a cup. She took a sip, wrinkled her nose and put the cup down again.

'I guess I should go home,' Johanne said, though it sounded like a question.

'Yes,' the other woman replied. 'You should.'

'Thank you for your help. For all your help over the past few months.'

'There's not much to thank me for.'

Johanne rubbed her lower back lightly before pushing her uncontrollable hair back behind her ears and straightening her glasses with a slim index finger.

'Yes, there is,' she said.

'I think you just have to learn to live with it. There's nothing you can do about the fact that she exists.'

'She threatened my children. She's dangerous. Talking to you, being taken seriously, being believed . . . it's at least made things easier.'

'It's nearly a year ago now,' the woman in the wheelchair continued. 'It was last year that things were really serious. What happened this winter . . . well, I can't help thinking that she's . . . teasing you.'

'Teasing me?'

10

'She triggers your curiosity. You are a seeking person, Johanne. That's why you do research. Your curiosity is what gets you involved in investigations that you actually want nothing to do with, and that's what is driving you to get to the bottom of what it is this woman wants from you. It was your curiosity that . . . that brought you here. And it is—'

'I have to go,' Johanne interrupted, with a fleeting smile. 'No point in going through it all again. But thank you all the same. I can see myself out.'

She stayed standing where she was for a moment. She was struck by how beautiful the paralysed woman was. She was slim, almost too thin, with an oval face and eyes that were remarkably like the little girl's: ice blue, clear, and nearly leached of colour, with a broad black ring round the iris. Her mouth was shapely, with a clearly defined upper lip, surrounded by delicate, beautiful wrinkles that indicated that she must be well over forty. She was elegantly dressed in a light blue V-necked cashmere sweater and jeans that were presumably not bought in Norway. A simple, big diamond hung, swinging gently, in the hollow of her neck.

'You look lovely, by the way!'

The woman smiled faintly, almost embarrassed.

'See you again soon,' she said and rolled over to the window, where she remained sitting with her back to her guest, without saying goodbye.

4

The snow lay knee-deep over the long strips of field. It had been frosty for a long time now. The naked trees in the woods to the west were glazed with ice. Every now and then his snowshoes broke through the rough crust on the snow, making him nearly lose his balance for a moment. Al Muffet stopped and caught his breath.

The sun was about to go down behind the hills to the west. Only the odd bird cry broke the silence. The snow glittered in the golden-red evening light and the man with the snowshoes stood for a moment to watch a hare that leapt out from the woods and zigzagged down to the stream on the other side of the field.

Al Muffet breathed in as deeply as he could.

He had never doubted that he had done the right thing. When his wife died and he was left with three daughters aged eight, eleven and sixteen, it took only a matter of weeks for him to realise that his career at one of Chicago's prestigious universities was simply not compatible with sole responsibility for his children. Their finances also implied that he should move what was left of his family to a quiet place in the country as soon as possible.

Three weeks and two days after the family had moved to their new home at Rural Route #4 in Farmington, Maine, two passenger planes each flew into a tower on Manhattan. A few minutes later, another thundered into the Pentagon. That same evening, Al Muffet closed his eyes in silent gratitude for his foresight: already, as a student, he had shed his real name, Ali Shaeed Muffasa. The children were sensibly called Sheryl, Catherine and Louise, and had all inherited their mother's delightful snub nose and ash-blonde hair.

Now, a good three years later, barely a day passed without him enjoying his country life. The girls were blossoming, and he had rediscovered the joys of clinical practice remarkably quickly. His practice was varied, a good mixture of small animals, pets and farm animals: poorly canaries, dogs giving birth, and every now and then an aggressive ox that needed a bullet through the head. Every Thursday he played chess down at the club. He went to the cinema with the girls on Saturdays. On Monday evenings he generally played a couple of games of squash with a neighbour who had a court in a converted barn. One day followed the next, a steady flow of pleasing monotony.

Only on Sundays were the Muffets any different from the rest of the community. They did not go to church. Al Muffet had lost any contact with Allah a long time ago, but had no plans of getting to know God. Initially, there was some reaction: veiled questions at parents' meetings, ambiguous remarks at the petrol station or by the popcorn machine at the cinema on a Saturday night.

But these gradually petered out.

Everything passes, Al Muffet thought to himself as he struggled to unearth his watch, which was buried under his mitten and his down jacket. He had to get a move on. His youngest daughter was going to make dinner, and from experience, he knew that it was worthwhile being at home when she did. Unless he wanted to be greeted by an extravagant meal and a bare goodies store. The last time Louise had made dinner it had been a Monday night and she had served up a four-course meal of foie gras, truffle risotto, and the venison he had got in the autumn and intended to have for their annual Christmas dinner with the neighbours.

The cold had more bite now that the sun had gone down. He took off his mittens and put his palms to his cheeks. A few seconds later he started to walk, with the long, slow snowshoe steps that he had finally mastered.

He had not watched the swearing-in of the President, but not because it would bother him in any way. When Helen Lardahl Bentley had entered the public arena, big time, ten years ago, he

13

had in fact been horrified. He remembered with unnerving clarity that morning in Chicago, when he was lying at home in bed with flu, channel-hopping through his fever. Helen Lardahl, so different from how he remembered her, making a speech in the Senate. Gone were the glasses. The puppy fat that had stayed with her far into her twenties had fallen away. Only characteristics such as the determined diagonal movement through the air with an open, flat hand to underline every second point convinced him that it really was the same woman.

How does she dare? he'd thought at the time.

And then he had gradually come to accept it.

Al Muffet stopped again and drew the ice-cold air into his lungs. He was down by the stream now, where the water was still running under a lid of clear ice.

She trusted him, it was simple. She must have chosen to trust the promise he had made back then, a lifetime ago, in another life and in a completely different place. Given her position, it would have been simple to find out whether he was still alive, still lived in the US.

But now she had got herself elected as the world's most powerful national leader, in a country where morality was a virtue and double standards a necessity.

He stepped across the stream and scrambled over the mounds of snow left by the snowplough. Suddenly his pulse was so fast that his ears were ringing. It was so long ago, he thought, and took off his snowshoes. With one in each hand, he started to run down the small, wintry road.

'We got away with it,' he whispered in rhythm with his own heavy steps. 'I am to be trusted. I am a man of honour. We got away with it.'

He was far too late. No doubt he would get home to oysters and an open bottle of champagne. Louise would say it was a celebration, in honour of the first female president of America.

Monday 16 May 2005

1

'Bloody great timing. Who the hell chose that date?'
The Director General of the Norwegian Police Security Service, PST, brushed a hand over his cropped ginger hair.

'You know perfectly well,' replied a slightly younger woman, who was watching an old TV screen that was balanced on a filing cabinet in the corner of the office. The colours were faded and a black stripe flickered at the bottom of the image. 'It was the Prime Minister. Great opportunity, you know, to show the old country in all its national romantic glory.'

'Drunkenness, trouble and rubbish everywhere,' grunted Peter Salhus. 'Not very romantic. Our national day has become pure hell. And how in God's name' – he was shouting now as he pointed at the TV – 'do they think it will be possible to look after that woman?'

Madam President was about to set foot on Norwegian soil. In front of her were three men in dark overcoats. The characteristic earpieces were clearly visible. Despite the low cloud, they were all wearing sunglasses, as if they were trying to parody themselves. Their doubles were coming down the steps from Air Force One behind the President; just as big, just as brooding and just as devoid of expression.

'Looks like they could do the job on their own,' Anna Birkeland quipped, nodding at the screen. 'And I hope that no one else shares your . . . pessimism, shall we say. I'm actually quite worried. You don't normally . . .'

She broke off. Peter Salhus didn't say anything either, his eyes fixed on the TV screen. It was not like him to have such an outburst. Quite the contrary: when, a couple of years previously, he was appointed as director general, a post that historically had some embarrassing blemishes, it was because of his placid and pleasant nature, and not because of his military background. The protests from the left had been muted by the revelation that Salhus had been a young socialist. He had joined the army at nineteen in order to 'expose American imperialism', he explained with a smile in an interview broadcast on TV. When he then gave an earnest one-and-a-half-minute account of the threats facing modern society, which most people could recognise, the battle was as good as won. Peter Salhus had changed out of his uniform and into a suit, and moved into the PST offices, if not with universal acclaim, then at least with cross-party support behind him. He was well liked by his staff and respected by his colleagues abroad. His cropped military hair and salt-and-pepper beard gave him an air of old-fashioned, masculine confidence. Paradoxically, he was in fact a popular head of security.

And Anna Birkeland had never seen this side of him.

The light in the ceiling was reflected in the sweat on his brow. He rocked his body backwards and forwards, apparently without realising. When Anna Birkeland looked at his hands, they were clenched tight.

'What is it?' she asked in such a quiet voice that it almost seemed she didn't want an answer.

'This was not a good idea.'

'Why haven't you stopped it, then? If you're as worried as you seem to be, you should have—'

'I've tried. And you know it.'

Anna Birkeland got up and walked over to the window. Spring was not springing in the pale grey afternoon light. She put her palm up to the glass. An outline of condensation flared up briefly, then disappeared.

'You had your objections, Peter. You outlined possible scenarios and pointed out possible problems. But that's not the same as trying to stop something.'

'We live in a democracy,' he said. As far as Anna could make out, there was no irony in his voice. 'It is the politicians who decide. In situations like this, I'm merely an adviser. If I could decide—'

'Then we would keep everyone out?' She turned suddenly. 'Everyone,' she repeated, louder this time. 'Everyone who might in any way threaten this idyllic village called Norway.'

'Yes,' he replied. 'Perhaps.'

His smile was difficult to interpret. On the TV screen, the President was being led from the enormous jet towards a temporary lectern. A man dressed in a dark suit fiddled with the microphone.

'Everything went well when Bill Clinton came,' Anna said and carefully bit her nail. 'He went walkabout in town, drank beer, and greeted every man and his dog. Even went for cake. Without it being planned and agreed in advance.'

'Yes, but that was before.'

'Before what?'

'Before nine/eleven.'

Anna sat down again. She ran her hands up her neck and lifted her shoulder-length hair. Then she looked down and took a breath as if about to say something, but instead released an audible sigh. The President had already finished her short speech on the silent TV.

'Oslo Police is responsible for the bodyguards now,' she said finally. 'So, strictly speaking, the President's visit is not your concern. Ours, I mean. And in any case . . .' she waved a hand at the filing cabinet under the TV, 'we've found nothing. No movement, no activity. Not among any of the groups we're aware of here. Not even on the peripheries. We've received nothing from elsewhere to indicate that this will be anything other than a friendly visit from . . .' her voice took on the intonation of a newsreader, 'a president who wishes to honour her homeland and the USA's great ally, Norway. There is nothing to indicate that anyone has other plans.'

'Which is strange, isn't it? This is . . .'

He held back. Madam President got into a dark limousine. A woman with lightning hands helped her with her coat. It was hanging out of the car and about to be caught by the door. The Norwegian prime minister smiled and waved at the cameras, a bit too vigorously, with childish delight at having such an important visitor.

'There goes the world's most hated person,' Peter finished and nodded at the screen. 'I know that plots are hatched to assassinate the woman every day. Every bloody day. In the States, in Europe. In the Middle East. Everywhere.'

Anna Birkeland sniffed, and wiped the tip of her nose with her finger.

'But that's always been the case, Peter. And she's not the only one that people want to assassinate. All over the world intelligence services are constantly uncovering irregularities so that they don't become realities. And America has got the world's best intelligence service, so—'

'People in the know might dispute that,' he interrupted.

'And the world's most efficient police organisation,' she continued, unaffected. 'I don't think you need lose any sleep worrying about the President of the United States of America.'

Peter Salhus got up and pressed the off button with his great index finger, just as the camera zoomed in for a close-up of the small American flag attached to the side of the bonnet. It was whipped into a frenzy of red, white and blue as the car accelerated.

The screen went black.

'It's not her I'm worried about,' Peter Salhus said. 'Not really.'

'Now I really don't know what you're talking about,' Anna exclaimed, with obvious impatience. 'I'm off. You know where to find me if you need me.'

She picked up a voluminous folder from the floor, straightened her back and walked to the door. She had half opened it when she turned and asked, 'If it's not Bentley you're worried about, who is it?'

'Us,' he replied, sharp and concise. 'I'm worried about what might happen to us.'

The door handle felt strangely cold against her palm. She took her hand away. The door slowly closed again.

'Not the two of us.' He smiled at the window; he knew she was blushing, and didn't want to look. 'I'm worried about . . .' He drew a big, vague circle of nothing with his hands. 'Norway,' he finished, and finally looked her in the eye. 'What the hell will happen to Norway if something goes wrong?'

She wasn't sure that she understood what he meant.

2

Madam President was finally alone.

She had a headache clinging to the bottom of her skull, as she always did at the end of a day like today. She sat down carefully in one of the cream armchairs. The headache was an old friend, a frequent visitor. Medicine didn't help, probably because she had never disclosed this problem to a doctor and therefore had never used anything other than over-the-counter painkillers. Her headache came at night, when everything was done and she could finally kick off her shoes and put her feet up. Read a book, or maybe close her eyes and think about nothing before falling asleep. But she couldn't. She had to sit still, leaning back, with her arms out from her body and her feet firmly on the ground. Her eyes half closed, never fully; the red darkness behind closed eyes just made the pain worse. She needed a bit of light. A sliver of light between her lashes. Loose arms with open hands. Relaxed torso. She had to shift her attention as far away from her head as possible, to her feet, which she pressed as hard as she could into the carpet. Again and again, to the beat of her pulse. Don't think. Don't close your eyes. Press your feet down. And again, and again.

Eventually, in a delicate balance between sleep, pain and wakefulness, the claws at the back of her head slowly loosened their grip. She never knew how long an attack would last. Generally it was about a quarter of an hour, though sometimes she stared in horror at her watch and could not believe that that was the time. Occasionally, it was only a matter of seconds.

As was the case this time, she realised when she looked at the alarm clock.

She tentatively lifted her right hand and wrapped it round her neck. She continued to sit absolutely still. Her feet were still pulsing against the floor, heel to toe and back again. The cool of her palm made the skin contract across her shoulders. The pain had really vanished, completely. She let out a sigh of relief and got up as slowly as she had sat down.

The worst thing about the attacks was perhaps not so much the pain as the fact that she felt so awake afterwards. Over the past twenty years or so, Helen Bentley had learnt to accept that sleep was something she sometimes just had to do without. She could go for months on end with no pain, but the armchair scenario had almost become a midnight ritual for her over the past year. And as she was a woman who never let anything go to waste, not even time, she constantly surprised her colleagues by how well prepared she was for early-morning meetings.

The US had, unwittingly, elected a president who normally had to make do with only four hours' sleep. And if it was up to her, her insomnia would remain a secret that she shared only with her husband, who had learnt after many years to sleep with the light on.

But now she was alone.

Neither Christopher nor her daughter, Billie, was with her on this trip. Madam President had gone to great pains to stop them. She still cringed when she remembered the astonished disappointment in her husband's eyes when she made the decision to travel alone. The trip to Norway was the President's first official visit abroad after having been sworn in, and it was of a purely representative nature. Not only that, it also was to a country that her twenty-one-year-old daughter would have had great pleasure and interest in visiting. There were a thousand and one good reasons why the family should go, as originally planned.

But she had made them stay at home, all the same.

Helen Bentley took a few cautious steps, as if she was afraid that the floor wouldn't hold. Her headache had definitely disappeared. She rubbed her forehead with her thumb and index finger as she looked around the room. It was the first time she had really noticed how beautifully the suite was designed. It was done out in cool Scandinavian style, with blond wood, light materials and perhaps a little too much glass and steel. The lights in particular caught her attention. The lamp bowls were made of sand-blasted glass. Though they were not all the same shape, they harmonised with each other in a way that meant that they somehow belonged together without her understanding why. She ran her hand over one of them. A delicate warmth seeped through from the low-wattage bulb.

They're everywhere, she thought to herself and stroked her fingers over the glass. They're everywhere, and they'll look after me.

She could not get used to it. No matter where she was, whatever the occasion, whoever she was with, with no consideration for time or discretion, they were always there. Of course she understood that it had to be like that. But equally, she had realised after barely a month in office that she would never actually get used to the more-or-less invisible bodyguards. The bodyguards who were around her during the day were one thing. She quickly learnt to accept them as part of daily life. She could distinguish them from one another. They had faces. Some of them even had names, names that she was allowed to use, even though she realised that they were likely to be false.

The other ones were worse. The countless invisible ones; the armed, concealed shadows that constantly surrounded her without her ever really knowing where they were. It made her feel uncomfortable; a misplaced sense of paranoia. They were watching over her. They wished her well, to the extent that they actually felt anything more than a sense of duty. She thought she had prepared herself for life as a target, until some weeks before she was sworn in as president, she realised it was impossible to prepare yourself for a life like this.

Not completely, anyway.

Throughout her political career, she had focused on opportunities and power, and judiciously manoeuvred herself in that direction. She had of course met with opposition en route, professional and political, but also a fair dose of ill will and agitation, envy and malevolence. She had chosen a political career in a country with a long history of personified hatred, organised slander, unprecedented misuse of power, and even assassination. On 22 November 1963, as a horrified thirteen-year-old, she had seen her father cry for the first time, and for some days afterwards had believed that the end of the world was nigh. She was still a teenager when Bobby Kennedy and Martin Luther King were killed in the same tempestuous decade. But she had never actually thought of the assassinations as personal. For the young Helen Lardahl, political assassination was an abominable attack on *ideals*, on the very values and attitudes that she greedily lapped up. Nearly forty years on, she still got shivers down her spine whenever she heard the start of the 'I have a dream' speech.

When two hijacked planes ripped through the World Trade Center in September 2001, she therefore interpreted it in the same way, as did nearly three hundred million of her compatriots – it was an attack against the American ideal. The close to three thousand victims, the unbelievable material damage, the permanent change to the Manhattan skyline all merged into a greater whole: the American dream.

Thus every victim, every courageous firefighter, every fatherless child and every broken family became a symbol of something far greater than themselves. And this made it easier for the nation and those left behind to bear the loss.

That was how she had experienced it. That was how she had felt.

Only now, now that she had taken on the role of Target No. 1, had she started to understand the underlying deceit. Now it was she who was the symbol. The problem was that she didn't feel that she was a symbol; she was more than that. She was a mother. She was a wife and a daughter, a friend and a sister. For nearly two decades she had worked solely towards achieving this goal of becoming the President of the United States. She wanted power, she wanted possibility. And she had succeeded.

At the same time, the deceit had become increasingly clear to her.

And it could be very bothersome on sleepless nights.

She remembered one of the funerals she had gone to, in the way that they had all attended funerals and memorial services – senators and congressmen, governors and other prominent figures, all wanting to be seen to be sharing the Great American Grief, in full view of photographers and journalists. The deceased was a woman who had recently been employed as a secretary in a company that had its offices on the seventy-third floor of the North Tower.

Her husband could not have been much more than thirty. He sat there, on the front bench in the chapel, with a toddler on each knee. A little girl of about six or seven sat beside him, stroking her father's hand over and over, almost manically, as if she already understood that he was about to lose his mind and needed to be reminded of her existence. The photographers concentrated on the children: the twins, aged one or two, and the lovely little girl, dressed in black, a colour that no child should have to wear. Helen Bentley, on the other hand, stared at the father as she passed the coffin. What she saw in his face was not grief, or certainly not grief as she knew it. His features were distorted by despair and anger, pure simple fear. This man could not understand how life would go on. He had no idea how he was going to manage to look after the children. He didn't know how he was going to make ends meet, to have enough money to pay the rent and school fees, to have the energy to raise three children on his own. He had achieved his fifteen minutes of fame because his wife had been in the wrong place at the wrong time and was now absurdly exalted as an American hero.

We used them, Helen Bentley thought to herself, and stared out of the panorama windows that faced south over the dark Oslo Fjord. There was still a strange, pale blue light in the sky, as if it wasn't quite ready to accept the night. We used them as symbols to make people toe the line. And we succeeded. But what is he doing now? What happened to him? And the kids? Why have I never dared to find out?

Her guardians were out there. In the corridors. In the rooms around her. On the roof and in parked cars; they were everywhere, looking after her.

She had to get some sleep. The bed looked inviting, with a big, down-filled duvet, like the one she'd had as a child in her grandmother's attic in Minnesota; when she was blissfully ignorant and could close the world out simply by pulling a checked duvet over her head.

This time 'the people' would not close ranks. That was why it was worse and so much more threatening.

The last thing she did before falling asleep was to set the alarm on her mobile phone. It was half past two, and bizarrely, it was already starting to get light again outside.

Tuesday 17 May 2005

1

As always, the Norwegian national day had started before the devil got his shoes on. Oslo Police had already arrested more than twenty teenagers out celebrating their final year in school, for being drunk and disorderly. They were now sleeping it off while they waited for their fathers to come and bail them out with indulgent smiles. The rest of the school-leavers, or 'Russ' as they were popularly called, were doing their best to ensure that nobody slept in or was late for the national-day parade. Cheap buses that had been converted and fitted with sound systems that cost the earth boomed through the streets. Here and there, a small child was already dressed up and out, and they ran like puppy dogs after the painted Russ buses and begged for the traditional Russ cards from the school-leavers. Groups of war veterans gathered in graveyards – fewer and fewer for each year that passed – to celebrate peace and freedom. Brass bands trudged through the town to a half-hearted march. Off-key trumpet notes ensured that anyone who might still against all odds be asleep could now just as well get up and have the first coffee of the day. In the city's parks, confused junkies emerged from under their blankets and plastic bags, unable to grasp what was happening.

The weather was the same as normal, with clouds breaking up to the south, but no sign that the temperature would rise. On the contrary, there was every reason to expect a shower or two, judging by the grey skies to the north. Most of the trees were still half naked, though the birch trees were now sporting buds and pollen-saturated catkins. All over the country, parents forced woollen underwear on their children, who had already started to pester them for ice cream and hot dogs, long before breakfast. Flags fluttered and flag ropes rattled on a brisk breeze.

The kingdom of Norway was ready to celebrate.

A policewoman stood shivering outside a hotel in the centre of Oslo. She had been standing there all night. As discreetly as possible, she looked at her watch at steadily shorter intervals. Someone would be coming to replace her soon so she could knock off. She had managed to snatch the occasional conversation with a colleague who was posted about fifty or sixty metres away, but apart from that, the night had been interminable. For a while she had tried to pass the time by guessing who was a bodyguard. But then, at around two in the morning, the steady stream of people coming and going had stopped. As far as she could see, there was no security on the roofs. No dark, easily identifiable cars with secret agents had cruised by since the American president had been dropped off and escorted into the hotel around midnight. They were, of course, still there. She knew that, even if she was only a constable who had been sent to decorate the outside of the hotel in a newly cleaned uniform – and to get cystitis.

A cortège of cars was approaching the main entrance of the hotel. The street was normally open to all traffic, but now it was closed, with loose metal barriers creating a temporary square outside the modest entrance.

The constable opened up two of the barriers, as she had been instructed to do in advance. Then she retreated to the pavement. She edged her way towards the entrance. Maybe she could catch a glimpse of the President up close, on her way to the national-day breakfast. That would be a welcome reward for a hellish night. Not that she was usually bothered about that sort of thing, but the woman was the most powerful person in the world, after all.

No one stopped her.

Just as the first car pulled up, a man came sprinting out of the hotel door. He had a bare head and was not wearing an overcoat. He had a walkie-talkie in a holster over his shoulder, and the constable could see the top of the butt of a gun just inside his open jacket. His face was remarkably devoid of expression.

A man in a dark suit got out of the passenger seat of the first car. He was small and compact. Before he was fully out of the car, the man with the walkie-talkie, who had come to meet him, grabbed hold of his arm. They stood like this for a few seconds, the larger man with his hand on the smaller man's arm, as they had a whispered conversation.

The small Norwegian did not have the same poker face as the American. His mouth fell open for a few seconds, before he pulled himself together and straightened up. The policewoman took a couple of tentative steps closer to the car. She still couldn't make out what they were saying.

Four other men had come out of the hotel. One of them was having a muted conversation on a mobile phone while he stared blankly at a ghastly polished steel sculpture of a man standing waiting for a taxi. The three other agents were gesturing to someone the policewoman couldn't see, and then, as if on command, they all looked in her direction.

'Hey, you! Officer! You!'

The policewoman gave an uncertain smile. Then she lifted her hand and pointed to herself with a questioning expression.

'Yes, you,' one of the men repeated, and bounded over to her. 'ID, please.'

She produced her police ID from her inside pocket. The man looked at the Norwegian coat of arms. Without even turning the card to check the photograph, he handed it back.

'The main door,' he hissed, as he turned to run back. 'No one in, no one out. Got it?'

'Yes, yes.' The policewoman swallowed, wide-eyed. 'Yes, sir!'

But the man was already too far away to hear that she had eventually remembered how to say it politely. Her colleague who been on the same night shift was also heading towards the main entrance. He had obviously been given the same instructions as she had, and seemed uncertain. All four cars in the cortège suddenly accelerated, spun out of the square and disappeared.

'What's going on?' whispered the constable, positioning herself in front of the double glass doors. Her colleague looked utterly confused. 'What the hell is going on?'

'We've just got to . . . We've just got to watch this door, I think.'

'Yeah, I realised that. But . . . why? What's happened?'

An elderly lady tried to get the doors to open from inside. She was wearing a dark red coat and a funny blue hat, with white flowers around the rim. Pinned to her chest she had a 17th of May ribbon that was so long it almost touched the ground. She eventually managed to fight her way out.

'Excuse me, ma'am. I'm afraid you'll have to wait a while.' The policewoman gave her friendliest smile.

'Wait?' the woman exclaimed in a hostile voice. 'I have to meet my daughter and granddaughter in quarter of an hour! I've got a place at—'

'I'm sure it won't be long,' the policewoman assured her. 'If you could just . . .'

'Can I be of help?' asked a man in a hotel uniform, as he strode quickly over from the reception desk. 'Madam, if you'd like to come this way . . .'

'*Oh, say! can you seeee, by the dawn's early liiight . . .*'

A deep voice suddenly resounded through the morning air. The policewoman spun round. A large man in a dark coat carrying a microphone was approaching from the north-west, where the blocked road led to a parking place on the south side of the main railway station. He was followed by a brass band.

'*What so prouuudly we hailed . . .*'

She recognised him immediately, and the musicians' white uniforms were unmistakable as well. She suddenly remembered that, according to plan, the Sinsen Youth Brass Band and the man with the powerful voice were going to help make the President feel at home at seven thirty sharp, before she was taken to the palace for breakfast.

A roll of drums grew into a roll of thunder. The singer took a

34

deep breath and gathered his strength for a new burst: '*At the twilight's last gleeeaming . . .*'

The brass band was trying to play something that resembled a march, whereas the singer obviously preferred a more theatrical style. He was always a note or two behind, and his exaggerated movements were somewhat in contrast with the musicians' military posture.

Madam President had still not appeared. It was a while since the cortège had driven off. The Americans had barely managed to bark out their instructions before dashing back into the hotel foyer, and were now nowhere to be seen behind the closed doors. Only the old woman with the hat was still there, fuming behind the glass. Someone had obviously immobilised the door-opener. The young policewoman was standing on her own and had no idea what to do. Her colleague had vanished without her knowing where to. She wasn't even sure if it was right for her to take orders from a foreigner. And no one had come to relieve her, as agreed.

She should perhaps call someone.

Maybe it was the cold, or the nerves that were inevitable with such a high-profile job. Whatever the reason, the forty-strong brass band and the theatrical singer continued doggedly with their rendition of 'The Star-Spangled Banner' on the closed road that was doubling up as an unsuccessful parade ground, with only a lone policewoman as audience.

'Jesus, Marianne! Jesus Christ!'

The policewoman turned around. Her colleague came tearing out of a side entrance. He had lost his hat, and she adjusted the peak of her own cap as a reprimand.

'The woman's disappeared, Marianne.' He was gasping for breath.

'What?'

'I overheard two . . . I just wanted to know what was going on, that's all, and—'

'We were told to stand here! To watch the door!'

'I don't need to take orders from them! They don't have juris-diction here. And we were supposed to knock off over half an hour ago. So I just went in there . . .' he pointed frantically, 'and the hotel staff, like, they didn't stop me, uniform and all that, so I—'

'Who's disappeared?'

'Bentley! The bloody president!'

'Disappeared?' she echoed in a flat voice.

'Vanished! And no one knows where! That is . . . I heard two of the guys talking together and . . .'

He stopped and pulled out his mobile phone.

'Who . . .' Marianne stuttered, covering one of her ears: the brass band was reaching a climax. 'Who are you calling?'

'The papers,' her colleague whispered. 'We'll get at least ten thousand kroner for this story from VG.'

She grabbed his phone from him in a flash.

'We will not,' she hissed. 'We have to get hold of . . . to get hold of . . .' She looked at the mobile phone as if it would give her the answer 'Who should we . . .?'

'. . . *and the hooome of the braaave!*'

The song was sung. The singer gave a hesitant bow. Someone in the brass band laughed. Then there was silence.

The policewoman's voice was uncertain and shrill. Her hand shook as she held out the phone to her colleague and continued: 'Who . . . who the hell should we ring?'

2

The Minister of Justice's personal assistant was alone in the office. She took three lever arch lever files from a metal cabinet in the locked archive: one yellow, one blue and one red. She laid them on the minister's desk and then went to put on some coffee. She went to the stationery cupboard and got pens, pencils and pads for the meeting room. With a deft hand, she switched on three computers, her own, the minister's and the Secretary General's. She picked up a stopwatch from her desk before going back to the archive. She pushed aside one set of bookshelves without much problem. A panel with red numbers on it came into view. She started the stopwatch, then punched in a ten-figure code and checked the time. Thirty-four seconds later she punched in a new code. Stared at the stopwatch. Waited. Waited. Ninety seconds later, another code.

The door opened.

She picked up the grey box and let the rest stay where it was. Then she went through an equally rigorous routine to lock everything and closed the door of the archive.

It had taken her exactly six minutes to get to the office. She and her husband had been on their way to visit a niece in Bærum to celebrate national day with egg-and-spoon races and waffles at Evje school when her mobile phone rang. As soon as she saw the number on the display, she asked her husband to turn round. He had driven her straight to the Ministry without any questions.

She was the first one there.

She sank slowly into a chair and smoothed down her hair.

Code Four, the voice on the mobile phone had said.

It could just be a practice – they had rehearsed the routines regularly for the past three years. It could of course just be a practice.

37

On the 17th of May?

A practice on Norway's national day?

The PA jumped when the door burst open with a bang. The Minister of Justice walked in without greeting her. He took short, measured steps, as if he was trying to control the urge to run.

'We've got procedures for situations like this,' he said a bit too loudly. 'Have you set everything in motion?'

He talked in the same way that he walked – staccato, tense. The PA was not sure if he was addressing her or one of the three men who came through the door behind him. She nodded, to be on the safe side.

'Good,' the minster said and continued to march towards his office. 'We've got routines. We're up and running. When are the Americans getting here?'

The Americans? the PA thought and felt a hot flush surge through her body. The Americans. She couldn't help looking over at the fat file containing the correspondence in connection with Helen Bentley's visit.

The Director General of the PST, Peter Salhus, did not follow the other three. Instead he came over to where she was sitting and held out his hand.

'It's been a while, Beate. I only wish it were under better circumstances.'

She got up, brushed down her skirt and took his hand.

'I'm not quite sure . . .' Her voice broke and she coughed.

'Soon,' he said. 'You'll know soon enough.'

His hand was warm and dry. She held it for a moment too long, as if she needed the reassurance that his firm handshake could give. Then she nodded briefly.

'Have you got the grey box?' he asked.

'Yes.'

She handed it over to him. All communication to and from the minister's office could be scrambled, coded and distorted with only a few extra tricks and no additional equipment. But it was seldom necessary. She couldn't remember the last time she had been asked about it. Perhaps a conversation with the Minister of Defence – just in case. But the box was only to be used under extraordinary circumstances. It had never been necessary, other than during practices.

'Just a couple of things . . .'

Salhus absent-mindedly weighed the box in his hand.

'This is not a practice, Beate. And you must be prepared to be here for some time. But . . . Does anyone know that you're here?'

'My husband, of course. We—'

'Don't ring him yet. Wait as long as you can before saying anything. It will all get out pretty soon. But until then we have to use what time we have. We have called in the National Security Council, and we would like them to be in place before this . . .' His smile did not reach his eyes.

'Coffee?' she asked. 'Shall I come in with drinks?'

'We'll sort that out ourselves. Over there, isn't it?'

He grabbed the full pot of coffee.

'There are cups, glasses and mineral water in there already,' the PA told him.

The last thing she heard as the door closed behind the Director General of the PST was the minister's hysterical voice: 'We've got procedures for this! Has no one been able to get hold of the Prime Minister? What? Where in God's name is the Prime Minister? We've got procedures!'

Then there was silence. There was soundproof glass in the windows, so she couldn't even hear the convoy of student buses that had decided it was a good idea to park right in the middle of Akersgate, outside the Ministry of Culture and Church Affairs.

All the windows were dark.

3

Johanne Vik had no idea how she was going to get through the day; she never knew how she would survive the 17th of May. She held the shirt of Kristiane's national costume up in front of her. This year she had thought ahead and was going to take a change of clothes for her daughter with them. The first outfit was already dirty by half past seven. And now this one had jam on the arm and a piece of melted chocolate on the collar. The ten-year-old was dancing around the floor naked, thin and fragile, with eyes that seldom focused on anyone or anything.

It was already nearly half past ten, and they didn't have much time.

'*Silent night,*' the small girl sang, '*holy night. All is calm, all is bright. Round yon virgin mother and child. Holy infant so tender and mild . . .*'

'You're a bit out on the date.' Adam Stubo laughed and ruffled his stepdaughter's hair. 'There are special songs for our national day too, you know. Do you know where my cufflinks are, Johanne?'

She didn't answer. If she had washed the first shirt and popped it in the tumble dryer, Kristiane could at least have started the party with clean clothes.

'Look at this,' she complained and showed the shirt to Adam.

'Doesn't really matter,' he said and carried on looking for his cufflinks. 'Kristiane has more white shirts in the cupboard.'

'More white shirts?' Johanne rolled her eyes. 'Do you know what my parents paid for this damn national costume? And do you know how offended my mother will be if we turn up with Kristiane in an ordinary shirt from H&M?'

'*A child is born in Bethlehem,*' Kristiane chanted. '*Hip-hip-hurrah!*'

Adam took the shirt and examined the stains.

'I'll sort it out,' he said. 'In five minutes, with a bit of washing-up liquid and a hairdryer. And by the way, you underestimate your mother. There are few people who understand Kristiane better than her. Why don't you get Ragnhild ready, so we can leave in quarter of an hour?'

The sixteen-month-old baby was sitting in deep concentration, playing with her building blocks in a corner of the sitting room. She was unperturbed by her sister's dancing and singing. With astonishing precision, she placed one block on top of another, and smiled when the tower was as high as her face.

Johanne didn't have the heart to disturb her. For a moment it struck her how different the two girls were. The older one thin and sensitive, the younger so very robust. Kristiane was difficult to understand; Ragnhild was healthy and direct. She lifted the block on top, saw her mother and grinned, revealing eight sparkling white teeth.

'Cudduwl, Mummy. Agni cudduwl. Look!'

'*On Christmas night all Christians sing,*' Kristiane sang, clear as a bell.

Johanne picked her elder daughter up. She was happy to be held like a baby, lying in her mother's arms with not a stitch on her body.

'It's not Christmas,' Johanne said quietly, puckering her lips against the child's warm, soft cheek. 'It's the seventeenth of May, national day.'

'I know,' Kristiane replied, looking straight at her mother for a second before continuing in a flat voice: 'Constitution day, when we celebrate independence and freedom. This year we can also celebrate the hundredth anniversary of our separation from Sweden. 1814 and 1905. That is what we're celebrating.'

'My little sweetheart,' Johanne whispered and kissed her again. 'You're so clever. And now you've got to get dressed again. OK?'

'Adam can do that.'

Kristiane wriggled out of her mother's arms and dashed, barefooted, across the room to the bathroom. She paused by the television for a moment, and turned it on. The Norwegian national anthem blared out of the loudspeakers. She had turned the volume right up the night before. Johanne grabbed the remote control and turned the noise down. Just as she was moving away to find her younger daughter's party frock, something caught her attention.

The scene was familiar enough. A sea of people dressed in all their finery in front of the royal palace. Large and small flags, rows of pensioners on the few seats that had been put out, just under the balcony. A close-up of a Pakistani girl in a Norwegian national costume; she smiled at the camera and waved her flag with great enthusiasm. As the picture swept over all the flags and then focused on the glamorous reporter, something happened. The woman put her hand to her ear. She smiled sheepishly, looked at something that was possibly a script and opened her mouth to say something, but nothing came out. Instead she turned away, as if she didn't want to be filmed. Two sudden, random and very short clips then followed. A sweep of the treetops just to the east of the palace, and a screaming child on its father's shoulders. The images were out of focus.

Johanne turned the volume back up.

The camera finally focused on the reporter again, who now had her hand over her left ear, listening intently. A teenager stuck his head up over her shoulder and shouted hurrah.

'And now,' the woman finally said, obviously flustered, 'and now we will leave the celebrations on Karl Johan for a moment . . . We'll return here shortly, but first . . .'

A young lad stuck his fingers up like rabbit ears behind the reporter's head and then howled with laughter.

'Back to the studio at Marienlyst for some breaking news,' the reporter said in a rush, and the picture was cut immediately.

Johanne looked at her watch. Seven minutes past eleven.

'Adam,' she called quietly.

Ragnhild toppled her tower. The news jingle played.

'Adam,' Johanne shouted. 'Adam, come quick.'

The man in the studio was in a dark suit. His normally wild curly hair looked greyer than usual and Johanne thought she saw him swallow a couple of times before opening his mouth.

'Someone must have died,' she said.

'What?' Adam came into the sitting room, carrying a fully dressed Kristiane. 'Has someone died?'

'Shhh.' She pointed at the TV screen, then put her finger to her lips.

'We repeat, the reports are still unconfirmed, but . . .' The lines of communication to NRK and the broadcasting house were obviously red hot. Even the experienced anchorman kept his finger on his earpiece and listened intently for a few seconds before he looked into the camera and continued: 'And now over to . . .'

He frowned, hesitated. Then he pulled out his earpiece, rested one hand on top of the other and went free-range: 'We have several reporters out following this story, and as you perhaps understand, there are some technical problems. We will talk to our reporters shortly. In the meantime, I repeat: the American President, Helen Lardahl Bentley, did not arrive as planned for the seventeenth of May breakfast at the palace this morning. No official reason has been given for her absence. Nor has a statement been given by the parliament, where the President was due to watch the parade with the President of the Storting, Jørgen Kosmo, and . . . One moment . . .'

'Is she . . . is she dead?'

'Dead and red with brown bread,' Kristiane chanted.

Adam lowered her gently to the floor.

'They don't know yet,' Johanne replied quickly. 'But it would seem that she—'

There was a sharp screech from the TV before the picture switched to a reporter who obviously had not had enough time to take off his national-day ribbon, for a more sombre effect.

'I am standing outside Oslo Police Headquarters,' he panted. His microphone was shaking. 'And one thing is certain: something has happened. Terje Bastesen, the Chief of Police, who normally leads the seventeenth of May procession, has just hurried up the road behind me together with . . .' he turned around and pointed up the gentle slope to the main entrance of the police HQ, 'together with . . . several others. At the same time, a number of marked police cars left the parking place behind the building, some of them with sirens blaring.'

'Harald,' the man in the studio tried, tentatively. 'Harald Hansen, can you hear me?'

'Yes, Christian, I can hear you.'

'Has anyone explained what has happened?'

'No, it's not even possible to get up to the entrance. But rumours are rampant. There must be twelve or thirteen journalists here already, and one thing at least is clear: that is that something has happened to President Bentley. She has not appeared at any of her official engagements this morning and there was absolutely no one at the announced press conference in the lobby of the Storting, just before the children's parade. The government press office appears to be non-functional and at the moment . . .'

'What the hell . . .' Adam whispered and sat down on the arm of the sofa.

'Shhh . . .'

'We have people at and near the main hospitals,' the reporter continued, breathless, 'where President Bentley would have been taken if her absence was due to . . . health reasons. However, there is nothing, and I repeat *nothing*, to indicate any form of extraordinary activity in the hospitals at this point. No obvious security measures, no unusual traffic, nothing. And—'

'Harald! Harald Hansen!'

'I can hear you, Christian!'

'I'm afraid I'm going to have to interrupt you there, as we have just got . . .'

44

The picture switched back to the studio. Johanne couldn't remember ever seeing a newsreader being physically handed a script in the studio. The courier's arm was caught on camera as the picture came on, and the anchorman fumbled for his glasses, which he hadn't needed until now.

'We have just received a press release from the Prime Minister's office.' He cleared his throat. 'I will now read . . .'

Ragnhild suddenly started to howl.

Johanne backed her way into the corner, where the toddler was screaming like one possessed, with her arms in the air.

'She's disappeared,' Adam said, in a trance. 'My God, the woman has just disappeared.'

'Who's disappeared?' Kristiane asked and took his hand.

'No one,' he replied, almost inaudibly.

'They have,' Kristiane insisted. 'You said a lady had disappeared.'

'No one we know,' he explained, then shushed her.

'Not Mummy, anyway. Mummy's here. And we're going to Grandma and Grandad. Mummy will never disappear.'

Ragnhild calmed down the minute she was in her mother's arms. She stuck her thumb in her mouth and burrowed her head into the hollow of Johanne's neck. Kristiane was still standing with her hand in Adam's, swaying backwards and forwards.

'Dam-di-rum-ram,' she whispered.

'There's nothing to worry about,' Adam said automatically. 'Nothing dangerous, my sweet.'

'Dam-di-rum-ram.'

She's going to close us off, Johanne thought in desperation. Kristiane was shutting everyone out as she did whenever she felt even the slightest bit threatened, or something unexpected happened.

'Everything's fine, sweetheart.' She stroked the girl's hair. 'And now we're all going to get ready to go to Grandma and Grandad. We're still going to see them, you know, just like we planned.'

But she couldn't pull her eyes from the TV screen.

The scene was being filmed from the air now, from a helicopter slowly circling over the centre of Oslo. The camera moved up the main drag, Karl Johan, from the Storting to the palace, at a snail's pace.

'Over a hundred thousand people,' Adam whispered, as he stood entranced. He didn't even notice when Kristiane let go of his hand. 'Maybe twice as many. How on earth are they going . . .?'

Kristiane was now banging her head against a cupboard in the corner of the room. She had taken her clothes off again.

'The lady's disappeared,' she hummed. 'Dam-di-rum-ram. The lady's gone.'

Then she started to cry, silently and inconsolably.

4

Abdallah al-Rahman was full. He stroked his firm stomach. For a short while he considered waiting to do his training. He had really eaten a bit too much. On the other hand, he had a lot to do for the rest of the day. If he didn't train now, the danger was that there wouldn't be time later. He opened the door to the big gym. The cool air was like a soothing breath on his face. He carefully closed the door before getting undressed. Then he stood there, barefoot as usual, and pulled on a large pair of white shorts.

He started the treadmill. Slow to begin with, a forty-five-minute interval programme. That would leave him half an hour for weights. Not what he would normally do, or a prospect that he relished, but it was better than nothing.

He had of course received nothing. No confirmation, no coded message, telephone call or cryptic email. Modern communication was a double-edged sword, effective, but still far too dangerous. He had instead had a breakfast meeting with a French business-man and done his morning prayers. He had then made a brief visit to the stud farm to inspect the new foal, which had been born during the night and was already a fabulous sight. Abdallah al-Rahman had not been interrupted by anything external to his day-to-day life here and now. And it wasn't necessary either.

It was a while now since CNN had given him the confirmation he needed.

Things had obviously gone according to plan.

5

Everything was running smoothly.

She realised that when she could finally sneak out for a cigarette. The Minster of Justice's PA, Beate Koss, was not a regular smoker, but generally had a packet of ten in her handbag. She had slipped on her coat and taken the lift down to the foyer. The building was closed to the public and armed guards stood on either side of the main entrance. She shivered, and nodded to the young lad who was doing his alternative service as a conscientious objector. He immediately let her through the barrier and out.

She crossed the street.

Everything was working. Everything that had previously been pure theory and locked-away directives had become reality in the course of a few hours that morning. The communication equipment and alarm procedures had functioned as they should. Key people had been called in, the committee was in place. Even the Minister of Defence, who had been celebrating the national day on Svalbard, was back in the office. Everyone knew their role and position in the complex machinery that seemed to run by itself once it had been set in motion. An hour or two too late, perhaps, as Peter Salhus so obviously thought, but Beate still couldn't help feeling a sort of pride in being part of something so important and historic.

'Shame on you,' she muttered to herself and lit a cigarette.

The news of the American president's disappearance had not yet made any visible or audible impact on the celebrations. Faint echoes of the shouts, hurrahs and general noise on Karl Johan bounced between the government buildings. The people who hurried past on the pavement were laughing and smiling. Maybe they didn't know. Even though the news had leaked several hours ago now, and the two main TV channels had interrupted the morning's programmes with regular newsflashes, it was as if the nation refused to be distracted from the great annual celebration of itself.

It felt good to have a smoke.

She hesitated for a moment before lighting up another cigarette. Her eyes roamed from a group of journalists who had gathered in front of the building, up to the green bulletproof windows on the sixth floor. They were so obviously different from the rest of the building. She had often wondered why the Minister of Justice should have bulletproof windows in his office, when he went shopping in the local supermarket on his own and had no more than an ordinary Securitas burglar alarm in his home. That's just the way it is, she said to herself; she always, with absolute loyalty, simply accepted things as they were and had been decided.

A man looked down at her.

She sheepishly lifted her hand in greeting. He waved back. It was Peter Salhus. A good man. A man you could trust. Always friendly whenever they met, attentive and alert, unlike so many of the other important people who came and went in the minister's office and barely even registered her existence.

Beate Koss dropped her cigarette butt on the ground, and stubbed it out with her shoe. She looked up again and thought she saw Salhus saying something, before he closed the curtains and turned back to the room.

A police car drove past, slowly and quietly, but with its blue light flashing.

'Now that we're alone,' Peter Salhus said when only the Minister of Justice and the Chief of Oslo Police were left in the office behind the green windows, 'I just wanted to ask . . .' He scratched his beard and swallowed. 'Hotel Opera,' he blurted out and looked directly at the Chief of Police, Bastesen. 'Hotel Opera!'

'Yes . . .'

'Why?'

'I don't quite understand your question,' Bastesen said, offended and with a furrow on his brow. 'It was—'

'When we've got the Continental and the Grand,' Salhus interrupted, making a great effort to keep his voice down. 'Wonderful, traditional, good hotels. We have elegant VIP accommodation and we have . . .' He lowered his voice even more and tapped the map of the centre of Oslo with his finger. 'Kings have stayed here. Princesses and presidents. *Albert bloody Einstein* . . .' He stopped and took a deep breath. 'God knows how many other celebrities, film stars and Nobel Prize winners have slept happily and safely in their beds just here . . .' He almost made a hole in the map with his index finger. 'And then someone decides to put the American president in a bloody transformer kiosk between a central station full of junkies and a bloody building site. Jesus Christ . . .'

He straightened his back and pulled a face. A faint humming from the air-conditioning was the only sound in the room. The minister and the Chief of Police leant forward and carefully studied the map on the table, as if Madam President might be hiding somewhere there, between the street names and the shaded blocks.

'What on earth were you thinking?'

The Minister of Justice took a couple of steps back. Bastesen brushed some invisible dust from the front of his uniform.

'Well, that attitude's not going to get us anywhere,' he said calmly. 'May I just remind you that we are responsible for bodyguard services now. That means the security of all objects, both nationals and non-nationals. And I can assure you that—'

'Terje,' Salhus cut in and puffed out his cheeks before exhaling slowly. 'I apologise. You are absolutely right. I shouldn't get so agitated. But . . . we *know* the Grand! We have *experience* in making the Continental secure. Why on earth . . .'

'Give me a chance to answer, man!'

'I suggest we sit down,' the Minister of Justice said in a tense voice.

Neither of the two took any notice of his suggestion.

'They had just completed the presidential suite,' Bastesen explained. 'The hotel is preparing to welcome the cultural elite. Major stars. Up until now, they've had a reputation for not quite . . . Well, let's just say they're not quite in the same class as the Grand, but when the new opera house is finished, the location will be a huge competitive advantage and . . .' He drew a circle round Bjørvika with his finger. 'Right now this is Spaghetti Junction and not particularly attractive, it's true. But the plans are . . . The presidential suite met all our requirements, in terms of aesthetics, practicality and security. Superb view. They added a couple of rooms on the ninth floor to an already existing suite, which is . . . And what's more . . .' he gave a crooked smile, 'it was actually quite reasonable.'

An angel passed through the room. Salhus stared at Bastesen in disbelief; Bastesen stared at the map.

Eventually the Director General of the PST groaned. 'Reasonable! The American president comes to Norway, the security operation is massive, perhaps the biggest we have ever had, and you choose a hotel that is . . . cheap! *Cheap!*'

'As I'm sure is also the case in your division,' Bastesen continued calmly, 'it is the responsibility of the head of every government agency to save public money wherever possible. We undertook a total analysis of Hotel Opera and compared it with the other hotels you just mentioned. The Opera came out best. Overall. And may I remind you that Madam President travels with a pretty large security operation herself. The Secret Service has of course inspected the area. Thoroughly. And had very few objections, as far as we were led to believe.'

'I think then we'll leave it at that,' the Minister of Justice said. 'Let's stick to the actual situation and not get distracted by what might, could or should have been done differently. I suggest that we . . .'

He went over to the door and opened it.

'Where are the drawings?' Peter Salhus asked and looked at the Chief of Police.

'Of the hotel?'

Salhus nodded.

'We've got them down at HQ. I'll get you copies straight away.'

'Thank you.'

Salhus held out his hand in a conciliatory gesture. Bastesen hesitated and then finally shook it.

It was already past two o'clock. Still no one had heard from Helen Bentley. Still no one knew exactly when she had disappeared. And the Director General of the PST and the Chief of Oslo Police still did not know that the architectural drawings of the Hotel Opera that they had back in that bleak, curved building at Grønlandsleiret 44 were incomplete and inaccurate.

6

The man woke up with his ear full of vomit.

The stench seared his nose and he tried to get up. His arms wouldn't do as he wanted. He lay back down, resigned. He was too far gone now. He had started to puke. He couldn't remember the last time he had had to get rid of all the shit he poured into himself. Several decades of practice had made his stomach immune to most things. The only thing he didn't drink was meths. Two years ago, after a real glut of contraband, he'd ended up in hospital with a couple of brethren spirits. All of them with methanol poisoning. One of them had died. The other one went blind. Whereas he got up after five days and walked straight home, more alert than he had been for a long time. The doctor had said he was lucky.

Practice, he had said to himself. It's having enough practice that counts.

But he avoided meths.

The flat was a tip. He knew that. He should do something about it. The neighbours had started to complain. About the smell, primarily. He had to do something, or they'd throw him out.

He tried to get up again.

Shit. The whole world was spinning.

He had an intense pain in his groin and sick in his hair. If he rolled his lower body off the sofa, he might be able to get up from there. If it weren't for the bloody cancer, he'd be doing all right. He wouldn't have thrown up. He would have had the energy to get up.

Slowly, to save what little muscle he had left in his scrawny body, he wedged his leg against the coffee table. He then managed to get up into a kind of sitting position, with his knees on

53

the matted carpet and his body in a resting position against the sofa, as if in prayer.

The TV was on, with the volume too loud.

He remembered now. He had turned it on when he came home at the crack of dawn. As in a distant dream, he remembered that someone had knocked on the door. Heavily and loudly, the way his bloody neighbours always did, to pester him both night and day. Fortunately nothing more had happened. No doubt the pigs had other things to do on a day like today, instead of coming to pick up a poor old soak.

'Hurrah for the seventeenth of May,' he wheezed with great effort, and finally managed to creep up on to the sofa.

'*It is still uncertain when President Bentley disappeared from the hotel . . .*'

The sound penetrated the man's tired brain. He tried to find the remote control in the chaos on the table. A packet of crisps that had spilled out over old newspapers was now drenched in beer from an upturned can. Someone had eaten nearly all the pizza that a mate in the backyard had given him the day before, and that he had been saving for today. He had no idea who.

'*As far as Dagsrevyen is aware, the American president is . . .*'

In many ways it had been a damn good night.

Real alcohol, not the usual rubbish and shit. He had had half a bottle of Upper Ten whisky to himself. And more, if he was honest. He had helped himself to some of the stuff the others had with them when he thought no one was looking, which had only resulted in one brawl. But that was what it was like when you were with your mates. He'd managed to stash a couple of minis in his inside pocket when it was all over. Hairymary wouldn't mind. What a girl, eh! She had landed on her feet when she was picked up by that policewoman and her filthy-rich dyke friend. Turned into a proper little lady's housekeeper in the West End. But Hairymary hadn't forgotten where she came from. She might never leave that fort of a flat that she had holed herself up in, but she did send money to Backyard Berit twice a year, on the

54

17th of May and Christmas Eve. Then the old gang had a party with food and the real thing.

He shouldn't be feeling so bad after such a good night.

It wasn't the alcohol, it was the bloody cancer in his balls.

The light on the fjord had been beautiful when he'd wandered through the town in the early morning – it must have been around four. The Russ was still being rowdy and carrying on, of course, but whenever there was a quiet moment he had taken time to sit down. On a bench or on that fence by the rubbish bin where he had found a full, unopened bottle of beer.

The light was so beautiful in spring. The trees somehow seemed friendlier, and even the hooting of car horns was less aggressive when he stumbled out on to the road a bit too suddenly and the drivers had to brake.

Oslo was his town.

'*The police ask anyone who might have seen anything to . . .*'

Where the hell was the remote control?

There. At last. It was hidden away under the pizza box. He turned down the volume and sank back into the sofa.

'Shit,' he said in a flat voice.

They were showing a picture of some clothes. A pair of blue trousers. A bright red jacket. Some shoes that just looked like any old shoes.

'*According to police information, this is the outfit that President Bentley was wearing when she disappeared. It is important that . . .*'

It was at ten past four.

He had just looked at the clock on the tower outside the old Østbanen station when she went by. Her and two men. Her jacket was red, but she was far too old to be one of the Russ.

Fucking hell, his balls were burning.

Had someone disappeared?

It had been a good night. He wasn't too bad, so he had managed to stagger home through the town, full and happy. The streets were decorated with colourful garlands and he had noticed how clean everywhere was.

The smell of sick was bothering him now. He had to do something. He had to tidy up a bit in here. Clean, so that he wouldn't get kicked out.

He closed his eyes.

This bloody cancer. Well, everyone dies of something or other, he comforted himself. That's life. He was only sixty-one, but that was old enough, really, when he thought about it.

Slowly he slipped sideways and into a deep sleep, with his ear in his own vomit once again.

7

'

. . . and there you have it.'

The Prime Minister sat back in his chair. There was silence in the large room. The air smelt dank. The place had been closed for a long time. Peter Salhus clasped his hands behind his neck and let his eyes wander round the room. There was a long, counter-like piece of furniture along one wall. Otherwise, the room was dominated by a huge meeting table with fourteen chairs around it. There was a plasma screen on one of the walls. The loudspeakers were on a glass shelf down by the floor. A faded map of the world hung on the wall opposite.

'So we're going to have these . . .' the Chief of Oslo Police, Terje Bastesen, looked as if he actually wanted to say *gorillas*, but tactfully said something else, 'these agents hanging over our shoulders. Sticking their noses into everything we find, everything we do, anything we might think or believe. OK.'

Before the Prime Minister had a chance to answer, Peter Salhus took a breath. He leant forward suddenly and propped his arms on the table. 'First of all, I think one thing should be made absolutely clear,' he said in a measured voice. 'And that is that the Americans will certainly not let their president disappear into thin air without doing their utmost, one . . .' he held a finger in the air, 'to find her. Two . . .' another finger pointed to the ceiling, 'to catch whoever it is who has kidnapped her. And three . . .' he broke into a smile, 'to move heaven and earth – and hell if needs be – to ensure that that person or those people are punished. And let's just say that that the punishment won't be meted out in this country.'

The Minister of Justice gave a dry cough. Everyone looked at him. It was the first time he had opened his mouth in the meeting.

'The Americans are our friends and allies,' he said. His voice had an edge of formal panic that made Peter Salhus close his eyes, so that he wouldn't interrupt. 'And we must of course do whatever we can to help them. But let me make clear . . .' the minister hit the table hard with his fist, 'that we are in Norway. Under Norwegian jurisdiction. The Norwegian police will lead the investigation. Let there be no doubt about that. And when the culprit has been caught, then a *Norwegian court . . .*'

He was shouting, and heard it himself. He broke off. Coughed again, and prepared to continue.

'With all due respect . . .' Peter Salhus' voice sounded rough in comparison. He got up from his chair. The Minister of Justice remained seated with his mouth open. 'Prime Minister,' Salhus continued, without even looking at the most senior politician responsible for the Norwegian police, 'I think we could do with a reality check.'

The Director of Police, a thin woman in full uniform who had largely sat and listened throughout the meeting, leaned back and crossed her arms. Her thoughts seemed to be elsewhere most of the time and on two occasions she had left the room to answer calls. Now she seemed to be more interested and looked straight at the Director General of the PST.

'I would just like to draw your attention to the fact that—' interjected the obviously angry Minister of Justice.

'I think we should take a moment to clear this up,' the Prime Minister interrupted, with a gesture that presumably was intended to reassure, but instead was more like one used when scolding a disobedient child. 'So, Salhus, in what respect do you think that we are not in touch with reality? What is it that you've seen that the rest of us haven't?'

His eyes, which naturally already looked narrow in his round face, were now like two slashes of a scalpel.

'Is it just me . . .' Salhus threw open his hands, 'is it just me to who finds this situation completely absurd?' Without waiting for an answer, he continued: 'An entire small air force, in addition to

Air Force One. Around fifty Secret Service agents. Two armoured cars. Sniffer dogs. A bunch of special advisers, which basically means FBI agents, if any of you were wondering . . .'

He tried not to look at the Minister of Justice, who was now sitting down and aggressively stirring his coffee with a pencil.

'That is the President's entourage on a state visit to Norway. And do you know what? That is surprisingly little!' He leant forward over the table with both his hands placed firmly on the tabletop. '*Little!*'

He let the word hang in the air, as if measuring the shock effect.

'I'm not quite sure that I understand what you're getting at,' the Director of Police said. 'We all know perfectly well how many people the President has with her, and it's not—'

'It's in fact very few,' Peter Salhus repeated. 'It's not unusual for the President to be accompanied by an army of two to three hundred agents. Personal cooks, a fleet of cars. A huge van full of modern communications equipment. Military ambulances. Bulletproof screens for use during official appearances, other IT equipment, entire kennels of sniffer dogs . . .' He pulled a face again as he straightened up. 'But the lady comes to Norway with a really rather meagre entourage. Sorry . . .'

The apology was slipped in quickly and he lifted an acknowledging hand to the Prime Minister.

'I mean the President, Madam President. And I'm sure you're wondering why. Why? Why on earth should the President embark on her first foreign visit with such limited protection from her own people?'

His audience did not appear to be pondering the question. Quite the opposite: the conversation up until that moment had focused on the overwhelming number of American agents, who were now knocking on doors, going into offices, confiscating equipment and generally making life difficult for the Norwegian police.

'Because – it – is – safe – here.' He said the words with an exaggerated delay. Then he repeated: 'Because Norway is safe. We thought. Look at us.' He hit himself gently on the chest. 'The whole thing is absurd,' he repeated quietly. His listeners were more attentive now. 'Nothing more than an intestine on this map, this . . .'

He surveyed the map of the world. The corners were worn. The word *Yugoslavia* was written in bold letters across the Balkans; Peter Salhus shook his head.

'Good old Norway,' he said, and stroked his country with his finger, from north to south. 'For many years now we've talked about what a colourful society we are and what a multicultural country we've become, and allowed ourselves to be lulled into a sense of security, peace, innocence – that we were somehow different. We're always saying that the world is pressing in on us from all sides, yet at the same time we get extremely offended if that very same world doesn't see us in exactly the same way that we have always perceived ourselves to be, as an idyllic place on earth. A peaceful corner of the world, rich and generous and kind to everyone.'

He bit a piece of dry skin on his lip.

'Right now we're caught up in a powerful and terrible head-on collision, I want you to realise that. This country is prepared for disasters to the extent that anyone can be prepared. We are prepared for epidemics and other catastrophes. Some people even believe that we are prepared for war . . .' He smiled vaguely at the Minister of Defence, who did not smile back. 'But what we were not prepared for in any way was this. What's happening now.'

'Which is?' asked the Director of Police, with a sharp edge to her voice.

'That we have managed to lose the American president.'

The Minister of Justice made an inappropriate noise that sounded like a stifled giggle.

'And they simply will not accept that,' Salhus continued, unperturbed. He went back to his chair. 'It's true that the

Americans have lost one or two presidents through assassinations, but they have never, *not even once*, lost a president on foreign soil. And you can be certain of one thing . . .' He sat down heavily. 'Every single one of those Secret Service agents who are now buzzing around making life difficult for our staff will take this personally. Very personally indeed. This happened on their watch, and they don't want that pinned on them. For them, that would be worse than . . . For them this is . . .'

He hesitated, and the Prime Minister managed to cut in with a question. 'Who . . . who can we actually compare them with?'

'No one.'

'No one? But it's a police force and—'

'Yes, but they have a number of other tasks as well. The body-guards are, if you like, the identity of the service, and have been ever since President McKinley was assassinated in 1901. And that identity has been seriously threatened by what happened last night. Not least because it's due to a big mistake. One that they themselves made.'

The Minister of Justice's body was still shaking, but there was no sound. This time no one used the pause to ask questions.

'They made an error of judgement,' Peter Salhus said. 'A gross error. We're not the only ones who think of this country as a peaceful corner in a big bad world. The Americans do too. And the most worrying thing about it, apart from the fact that the President has simply vanished, is that the Americans actually thought it was safe here. They are in a far better position to assess that sort of thing than we are. And they should have known better, as—'

'As they have far more intelligence,' the Director of Police chimed in.

'Yes.'

'I see,' said the Prime Minister.

'Exactly.' The Minister of Justice nodded.

'Yes,' Peter Salhus said again.

Then there was silence. Even the Minister of Justice left his cup of coffee in peace. The plasma screen on the wall shone a uniform blue and told them nothing. The neon strip light on the ceiling had started to blink, off beat and without a sound. When a fly broke the silence with a lazy buzz, Peter Salhus followed it with his eyes until the silence started to feel uncomfortable.

'The Americans have absolutely no idea what is happening,' the Prime Minister concluded.

He gathered the papers in front of him into a pile, without indicating that the meeting was over.

'I mean, they don't either.'

'I would perhaps say that they *had* no idea,' Salhus corrected, with some hesitation. 'Beforehand, I mean. The challenge for them now is to sift through all the material that they have at any given time. To lay their cards on the table in a different way and see what emerges.'

'But the problem is,' the Director of Police said, swatting at the fly, which had come a bit too close, 'that they have too many cards.'

Salhus nodded. 'You can't even begin to imagine,' he said. His eyes felt dry and he chewed at this thumb. 'It's hard for us to comprehend all the information they have. And that they receive all the time, every minute, every hour, every day. The FBI has multiplied in both size and budget since nine/eleven. From being a relatively traditional police organisation with clear professional and largely internal American responsibilities, the greater part of its budget and staff are now earmarked for anti-terrorist activities. And this, ladies and gentlemen . . .'

He picked up an official portrait of Helen Lardahl Bentley from the table.

'Kidnapping a president definitely falls under the category of terrorism in the US. They will come storming over here, be sure of it. As I said, a number of FBI people are probably already here with the President. But we ain't seen nothing yet.'

He gave a feeble smile and ran his finger round his collar while absently staring at the photograph of the President.

'According to my reports, a special flight is in fact due to land in three hours' time,' the Director of Police confirmed. 'And there are more scheduled to arrive after that.'

The Prime Minister traced his finger over the top of the table. He stopped at a spot of coffee. Two deep furrows could be seen in the folds of skin on his face, and it was only the light reflecting on his glasses that indicated that there was a pair of eyes there too.

'Yes, but we're not talking about an invasion,' he said, obviously irritated. 'You make it sound as if we're completely at the mercy of the Americans, Salhus. And let me reiterate . . .' he raised his voice a notch or two, 'that this has happened on Norwegian soil. We will of course spare no effort or money and the Americans will be treated with the utmost respect. But this is a *Norwegian* case, to be dealt with by the *Norwegian* police and legal system.'

'Good luck,' Peter Salhus muttered, and rubbed his forehead with his knuckles.

'I will let nothing of the sort . . .' The Prime Minister paused and raised his glass to his mouth. His hand was shaking and he put the glass down again without drinking any water. Before he had a chance to continue, the Director of Police leant over the table.

'Peter, what do you actually mean? That we should leave the whole puzzle to the Americans? Give up our sovereignty and jurisdiction? You can't be serious!'

'Of course I don't mean that,' Salhus replied. He seemed surprised by her familiarity and hesitated a bit. 'I mean that . . . I in fact mean the opposite. All our experience – political, professional and for that matter military – means that we have a huge advantage over the Americans in this case.'

Someone knocked on the door and a red light flashed by the door frame.

No one reacted.

'We are Norwegian,' Peter Salhus said. 'We know this country.

We know the language. The infrastructure. The geography, the topography. The architecture, the town. We are Norwegian and they are American.'

There was another knock at the door, more agitated this time.

'We've started,' Salhus continued and shrugged. 'Things are working. We're all here, everyone who should be here. The contingency plans work. Staff have been called in. The machinery was started up hours ago, in all the ministries. The Ministry of Foreign Affairs and the Storting are taking responsibility for protocol at the moment. My point is just that—'

He stopped when a round middle-aged woman came into the room. She silently placed a piece of paper in front of the Prime Minister, who made no attempt to read it. Instead, he nodded to Salhus. 'Carry on,' he said curtly.

'My point is that we have to understand what we are dealing with. We can have no illusions that the Americans will be happy to take instructions in a situation like this. They will overstep the mark, again and again. At the same time, we have to acknowledge that they have qualifications, equipment and intelligence that will be essential for the case. To put it simply, we need them. The most important thing will be to convince them that . . .' He lifted his glass and looked at it, distracted. The fly had settled on the inside and was attempting to open its wings, feeble and half dead. 'That they need us just as much,' he said emphatically, turning the empty glass in his hands. 'If not, they'll bulldoze us. And if we are going to achieve mutual understanding and trust, then I think we should stop banging on about words like jurisdiction, territory and sovereignty.'

'Which is more or less what Vidkun Quisling must have said,' the Minister of Justice objected, 'in April 1940.'

The silence that followed was almost deafening. Even the fly had capitulated and lay with its legs in the air at the bottom of the glass. The Prime Minister's incessant rummaging in his papers stopped abruptly. The Director of Police sat bolt upright in her chair, without leaning back. The Minister of Foreign Affairs, who had barely said a word throughout the meeting, sat petrified, with his mouth open.

'No,' Peter Salhus said eventually, and so quietly that the Prime Minister on the other side of the enormous table nearly missed it. 'It is not. It is not in any way the same.'

He was stiff and slow when he got up.

'I assume that this meeting is over,' he said, without looking at the Prime Minister.

Salhus walked over to the door. He held his documents loosely in his hand, and looked at no one. They were all staring at him. As he passed the last chair before the door, the Prime Minister put a conciliatory hand on his arm.

'Thank you for your efforts so far,' he said.

Salhus did not reply.

The Prime Minister didn't take his hand away.

'You . . . you really admire these FBI people.'

Peter Salhus couldn't understand what the man wanted. So he didn't answer.

'And these Secret Service agents. You really admire them, don't you?'

'Admire.' Peter Salhus said the word slowly to himself, as if he wasn't quite sure what it meant. Then he reclaimed his arm and looked the Prime Minister straight in the eye.

'Perhaps, yes.' He nodded. 'But first and foremost . . . I fear them. And so should you all.'

He left the government's secret crisis meeting with the faint smell of decay in his nostrils.

8

The young man at the petrol station was thoroughly pissed off. It was the second year in a row that he had had to work on the 17th of May. OK, so he was only nineteen and the youngest employee, but it just wasn't fair that he should have to die of boredom at work on a day when practically no one needed petrol. And not many people would come to buy hot dogs either, as the station was too far from the centre of town. They should just close the damn place. If anyone was desperate for fuel, the card-payment-only pumps were still available.

'Junior'll do it,' the boss had boomed when they were arguing about shifts a couple of weeks before.

Junior'll do it. As if the boss was his dad or something.

Two boys of about ten came running in. They were wearing maroon band uniforms, black hats and white patent-leather bandoliers. They had obviously left their drums somewhere and were fencing energetically with their sticks.

'En garde,' one of them shouted and made a hit.

'Ow! That hurt!'

The smaller of the two dropped his drumsticks and clutched his shoulder.

'Stop making such a racket,' the assistant said. 'You going to buy anything, or what?'

Without saying anything, the two boys rushed over to the freezer. It was a bit too high for them. One of them used the shelf with chocolates on it as a ladder.

'Cornetto,' screamed the other.

'Leave it out.' The assistant hit the counter.

The cheeky bugger who had climbed on the shelf was an Asian.

They could camouflage themselves in band uniforms and

national costumes if that was what they wanted. They were still bloody foreigners. It was really pathetic the way they tried to Norwegianify themselves. Earlier that day a whole flock of little black kids had come in. They'd chatted and made a noise and took over the whole shop, as if they were at home in Tamil-land or Africa or wherever they came from. And they didn't buy much. But they were all wearing 17th of May ribbons. Great red, white and blue ribbons on their jacket collars and Salvation Army coats. Grinning and laughing and ruining the national day for everyone else.

'Hey, you!'

The assistant came out from behind the counter and went over to the boys. He took hold of the Paki by the scruff of the neck.

'Drop the ice-cream.'

'I'm going to pay for it! I was going to pay!'

'Drop the bloody ice cream!'

'Ow, that hurts!'

His voice wasn't as cocky now. The assistant could have sworn the kid was about to cry. He let go.

'Hi.'

A man came in. He stood for a moment looking askance at the two boys. The assistant mumbled hello.

'Sorry to park right up by the window,' the man said and nodded towards a blue Ford on the other side of the glass. 'I didn't see the sign until I was out of the car. I just want some mineral water, so . . .'

The assistant lifted his chin in the direction of the fridge and returned to his place behind the counter. The younger of the boys, his blond hair curling out from under his hat, slapped a fifty-krone note down in front of him.

'Two ice creams,' he hissed through gritted teeth. 'Two Cornettos, you creep.'

The man from the Ford came up behind him. The boy took his change without a word and turned away. Then he held one of the ice creams out towards his friend, who had sought refuge by the door.

'*Dickhead!*' they chorused as the door closed behind them.

'Three mineral waters,' the man said.

'You paying by card?' the assistant asked, curtly.

'No. Here.'

The man took his change from the one-hundred-kroner note and stuffed it in his pocket.

The assistant glanced over at the car. It was parked so the driver's seat was right up by the window, less than a metre away. He thought he saw someone in the passenger seat, a thigh, and a hand that reached out for something. There was a woman in the back, sleeping. Her head was leant against the window. Her jacket had somehow got caught around her shoulders and it made the angle of her neck look unnatural. The skin on her neck was almost as red as the jacket.

'Bye, thank you,' said the man. He pulled his cap down over his forehead and disappeared out the door.

Bloody 17th of May. It was almost four o'clock. At least his shift would be finished soon, if the boss bothered to turn up, that is. You never knew. What a crap day.

He took his time, dropped the sausage into a roll, then covered it with prawn mayonnaise, relish and loads of mustard before wolfing it down.

It was his ninth hot dog since the morning, and it didn't taste good.

9

'The palace is just up there,' Ambassador George A. Wells said, and nodded towards the park on the other side of Drammensveien. 'And it's not just a monument, they actually live there. The royal family. Nice people. Very nice people.'

The men looked quite similar, standing as they were with their backs to the room, looking out over the street behind the fortifications that surrounded the triangular building. They might easily be mistaken for brothers. The ambassador had to put up with his wife nagging him daily about losing some of the extra pounds round his stomach. But the two men standing in front of the window of the American Embassy in Oslo, watching the Norwegian people celebrate in all their finery on the other side of the aggressive metal barriers, both took their food and golf very seriously. And they both looked good on it. George Wells was nearly seventy, but was still blessed with thick silver hair. His guest was younger and had the same thick hair, though not as well groomed. They both had their hands in their pockets. Their jackets had been abandoned long ago.

'The royal family appears to be less well protected than we are,' the guest said, and pointed towards the park around the palace. 'Anyone can walk right up to the palace.'

'Not only can, but do. The endless parade they have every year to mark the seventeenth of May passes right under the balcony where the royals stand waving to the crowd. There's never been a problem. But then they . . .' he gave a wan smile and ran his fingers through his hair, 'are a bit more popular than us.'

Neither of the men said anything for a while. They looked down at the street, where it was difficult to tell whether people were coming or going. Suddenly, and at the same time, they both caught sight of a little boy with an American flag. He was probably about five or six years old and was wearing dark blue trousers and a bright red V-neck sweater with a white T-shirt underneath. He stopped and looked up. There was no way that he could see them; he was too far away, and the smoked windows made it impossible to see in. He smiled all the same and timidly waved his flag. His mother turned round and grabbed him by the arm, irritated. The boy carried on waving until he was out of sight.

'He can get away with that because he's little,' the ambassador said. 'He's a sweet little Afro-American boy, so he's allowed to wave the Star-Spangled Banner on the Norwegian national day. Won't be like that in a few years' time.'

Silence again. The guest seemed to be fascinated by what was going on down on the street and remained standing at the window. The ambassador showed no sign of wanting to sit down either. A large group of young people came storming down from the Nobel Institute. They were singing so loudly and out of tune that it penetrated even through the reinforced glass. One of the girls was around eighteen and was so drunk that she had to be supported by two friends. One had his left hand cupped around her breast, which didn't seem to bother her in the slightest. Coming towards them was a primary-school class, walking hand-in-hand in a crocodile. The front pair, two girls with blonde plaits, burst out crying when one of the youths roared in their faces. The furious parents came rushing over. A young man in blue overalls poured beer all over the angriest father.

A police car was trying to force its way through the crowd. It had to give up halfway and stop. Two of the youths sat down on the bonnet. One girl insisted on kissing the policeman who got out of the car to sort things out. Several others ran over. A whole flock of girls in red overalls badgered the uniformed policeman for a kiss.

'What is this?' the guest mumbled. 'What kind of a country is this?'

'Strictly speaking, you should have known that,' the ambassador responded, 'before sending Madam President here. On a day like this.'

The guest gave an audible sigh, almost demonstrative. He went over to a table where mineral water and glasses were set out on a silver tray. He lifted one of the bottles and looked sidelong at the ambassador.

'Go ahead. Please, help yourself.'

The ambassador also appeared to have had enough of the Norwegian people. He picked up a remote control and pushed a button. The curtains closed.

'I apologise for making that comment, Warren.'

The ambassador sat down. His movements were heavier now, as if the day so far had already been too long and his age was becoming a burden.

'That's fine,' Warren Scifford assured him. 'And in any case, you're right. I should have known. The point is that I do know. I know everything there is to read or hear about this place. You know the procedures, George. You know how we work.'

He held a bottle of Farris mineral water at arm's length and looked at the label with suspicion. Then he shrugged and poured himself a glass.

'We've been working on it for two months,' he said. 'And in fact we thought it was a great idea when Madam President first suggested Norway as the destination of her first overseas visit. An . . .' he lifted his glass in a silent cheers, 'an excellent idea. And you, of course, know why.'

The ambassador said nothing.

'We have a scale,' Warren Scifford continued. 'Completely unofficial, naturally, but still fairly serious. With the exception of a handful of Pacific states where there are only a few thousand friendly inhabitants and the only threat to the President would be an unexpected tsunami . . .' he took a sip of water, swallowed and wiped his mouth with his shirt sleeve, 'Norway is the safest country to visit in the world. Last time . . .' He shook his head slightly. 'President Clinton behaved like he was on some scout trip in

71

Little Rock when he was here. That was before your time, and before . . .' He suddenly rubbed his temples.

'Everything OK?' asked the ambassador.

Warren Scifford frowned and rolled his neck. 'Tiring flight,' he mumbled. 'In fact, I haven't slept for twenty-four hours. It all happened a bit fast, you might say. When's this guy coming? And when can I—?'

The telephone on the vast desk started to ring.

'Yes?' The ambassador held the receiver a few centimetres from his ear. 'Yes,' he said again and put the receiver down.

Warren Scifford put the glass back on the tray.

'He's not coming,' the ambassador said and got up.

'What?'

'We're going to them.' He grabbed his jacket and pulled it on.

'But we had *an agreement* . . .'

'Well, actually, it was more of an order.' The ambassador pointed at Scifford's jacket. 'An order from us to them. Put your jacket on. They won't tolerate that. They want us to go there.'

Before Warren Scifford could complain again, the ambassador put a fatherly hand on the younger man's arm. 'You would do exactly the same, Warren. We're guests in this country. They want to play at home. And even though there aren't many of them, be prepared for . . .'

He stopped and laughed, a surprisingly high whinny. Then he went over to the door before finishing the conversation. 'There may not be many people in this country, but they are incredibly stubborn. Every single one of them. You might as well get used to it, son. Get used to it!'

10

'**M**um! It's true! Just ask Caroline!'

She crumpled over the table and hit the surface with her left hand. Her eyes were red and her make-up had run in grey streaks down her cheeks. Her hair, which the evening before had been tied up with colourful ribbons and shoelaces in an eighties-style fashion, was now hanging down her back in bedraggled knots after what had been a slightly too successful party. She had her overalls half down. The arms were tied loosely around her waist and she had stuffed a half-litre bottle of Coke in the waistband.

'Why won't you believe me? You *never* believe what I say!'

'Of course I do,' her mother said calmly and put a dish in the oven.

'No you don't. You just think that I drink and fu—'

'Careful, young lady!' The mother's voice was sharper and she slammed the oven door shut with a bang. 'You may be moving away from home this autumn, and then you can do what you like. But until then . . .'

The woman turned to her daughter. She put her hands on her hips and opened her mouth to say something else. Then she closed it again and smoothed down her hair in exasperation.

'Just ask Caroline,' sobbed the daughter and grabbed hold of a half-full glass of milk. 'We were both there. I don't know where they came from, but they got into a car. A blue car. It's true. It's the truth, Mum!'

'I don't doubt that you're telling the truth,' her mother replied in a strained voice. 'I'm just trying to point out that it couldn't have been the American president that you saw. It must have been someone else. Don't you understand? Don't you realise . . .'

With a groan, she sat down at the table and tried to hold her daughter's hand. 'If someone had just kidnapped the American president, they wouldn't calmly walk over to a car parked by the Central Station on the morning of the seventeenth of May, where everyone could see them. You'll have to stop—'

The girl pulled her hand away.

'Where everyone could see them? *Where everyone could see them?* There was no one bloody else there. It was only me and Caroline and—'

'You must try to stop being so dramatic all the time! Surely you understand that—'

'I'm going to call the pigs. The woman was wearing the same clothes as on TV. Exactly the same. I'm going to phone, Mum.'

'Well, if that's what you want to do. But you'll just make a fool of yourself. And remember that they call themselves the police. Not pigs. Phone away.'

The mother got up. There was a strong smell of cooking. She opened the window a bit.

'Who the hell has a dinner party on the seventeenth of May, anyway?' the girl muttered and finished the glass of milk.

'Now you watch yourself, my girl. And stop all that unnecessary swearing!'

'People have breakfast on the seventeenth of May, Mum. Breakfast, or at a push a nice lunch. I have never heard of anyone having a bloody—'

A casserole was thumped down on the worktop. The woman pulled off her apron and took two neat steps towards her daughter. Then she slapped the table.

'*We* have a dinner party on the seventeenth of May, Pernille. *We, the Schou family*. And we have done so for generations, and *you* . . .' She lifted a finger. It was trembling. 'You had better be in the dining room at six o'clock sharp, and in a better state than you are now. Understood?'

The mother interpreted her daughter's muttering as agreement.

'But I *did* see the President,' the girl insisted, almost inaudibly. 'And she didn't bloody well look like she'd been kidnapped.'

11

The model of the Hotel Opera was made to a scale of one to fifty. It was mounted on a free-standing solid column, like a miniature accommodation platform. The details were impressive. The small swing doors in the entrance moved. The windows were made out of the thinnest glass possible, and even the curtains had the right pattern. When Warren Scifford bent his knees and peered into the foyer, he could see the yellow sofas facing each other with tiny tables in between. The lamps gave a yellow glow and the royal-blue armchairs looked temptingly comfortable.

'But this is not the building as it stands,' he mumbled and scratched his stubble.

'No,' replied the Chief of Police, Terje Bastesen. 'It was made in connection with the renovations. The hotel management have of course been extremely . . .' he searched for the right word, 'obliging. The roof can also be removed.'

His hands were coarse and he was shaking slightly. As he put his fingers gently round the roof, it slipped. A rasping sound made a young policeman who had been in the background, in the corner of the room, rush forwards. He lifted the roof with the utmost care to reveal the hotel's ninth floor.

'Look at that,' Warren Scifford exclaimed. 'And that is where she was staying.'

The presidential suite was in the left wing of the hotel, facing south. Even when the roof had been removed from the model, the windows overlooking the fjord stayed in place. There were sliding doors leading out on to the roof terrace, which was bordered with minute flowerpots. The suite was tastefully furnished down to the smallest detail, like a doll's house for a rich man's spoilt daughter.

'So you come in here . . .' Bastesen used a laser pen to point; the red spot danced and shook, 'straight into the reception room. Then you can go through here . . .' the spot hopped to the east, 'to the office. Well, it's supposed to be some kind of office. And here we have . . .' He bent down and peered short-sightedly at the model. 'Here we have a PC and a minuscule printer. And as you can see, the bedroom is at the far end of the reception room. We assume that the Presi— that Madam President was sleeping when the kidnappers came in.'

'Kidnappers,' Warren Scifford repeated, carefully touching the bedclothes with his index finger. 'As far as I know, there is no information to indicate how many there were.'

The Chief of Police nodded and popped the laser pen back in his breast pocket.

'No, that is correct. What I'm saying is based on the message. *We'll be in touch*, it says. "We". Not "I". *We've got her. We'll be in touch*.'

Warren Scifford straightened up and was handed a piece of laminated paper.

'I take it this is a copy,' he said.

'Of course. The original has been sent for analysis. It was your men who found it, and they . . . they had the sense not to touch it until it could be handled correctly.'

'Times New Roman,' Scifford stated. 'The most common font of all. I assume there are no fingerprints? And it's the sort of paper that can be found in every office and home?'

He didn't even bother to look up to see the Chief of Police's affirmative nod. Instead, he handed the sheet back and focused on the model again.

'By the way, they're not my men,' he said, slowly moving a couple of steps to the left to get a new perspective on the entrance to the presidential suite.

'Excuse me?'

'You said that it was my men who found the note.'

'Yes . . .'

'They're not my men. They're from the Secret Service. And as I assume you know, I am . . .' His hair flopped over his forehead as he bent down and closed one eye. He squinted along the corridor outside the presidential suite. 'I am from the FBI. Different organisations.'

His voice was cool. He had still made no eye contact with the Chief of Police. But he did put his hand on the other man's arm, as if he wanted to move an obstinate schoolboy.

'Give me some room,' he muttered, and once again became totally focused on the model of the Hotel Opera. 'Is this as exact as it appears to be?'

The Chief of Police didn't answer. A flush spread over his cheeks. He blinked several times before brushing some dust off his uniform jacket and clearing his throat.

'Mr Scyfford,' he said. His voice was deeper and raspier.

'Scifford,' the FBI agent corrected. '*Ski*, like the planks you use to walk on snow with in winter. Not *sky* as in clouds.' He pointed at the ceiling.

'I apologise, and take note of the correct pronunciation,' the Chief of Police said slowly. 'But before we go any further, I would just like to clarify a couple of things. First of all—'

'Just a moment, please.' Warren Scifford lifted a hand. 'There's a camera installed here, is that correct?'

He fished a pen out of his pocket and pointed towards the corridor.

'Yes,' Bastesen replied hesitantly. 'And over here. Just where there's a bend in the corridor. That way the whole corridor is kept under surveillance. From both sides. There's also a camera here . . .' He pointed to the area by the lifts. 'And here, on the stairs. The emergency exit. But before we go any further, I just want—'

'Please wait. Just a moment.'

Warren Scifford circled the model in deep concentration. Every now and then he stopped, bent down so his face was level with the wall and squinted down the corridor. His dark grey wavy hair was constantly falling over his face. He pursed and smacked his lips, before going round again. Slowly.

'I'll obviously have to go and see the actual hotel,' he said without moving his eyes from the model. 'This evening, preferably. But you're right. The whole corridor does seem to be covered. What about the terrace?'

'Well, it's not possible to get up there from the outside, unless you—'

'Nothing is impossible,' Warren Scifford interrupted, adding with a smile that was impossible to interpret: 'My question was about the camera coverage.'

'Well, Madam President didn't want cameras in the suite. Apparently she was very insistent. Both we and—'

Warren Scifford raised both his hands. The Chief of Police allowed himself to be interrupted again. The young policeman, who had withdrawn to the corner by the door again, looked uncomfortable, and was staring at the floor. The room was starting to feel stuffy, really too hot. Bastesen was sweating in his uniform. The flush on his cheeks had spread over his whole face. His thin hair was sticking to his forehead. Scifford had thrown off his jacket and rolled up his shirt sleeves some time ago. His tie was hanging loose and the top button of his shirt was undone. His eyes were deep-set and dark brown, with unusually long lashes. His curls and unkempt hair made him look younger than he presumably was. He looked directly at the Chief of Police. Bastesen stared back.

'I know my president,' Warren Scifford said deliberately. 'I know her very well and I therefore feel it is unnecessary for you to inform me of her habits. I think we would both benefit from keeping this . . . conversation . . . strictly to what I need to know. To put it simply, you answer my questions. OK?'

The Chief of Police took a deep breath. Then he suddenly smiled, unexpectedly. He took his time unbuttoning his jacket and pulled it off. He didn't seem to be embarrassed by the large sweat marks under his arms as he brushed his hair back with both hands. He then gave an even broader smile, put his hands behind his back and slowly rolled backwards and forwards on the balls of his feet, like an old-fashioned bobby. His shoes squeaked.

'No,' he said cheerfully. 'That's not OK.'

Warren Scifford lifted an eyebrow.

'I think that what is most important right now,' Bastesen continued, 'is that you understand what your role is here. And what my role is.'

He stood up on his toes for a moment, before rolling back down and continuing. 'I am the Chief of Police here in Oslo. A crime has been committed here, in my town and my country. In Norway, an independent state. The investigation of this crime falls under my governance. And the fact that the victim is a . . . a prominent person from another country . . .' His hands were no longer shaking as he carefully touched the flowerpots on the terrace outside the presidential suite. It was so quiet in the room that they heard the sound of the paper against his skin. '. . . means that out of common courtesy to you as a close ally, and respect for the importance of this case, we will keep you informed. And that is the key word. Information. You will provide us with the information necessary to solve the case as speedily as possible. We will inform you of developments in the case and what is going on. *To the extent that it does not jeopardise the investigation.*'

The sudden increase in the volume of his voice made the policeman in the corner jump. Then there was silence.

Warren Scifford pulled at his ear lobe. He was tanned for the time of year. There was a white bracelet round his left wrist where a watch had presumably prevented the sun from touching his skin.

'Sure,' he said in a friendly voice, and nodded.

'I hope so,' Bastesen said, and this time he did not return the smile. 'And if I may get to the point now?'

Scifford just nodded.

'She didn't want any sort of surveillance in the suite itself. And that was why we were so particular about the corridor.'

He turned his laser pen on again and pointed.

'As you already know, the cameras show no movement whatsoever either in or out of the room between twenty to one, when Madam President returned from an official dinner, and twenty past seven in the morning, when your men . . .' He stopped himself and started again: 'Twenty past seven in the morning, when the Secret Service thought it necessary to enter the suite. She was due to report to them at seven a.m. The cortège that was to take her to breakfast at the palace was due at seven thirty. And as far as the terrace is concerned . . .'

He walked around the model and pointed to the sliding glass doors.

'It was of course difficult to install a camera on the terrace without this conflicting with the President's explicit wish not be under surveillance in her room. It was a problem. So we fitted the doors with sensors.'

Bastesen allowed a short pause before he concluded: 'An alarm would have gone off if the doors had been opened. And they weren't. The sensors have, obviously, since been tested and are in perfect order. So we have to conclude that no one went in or out through these doors.'

'No one has come in and no one has left.' Warren Scifford ran his fingers through his hair. 'Quite apart from the fact that Madam President has disappeared and someone has left a note in her room.'

If the Chief of Police had been better at English, he would have noticed the biting sarcasm. However, he now just gave an affirmative nod.

'That aside, yes.'

'The air vents,' Warren Scifford said mechanically, without looking away from the model. 'Emergency exits. Other windows.'

'They are all being investigated. Everything will, of course, be examined in detail. But we have already spoken to the hotel's technical operations manager and he has ruled out any possibility that the air vents may have been used to get in or out of the room. He said that they're not big enough, and furthermore, they're blocked by fixed grates at fairly regular intervals. As far as the windows go, they're all alarmed, as I said. And they, quite simply, have not been opened. Emergency exits?'

He swept the red spot over a door from the office into the corridor.

'Well, the lock is sealed with one of those green plastic cases that have to be broken before the door can be opened. The mechanism is intact. The door has not been opened. And in any case, the exit is covered by the cameras in the corridor, and as I said . . .'

'No one went in,' Warren Scifford repeated, 'and no one went out.'

There was a knock at the door. The policeman looked at Bastesen, who nodded.

'Ambassador Wells and the Minister of Foreign Affairs are waiting for Mr Scifford,' a young woman said in Norwegian. 'I got the impression that they were getting a bit impatient.'

'They're asking for you,' Bastesen translated, and handed Scifford his jacket.

He didn't take it. Instead he loosened his tie even more, and produced a notebook from his back pocket.

'I suggest that for the time being, we have three meetings a day,' he said and wiped his nose with a finger. 'I would also like to have a liaison person.' His smile was almost boyish, as if he was apologising without really meaning it. 'If that suits you and your people,' he added. 'If you think that is the best way to exchange information.'

Bastesen nodded and shrugged. He was still holding Scifford's jacket.

'And I would really like to have . . .' Scifford scribbled a name down on a sheet of paper and gave it to the Chief of Police, 'her. Do you know the name?'

Bastesen's eyebrows shot up in surprise as he studied the piece of paper.

'Yes, but that's impossible, I'm afraid. She doesn't work for us. She never has done, even though she . . .' He hung the jacket over the back of a chair. 'She has helped the police on a couple of occasions,' he continued. 'Completely informally. But in the current situation, it would not be possible to use—'

'Well, I almost insist,' Warren Scifford replied.

His voice was different. The arrogance was gone. The drawling, slow manner of speaking had been replaced by an almost pleading tone.

'No,' Bastesen repeated and tried to give the American his jacket again. 'I'm afraid it's not possible. But I'll find the best person for you, immediately. I think you should go now. Apparently they were very impatient.'

'Wait,' Scifford said and scribbled down another name on his pad. 'Can I have him, then? He should at least . . .'

'Adrian Stubburt,' Bastesen read out slowly and gave a slight shake of the head. 'I don't know anyone by that name. But I—'

'Adam Stubo,' came from the door.

Both men turned round. The policeman blushed.

'I'm sure he means Adam Stubo,' he stuttered. 'He's in the NCIS. He lectured us in—'

'Adam Stubo,' Bastesen repeated, waving the first piece of paper that Scifford had given him. 'He's in fact married to this lady here! Do you know them?'

Warren Scifford straightened his collar. Finally he put his jacket on.

'I've met Stubburt on two occasions,' he said. 'But I don't know him. Johanne Vik, on the other hand . . . I knew Johanne well once upon a time. Can I use Stubburt?'

'Stubo,' Bastesen corrected him. 'Stubooooo. I'll see what I can do.'

They walked towards the door together. Bastesen stopped

abruptly, his face full of curiosity as he put a hand on the American's arm and exclaimed: 'That's right! Johanne Vik has a connection with the FBI. Something that I've never really worked out. Is that how you know each other?'

Warren Scifford didn't answer. Instead he tightened his tie, straightened his jacket and went to meet his ambassador.

12

Abdallah al-Rahman was still a good swimmer. He cut through the water with long, steady strokes. His rhythm was slow, but the efficiency of his long arms and unusually large hands meant he kept his speed. The water was not chlorinated. Chemicals made him feel nauseous, and as no else had permission to use the large pool, it was filled with salt water. The water was changed frequently, so it never made him ill.

The man sitting by the edge of the pool in a comfortable chair full of cushions, smiled at the beauty of the mosaics in and around the pool: tiny pieces of tile in myriad shades of blue that glittered in the light from the flares along the stone wall to the east. The evening air was gentle compared with the harsh heat that had harassed him all day. He would never get used to the heat. But he loved what was left behind, the stored warmth of the sun that made the evenings balmy and eased the pain in his damaged knee.

The Arab's body ploughed through the water. The man by the pool was drinking tea as he followed his friend's progress.

His name was Tom Patrick O'Reilly and he had been born into appalling poverty in a small town in Virginia in 1959. And things had got worse. His father had disappeared when the boy was barely two. He went out to fill up the car one day and his family had seen neither hide nor hair of him or the twelve-year-old pick-up, the family's only car, since. His mother literally killed herself trying to feed the four children. She died when Tom was sixteen, in 1975, and already at her modest funeral, Tom had decided to invest everything in the only good card he'd ever been dealt. From being a talented player in the local football team in his last two years at high school, he managed to become the most promising quarterback that Virginia had produced in

84

decades. He was given a scholarship to Stanford and left his home town with only a rucksack for his clothes, three one-hundred-dollar bills in his back pocket and the absolute certainty that he would never set foot in the town again.

He injured his knee in the first year. Lateral and cruciate ligaments, and meniscus. Tom O'Reilly was twenty years old and saw no future for himself. His academic performance was at best mediocre, so the only way he could continue his education was to pay with his spectacular passes.

He had been sitting in his room crying when Abdallah came in without knocking. The young man, whom Tom had only spoken to a couple of times, sat down on a stool and looked out the window. He said nothing.

Tom O'Reilly remembered drying his eyes. He gave a forced smile and pulled at the arms of his sweater, which was too small for him. Tom's training meant that he was getting bigger. His scholarship only covered absolute necessities, fees and a modest living. Clothes were a luxury. The young man who had come uninvited into his room and started to finger the few belongings that Tom had stuffed into his rucksack was dressed in expensive jeans and a silk shirt. His shoes alone would cost more than Tom's annual clothes budget.

Now, sitting in this palace outside Riyadh, drinking sweet tea and managing a fortune that he could never have even dreamt of at the time when he stood on the threshold of a promising career as a sportsman, it struck Tom that what had happened that warm spring day in 1978 was absurd.

He didn't know Abdallah. No one at Stanford knew him. Not really, even though he was invited to the most popular parties and occasionally turned up, sauntering in with an enigmatic smile. The young man was filthy rich. Oil, everyone thought when they saw his black hair and sharp profile. No doubt it was oil, but no one asked. Abdallah al-Rahman did not invite questions about his private life. He was friendly enough, though, and a very good swimmer in the university team. He didn't seek the company of his peers in the way that others did, but he was not a loner either. Girls always turned their heads. He was broad-shouldered and tall, and his eyes were unusually large. But nothing ever happened; after all, he was a foreigner.

And it seemed he was happy to keep it that way.

And then suddenly there he was, sitting in the messy student room that smelt of boys' socks. When he threw Tom O'Reilly a lifeline, the penniless young man grabbed it with both hands.

And he had never let go since.

The tea was so sweet that his tongue felt furry. Tom O'Reilly put the glass down. He ran his fingers through his strawberry-blond hair and smiled at the Arab, who, with one graceful movement, emerged from the water.

'Good to see you,' Abdallah said, and shook his hand. 'Sorry to make you wait.'

Always a handshake, Tom O'Reilly thought to himself. Never a traditional embrace or kiss. Nothing more, nothing less, a simple handshake. It was cold and wet and Tom O'Reilly shivered slightly.

'You've had too much sun,' Abdallah told him and picked up a towel to dry his hair. 'As usual. I hope you haven't been bored. I've had quite a bit to do.'

Tom just smiled.

'How is Judith? And the kids?'

'Well,' Tom replied. 'Very well, thank you. Garry is starting to get good now. Will never be much of a quarterback. Too big and heavy. But he might have a future as a defence player. I'm trying to pull some strings.'

'Don't pull too hard,' Abdallah advised him, and tugged a white tunic over his head before sitting down on one of the empty chairs. 'Children should learn to look after themselves. More tea?'

'No thanks.'

Abdallah poured himself some from a silver pot.

They sat in silence. Tom caught himself studying Abdallah

when he thought he wasn't looking. The Arab had an unusual calm that never ceased to fascinate him. They had known each other for nearly thirty years now. Abdallah knew everything there was to know about Tom. The American had shared his sad story with his friend on that first night, and since then he had kept Abdallah informed of everything, big and small, that happened in his life: girls and stories, work, love and political preferences. Sometimes, when Tom was lying awake in bed and couldn't sleep, he would look at his wife in the dark and think that Abdallah knew more about him than she did. Even after nearly twenty years of marriage.

That was the deal.

Even way back then, on that warm afternoon when spring had finally arrived and Tom had received the letter saying that his scholarship would be withdrawn from the following school year, *due to medical circumstances*, he was clear what the price of this fantastic gift would be.

Abdallah would know everything about him.

But both then and now, Tom felt it was a small price to pay. It was always a pleasure to be with Abdallah. At school they hung out every now and then, but were never seen to be good friends. At least not by others. And when they had finished school, they never met in the US. Their paths sometimes crossed in Europe. Tom often had meetings in metropolises where Abdallah happened to be on business. Then they would meet for dinner at some local Arabic café in London, or for a walk in the Champ de Mars by the Eiffel Tower, or along the Tiber, after a couple of coffees at a Roman café.

Occasionally Tom was called to Riyadh.

'How was the journey?' Abdallah poured himself more tea.

'Fine.'

Tom O'Reilly liked being in Riyadh. He was always taken to this place, even though he knew there were other palaces, which he was led to believe were bigger and more impressive. The invitations were always sudden, never more than three hours' notice.

Always from a local telephone number. A private jet was ready for departure at the nearest airport. All Tom had to do was turn up. He might be in Madrid or Cairo, or Stockholm for that matter, when the invitation came. His work as the CEO of ColonelCars took him all over the world. In the days when he was lower down the ladder, it was sometimes difficult to suddenly rearrange everything. That was easier now, and in any case, the invitations had become less and less frequent.

It was a year and a half since he had last been here.

'This will be the last time we meet,' Abdallah said out of the blue and smiled. Tom O'Reilly tried to straighten up in the sea of soft cushions. His knee was hurting again. He had been sitting in the same position for too long. He didn't know what to say, but he knew that he had to say something.

'That's a shame,' he murmured, and felt like an idiot.

Abdallah al-Rahman's smile widened. His teeth were pearly white against his dark skin. He drank down the rest of his tea in one go and put the glass down carefully.

'It has been a pleasure, Tom, a real pleasure.'

The affection in his voice surprised Tom; it was as if Abdallah was talking to a favoured child.

'Likewise,' he mumbled, clasping his hand round the glass so his fingers had something to do.

Again they were both silent. The only thing that broke the vast, warm silence of the palace was a dog barking in the distance. The water in the pool was like a mirror. The gentle breeze at sunset that had made the air so pleasant earlier had now died down. Certainly in here behind the high old walls that surrounded the garden.

When Tom O'Reilly had accepted Abdallah's generous offer in 1978, he had done so without any great reservations. He had swiftly managed to suppress the faint twinge of something that might be bad conscience. It was just stupid to question things that you didn't quite know the answer to. The remainder of his studies would be paid for in return for no more than a small favour. The money would not only cover his school fees, but would also afford him a generous lifestyle. He could stop taking on extra jobs and concentrate on his studies. And as he was no longer training four hours a day, his academic work improved immensely. He qualified with a good grade, a valuable network of contacts from Stanford and the will to succeed that so often drives those who have found themselves on the edge.

But as he got older, doubts crept in.

Not overwhelming, but enough for him, in his thirties, to try to find out more about the foundation that had made it possible for a poor and not particularly promising student to finish his studies at one of the world's most prestigious universities. As a student, the only thing that had concerned him was that a sizeable sum was paid into his account every summer and every Christmas, from the anonymous 'Student Achievement Foundation'.

The foundation did not exist.

That worried him and gave him a couple of sleepless nights. However, he quelled his doubts after a while and assumed that it might well have been disbanded. Nothing strange about that, really, when he thought about it. No point in wasting valuable time investigating any closer.

Tom O'Reilly was an intelligent man. When Abdallah al-Rahman started to contact him in Europe, he of course realised that it could be misconstrued by others. By those who couldn't understand that they were, in fact, good friends from university. By those who didn't realise that the conversations they had were completely innocent.

'Has life turned out the way you hoped it would?' Abdallah asked him now in a calm voice, almost uninterested.

'Yes.'

Tom had everything. He was faithful to his wife, though there had been temptations along the way. Even as a student, he had sworn that his father's legacy would not cast any shadows in his own life. He was blessed with four children and an income that meant he could afford to house his family in a twelve-bedroom villa in one of Chicago's best suburbs. He worked hard, and long hours, but had worked his way high up enough in the system to safeguard his weekends and holidays. Tom O'Reilly was a respected man. In quiet moments, when the children were younger and he tucked them in before he went to bed, he felt that he epitomised the American dream. He was content.

'Yes,' he repeated and coughed. 'I am extremely grateful.'

'You have only yourself to thank. I just helped when the system turned its back on you. You did the rest yourself. You've done well, Tom.'

'Thank you. But I am . . . grateful. Thank you.'

Abdallah's choice of words made him feel uncomfortable.

The system.

He had used a concept that Tom did not like. Not in the way that Abdallah had used it; to refer to the system in that way seemed . . .

Abdallah is not like them. He understands us. He operates within our system, our economy, and has never, not once, said anything that would indicate that he is like them. Quite the opposite. He respects me. He respects American values. He is practically . . . American.

'The system is harsh.' Tom nodded. 'But it's fair. I would in no way underestimate what you've done for me. As I said, I am deeply grateful. But with all due respect . . .'

He hesitated, and studied the chased-metal circles on the glass.

'With all due respect, I would probably have managed to get by on my own. I had the ambition. I was willing to work hard. The system repays those who work hard.'

It was impossible to read in Abdallah's face what he was thinking. He was obviously relaxed. His eyes were half closed, and a faint smile played on his mouth, as if he was thinking about something amusing that had nothing whatsoever to do with the conversation.

'We're both examples of that,' he replied eventually. 'The system repays those who work hard and who are focused. Those who set themselves long-term goals and don't think only about short-term gain.'

Tom was reassured. He shrugged and smiled.

'Exactly.'

'And now I want you to do me a favour,' Abdallah said, the distant expression still in his eyes, as if he was actually thinking about something else.

He gestured to a servant whom Tom had not noticed earlier. He was standing half hidden behind a gigantic pot with three palm trees in it over by the terrace entrance some twenty metres away. The servant approached on silent feet and handed an envelope to Abdallah. Then he withdrew, equally silently.

'A favour,' Tom muttered. 'What is it?'

You've never asked me to do anything before. You've only asked about my life. About me and what I'm doing. That was the deal. I was to stay in touch. Meet you whenever you asked me to. That was the agreement. You said nothing about favours, Abdallah. I've kept my promise for nearly thirty years. I never promised to do any more than that – than to give of myself.

'Something very simple.' Abdallah smiled. 'I just want you to take this back to the US and post it. And then we're quits, Tom. Then you will have paid back what you owe me. And just so that you don't think this is anything dangerous . . .'

Tom sat paralysed as Abdallah opened the envelope. Inside there was another, smaller envelope. It was not sealed. Abdallah stuck his nose down into it and took a deep breath. Then he smiled and held the envelope open for Tom.

'Look, no poison. You are, and I think I'm justified in saying this, a bit hysterical about postal correspondence. This is quite simply a letter.'

Tom saw the folded paper. It looked like there might be several sheets. The letter was folded so the writing was on the inside. It was ordinary white paper. Abdallah licked the envelope and sealed it. Then he put it back into the bigger envelope and sealed that too.

'All you have to do,' he said calmly, 'is to take it home with you. Then you need to find a postbox. It's of no importance to me whatsoever where in the US that might be. Then you open the big envelope and pop the smaller one in the box and throw away the big one. That's all.'

Tom O'Reilly didn't answer. He felt his throat constrict, as if he was about to cry. He swallowed. Tried to cough.

'Why?' he stuttered.

'Business,' Abdallah replied indifferently. 'I don't trust the post here. And certainly not all this modern communications technology. Too many eyes and ears. It's important that this reaches its destination. Simply business.'

How can you lie outright to me? Tom thought to himself and tried to keep his composure. How can you insult me like this? After thirty years? You have an entire fleet of planes and an army of employees at your disposal. But you've chosen me as a courier for that letter. What is this? What should I do?

'You will do this,' Abdallah added deliberately, 'primarily because you owe it to me. And if that is not enough . . .'

He didn't finish his sentence but looked the American straight in the eye.

You know everything about me, Tom thought and rubbed his sweaty palms together. More than anyone else. We have talked together for twenty-eight years, always about me, and seldom about you. You have been my confidant in everything. Everything. You know about my good and bad habits, my dreams and nightmares. You know my wife without ever having met her. You know how my children . . .

'I understand,' he said abruptly and took the letter. 'I understand.'

'Then we're quits. The plane will be ready to take you back to Rome tomorrow morning. Is seven too early? No. Good, I'm hungry. Let's go and eat, Tom. It's cool enough to eat now.'

He stood up and offered the American his hand to help him out of the low chair. Tom automatically took it. When he was on his feet, the Arab put his arm around his shoulder and kissed him.

'It's been a joy to have you as a friend,' he said softly. 'A real joy.'

And as the American stumbled, bewildered, over the flag-stones behind him, through the glass doors into the beautiful palace, a thought struck him for the first time: *How many Tom O'Reillys do you have, Abdallah? How many people are there like me?*

13

Detective Chief Inspector Adam Stubo walked home from his parents-in-law after a far too long and rather unusual national-day celebration.

He could, of course, have gone in the car with Johanne when she was finally allowed by her mother to go home. Ragnhild had fallen asleep long before. Kristiane was absolutely exhausted and confused when Isak, her biological father, turned up to collect her around seven. Even though they were all affected by the day's events, it was Kristiane who had taken it most to heart. They had managed to calm her down in the morning, and the girl had enjoyed being in the parade, though she hadn't let go of Adam's hand for a second. But things had got gradually worse throughout the day. She was obsessed with the lady who had disappeared and clung to her mother, terrified, until her father finally came and tempted her away by telling her about a new train set that only she could look after.

Adam could have gone in the car, but he chose to walk.

Instead of cutting down to Kjelsåsveien and crossing Storo, then heading towards Tåsen and home, he took a detour over the hill at Grefsen. The air was cool and fresh and the May light was still hovering in the western sky. His feet crunched on the asphalt. The council hadn't removed all the grit from the winter. It had rained earlier in the day, and the smell of last year's rotten leaves wafted over from the gardens. The flowerbeds were full of tulips that were past their best. Behind every window a TV screen flickered.

He stopped by a white picket fence.

The house was also white, but the evening light made it look almost blue. The curtains were open. An elderly couple were watching the news. He saw the woman lift her coffee cup. When she put it down again, she clasped the man's hand. They stayed sitting like that, frozen, hand in hand, as they watched the news that presumably told them nothing more than they had heard ten times already over the course of the day.

Adam stood there for a while.

He was cold, but it felt good. It cleared his brain. He couldn't drag himself away. The old couple in the small white house with tulips outside the sitting room window and the news on the TV somehow epitomised what had happened in Norway on this strange day that had started with celebrations and was now about to end with a threat that no one fully understood yet.

An assassination would, paradoxically, have been easier to accept, he thought. Death might be a sudden end, but it was also the start of something else. Death was something that could be mourned. A disappearance was endless purgatory, impossible to bear.

The man in the house got up stiffly. He shuffled over to the window and for an embarrassing moment Adam thought he had been seen and took two quick steps back. The man pulled the curtains shut; heavy, flowery material that closed out the rest of the world for the night.

Adam decided to go all the way up to Stilla, and then follow the path along the river. The water was breaking the banks. The geese had returned after winter a while ago, and here and there a mallard struggled against the stream, ducking down at regular intervals for some night food. Adam started to walk faster. He tried to keep up with the swollen spring river; he had to jog.

They chose not to assassinate her, he thought, out of breath. If there is such a thing as 'they'. They chose not to kill her. Was that what they wanted? The purgatory? And if they wanted to create a confused vacuum, they . . .

He was running as fast as he could now, in his good shoes, a suit, and a coat that was a touch on the tight side. He stumbled here and there, but found his balance again and stormed on.

95

He wanted to get home. He ran and tried to think about something else. About summer, which was just around the corner; about the horse he was thinking about buying, though Johanne had refused to have any more pets other than the yellowy-brown slavering dog that Kristiane called Jack, King of America.

How were they going to use that vacuum?

14

It was nearly eleven o'clock. Johanne was too tired to get up from the sofa and too restless to sleep. She tried to relish the thought of not having the children tonight and tomorrow, but couldn't do anything other than stare at the news, which was only serving up pointless repeats and regurgitated speculation. The only thing the authorities were clear about, nearly sixteen hours after the disappearance of the American president had been discovered, was that she had not reappeared. Representatives of official Norway were still reluctant to use the word 'kidnapping', but journalists showed no such restraint. One commentator after another expanded on the more-or-less ridiculous theories. The police just kept quiet. No one leading the investigation had been willing to give an interview since early afternoon.

'I agree with them about that,' Adam said and sat down beside her on the sofa. 'There are limits as to how many times they can be forced to say exactly the same thing. Which generally has been nothing. Bastesen looked pretty sheepish the last couple of times.'

'I hope they're lying.'

'Lying?'

She gave a faint smile and moved until she was more comfortable. 'Yes, that they know more than they're letting on. And I'm sure they do.'

'I'm not so sure. I have seldom seen a grimmer-looking bunch of people than whose who were filmed on their way out from . . .'

Johanne zapped over to CNN.

Wolf Blitzer himself was in the studio, as he had been for the past fourteen hours. The programme, *The Situation Room*, had taken over the entire broadcasting network, and judging by the activity in the studio, they had no intention of ending soon. The anchorman was, as usual, immaculately dressed. Only his tie was a smidgen looser than earlier in the day. With expert ease, he switched from a correspondent in Washington DC over to New York, before politely interrupting the journalist to give the word to Christiane Amanpour. The world-famous journalist was on the slope in front of an illuminated Norwegian royal palace. She was wearing thin clothes, and she seemed to be shivering.

'It's impressive how quick they are,' Adam mumbled. 'They're up and running within a few hours.'

'I don't see what the palace has got to do with the case.' Johanne stifled a yawn. 'But it's a good report, I agree. Everything is getting slicker and quicker. Did you run? You're sweating, my love.'

'Picked up speed a bit towards the end. It was great. More like jogging.'

'In a suit?'

He smiled disarmingly and kissed her. She plaited her fingers into his.

'Strange, really . . .' She stopped and stretched to get her wine glass. 'Can you tell the difference?'

'Between what?'

'The Norwegian and the American programmes. The mood, I mean. The Americans seem to be efficient, quick, nearly . . . aggressive. Everything here is a bit more . . . restrained. People seem to be paralysed in a way. Almost passive. At least, the interviewees certainly do. It's as if they're frightened to say too much, and so what little they do say just sounds silly. It all feels a bit like a parody. Look at the Americans, they're so much better at it.'

'But then they've had more opportunities to practise,' Adam said, trying to hide the irritation he always felt when confronted with Johanne's ambiguous relationship with anything American.

On the one hand, she never wanted to talk about the period when she had studied in the US. The two of them had known each other for many years now. They were married; they had children and a mortgage together. They shared dreams and daily life.

But there was still a substantial part of Johanne's past that was secret, that she protected more vehemently than even the children. The night before their wedding, she had forced him to take an oath: that he would never, under any circumstances, ask her why she had suddenly broken off her psychology studies at the FBI's academy in Quantico. He had sworn on his dead daughter's grave. Both the formulation of the oath and the consequences of it made him feel unwell whenever the topic was raised, and Johanne was consumed by a rage that she never demonstrated otherwise.

But at the same time, Johanne's fascination with everything American was bordering on manic. She read almost exclusively American literature and had a large collection of American low-budget films, which she bought over the Internet or got a friend of hers in Boston, whom he had never met and knew practically nothing about, to send. The shelves in her small office were full of reference books about American history, politics and society. He was never allowed to borrow any of them, and it really bothered him that she locked the door on the rare occasions that she went away on her own.

'Not really,' she said after a long silence.

'What?'

'You said that they'd had more opportunity to practise.'

'I meant . . .'

'They have never lost a president outside the country's borders. American presidents have been killed by random madmen in their own country. Never abroad. And never as part of a conspiracy, for that matter. Did you know that?'

Something in her voice made him not answer. He knew her well enough to know that if he turned this into a dialogue, she would quickly change the subject. If she was left to carrying on talking without interruption, she did.

'Four out of forty-four presidents have been assassinated,' Johanne said thoughtfully, as if she was actually talking to herself. 'Is that not nearly ten per cent?'

He tried to withstand the urge to interrupt.

'Kennedy.' She gave a faint smile and beat him to it. 'Forget it. Lee Harvey Oswald was a strange man who may have planned it with another couple of weirdos. Possibly not. It was certainly no great conspiracy. Except for in the film.'

She reached out for the bottle of wine. It was too far away. Adam grabbed it and poured some into her glass. The TV was still on. Wolf Blitzer's forehead now looked slightly damp, and when he handed over to a reporter in front of the White House, you could see the shadows under the anchorman's eyes. No doubt they would be concealed with make-up after the adverts.

'Lincoln, Garfield and McKinley,' Johanne continued, without touching her glass. 'They were all killed by lone fanatics. A confederate sympathiser, someone with mental-health problems and a mad anarchist, if I'm not wrong. Mad fellow countrymen. The same is true of all the many attempted assassinations. The guy who tried to kill Reagan wanted to make an impression on Jodie Foster, and the man who tried to bump off Theodore Roosevelt thought that he would get rid of the pain in his stomach if he killed the President. Only the two Puerto Ricans who . . .'

Christiane Amanpour was on the screen again. She had a warmer jacket on. The fur collar was perhaps intended to give a more Arctic mood. She was trying to keep it shut with one hand. This time she was standing outside the police headquarters in Grønland. Nothing new from there either. Johanne squinted at the screen. Adam turned down the volume with the remote control and asked: 'What about the Puerto—'

'Forget it,' Johanne interrupted. 'My point wasn't to lecture you in elementary American history.'

'What *was* the point then?' he asked, and tried to keep a friendly tone in his voice.

'You seemed to think the Americans were prepared. And they are, of course, in many ways. Certainly the television stations are.'

She nodded at Christiane Amanpour, who was having difficulties with her microphone. Behind her, a group of men in dark

100

suits hurried down the slope to Grønlandsleiret. They turned their collars up at the TV cameras and were not to be stopped by the questions shouted by around thirty journalists who obviously had bunkered down for the night. Adam immediately recognised the Chief of Police. Terje Bastesen turned away from the press and pulled his uniform hat down lower than regulated as he strode towards the cars that waited by the road.

'But the American people,' Johanne said, focusing on a point far above the television. 'They're hardly prepared. Not completely, not for this. Their entire history tells them that when it comes to the assassination of presidents, they have to watch out for confused fellow Americans. I should imagine that the Secret Service has outlined a number of assassination scenarios, mostly involving anti-abortionists, women-haters and the most zealous supporters of the war in Iraq – groups that include Helen Bentley's most ferocious opponents on the home front, and the sort of environment that fosters the kind of fanaticism that is empirically proven to be requisite. America's more recent history . . .'

She paused for a moment. 'More recent history has, of course, generated other scenarios. Post-nine eleven, I assume that the Secret Service would ultimately like to keep their president in a cement bunker. The US has never been so unpopular with the rest of the world at any time since the War of Independence. And as the concept of terrorism has been extended in recent years, certainly for the Americans, their fears of what might happen to the president have also changed. The fact that she would simply disappear into thin air on a state visit to a small, friendly country was probably a long way off what they anticipated. But . . .' The wine glass nearly toppled over as she suddenly reached out for it. '. . . what do I know about that?' She finished on a light note. 'Cheers, my love. Let's go to bed soon.'

'What's it like in the real Situation Room at the moment then, Johanne?'

She extracted herself from his arm.

'How should I know? I have no idea about—'

'Yes you do. If nothing else, because you've got a book that's actually called *The Situation Room* . . .' now it was Adam who could not restrain his irritation, which was about to spill over into real anger, 'that's lying on your bedside table. For Christ's sake, Johanne, it must be possible to share . . .'

In one swift movement she got up from the sofa and was on her way to the bedroom. A few seconds later she came back. Her face was bright red.

'Here,' she said. 'You've got the title wrong. And if you're so interested, you're free to read it. It's not exactly secret as it's lying beside our bed. So here you are.'

Her glasses were starting to steam up and sweat was visible on her nose.

'Johanne,' Adam groaned, exasperated. 'For God's sake, we can't carry on like this . . .'

I'm starting to get sick of this, he thought to himself. Be careful, Johanne. I don't know how much longer I can stand your ambiguity. This transformation of my intelligent, lovely, sensible wife into an ill-tempered creature that rolls into a ball with all its spines out for no understandable reason is wearing me out. Your secrets are too big, Johanne. Too big for me, and far too big for you.

There was a ring at the door.

They both jumped. Johanne dropped the book on the floor, as if she had been caught red-handed with stolen goods.

'Who could that be?' Adam mumbled and looked at the clock. 'Twenty past eleven . . .'

He was stiff when he got up and went to open the door.

Johanne stayed standing where she was, half turned towards the TV. The images that flickered across the screen were being watched all over the world at this very moment, irrespective of time zone or political regime, religion or ethnicity. CNN hadn't had so many viewers since the catastrophe on Manhattan, and seemed to be greedily taking advantage of the situation. It was nearly six in the evening on the east coast. Americans, hungry for news, were on their way home from work; they had felt compelled to go, despite the morning's terrible news. The news programme packed in more reporters, analysts, commentators and experts. They seemed more engaged than tired, as if the knowledge that they were nearing prime time gave them all renewed energy. Solemn men and women with impressive titles discussed the constitutional consequences and national contingency plans, short- and long-term crisis scenarios, terrorist organisations and the vice president's highly criticised absence. As far as Johanne could make out, he was hidden away either in a plane somewhere over Nevada, or in a bunker in Arkansas, as one of the experts claimed. Another insisted that he knew that the vice president was already out of harm's way at an American naval base far from the country's shores. They discussed the twenty-fifth constitutional amendment, and everyone agreed that it was scandalous that the White House had not made it clear whether this had been activated yet or not.

That's what they're discussing in the real situation room, Johanne thought to herself.

She could image all the plasma screens on the walls of a cramped room in the White House, somewhere on the ground floor of the West Wing, with red geraniums outside the windows. More than six thousand kilometres away from the semi-detached house in Tåsen in Oslo, a group of people were at that moment working frantically in an uncertain crisis situation, keeping a watchful eye on the same TV programmes as everyone else, while they tried to prevent the world from becoming a considerably changed place the following morning.

Every day, the many departments and agencies connected with national security received more than half a million electronic messages from embassies, military bases and other intelligence sources all over the world. They included warnings of vital importance to the nation's security as well as insignificant memorandums they would rather be spared. Routine reports came in

103

alongside reports of worrying enemy activity. The CIA, the FBI, the NSA and the Department of State all had their own operations centres that separated the wheat from the chaff in the incessant flow of information. Information of no importance was sent where it would do least harm, whereas important and dangerous information was tapped into messages to those who were there to deal with such matters: the Situation Room staff, a tight-knit core that had the authority to raise or lower the threshold for information, to demand more reports about particularly worrying developments, and who, most importantly, worked directly for the President.

Under George W. Bush, the screens were locked on to Fox News.

But now they once again watched CNN in the Situation Room.

Everyone did. Johanne nodded and sat down again.

The Americans were swimming in a sea of information with undercurrents that constantly threatened to pull them under. Agencies and departments, operations centres and foreign outposts, military and civil organisations – the flow of information in a crisis such as this was unbelievable. The entire American system would be on its knees by now, both domestic and international, in Washington DC and countless other cities and towns. When Johanne closed her eyes and acknowledged the indescribable fatigue that made it impossible to open them again, she thought she could hear a faint hum, like a swarm of bees in summer: tens of thousands of American civil servants who had only one aim, to bring the American president safely back home again.

And they were watching CNN.

She turned the TV off.

She felt so small. She went over to the kitchen window, which had finally been fixed. There was no longer a cold draught when she ran her hand along the windowsill. It was almost dark outside, but not quite. The spring brought with it the return of this beautiful light that made the evenings less threatening and the mornings easier.

She spun round. 'Who was it?'

'Work,' he mumbled.

'Work? At midnight on the seventeenth of May?'

He walked over to her. She was staring out of the window again. He put his arms round her slowly. She smiled and felt the goodness of his body warm her back. She relaxed. Closed her eyes.

'I want to go to sleep,' she whispered and ran a finger down his underarm. 'Please take me to bed.'

'Warren is in Oslo,' he whispered, not letting her go, even though he felt her stiffen. 'Warren Scifford.'

'What?'

'He's here in connection with . . .'

Johanne was no longer listening. Her head felt light and detached, as if it was no longer her own. A flush of heat pulsed down her arms into her hands, which she lifted and pressed to the window pane. She saw the lights of an aeroplane in the sky to the north, and could not understand what it was doing there at this time of night, on a day like today. She found herself smiling without knowing why.

'Don't want to know,' she said lightly. 'You know that. Don't want to hear about it.'

Adam refused to let her go. Her body felt smaller now; she was positively skinny. And stiff as a poker.

Warren Scifford, *the Chief*, had been Johanne's teacher at the FBI Academy. And more than just a teacher, Adam had soon understood. Johanne was very young at the time, only twenty-three, whereas Warren must have been well into his forties. A love affair that happened an eternity ago. Adam had not felt even a hint of jealousy on the few occasions that he and Warren had bumped into each other. The last time must have been three or four years ago at an Interpol meeting in New Orleans, when they had even had dinner together. But for reasons that he could not explain, he had felt uncomfortable when Warren started to ask lots of questions about Johanne. He had avoided answering in any detail, and for the rest of the meal they had talked about their work and American football.

Warren Scifford played a leading role in Johanne's great secret. Any talk of the man was forbidden, a fact that only told Adam the obvious: that he had at some point hurt her deeply.

But shit happens, he thought, and held on to Johanne. It's horrible and can be very difficult at the time. But you get over it. It's almost fifteen years ago now, my love. Forget it. Get over it, for God's sake. Or is there something more?

'Talk to me,' he whispered in her ear. 'Can't you just tell me what this is all about?'

'No.' Her voice was no more than breath.

'I'm going to have to work with him,' he said. 'I'm sorry.'

He still tried to hold on to her, but she pulled herself loose with surprising strength and pushed him away. The look in her eyes frightened him when she asked: 'What did you say?'

'He needs a liaison.'

'And it has to be you. Of all the hundreds of . . . You said no, of course.'

In a way she suddenly seemed more present, as if she had woken up when he let go of her body.

'I was given an order, Johanne. I work for an organisation that gives orders. Saying no is not an option.' He made quote marks with his fingers.

Johanne turned away from him and went into the sitting room. She twisted the cork from the corkscrew and put it back into the half-empty wine bottle. Then she grabbed the glasses and took them out into the kitchen, where she put them down on the worktop. Then she checked that the dishwasher was full, put some soap in the dispenser, closed the metal door and started the machine. She snatched up a cloth, wrung it under running water and wiped the surfaces. Then she carefully shook the cloth over the sink, rinsed it again and folded it before hanging it over the edge.

Adam followed her every movement without saying a word.

Finally, Johanne looked at him.

'I just want to make one thing absolutely clear before we go to bed,' she said. Her voice was calm and enunciated, just as it was when she was giving Kristiane a telling-off. 'If you say yes to being Warren Scifford's liaison, this marriage is over.'

He didn't know what to say, so he said nothing.

'I'll leave you, Adam. If you say yes, I'll leave you.'

Then she went and got ready for bed.

Finally, the Norwegian national day had come to an end.

Wednesday 18 May 2005

1

When Warren Scifford woke up, he didn't know whether it was the jet lag, the fact that he hadn't had enough sleep or a latent flu that was making him feel so awful. He lay in bed for a while, staring at the ceiling. The airy sky-blue curtains let the sunlight in. His bed was bathed in morning light. When he finally lifted his head to look at the digital clock on the TV, he furrowed his brow in disbelief.

Half past four in the morning.

Now he understood the point of those hideous rubber blackout curtains he had ignored when he flopped into bed at around one. He struggled out of bed and padded over to the window to close the curtains. Darkness fell in the room. Only a sliver of light that prised its way through the opening between the curtains made it possible to see anything at all.

He turned on the bedside lamp and lay down again without pulling the duvet over him. His naked skin contracted in the breeze from the air-conditioning. His neck was stiff and he could feel a headache lurking behind his eyes. He was exhausted and yet alert at the same time, and he knew that he wouldn't go back to sleep. After a few minutes, he got up again and put on a peacock-blue silk dressing gown. There was an electric kettle on the shelf by the TV. Three minutes later he was stirring a cup of bitter, strong instant coffee, which he drank as soon as he could. It helped, but he still felt so drained that in other circumstances he might have been worried.

He quickly worked out that it would be half past ten in the evening in Washington DC. This raised his spirits a notch. He could still count on a couple of problem-free hours, should it be necessary to contact anyone. He quickly set up his portable office on the desk that he had got the hotel to install. When he had arrived in the afternoon, there had been a great rococo table with a huge vase of flowers in the room, which would hardly have done the job. The desk he had now was simple and unpretentious, but massive. He took out an unusually large laptop from the metal case standing by the bed, then four mobile phones and a pile of pastel-coloured paper. He placed them all neatly in a row with meticulous precision. On top of the paper he laid three pens, equally spaced. A black pen, a red pen and a blue pen. The four mobile phones were of different appearance and made by different manufacturers, and he placed them, as if on display, to the left of the laptop. Finally he took a small printer, in three detachable parts, out of the suitcase, attached it to the computer and plugged it into the socket under the window. The laptop immediately turned itself on. The hotel boasted about its complimentary wireless connection, but he instead tapped in an American number. Seconds later he had accessed one of his mailboxes, which only four people knew about. The encryption code scrambled briefly, as it always did, showing him a chaos of characters before settling down into a well-known image.

Warren Scifford yawned and then blinked away the tears that had been squeezed out. He had received a reply to the query he had sent before he went to bed. He opened the email with a single click.

He read slowly. Then he read the whole thing again before clicking on the print icon and waiting for the whirring sound that told him that the document was being transferred to the printer and about to come out. He swiftly logged out and turned off the laptop. Then he went over to the door to check that the security lock was still on. No one had touched it.

He needed a shower.

He stood under the rushing, too-hot water for several minutes. To begin with it burnt on his skin, before a comfortable numbness spread down his spine. His neck already felt more flexible and his sinuses unblocked. He gave himself a good lather and washed his hair. Then he turned off the hot water and gasped in an ice-cold cascade.

Now he was certainly wide awake. He dried himself briskly and took some clean clothes from his suitcase, having confirmed behind the blackout curtains that it looked like it would be a sunny day. He got dressed, grabbed the printout and threw himself down on the bed, pushing three pillows behind his head.

The Trojan Horse link was not just warm, it was burning hot.

It was six weeks since one of the special agents had come into his office with a small pile of paper and a worried look on his face. When the man left half an hour later, Warren Scifford had put his elbows on the table, clasped his hands behind his neck and stared at the desktop for ages while silently cursing his own vanity.

He could have stayed where he felt comfortable. Warren Scifford was the best in his field; he was an expert in behavioural psychology, and the FBI had nurtured and developed him for over three decades now. He could have continued being a super-hero in his own universe. Paradoxically, there was something safe and manageable about pursuing bizarre serial murderers and perverted rapists. Warren Scifford had done it for so long and seen so much that the crimes no longer made any real impact. His emotions did not cloud an increasingly sharp eye and growing insight.

He was the very best hunter.

But then he was tempted.

President Bentley had called him personally in November, well before she was sworn in, to persuade him. Warren could still remember the feeling of intoxication when she contacted him. The sweet taste of success made him soft, and he laughed out loud and punched the air with his fist when the conversation was over. Not only was he wanted by America's commander-in-chief for an important position, she had in fact begged him. Even though Helen Bentley had been a close friend for more than six years, he knew that that gave him no advantages in the extensive jigsaw puzzle she had started to piece together when George W. Bush had finally and unwillingly given his concession speech.

Quite the opposite, in fact. Commentators had praised Madam President as the various appointments were announced. The extent to which she had steered clear of friends and loyal supporters in favour of candidates who were indisputably competent and independent was admirable.

But Warren was to be one of them, and he became a daily visitor to the West Wing.

The group he had been appointed to lead was part of the FBI. But he was to report directly to the President all the same, something that had caused a serious rift with the director of the FBI before the intelligence group had even been established. The entire procedure was completely at odds with FBI tradition. Of course, the director had to back down, but Warren's pride in being given the prestigious position waned somewhat when he had to acknowledge that he was no longer deemed to be a true Bureau man. For a short while he had considered changing his mind. But he quickly understood that that wouldn't be possible.

After 9/11, things had changed in the FBI. The Bureau had very quickly gone from being a police organisation that focused mainly on traditional, domestic crime to spearheading the fight against terrorism. Restructures that would have taken years to implement before were now completed within weeks. A storm of patriotic efficiency swept through all government organisations, institutions and departments that had anything to do with national security. The process was greatly helped by more or less unlimited resources and a legislative authority that proved to be more flexible than Americans might otherwise have thought before that catastrophic morning in September.

The image of the enemy had changed too.

There were still countries and states that were a threat to the world's most powerful nation. Following the disintegration and dissolution of the Soviet Union, the prospect of a traditional attack had as good as disappeared. But as the US had interests all over the world, it was still important to focus attention on unfriendly nations and hostile states that could attack for ideological, economic or territorial reasons.

So those functions continued, now as ever.

But it was not a state that had attacked the US on the 11th of September. There was no country to strike back at. The men who had hijacked the four planes and crashed them on American soil were individuals, of different origins and diverse backgrounds. While the political machinery surrounding President Bush had constructed a classical enemy in the form of the axis of evil, and targeted all its aggression towards existing nations, Helen Lardahl Bentley was convinced that the attackers were far more dangerous than that.

They were people.

They had not been recruited to fight, like the terrified soldiers through the ages who had faced death for a flag and a country they would never see again. The battlefields were no longer drawn up by generals on both sides of the front, who basically fought with the same parameters for victory and defeat: territory won and battles lost.

America's new enemies were individuals, with an individual's experience, greatness and flaws. They did not live in one place, in one system, and they did not wave a visible flag. They did not go to war because they had been ordered to, but because of their own conviction. They were not bound together by the same nationality and sense of belonging, but by belief and distrust, hate and love.

America's new enemies were everywhere, and Helen Lardahl Bentley was convinced that the only way to uncover them and render them harmless was to get to know them. The first thing she did in office was to establish the Behavioural Science Counter-terror Unit. Their remit was to transform dry facts and random intelligence into living images. The BSC Unit was to see people where the rest of the extensive domestic security system saw only possible attacks and potential terrorists, bombs and hi-tech equipment. By analysing, understanding and explaining

115

what made men of different nationalities and from different backgrounds choose a martyr's death in their collective hate of the US, the States would become better at forestalling them.

Warren Scifford had been allowed to choose from the most talented people. The group of nearly forty special agents included some of the best profilers in the FBI. Every single one of them had accepted eagerly.

But Warren had begun to regret his decision.

When one of the special agents had wandered into his office six weeks ago, with four sheets of paper in his hand, and in a quiet voice had shared his concerns with his boss, Warren Scifford had for the first time in his fifty-six years been truly scared.

A Trojan horse attack did not fit in with the picture they had drawn.

It didn't make sense. It was neither spectacular nor symbolic. It would not generate terrifying, unforgettable images like those of the planes crashing into the World Trade Center. No hordes of people fleeing in fright and tears, panic and disbelief to frame in powerful TV images. The Trojan Horse would not attract attention to the enemy; there was no honour, no matter how twisted, to be gained from this.

The rest of the system had done everything it could to link al-Qaeda or related organisations to the Trojan Horse. Warren Scifford and his men and women had protested violently. Something wasn't right, they argued. That wasn't the way al-Qaeda operated. They didn't think like that. And it certainly wasn't the way they wanted to punish the US. As the BSC Unit had already been frozen out by everyone other than the President, what they said generally fell on deaf ears. After a couple of weeks of intense and focused work, trying to find a link with existing terrorist networks, without so much as a hint of success, it was concluded that Warren Scifford's group had been right after all. Al-Qaeda was not behind this. The diffuse, incomplete information was therefore no longer of interest. The vast US intelligence apparatus received so much; there was almost too

116

much to deal with. So as more incomprehensible and chaotic information about more potential attacks ticked in, every hour, every day, the Trojan Horse was parked in a quiet back alley.

But Warren Scifford was still worried.

And so was Madam President.

And now Warren was lying in bed in a Norwegian hotel room with a gnawing feeling in his belly. He read the memo for the fourth time. Then he got up and went to the bathroom. He took a lighter out of his pocket, held the document over the toilet pan and set light to it.

The thing that made him most uneasy was the feeling that someone was taking him for a ride.

For a few weeks now, he had been dogged by a nagging suspicion that the information was planted. Having thoroughly studied the document, which included all the new information they had received in the past twenty-four hours relating to the complex he had chosen to call Trojan Horse – searching up and down, left to right, until nothing made any sense any more – he was still completely at a loss.

The flames licked the paper. Small flakes of soot drifted down towards the white porcelain.

If everything was planted, the whole thing was a red herring. And if that was the case, the President could be the actual target. And in that case, they were facing an enemy they knew nothing about. Not Osama bin Laden, not the many terrorist organisations based in . . .

'It can't be true,' Warren said out loud to himself, to interrupt his own thoughts. 'No one has the apparatus to plant something like this. It's too good to be planted.'

He had to let go of the last tiny scrap of the paper. He flushed the toilet. Small black flakes still clung to the pan, and he had to use the toilet brush to get rid of it all.

He went back to the desk and picked up a copy of the note that had been left in the President's hotel suite.

'We'll be in touch,' muttered Warren Scifford. 'But when?'

He dropped the note suddenly as if it had burnt him.

He had to eat.

The clock on the TV told him that breakfast was now being served. It took him three minutes to pack up his office and put the locked suitcase back in the cupboard. Only the pile of coloured paper was left on the desk, with the three pens lined up like tin soldiers on top.

He put one of the mobile phones in his pocket before he left. It hadn't been necessary to call anyone after all. And to be honest, he wasn't sure who he should ring anyway.

2

The customs officer at Oslo Airport Gardermoen could scarcely believe his own eyes. The gang of Americans had arrived on a charter flight, but their arrogance in relation to the security and laws of another country still beggared belief.

'Excuse me!' He held up his hand, then took a couple of steps out from behind the counter where he had been standing getting bored for the last hour and a half.

'What is that?' he asked in English, with an accent that made the American smile.

'This?' The man lifted his jacket, so that his government-issue firearm was visible.

The customs officer shook his head in disbelief. There were more of them coming through now, all with that characteristic bulge under their ribcage. They descended on him, wanting to get past, but he stood there with his arms held out and shouted: 'Stop! Wait just a moment!'

An irritated mumble spread quickly among the new arrivals, who must have numbered some fifteen or sixteen men and a couple of women.

'No guns,' the customs officer said firmly and pointed at the wide, low counter. 'Put all your weapons here. Then form a queue and you will get a receipt for each one.'

'Now listen here,' said the man who had come first. He was in his fifties and a good head taller than the small, rotund customs officer. 'Our arrival has been cleared with the Norwegian authorities, as you no doubt know. According to the messages I've received, we were to be met by a police office as soon as we—'

'Makes no difference,' the customs officer persisted, and for safety's sake pressed the button under the counter that closed the mechanised doors further down the corridor. 'I'm the one in charge here. Do you have papers for these weapons?'

'Papers? Now listen—'

'No papers, no weapons. Please form a queue here, then I'll—'

'I think it would be best if I spoke to your boss,' the American said.

'He's not here,' the customs officer replied. He had big blue eyes and a friendly smile. 'Now, let's get this sorted as quickly as possible.'

The American turned towards his increasingly impatient colleagues and started a somewhat muted conversation. One of the women took out her mobile phone. She tapped in a number with nimble fingers.

'There's no reception in here,' the customs officer said gleefully. 'So you can just forget about that.'

The woman continued to listen for any sign of life at the other end. Then she shrugged and gave the man, who was obviously some kind of boss, a look of exasperation.

'I really must protest,' he said to the customs man, with a look that stopped the short duty officer from interrupting again. 'There has obviously been a breakdown in communications on several fronts. To begin with, we were supposed to be met off the plane by our Norwegian colleagues. But instead we've been shown into this . . . labyrinth, without anyone to accompany us, and without knowing where to go.'

'You have to go out through there,' the customs officer said, pointing to the closed door.

'Then I suggest that you open it. Now. This is an embarrassing error on your part, and I'm losing patience.'

'I suggest . . .' the customs officer said, with a slight pause that gave him enough time to jump up on to the counter, with an agility that no one would have expected of him, 'that you do as I say. Out there . . .' his voice rose to a shout as he pointed towards the arrivals hall, 'other people decide. But in here, in this corridor, at this desk where you're now standing, it's me who knows the rules. And according to those rules, it is strictly forbidden to bring weapons into *my country* . . .' he was nearly screaming now, 'without the required papers. So please, start queuing, for God's sake!'

He broke into Norwegian. His face was flushed and he was sweating. The Americans stared at each other. Someone muttered something. The woman with the mobile phone made another equally unsuccessful attempt to call for help. There was a pause of about thirty seconds. The customs officer hopped down from the counter and stood arms akimbo. Another thirty seconds passed.

'Here,' said the boss suddenly, and put his weapon on the counter. 'But I can assure you, there will be consequences.'

'Only doing my job, sir!'

The customs officer was grinning from ear to ear. It took him nearly half an hour to collect in all the guns and place them in the plastic containers that were stored on a shelf at the far end of the room. When he had finished, he gave a two-fingered salute and pressed the button to open the doors.

'Have a nice stay,' he said and laughed when nobody answered.

He was only doing his job. Surely they could understand that.

3

When Johanne woke up, work was the first thing she thought about. She lay there without moving and squinted at the morning light. She had just finished a research project before having Ragnhild and hadn't really started on anything else since, so neither she nor the university would suffer too much if she took the two years' unpaid maternity leave to which she was entitled. She and Adam had agreed on that, as they were afraid that they might not get a nursery place for Ragnhild. They had both been well established when they met, and could pay the mortgage with only one income. They lived a simple, quiet and good life. Kristiane was improving too. They were all in a better place.

Johanne liked the routine of being at home. Life went at a different pace when she was with the children. She had always enjoyed making food, and the long mornings gave her the opportunity to do it from scratch. They had let the cleaner go, and even the cleaning was now part of the contemplative boredom that she had come to appreciate. Ragnhild slept for a couple of hours in the middle of the day, and sometimes Johanne felt that she really had time to think, for the first time in years.

It was a good life. For a while.

Maybe that time was over now.

Suddenly the idea of quiet mornings in the house was not so appealing. She listened for the sound of Ragnhild's chattering, but then remembered that the one-year-old was still with her grandparents. She felt unusually stiff. Slowly she stretched her arms over her head and turned over.

Adam wasn't there.

It was not like her to sleep so heavily. She usually woke up several times during the night, and would be wide awake within seconds if there was the slightest noise from the kids.

She sat bolt upright, cocked her head and held her breath so she could listen better. But the only thing she could hear was a car engine idling some way off and the spring chirping of ecstatic birds outside the bedroom window.

'Adam?'

She got up and pulled on her dressing gown, then padded out to the kitchen. The clock on the cooker said it was nearly quarter past eight. Silence everywhere. There was a half-finished cup of coffee on the worktop. When she picked it up, she could feel it was still warm, so it wasn't long since he'd left. There was a note beside the cup.

My love, I have to do my job, I'm sure you understand. And when you don't even give me a good reason to try to get out of it, I have no choice other than to go. Not easy to say when I'll be home, as I don't even know what the job entails. I'll ring as soon as I can. Your Adam.

Johanne took a sip of the lukewarm coffee.

Adam was going to be Warren's liaison. She had asked him not to. She had threatened him with what she thought was his worst nightmare. And yet he had got up as she slept, quietly made some coffee, written a short, cool note, then slipped out.

She stood with the sheet of paper in one hand and the cup in the other for a long time.

She couldn't go to her parents. Her mother would just get hysterical and her father would take it to heart, as he always did when the world was against him. Johanne often wondered if her parents were fonder of Adam than they were of her. Her mother certainly always bragged about him to anyone who bothered to listen. Adam was showered with attention by his in-laws, and he was the one who got all the honour every time Ragnhild impressed anyone with her language and motor skills.

'It's actually me who's at home with her all the time,' Johanne would sigh, before masking her irritation with a smile.

She couldn't go to her sister's either. Marie's perfection had become an insurmountable hurdle between them. She was beautiful, well dressed and childless. The very thought of invading her harbourside flat with baby food and smelly nappies made Johanne hyperventilate.

She read the short note again. The letters became unclear. She tried to blink away the tears. They coursed their way down her nose and she wiped away some snot on her sleeve.

When they had gone to bed the night before, she had been certain that he had understood. He had snuggled up to her in bed, without saying a word, his hands warm and strong, just the way she loved them. Adam knew that she needed protection and that Warren Scifford must not be allowed anywhere near their safe, routined life in Haugesvei. When he stroked her hair, she had been convinced that he realised all this. She was certain that she'd seen the acknowledgement in his eyes that Warren's very presence threatened all that they had that was beautiful and true and pure. And she had fallen into a deep, blissful sleep.

Then Adam had just left.

He hadn't taken her threat seriously. He hadn't taken *her* seriously. Well, he was going to find out how just serious she was.

Johanne packed the bare necessities. She folded enough clothes for a few days for herself and their younger daughter, and put them in a small suitcase.

'Kristiane can stay with Isak,' she whispered to herself as she tried to stop crying. She had to collect Ragnhild. Her mother would immediately notice her red eyes, the way she always noticed when anything was wrong with her daughter.

'Pull yourself together,' Johanne hissed and sniffed.

She didn't know where to go. But she continued to pack. The suitcase was eventually so full that she struggled to close it. With some florid language and a forceful arm she finally managed to zip it up.

She had to seek refuge with someone who would leave her in peace. Not her family, or friends. She couldn't go to anyone who might tell her how childish and irresponsible her behaviour was. She didn't want to go to anyone who might state the obvious: that the drama would be over in a few days, and that she wouldn't leave Adam, so she might as well go home again. And under no circumstances would she go to Line, her sociable best friend, who would undoubtedly drum up a party in the belief that there wasn't a problem in the world that couldn't be fixed with good food, good friends and buckets of drink.

The wind still felt cool as Johanne locked the front door behind her, even though the garden was bathed in sunlight. Then it struck her: there was only one place to go.

She dried her tears and forced a smile to a neighbour who waved to her from the road. Then she took a deep breath and got into the car. She had to collect Ragnhild. She should be able to think up a plausible lie for her mother as she drove over.

Johanne didn't feel any better about things, but at least she knew where she was going.

4

It was half past two in the morning in Farmington, Maine.

Al Muffet had been woken by a dream he couldn't remember. It was impossible to get back to sleep. His sheets were sweaty against his skin and his quilt had bunched into a nest at his feet. He changed position. It didn't help.

He had watched the news on TV all day. The disappearance of the President had shaken him as much as it had shocked the rest of the nation, but he also felt an inexplicable twinge of alarm.

His brother had phoned.

The last time his brother had called was three years ago, when their mother was dying. A stroke had stopped the industrious woman in her tracks, and she only had a matter of hours left. He had caught the first flight back to Chicago, but got there too late. His mother was already laid out in an open coffin, beautifully made up and dressed in her finest.

Even though she, like her husband, had maintained the Muslim faith of her childhood, the Muffasa family religion was flexible and well adapted to life in a suburb where there were few, if any, other Arabs. Mrs Muffasa was a highly appreciated asset to the Episcopal church that lay only a block away from the house. The best cakes at the harvest fete always came from her oven. She ran a youth club for young people from less fortunate backgrounds. No one could do flowers like Mrs Muffasa, and she looked after the reverend's numerous children whenever his wife gave birth to another and was out of action for a couple of weeks.

But the Muffasa family never went to church.

In their own quiet way, they tried to keep Ramadan. They celebrated Eid with relatives from Los Angeles, who always took the time to come. And if Mr Muffasa didn't actually face Mecca

126

and pray five times a day, he often found time to pray when the garage was empty and quiet before closing time.

Mr and Mrs Muffasa read the Koran in the most user-friendly way. They honoured the prophet Muhammad and prayed that peace be with him, without that preventing them from decorating a Christmas tree so that the children wouldn't feel left out.

When she died, Mrs Muffasa's children found a kind of will in the drawer of her bedside table. Her memorial service was to be held in the Church of the Epiphany, and was to be organised by the reverend's wife.

This caused rumblings in the family ranks, and their mother's eldest sister threw herself in hysterical tears over the washed and dressed body that lay with folded hands in the coffin, with a cross on either side. But Mr Muffasa insisted. His wife had been of sound mind when she decided on how she wanted to be remembered. No one could dissuade him from fulfilling her final wish, and so Mrs Muffasa was buried in consecrated ground in front of a full Christian congregation.

The funeral was the last time Al Muffet had seen his older brother.

Three years of silence. And then he rang last night.

Al Muffet got out of bed and dressed himself with swift, silent movements. He had some paperwork he could do to pass the time. Anything was better than lying in bed not being able to sleep, plagued by this anxiety that he could not explain.

He and Fayed had never been friends. They put up with each other, as brothers do, but they had never understood each other. While little Ali hid behind his mother's skirt and was adored by all her Episcopalian friends, Fayed wandered the streets alone and yearned to be with the extended family in Los Angeles, where he could go to the mosque with his uncle every day. There he could eat traditional food and learn more Arabic than the few words he managed to grasp from his father's mumbled prayers. As an adult, he didn't deserve to be called a practising Muslim, but on the whole, he upheld the traditions and married a Muslim woman. And when Ali Shaeed Muffasa became Al Muffet in the seventies, his brother Fayed accused him of being an Arab Uncle Tom. The brothers had barely spoken since.

Al Muffet had no idea what Fayed wanted. He had asked outright, but had avoided being positively rude. After all, they were brothers, and as their father was still alive, he didn't want any dramatic bust-ups in the family, as that would kill the old man.

Fayed was coming to visit.

Fayed, who was a middle manager for a gigantic electronics company based in Atlanta, and who barely had time to see his own children, had phoned to say that he would drop by on the 18th of May. A curt comment that it wasn't so strange that he wanted to know how Al and the girls were getting on out in the sticks was the closest he came to an explanation.

'I'll drop by,' he had said.

Al Muffet crept past his daughters' bedrooms. He knew the old house well enough now to step carefully over all the boards that creaked. At the top of the stairs he stood listening for a moment. Catherine's steady breathing and Louise's snoring made him smile. He felt calmer. It was his house and his life. Fayed could drop by as much as he liked. No one could harm Al Muffet or his daughters.

He went quietly downstairs and turned on the lights in the kitchen. He put on the kettle and took the cafetière out of the dishwasher, before getting the file he had brought home from the office from his bag.

'Dad?' Louise looked at him in surprise from the doorway.

He jumped and dropped the cafetière on the floor.

'Is anything the matter?' his daughter asked. Her hair was tangled and her pyjamas were too big.

'No, sweetpea. I just woke up and couldn't get back to sleep.'

He found the dustpan and brush in the scullery.

'But why are you dressed, Dad?' Louise sounded quite anxious now, and came closer.

'Watch out for the glass,' he warned. 'Nothing's wrong, nothing

128

at all. I just thought that I could use my sleepless night to do some work. Shall I make some warm milk for us both? Then we can have a natter before you go back to bed. Would you like that?'

She gave a big smile and sat down at the table.

'What fun,' she said and grabbed an apple. 'Just like when I was little. I must tell you what happened when Jody and I got . . .'

Al Muffet half listened as he swept up the broken glass. At least Louise had been reassured. He only wished he could say the same about himself.

5

The young police lawyer was bored. He had been fining people for nearly three hours in an attempt to empty the overcrowded cells. Over half of them were teenagers whose bodies were still not rid of the national-day celebrations. They stood in front of him, one after the other, with hangovers, staring at the floor as they stammered their polite apologies and promised never to do it again. A couple of older drunk drivers tried to drum up an argument, but piped down when threatened with continued detention, and were then released on bail.

The remainder were old acquaintances. Most of them were in fact grateful for free accommodation in a place that was at least warm and dry. The police lawyer had never seen the point in fining people who then had to go to social services to get the money to pay the fine. But he was just doing his job, and soon enough he'd gone through the list.

'How's things?'

The young man held out his hand to Bugs Bunny. He normally gave arrestees nothing more than a nod, but Bugsy was in a class of his own. He was a thief by profession and had been a very good one in his day. But he had lost all the fingers on his left hand during a disastrous attempt to blow a safe in the seventies, and alcohol had consumed the rest of his body since then. His real name was Snorre. He had been given his nickname in the days when he still had teeth, because they were so big, and it had stuck ever since. Now he kept himself busy by stealing from lorries that had been left open, cellar storerooms with simple padlocks, and the odd shop. But he was always caught. The notion of modern surveillance equipment had passed him by. He would stand there, resigned, with the stolen goods under his arm as the alarm sounded and the security guards came bounding over.

Bugs Bunny had never physically hurt another person.

'Not good,' he complained and sat down carefully on the spindly chair.

'You don't look good either,' the police lawyer said.

'Cancer. Down below. Really bad.'

'Are you getting any help?'

'Pah, not a lot they can do now, you see.'

'So why did you attempt to break into a chemist shop then?'

'The pain. The bloody pain.'

'You're not up to a chemist shop, Bugsy. Alarms and all that. And the stronger drugs are locked away in a store cupboard that I quite honestly don't think you could bust, even if you did, against all odds, manage to get into the shop. It was a bit stupid of you, you know.'

Bugsy moaned and rubbed his neck with his left hand.

'Yes,' he mumbled. 'But fucking hell, it hurts.'

The police lawyer tipped his chair back. It was quiet in the small room, and they could hear an argument going on out by the front desk. Someone was crying – it sounded like a young woman. The police lawyer looked at Bugs Bunny's face, and he could have sworn he saw tears in the worn old man's eyes.

'Here,' he said suddenly and took his wallet out of his jacket pocket. 'The offies are open again today. Get yourself something strong.'

He handed him a five-hundred-kroner note. Bugs Bunny's toothless mouth dropped open in disbelief. He shot a glance at the uniformed policeman on duty by the door, who just smiled and looked away.

'Thanks,' Bugs Bunny whispered. 'You guys are something else.'

'Yes, but I can't get rid of these,' the police lawyer said with his hand on the documents. 'I assume that you'll be up in the magistrates' court, as usual.'

'Course, yeah. I stand for what I've done, you know. Always. Thank you, thanks.' He stroked the banknote.

'You can go then. And stop breaking into places. You're not up to it any more, OK?'

Bugs Bunny got up as carefully as he had sat down. He stuffed the money in his pocket. Normally he would be out of the station as fast as his thin legs would carry him. But now he stood there, swaying slightly, apparently in his own world.

'Ten past four, it was,' he said suddenly. 'That's when the President got in the car.'

'What?'

'Was watching TV yesterday, and realised that the lady I'd seen in the morning was the one you're all after.'

The police lawyer peered at him as if he hadn't quite understood what he'd said. Then the uniformed policeman by the door took a step towards the arrestee.

'Sit back down,' the police lawyer said.

'You said I could go.'

'Sit down, Bugsy. Let's go over this first.'

The old man sat down again, reluctantly.

'I've just told you all there is to tell,' he said sullenly.

'I just want to get this completely clear. Where were you yesterday morning?'

'I'd been at a party at Backyard Berit's. Lives down in Skippergata. Was going home, you know. I looked at the clock as I passed Central Station. Ten past four. Then a woman and two blokes crossed the square. They got in a car. The woman was blonde in that way older women are. Bottle blonde. Was wearing a red jacket, just like the one on TV.'

The police lawyer said nothing. He got hold of his snus box and put a pillow under his lip. Then he held the box out to Bugsy, who packed half the contents over his destroyed gums. The man in uniform put a hand on his shoulder, as if to prevent him from running away.

'And this was yesterday,' the policeman said slowly. 'The seventeenth of May?'

'Yep,' Bugsy replied, irritated, and spat out a black gob. 'I might not be at my best, but I'm not so bloody gone that I can't remember national day!'

'And it was ten past four. In the morning. Are you sure of that?'

'Yes, I just said. And now I want to go to the offy.'

He pulled out the five-hundred-kroner note and smoothed it over his knee. Then he neatly and carefully folded it again and put it back in the other pocket. The police lawyer exchanged looks with the policeman.

'I'm afraid that may have to wait,' he said. 'But we'll get you some painkillers in the meantime.'

He picked up the phone, but had problems hitting the right numbers.

6

'They're starting to get really pissed off.'

'Who?'

'The FBI. Or whoever all these Americans are.'

The Director General of the PST, Peter Salhus, wrinkled his nose.

'What is it now?' he asked in exasperation.

'I get the impression it's everything.' Bastesen, the Chief of Oslo Police, shrugged and held out a cup of coffee. 'Apparently there was an episode out at Gardermoen. First of all there was a misunderstanding about who was to collect the twenty or so agents who arrived this morning. And then . . .' He chuckled, but as the corners of Salhus' mouth didn't even twitch, he covered his mouth with his hand, gave a discreet cough and then continued in a serious voice: 'A rather zealous customs officer confiscated all their handguns, which, to be fair, is legally correct. What do they need weapons for in this country? These Secret Service guys are armed all the time, and see what difference that made! But apparently the customs officer was a bit . . . undiplomatic.'

The gym in the police HQ had no windows. The Chief of Police had already started to pull at his collar. Fifty people were sitting in deep concentration at desks placed in a horseshoe around a huge round table. Charts and maps were hanging from the stall bars. The technical equipment gave off a suffocating waft of dust that mixed with the remains of sweat and smelly trainers.

'They're not happy with their offices either.' Bastesen emptied his coffee cup in one final gulp. 'We've given them three offices on the second floor, the red zone, but they don't appear to be using them. Which is no skin off my nose. And here we've got together your guys from PST, the best people from the NCIS and my men. It's—'

'And women,' Salhus interrupted.

'And women.' Bastesen nodded. 'It was more a figure of speech. My point is that we can't let the Americans just do as they please and trample on everything. I don't see how that will help the investigation. The language barrier alone would . . . And so far they have given us nothing. Tight as clams.'

'The reports suggest that they've decided to set up shop at the embassy,' Salhus said. 'To be expected. The traffic in and out of Drammensveien has increased considerably, and all public services have been closed. They can do what they want in the embassy. I'm sure we would have done the same. And as for their lack of communication . . .' He turned towards the Chief of Police. He wavered for a moment, then put his hand on Bastesen's arm in an unexpected friendly gesture. 'The Americans don't give anything away unless it's to their advantage,' he continued. 'And certainly not when they don't trust the other party. Strictly speaking, I can understand why their trust and confidence in us is not optimal at the moment.'

Without waiting for a response, he stepped down from the raised platform in the far corner of the hall. He was still holding his cup of coffee when he stopped beside an overweight man in his forties, who was sitting with his chin cupped in his hands, staring at a computer screen.

'Still nothing?' Salhus asked in a quiet voice.

'Nope.'

The officer rubbed his red eyes. He grabbed a bottle of mineral water and drank half of it before suppressing a burp and screwing the top back on.

'I've watched all the videos three times. In slow motion, fast and real time. Nothing. No one comes and no one goes. The woman must have flown out the window.'

'No,' was Salhus' measured response. 'She didn't do that. As you know, Secret Services had someone standing . . . here.'

An aerial photograph of the area around the Hotel Opera was hanging on the wall behind the monitor. Salhus pointed to the roof of the neighbouring building.

'And all the equipment is in good working order? No one's tampered with anything? No short circuits or loops?'

'Well if there are, they've been bloody well perfectly done,' sighed the policeman, scratching his neck. 'Basically, we've found absolutely nothing. I don't get it . . .'

He looked up, obviously distracted by the sharp clacking of heels across the floor. The atmosphere in the provisional incident room was subdued. Most people tiptoed around. Even the whir of the technical equipment was dampened by lined cases and rubber mats.

A red-haired woman hotfooted over the floor. She was waving a phone enthusiastically in her hand, as if she had won a prize.

'Witnesses,' she exclaimed when she reached the Chief of Police, who had followed Salhus and was watching the empty corridor on the ninth floor of the Hotel Opera. 'People are finally starting to ring in with sightings, and lots of them!'

'Witnesses?' Bastesen repeated dubiously. 'Witnesses to what?'

The woman took a deep breath, and tucked her red hair behind her ear. 'The kidnapping,' she panted.

The corpulent policeman stared at her, as if he was having difficulty understanding the language.

'There are no witnesses,' he said aggressively and pointed at the monitor. 'There's not a fucking person to be seen!'

'Not there,' the woman said. 'Outside. Later, I mean. Outside the hotel.'

'Where?'

Salhus put a hand on her shoulder, but removed it immediately when he detected a slight frown on the woman's face.

'A young woman,' she said, more evenly now. 'A Russ. She

was sitting with a friend in the parking place on the fjord side of Central Station when two men and a woman who fits the description of Helen Bentley went past . . .' she glanced around swiftly and then leant towards the aerial photograph, 'from here. They got into a blue Ford.'

'Hmmm,' the Chief of Police muttered. 'Well, well.'

He had crossed his arms and was staring blankly at the wall. Peter Salhus was pensively pulling his earlobe. The policeman sitting in front of the screen couldn't hide his grin.

'We believe, tra-la-la,' he muttered.

'And she's not the only one,' the woman added quickly. 'She and her friend, that is. Last night one of the old boys was picked up, and when he was questioned this morning before being released, it turns out that he'd been in the same place at the same time. And he says exactly the same thing.'

'Same time,' Peter Salhus said, and let go of his ear. 'And what time was that?'

'Around four, the two girls said. The old alcoholic said ten past four, because he'd just looked at the clock. And then . . .' She fumbled eagerly in her jacket pocket for her notebook. 'Three witnesses have, independent of each other, phoned in to report sightings of a blue Ford with two men and a sleeping woman in a red jacket in it, heading towards Svinesund. They've been seen in . . .' She leafed through her book. She was now surrounded by an audience. No one said anything. The woman with the red hair licked her finger and turned another page. 'At a petrol station on the E6, close to Moss. In a lay-by outside Fredrikstad, and . . .' she stopped abruptly and shook her head, 'in Larvik,' she finished off in disappointment. 'In Larvik, which is not on the way to Sweden.'

'Not really,' said the monitor man and laughed.

'But we're used to that,' Bastesen said. 'Some witnesses have actually seen something and others just want attention, or have remembered incorrectly. It's something to be going on, though. Let me see the reports.'

He gave the woman an encouraging pat on the shoulder and followed her out of the gym. Peter Salhus stayed standing where he was. He stared blankly at the monitor while the officer fast-forwarded to a picture of the door to the President's suite at four a.m.

'Nothing,' the officer said and threw up his hands in exasperation. 'Maybe it's an episode of *Star Trek* and she just, like, beamed herself down to the car park?'

'Rewind it to . . . When did the President come back to her room? Was it twenty past midnight?'

The man nodded and typed the time into the computer.

The President looked tired. She walked slowly and rubbed the back of her head as she stood waiting for the door to open. The fleeting smile that she gave to the two men with her did not reach her eyes. Then she nodded, said something to one of them, and went in. The door closed behind her. The agents walked towards the camera, got closer and closer, then disappeared from view. The corridor was empty again.

'Do these images say anything at all to you?' the policeman asked.

'What?' Peter Salhus straightened up.

'Do these images say anything at all to you?'

Two Russ girls and an alky, Salhus thought to himself. Witnesses ringing in from petrol stations and lay-bys on both sides of the Oslo Fjord. They've all seen the same thing, independent of each other: a blue Ford, two men, and a woman in a red jacket.

He suddenly realised that more people would ring. And not just from the neighbouring counties. More witnesses would call in, some reliable, others attention-seekers, but they would all swear that they had seen two men and a woman in red in a blue Ford.

The realisation made his cheeks flush. The air was heavy and sticky. He loosened his tie and his breathing quickened.

'Do these images say anything to you?' the policeman repeated.

'No,' Peter Salhus replied. 'They confuse me just as much as the rest of this case.'

And with that he stuffed his tie in his pocket and went in search of more coffee and a couple of paracetamol.

7

Little Ragnhild had fallen asleep in the car. Johanne drove past an empty parking place just by the gate in the low stone wall. A block further down, in Lille Frogner Allé, she found another one and slipped into the space vacated by a lorry with a broken exhaust pipe. Ragnhild whimpered a bit as she braked, but didn't wake up.

Johanne felt sure and unsure at the same time.

She would be welcome here. She knew that. The flat was pervaded by a peculiar atmosphere of friendliness and isolation, like a sun-soaked island that lies far from the shore. The family generally seemed to stay at home. The funny old housekeeper in fact never went out, and Johanne was sure she had heard groceries and goods being delivered to the door. She had been there quite often over the past six months, every third week or so. To begin with, she came because she needed help. But then gradually her visits to Krusesgate became a pleasant habit. The flat and everyone in it was hers, and hers alone, an oasis, somewhere without Adam and the rest of the family. The housekeeper always looked after Ragnhild and the two women were left in peace.

They sat there and talked openly and sincerely, like two old friends.

Johanne had never felt anything other than welcome. And yet she hesitated. She could leave the bags in the car. That way she wouldn't seem so obtrusive. Maybe she should test the waters first. Act as if she was just dropping by and see how the land lay. If it was appropriate. If it was all right to turn up with a baby in tow looking for refuge with someone she had only recently got to know.

Johanne made a snap decision.

She turned off the engine and took out the ignition key.

Ragnhild woke up, as she always did when it suddenly went quiet. She was delighted when her mother got her out of the child seat.

'Agni sthleep,' she piped happily as she was picked up.

Johanne walked briskly along the stone wall, in through the gate and up to the front door. She looked up at the top floor. The curtains in the sitting room were half drawn. No lights were on; after all, it was the middle of the day. The large oak trees cast sharp shadows on the asphalt, and as she approached the building she was blinded for a moment by the flashing reflection of the sun in one of the windows.

She took the lift up and rang the doorbell without any hesitation.

It was a long time before anyone came. Finally Johanne heard someone rattling with the security locks. The door opened.

'Well, if it's no' my wee darlin'!'

The housekeeper didn't even say hallo to Johanne. She picked Ragnhild up in a firm grasp and sat her on her hip while she babbled away. The little girl reached up and grabbed the necklace of extremely large colourful wooden beads that the housekeeper was wearing. Mary then limped into the kitchen and closed the door, still without having said a word to Johanne.

The wall at the end of the hall was glass. The woman in the wheelchair had come out of the sitting room, and was now a black silhouette against the sunlight that streamed in through the bare window panes.

'Hi,' Johanne said.

'Hello,' said the other woman, and rolled her chair nearer.

'Is it all right if I stay here for a while?'

'Yes, come in.'

'I mean,' Johanne swallowed, 'can I . . . Could Ragnhild and I . . . could we stay here . . . for a few days only?'

The woman came closer. Her wheels squeaked slightly, but it was perhaps only the rubber against the parquet. Her fingers fumbled on a panel on the wall and then there was a low humming sound as the curtains closed in front of the window and the hall darkened into a comforting half-light.

'Of course you can,' she said. 'Come in. Shut the door.'

'Just for a couple of days.'

'You're always welcome here.'

'Thank you.' Johanne felt something catch in her throat and she didn't move. The woman in the wheelchair came even closer and held out her hand.

'I take it no one's died,' she said calmly. 'Because then you wouldn't have come here.'

'No one's died,' Johanne sobbed. 'No one has died.'

'You can stay as long as you like,' the woman said. 'But first you should come in and shut the door. I'm quite hungry, so I'd thought of getting something to eat.'

Hanne Wilhelmsen retracted her hand, turned the wheelchair round and steered slowly towards the kitchen, from where they could hear Ragnhild's bubbling, happy laugh.

8

Warren Scifford's eyes wandered from the ancient television set with its internal aerial over to the cork noticeboard with a broken frame. His roaming gaze stopped at the office chair. One of the armrests was missing. Then he almost imperceptibly sniffed the air. There were three brown apple cores in the rubbish bin.

'I'm a bit superstitious,' Peter Salhus admitted. 'I've been in high-risk jobs since my early twenties and nothing has ever gone seriously wrong. So I keep my chair with me. And as for the rest of the office . . .' He shrugged. 'Well, the whole organisation is moving to new premises in June. No point putting much effort into the room. Please sit down.'

Warren Scifford hesitated, as if he was afraid of ruining his expensive suit. There was a kidney-shaped stain in the middle of the back of the chair. He carefully placed his hand over the dark patch before sitting down. Adam Stubo sat beside him, fiddling with a silver cigar case.

'You still got that bad habit?' Warren smiled.

Adam shook his head. 'No, not really. One on Christmas Eve and perhaps a few puffs on my birthday. That's all. But we all have our dreams. I can still sniff them and dream.'

He opened the case and wafted it under his nose. With an audible sigh, he then twisted it shut and popped it back in his inner pocket.

'These witnesses,' he said to Peter Salhus, who had poured three glasses of mineral water without asking whether they wanted any. 'Have you heard any more about them from the police?'

The Director General of the PST sent him a look that he couldn't interpret. Perhaps it was a warning. Perhaps it was nothing.

'I'm fairly sure that Mr Scifford has—'

'Warren. Please call me Warren.'

Scifford held out his hand as if he were honouring Peter Salhus with a gift. The glasses of mineral water stood untouched in front of him on the desk. It was so quiet in the office that you could hear the bubbles bursting.

'I'm glad that you now have the liaison contact you wanted,' Peter Salhus said finally. 'Adam Stubo will definitely be of help to you. I'd also like you to know that I fully appreciate your . . . impatience regarding the investigation. The problem is, as I'm sure you'll understand—'

'The problem is the lack of results,' Warren Scifford interrupted, with a smile. 'Plus, it seems that the investigation has no real leadership, is totally unorganised and furthermore . . .' His smile had vanished now. He imperceptibly pushed the chair back and straightened his small, thin glasses. 'We have also experienced some animosity from the police, which is unacceptable.'

Again there was silence in the room. Peter Salhus picked up a polished egg-shaped stone from his desk. He let it rest in the palm of his hand and then ran his thumb over the smooth surface. Adam coughed and sat up straight in his chair. The Director General of the PST looked up and stared at the American.

'The fact that you are in my office right now,' he said in a friendly voice, 'is proof that we are going out of our way, well out of our way, to keep you and your people happy. I am under no obligation to talk to you, and I don't really have the time. But you requested it. And I chose to honour that request. Now, I could of course give you a crash course in the structure of the Norwegian police and criminal investigation service . . .'

'I don't have—'

'Just one moment!' Peter Salhus raised his voice sufficiently to allow him to continue. 'And perhaps that might not be so stupid. But to keep things simple, and in the hope of reassuring you . . .' He looked quickly at his watch. His mouth moved very slightly, without a sound, as he calculated something. 'It's only twenty-seven hours since the disappearance of the President was discovered,' he said, leaning across the table. 'Just over twenty-seven hours. And within that time we have set up an investigation organisation that is unparalleled in this country. Oslo Police have put in all their resources, and a bit more.'

He turned up his shirt sleeves before grabbing hold of his left index finger with his right hand.

'They are working closely with us,' he said and shook his finger as if it was the PST he was holding on to, 'as there is reason to believe that this case may be connected to our daily work and field of responsibility. What's more . . .' he clasped two fingers with his right hand, 'the NCIS is heavily involved, with their specialist knowledge. Not least in terms of technical work. In other words, every man and beast that creeps and walks has been put on the job. And the staff are *extremely* competent, though I say so myself. The government has also instigated full contingency operations, with all that that entails, even in organisations and directorates that are not directly linked to the police. Our governments are in constant contact at the highest level. The very highest level.'

'But—' Warren Scifford straightened his tie. He was smiling broadly now. Peter Salhus held up a hand in warning.

'Jack Bauer will not be coming,' he said in all seriousness. 'His deadline passed . . .' he looked at his watch again, 'three hours ago. We will have to put our faith in good and modern, if not quite so spectacular, police work. Norwegian police work.'

The silence lasted for several seconds. Then Warren Scifford started to laugh. His laugh was warm, deep and contagious. Adam chuckled and Peter Salhus grinned.

'And what's more, you're mistaken,' he added. 'As you will be informed at the meeting with the Chief of Police in an hour's time, there have absolutely been developments.'

'I see.'

'The question is whether . . .'

The Director General of the PST leaned back and clasped his hands behind his neck. He appeared to be studying a spot on the ceiling. This went on for so long that Adam looked up to see if there really was anything there. He felt dishearteningly superfluous.

No one had actually told him what he was supposed to do. The Chief of Police had seemed distracted when he'd quickly introduced them to each other about an hour ago. He had obviously forgotten that they already knew each other, and after a few minutes, had abandoned them without giving any further instructions. Adam had the feeling that he was to function as an alibi; a piece of meat thrown to the Americans to keep them happy.

And he hadn't had time to phone home yet.

'The question is whether I decide to be straightforward or not,' Peter Salhus concluded suddenly, looking the American straight in the eye and holding his gaze.

Warren did not back off.

Did not blink.

'Yes,' Peter Salhus said at last. 'I think I should.'

He pushed one of the glasses over to Warren Scifford. The American didn't touch it.

'First of all,' Salhus said, 'I want to stress that I have the utmost confidence in Oslo Police. Terje Bastesen has been in the force for nearly forty years, and was an officer before he became a lawyer. He can seem a bit . . .' He cocked his head and searched for a suitable phrase.

'Very Norwegian,' Warren suggested.

'Perhaps,' replied the Director General of the PST, without smiling. 'But don't underestimate him. I think that we have to pin our hopes on the police in this case. Here at the PST we've spent the past twenty-four hours going through all the intelligence we received prior to the President's visit. We have combed through every report and analysis to see if there's anything we might have missed, something we didn't attach importance to but that might have told us something. Something that might have

146

warned us. And we've gathered all relevant information about any known groups, vague constellations, individuals throughout Europe . . .'

He clasped his hands behind his head.

'Nothing. At least not at the moment.'

Warren Scifford took off his glasses and pulled a cloth from his back pocket. Slowly, almost lovingly, he polished his lenses.

'We had something,' he said quietly. 'Before nine/eleven, that is. The information was there. It existed and we had it. We just didn't pay any attention to it. The intelligence that could have saved the lives of nearly three thousand people just drowned in the great sea of information. All the . . .'

He put his glasses on again, without finishing his sentence.

'That's the way it is,' Salhus nodded, 'in this business. I have to admit that yesterday morning I dreaded one thing more than anything else: the moment when one of my staff came to me with some information that we'd overlooked. The piece of the jigsaw puzzle we'd put to one side because we couldn't get it to fit. I was absolutely positive that would happen. But, until now . . .' He threw open his hands, and repeated: 'Nothing.'

Then, after a short pause, he added, pushing: 'And what about you? Have you found anything?'

His voice was light and the question friendly. Warren responded with an imperceptible arch of the eyebrow. Then he picked up the glass of mineral water, but didn't take a drink.

'You said something about witnesses,' he said and looked at Adam Stubo.

'So, you have got something,' Salhus commented.

Warren emptied the glass in one go. He took his time. When he had finished, he dried his mouth with a handkerchief and put the glass down. When he looked up at the Director General of the PST, his face was blank.

'Witnesses,' he reminded him.

'I was trying to gain your confidence.'

'You have my confidence.'

'No.'

'Yes, absolutely. In our business there's a big difference between confidence and being loose-tongued. And you know that. The moment I see that you and your people need any of the information that we have, then you'll be given it. You. Personally. You have my word. And right now, *I* need to know what all this talk of witnesses is about.'

Salhus got up and went over to the window. It had been a lovely morning, with bright sunshine and only a few fluffy summer clouds. But they were getting darker now and were preparing to attack from the south. He could already see a bank of rain moving up the Oslo Fjord. He stood for a while, watching the weather.

The feeling of being superfluous was so strong now that Adam considered getting up to leave. He should have phoned home long ago. When he had made his decision early that morning, he had been convinced that the only right thing to do was to follow orders. He had been seized by an uncharacteristic rage when he woke up and crept out of bed. His stomach was knotted and he couldn't eat. Adam couldn't remember a time when he had ever voluntarily skipped a meal. And now there were rumbles coming from under his shirt. He just wanted to leave. This case was so unlike anything he'd ever dealt with before that he had nothing to offer. If the intention was that he should shuttle Warren Scifford between various public offices in Norway, then the job was an insult.

The note he'd left for Johanne could perhaps have been friendlier.

He had to phone home as soon as possible.

'Stubo,' the Director General of the PST said suddenly, and turned round. 'This is something for you.'

Adam looked up. Bewildered, he sat up straight in his chair, like a pupil who has been caught daydreaming.

'Really?'

Peter Salhus took five minutes to tell them about the various witnesses. Around thirty people had contacted the police to report what they had seen and they all said the same thing. Two men and a woman who looked like Madam President in a blue car. Half of them thought it was a Ford. The others were only certain about the colour. But they all said that the driver of the car had made no obvious efforts to be discreet.

'And there we have a problem,' he concluded, and pointed at the map he had drawn.

The sketch of Norway looked like a well-worn mitten that had been hung up to dry. Peter Salhus put his pen down and crossed his arms. The two other men leant over the drawing.

'That can't be right,' Adam said.

'It is,' Salhus replied. 'It is completely correct.'

Then he too leant forwards and added: 'These are the sightings we've received. But even if we take into account the usual reservations that some of them are wrong and others simply lies, it still doesn't make sense. You're absolutely right.'

Adam went slowly over the map again, moving from point to point. The Director General of the PST had scribbled down the times of all the observations beside the red dots.

'This is the E6 heading towards Sweden,' Adam said and ran his finger over Østfold county. 'And here is the E18 to Kristiansand. And here . . .' His finger traced the route to Trondheim.

'It's not my area of responsibility,' Salhus said quietly, scratching his beard. 'I'm sure the police will sort it out. For all I know, they may have already done so. It's pretty obvious.'

'The whole thing's a wild goose chase,' Adam exclaimed. 'It's all just nonsense!'

'Yes.'

Warren Scifford hadn't said a word while Salhus was drawing and explaining. Now he picked up the map in his right hand and stared at the pearl string of sightings across the whole of southern Norway. He then queried: 'You know the distances. Have you worked out how many Fords and women dressed in red might be involved?'

'At least two,' Salhus replied. 'Probably three. It's physically possible to get from here . . .' he took the map and pointed, 'to here within the given time frame. You could also drive between these two towns . . .' his finger moved from Larvik to Hamar, 'in three and a half hours. But it would be tight. As everyone was celebrating Norway's national day, there wouldn't be much traffic, so it is possible.'

'Two groups,' Warren Scifford muttered. 'Probably three.'

'Driving around Norway, making sure that they were seen,' Adam said. 'Why would anyone go to all that trouble? They must know that it would only be a matter of time before they were exposed.'

The light was no longer as bright. The wind had picked up and suddenly a heavy shower battered the window. A seagull perched on the windowsill. Its beady black eyes stared intently at something in the room. Then it opened its beak to screech.

'Time,' Salhus said loudly. 'They wanted to waste time and create confusion.'

The seagull took off and swooped down towards the ground. It had started to hail. The hailstones were as large as peppercorns and rattled on the glass panes.

'But everything has its positive side,' Salhus said suddenly and with forced cheer. 'There are several excellent pictures of the driver. Or drivers. From at least two petrol stations, from what I've heard. And even if the whole manoeuvre is lookalikes out for a ride, it would be very interesting to know who sent them. Ask the Chief of Police about it, Warren. As I said, this is not my business. Talk to the police. But before you go . . .' Peter Salhus bit his lip and hesitated before adding: 'Why are you actually here?'

Warren Scifford looked at him and raised an eyebrow.

'Why did they send you?' Salhus asked. 'As far as I understand, you head a kind of . . . behavioural psychology anti-terrorist group. Is that right?'

The American nodded indifferently.

'So you're not a head in the FBI. You're not head of any operative group whatsoever. But still they send—'

'That's where you're wrong. We are highly operative.'

'But I still can't understand,' Peter Salhus insisted and leant forwards across the desk, 'why they didn't send a—'

'Well observed,' Warren Scifford interrupted. 'Very well observed. You do, of course, have a point.'

For the first time, Adam thought he saw something helpless in the self-assured man. His eyes wavered for a second, a pull at his mouth aged him, even made him look old. But he said nothing. The hailstorm had stopped just as abruptly as it had started.

'So what's the point?' Peter Salhus asked quietly.

'That my colleagues don't believe the answer to this mystery lies in Norway,' Warren Scifford replied and took a deep breath. 'The point is that they've sent me because they don't want me at home. They're convinced that we can find the answer in the chaos of intelligence that we already have, combined with our own ongoing investigation. It is . . . intense. To say the least. Heavy-handed, you Europeans might say.'

He picked up the glass again, paused, then put it back down. It was empty.

'The FBI believes that the President's disappearance is a terrorist plot that only the US can deal with,' he continued. 'In that context, Norway is nothing more than a little . . . a very little and insignificant . . .' He smiled briefly, almost apologetically, and shrugged. 'I'm sure you understand. And as I and my men differ slightly from the top leaders in our view of what constitutes a terrorist, what terrorists are trying to achieve and . . .'

He stopped suddenly again. He sat up straight in the chair, smoothed down the front of his jacket, then leant forward and looked Salhus straight in the eye.

'Internal FBI conflicts are hardly of any interest to you,' he said. 'And I don't need to discuss them, either. But I'm not giving away too much when I say that the US' main suspect in this case is unambiguous: al-Qaeda. They have money. They have a network.

They have a motive. And as is well known, they have attacked us before.'

'But not yours,' Salhus commented.

'What?'

'Your suspicions are not focused on al-Qaeda.'

Warren Scifford didn't answer. He ran his fingers through his hair. A vague scent of shampoo wafted around him.

'You're director general of the security services,' he said, finally, a bit too loud. 'What do you think?'

Now it was Peter Salhus' turn not to say anything. He beat a rhythm on his desk with a pen.

'I thought as much,' Warren Scifford said.

'I haven't said anything.'

'Not in as many words. But both you and I know that this is far removed from al-Qaeda. Osama bin Laden wants to spread fear, Salhus. Al-Qaeda are holy warriors, driven by a burning hate. They want spectacular scenes of absolute . . . terror. They are *terrorists*, in the purest sense.'

'Terrorism,' Salhus said and put the pen back in a drawer, 'is defined roughly as an illegal action where the victim of violence or threats of violence is not the main target, but a means to impact on a larger group of people. Through terror and fear, quite simply. Is kidnapping the American president not an act of terrorism? As far as I can make out from the news broadcasts . . .' he nodded at the ancient TV screen, 'terror is rife in your country right now.'

'Or uncertainty,' Adam said and coughed. 'A tortuous uncertainty. Which is perhaps even worse. To me, this seems very different from what I would normally associate with terrorism. It seems more like someone . . .' He held his breath, searching for the right word, as he looked at Salhus' sketchy map of Norway, scattered with red dots. 'Like someone is playing with us,' he said, finally. 'It feels like someone is taking us for a ride. Which isn't really Osama bin Laden's style.'

The two other men looked at him. Salhus nodded in surprise

152

and then shrugged. He was just about to say something when Warren Scifford suddenly got up.

'We have to go.'

Adam still felt uncomfortable when he took Salhus' hand at the door. The American had his mobile phone pressed to his ear and was heading for the lift.

'You're absolutely right,' Salhus said very quietly, in Norwegian. 'They're playing with us. Someone has the motive, the resources and the opportunity to take us for a ride, big time. And I'm damned if your friend over there doesn't have an idea of who it is. If you get so much as a hint of what this is all about, contact me immediately. OK?'

Adam gave a weak nod and was astonished to discover that the Director General of the PST's hand was cold and sweaty.

9

Abdallah al-Rahman loved the newly born foal. She was jet black, just like her mother, and the lighter patch between her eyes gave him hope that she had inherited her father's white blaze. Her legs were disproportionately long, as they are on a one-day-old foal. Her body was promising and her coat was already polished and shiny. She tottered backwards when he slowly entered the box with his hand outstretched. The mare whinnied aggressively, but he quickly calmed her with some soft words and a stroke on the muzzle.

Abdallah al-Rahman was happy. Everything was going according to plan. He still hadn't had direct contact with anyone. It wasn't necessary. As an adult, he had never done anything unnecessary. As human beings were only granted a limited amount of time on this earth, he believed it was important to keep the balance, to follow a strategy. He looked at his life in the same way that he looked at the fantastic carpets that adorned the floors of the three palaces he felt he needed at the moment.

A carpet weaver always had a plan. She didn't start in one corner and then work willy-nilly until the carpet was finished. She knew where she was going, and it took time. Sometimes she was inspired and might include the most beautiful details, on impulse. The perfection of a hand-made carpet lay in its imperfection, in the tiny deviations from a preordained yet strict symmetry and order.

The most beautiful carpet of all was in his bedroom. His mother had knotted it, and it had taken her eight years to make it. Abdallah was thirteen when it was finished and she gave it to him as a present. No one had ever seen its like before. The golden hues changed according to the light, making it difficult to say what the colours actually were. No one had ever seen such close knots or felt such indescribably soft, thick silk.

The foal came up to him. She had pitch-black eyes, and she opened them wide as she tottered sideways, tossing her head to keep her balance. She snorted helplessly and pressed into her mother's flank before trying once again to walk towards him.

Abdallah's life was like a carpet, and when his brother died, he had decided what the pattern would be. He had made some small changes along the way, some minor adjustments, but never any more than his mother had done: a deeper, darker thread here and there, or another shade because it was beautiful and fitted in.

His brother was three years older than him and had been killed in Brooklyn on the 20th of August 1974. He had been on his way home from seeing an American girlfriend that his parents knew nothing about, and it was very late. When he was found by an elderly woman the next morning, his genitals were a bloody mess from all the punches and kicks. Their father flew immediately to the US and returned one month later, an old man.

The murder was never solved. The father's powerful position in his home country and his indisputable authority, even in his meetings with the American authorities, had made no difference. After fourteen days, the chief investigator shrugged and looked away when he admitted that those responsible would never be caught. There were so many murders, so many young men who didn't understand that they should avoid dangerous areas and stay indoors after midnight. He complained that there weren't enough resources, and then closed the thin case file for good.

The father knew the man who much later became the first President Bush. The Arab had done him several favours, so now it was time to ask for one in return. But he wasn't able to contact his influential friend. Richard Nixon had been forced from office some days earlier and Gerald Ford was the new president of the US. On the same evening that a young foreigner was kicked to death in a back street in Brooklyn, President Ford had announced that Nelson Rockefeller was to be appointed as America's forty-first vice president. A deeply disappointed and hurt George Bush Senior had more important things to think about than a forgotten Arab acquaintance, and later that year escaped to China to lick his political wounds.

Abdallah grew up that autumn. He was only sixteen, and his father never really recovered. The old man managed to carry on the business. He had dependable people around him, and even though the oil industry went through a turbulent time at the start of the seventies, the family's wealth grew steadily, but he was never the same again. With increasing frequency, he withdrew into religious meditation and hardly ate. He made no protest when Abdallah left his parents and six sisters to go to the West to get the schooling that his brother had been denied.

The people who ran the business were good, but gradually their numbers dwindled. Abdallah trusted them, but already by the time he was twenty he had a finger in most pies. He went home as often as he could. The summer he turned twenty-five, his father died of grief, ten years after losing his son.

Abdallah had seen it coming and had included it in the tapestry of his life, so that nothing would ever surprise him again. He was the head and sole owner of a conglomerate that no one had sufficient insight into to value. He was the only one who could estimate a reasonable figure, and he never told anyone what that was.

The absence of anger was the only unexpected thing.

He had been exhausted by anger about six months after his brother's death and fell ill. A stay in a convalescence home in Switzerland got him back on his feet, and the anger was replaced by a calculating calm that was much easier to live with. His rage had wormed its way into everything and eaten him up from inside, in the same way that grief had consumed his father, whereas calculating cynicism was something he could ration. Abdallah discovered the value of long-term planning and well-thought-out strategies, and he moved his mother's present into his room so that he could study the carpet before falling asleep and on the rare occasion when he was woken at night by dreams of his brother.

The foal was one of the most beautiful things he had seen. Her muzzle was perfect, with unusually small vibrating nostrils. Her eyes were no longer so timid, and her eyelashes were like butterfly wings. She came right up to him as he sat on the bale of hay, waiting to win her trust.

'Father!'

Abdallah turned around slowly. Over the top of the stable door he could see the fringe of his youngest son, who was trying to pull himself up with his hands so he could see the foal.

'Just a minute,' he said in a friendly voice. 'I'm coming out.'

He very carefully stroked the foal. She arched her neck where he touched her and quivered. Abdallah smiled and put his hand on her tiny muzzle. She pulled back nervously. The man got up, walked slowly out of the stall and closed the door.

'Father!' the boy cried in delight. 'We were going to watch a film today! You promised me!'

'Wouldn't you rather do some riding? In the ring, where it's cooler?'

'No! You said I could watch a film.'

Abdallah lifted the six-year-old up and carried him on one arm out through the massive stable doors. For want of legal cinemas in Saudi Arabia, Abdallah had made his own, with ten seats and a silver screen.

'You promised me I could,' the boy complained.

'Later on. This evening is what I said.'

The boy's hair smelt clean and tickled his nose. He smiled and kissed him before putting him down.

His youngest son was called Rashid, after his dead uncle. None of the four older boys would have suited the name. They all had the characteristics of their mother's family. Then came the fifth son. The moment he was born, Abdallah saw his square chin with the tiny cleft in it. When the boy was two days old and had finally opened his eyes, he had a slight squint in his left eye. Abdullah laughed happily and named him Rashid.

Abdallah had never thought about avenging his brother's

death. Certainly not once the first surge of anger had died down and he had returned from Switzerland. He didn't know who to take revenge on. The culprits were never caught and it would be impossible for an Arab boy to investigate a murder in the US on his own, no matter how much money he had. The policeman who closed the case was as much a victim of the system as he was himself, and it was hardly worth the time and effort to punish him.

The only real hatred that Abdallah al-Rahman allowed himself to nurture was for George Bush Senior. The man who became head of the CIA had owed his father a favour back then in 1974, and was obviously influential. He could have reopened the closed investigation with a simple telephone call. As it appeared that Rashid had been murdered by a gang of racist youths, surely it wouldn't have been that difficult to solve the case – if only they had wanted to, and been given the permission to prioritise it.

But George Herbert Walker Bush was so preoccupied with the insult of not being offered the vice presidency that he didn't have the time to answer the calls of a business contact he had chosen to forget.

As time passed, Abdallah understood that the most important lesson to learn from the circumstances surrounding his brother's death was that favours did not always lead to favours in return. Unless you had something up your sleeve. Something that made it impossible to forget the debt, whether you wanted to or not. Abdallah had spent the last thirty years being generous without asking for anything in return, so now a lot of people owed him favours.

The time had never been right. Not until Helen Lardahl Bentley had given him final confirmation of his experience in life: never, never trust an American.

'Can I watch an action film, Father? Can I watch—'

'No. You know very well that they are not good for you.'

Abdallah ruffled his son's hair. The boy looked up with a sulky pout, before slouching off with bowed head to find his brothers, who had arrived from Riyadh the night before, and were going to stay at home for the whole week.

Abdallah stood and watched his son until he disappeared round the corner of the huge stable building. Then he wandered towards the shady garden. He wanted to take a dip.

10

Hanne Wilhelmsen was a person who did not have friends. She had chosen to live like this, but it hadn't always been the case.

She was forty-five years old and had worked for the police for twenty of them. Her career ended abruptly between Christmas and New Year of 2002 when she was shot during the arrest of a quadruple murderer. A heavy-calibre bullet hit her between the tenth and eleventh thoracic vertebrae and for reasons that the doctors could not understand became lodged there. When the foreign object was subsequently removed, the surgeon was so fascinated by the porridge-like remains of what had once been functioning nerves that he photographed them; he kept it to himself that he had never seen a worse injury.

The Chief of Police had begged her to stay on in the force.

He came to visit her frequently during her convalescence, even though she became more and more withdrawn. He offered her special arrangements and equipment. She could choose from the top positions and would want for nothing when it came to aids and assistance.

She didn't want any of it and resigned from her job two months after the operation.

No one had doubted that Hanne Wilhelmsen had exceptional talents. Younger officers, in particular, looked up to her. They didn't know her, and had not yet grown weary of the distant, odd behaviour that was increasingly characteristic. Before the catastrophic shooting, she would occasionally take on what amounted to a protégé. She could cope with the admiration, because admiration meant distance, and distance was important to Hanne Wilhelmsen. And she was a good teacher.

Her peers and older colleagues had long since had enough.

They never tried to deny the fact that she was one of the best investigators that Oslo Police had ever had, but as the years went by, they had tired of her pigheadedness and her sullen opposition to working in a team. And even though everyone in the force was shocked by the fact that a colleague had been seriously injured in the line of duty, there were whispers in several corners that it was a relief to be rid of the woman. Then the waters calmed again and most people forgot about her – out of sight, out of mind.

In all the years that she worked in the force, she really only kept one friend, and when she was lying unconscious in that hut in the forest outside Oslo, bleeding to death, he was the one who saved her life. He had watched over her in hospital for three days and nights, until he smelt so bad that one of the nurses had pushed him out the door, saying that it would be best for everyone if he went home. When it then became obvious that Hanne would survive, he had grasped her hand and cried like a baby.

Hanne had rejected him too.

It was over a year ago now since he last dropped by to see if anything remained of the friendship that could be rekindled. After she had closed the front door behind his broad, stooped back quarter of an hour later, Hanne Wilhelmsen proceeded to get drunk on champagne, lock herself in the bedroom and cut her police uniform to shreds, which she then later burnt in the fire.

For the first time in her strange, twisted life, Hanne Wilhelmsen was happy.

She lived with a woman who had gradually come to accept a divided life. Nefis worked at the university and had her own friends and a life outside the flat, in which her partner played no part. Hanne would wait for her at home in Krusesgate and was always quietly pleased to see her again and never asked questions.

What they did share was their delight in Ida.

'Where's Ida?' Johanne asked.

She was sitting on the sofa with her legs tucked underneath her, watching the newscasts on a huge plasma screen.

'She's in Turkey with Nefis. Visiting her grandparents.'

Johanne didn't say any more.

Hanne liked Johanne. She liked her because she wasn't a friend and didn't demand to be one. She knew nothing about Hanne, other than what she had heard and picked up from others. Which could be anything, of course, but she never seemed tempted to dig and ask or demand. She talked a lot, but never about Hanne. As Johanne was the most genuinely curious person Hanne had ever met, this apparent lack of interest was proof of how well Johanne knew her subject. She was a real profiler.

Johanne understood Hanne Wilhelmsen and let her be. And she seemed to appreciate her company.

'Oh no,' Johanne exclaimed quietly, and closed her eyes. 'Not her.'

Hanne, who was sitting reading a novel, looked over at the screen.

'She won't jump out of the TV to get you,' she said and continued to read.

'But why do they always . . .' Johanne sighed and took a deep breath. 'Why does *she* have to be the great oracle in any discussion about crime and criminals?'

'Because you won't do it,' Hanne said and smiled. Johanne had once stormed out of a television studio in protest during a live debate, and had never been invited back.

Wencke Bencke was the most famous crime writer in the country. For years she had been regarded as an eccentric, who was difficult and unapproachable. Then suddenly, a year ago, she had stepped into the limelight. A string of celebrities were killed in a case that the police never got to the bottom of. Johanne had been dragged reluctantly into the investigation, but for a long time the murders seemed to be without motive and random, even to her. And Wencke Bencke became the media's favourite expert. She glowed as she shared her insight into the character and absurd logic of criminals, and at the same time maintained an ironic distance from the police. Which all made for good TV.

The same autumn, she published her eighteenth and best novel. It was about a crime writer who started to kill out of sheer boredom. In three months, 120,000 copies of the book were sold, and the rights were promptly bought by publishers in more than twenty countries.

Only a handful of people, including Johanne and Adam, knew that the book was in fact about Wencke Bencke herself. They could never prove it, but knew everything. The crime writer had also made sure of that. The clues she had given were useless as evidence, but sufficient for Johanne Vik, and she was certain that they had been left to tease her.

Wencke Bencke had got away with murder.

And every now and then, on sleepless nights, when she had seen Wencke Bencke smiling at her across the freezer in the supermarket, or seen her waving from Haugesvei late in the evening, Johanne found herself thinking that the murders had been committed to provoke her. She just couldn't understand why. Last autumn, when she was on her way to the cabin with both the children in the back, a car had driven up beside her at the traffic lights on Ullernchausseen; the driver gave her a thumbs-up, honked her horn and then turned right. It was Wencke Bencke.

A coincidence, Adam said, exasperated, time and again. Oslo was a small town, and sooner or later Johanne would have to put the damn case behind her.

Instead, she went to Hanne Wilhelmsen. To begin with, it was curiosity that spurred her. Hanne was a legend among the few left who still talked about her. If anyone was able to help Johanne understand Wencke Bencke, it would be her. The former detective inspector's calm, almost blasé nature was reassuring. She was coldly analytical where Johanne was intuitive; indifferent where Johanne allowed herself to be provoked. But Hanne took the time to listen; she always had time to listen.

163

'The police are at a complete loss,' the crime writer said in the studio, and straightened her glasses. 'It's rare to see them in quite such disarray. From what I've gleaned, they're dealing with a problem that would be more fitting in a good old-fashioned thriller than in the real world.'

The presenter leant forward. The picture cut to a camera that showed them both. They huddled together as if they were sharing a secret.

'I see,' said the man, in a grave tone.

'The President is of course the subject of an extensive security operation, as many of the reports over the last twenty-four hours have shown. Among other things, the CCTV cameras in the corridors around . . .'

'Don't let it bother you,' Hanne said quietly. 'We can turn it off.'

Johanne had grabbed a cushion and was clutching it hard, without realising.

'No,' she said. 'I want to listen.'

'Are you sure?'

Johanne nodded and stared at the screen. Hanne looked at her for a few seconds, before giving the slightest of shrugs and returning to her book.

'. . . in other words, a kind of "closed room" mystery,' Wencke Bencke said and smiled. 'No one goes into the room and no one comes out . . .'

'How does she know that?' Johanne asked. 'How in the world does she always know what the police are doing? They can't stand her down there and —'

'The police HQ leaks more than a colander from IKEA,' Hanne retorted. She finally seemed to be interested in the conversation on the TV. 'It's always been like that.'

Johanne caught herself studying her. Hanne had closed the book, which was about to fall off her lap without her noticing. The wheelchair rolled forwards a bit, and she picked up the remote control to turn up the volume. Her body was leaning forwards as if she was afraid of missing the slightest nuance of the crime writer's story. She slowly took off her glasses, without her eyes leaving the screen for a second.

That's how she must have been, once upon a time, Johanne thought in surprise. So alert and intense. Such a contrast to the indifferent character who had willingly imprisoned herself in this lavish flat in Oslo's West End, and now spent her time reading novels. Hanne seemed younger now, almost youthful. Her eyes were shining, and she moistened her lips before carefully tucking her hair behind her ear. A diamond caught the light in a flash. When Johanne opened her mouth to say something, Hanne lifted a cautionary finger, with barely a movement.

'And now we'll go over to the government offices,' the presenter said at last, and nodded his thanks to the writer, 'where the Prime Minister is about to meet . . .'

'You have to ring,' Hanne Wilhelmsen said, and turned off the TV.

'Ring? Who do I have to ring?'

'You have to call the police. I think they've made a mistake.'

'But . . . call them yourself then! I don't know what . . . I don't know any . . .'

'Listen!' Hanne turned the wheelchair to face her. 'Call Adam.'

'I can't.'

'You've had an argument. I realised that much when you came here to hide. It must be serious, or you wouldn't have upped and run with the baby. But I don't give a damn. I'm not interested.'

Johanne realised that her mouth was open, and she closed it with an audible snap.

'At any rate, this is more important,' Hanne continued. 'If what Wencke Bencke says is right, and there is every reason to assume that it is, they've made such a major mistake that . . .'

She hesitated, as if she didn't dare to believe her own theory.

'You're the one who knows Oslo Police,' Johanne said feebly.

'No, I don't know anyone any more. You have to phone. If you call Adam, he'll know what to do.'

'Tell me then,' Johanne said, with some doubt in her voice. She put down the cushion. 'What is it that's so important? What have the police done?'

'It's more what they haven't done,' Hanne replied. 'And as a rule, that's worse.'

11

Adam Stubo stood by the lifts on the third floor of the police headquarters, feeling anxious. He still hadn't had the opportunity to phone home. The sense of apprehension that he had done something wrong by sneaking out of the sleeping house first thing that morning, without speaking to Johanne, got stronger with every hour that passed.

Warren Scifford must have eaten an enormous breakfast, as he had declined the offer of lunch twice. Adam was starving and had started to be irritated by the American's apparently random visits to various offices at Grønlandsleiret 44. The man was communicating less and less with his Norwegian liaison. Sometimes he excused himself to make a phone call, but then moved too far away for Adam to catch any of the conversation. As he never knew how long Warren would be on the phone, he couldn't take the opportunity to try to get hold of Johanne.

'Have to go,' Warren said and closed his mobile phone as he rushed over to Adam.

'Where to now?'

Adam had been waiting for him for nearly quarter of an hour. But he still tried to be friendly.

'I don't need you. Not right now. I have to go back to the hotel. What's your phone number?'

Adam took out a business card.

'My mobile,' he said, pointing. 'Ring that number when you need me. Should I take you there? Call a car?'

'The embassy has already sent one,' Warren said lightly. 'Thanks for all your help. So far.'

Then he ran towards the stairs and disappeared.

'Adam? Adam Stubo?

A petite, slim woman walked over to him. Adam immediately

167

noticed her shoes. The heels were so high that it was difficult to understand how she stayed on her feet. Her face lit up when she saw that it was really him. She stood up on her toes and gave him a quick kiss on the cheek.

'What a lovely surprise.' Adam's smile was genuine this time. 'It's been a long time, Silje. How are you?'

'Pah . . .' She inflated her cheeks and then let the air out slowly.

'It's very busy here, you know. Everyone's working on the President's case. I've been here for over twenty-four hours now, and I'll be lucky if I get away within the next six or so. And you?'

'Yeah, fine. I . . .'

Silje Sørensen looked up at him suddenly, as if she had just seen a new side of the handsome man who looked like he had been forced into a slightly too tight jacket. Adam stopped himself, at a loss, and pulled his nose.

'Adam, you worked on the Munch thefts, didn't you?' she asked quickly. 'And the Norwegian Cash Service robbery?'

'Yes and no,' Adam replied and looked around. 'I worked on the Munch case, but not directly with the NOKAS robbery. But I—'

'You know a lot about the armed robbery league. More than most, at least.'

'Yes, I've worked with—'

'Come with me!'

Police Sergeant Silje Sørensen took him by the arm and started to walk. He followed without really wanting to. The feeling of being treated like a stray dog mushroomed. He had himself worked in the police HQ when he was younger, but had never felt at home there, and he had no idea where Silje was taking him.

'What are you doing here?' she asked, out of breath, as she hurried down the corridor, her heels clacking on the floor.

'To be honest, I'm not sure myself.'

'No one's sure of anything these days.' She smiled.

They finally stopped outside a blue door with no name on it. Silje Sørensen knocked, then opened the door without waiting for an answer. Adam followed her in. A middle-aged man was sitting in front of three monitors and something that looked like a sound studio mixing desk. He swung round and muttered hello before turning back and concentrating on his work again.

'This is Detective Chief Inspector Adam Stubo, from the NCIS,' Silje explained.

'The New NCIS,' Adam corrected her, with a smile.

'Stupid name,' grumbled the man by the mixing desk. 'Frank Larsen's the name. Police Sergeant.'

He didn't hold out his hand and his eyes were still glued to the monitors. Black-and-white images from a petrol station, with customers coming and going, were being shown fast-forward on the screen.

'There aren't many people who know as much about the armed robbery brigade here in Østlandet as Adam,' Silje Sørensen said, pulling two chairs up to the large table. 'Sit down, Adam.'

Sergeant Larsen seemed more interested now. He gave Adam a brief smile, while his fingers danced across the keyboard. The screen went blank, and a few seconds later a new image appeared: a man who was leaving the shop through an open sliding door. The camera must have been mounted on the ceiling, as the man could only be seen at an angle, from above. He just about collided with the newspaper stand, and then pulled his cap further down on his forehead.

'We haven't managed to systematise the questioning of witnesses yet,' Silje said in a low voice, while the sergeant manipulated the picture to make it clearer. 'But there's at least one thing that strikes me. This man, or these men – we currently think there are two – want to be noticed by the people working in the petrol station. He's chatted with the assistant and made himself obvious. But he doesn't want to get caught on camera. We don't have a single clear picture of his face – or their faces, to be precise.'

Frank Larsen pulled up another picture on a second monitor.

'Look.' He pointed. 'He obviously knows where the cameras are. He pulls down his hat, here . . .' All three of them looked at the monitor that was marked A. 'And then looks away, here.'

Monitor B showed a man almost sidling up to the counter.

'If they know where the cameras are, they've been there before.' Adam spoke quietly, and stared in fascination at Monitor C, where an unclear, grainy picture of a man was gradually becoming sharper. It was filmed from behind, at an angle. The peak of his cap covered most of his face, but his chin and big nose were visible. It was too early to say for definite, but Adam was sure he could make out a trimmed beard.

'And if they've done a recce beforehand,' he continued, 'there should be better pictures from previous visits.'

'Hardly,' Frank Larsen said sullenly, as if the thought of going through even more material depressed him. 'The stations generally delete them after a couple of weeks. Every crook knows that. These guys too, no doubt. So all you have to do is have a look around well in advance, that's it. There's this one too, by the way.'

A pudgy finger touched a button on Monitor C.

The man in the picture was broad-shouldered, and sure enough, his chin was covered by a short, trimmed beard. His eyes were hidden by the peak of his cap, but it did not cover his unusually large and hooked nose. The man had a crew cut under his cap, and a small solid gold earring in his right ear.

'I'm sure I've seen him before,' Silje said. 'And something tells me that it's to do with the armed robbery. But it—'

'He's cut his hair,' Adam said and pulled his chair closer to the table. 'And grown a beard. The earring's new, as well. The only problem is . . .' he was smiling now, and ran his finger over the screen, 'you can't disguise that nose.'

'D'you know who it is?' Frank Larsen sounded sceptical. 'It's not as if you can see a lot of the guy.'

'It's Gerhard Skrøder,' Adam said and leant back in his chair.

'They call him the Chancellor. He's such a big mouth about town that for a while we thought he was involved in the NOKAS robbery. But it was just boasting in the end. The Munch paintings, on the other hand . . .'

Frank Larsen's fingers were working while Adam spoke. A printer in the corner of the room started to rumble.

'We've never managed to get anything on him, but if you ask me, he was involved.'

Silje Sørensen got the printout and studied it for a moment before passing it to Adam.

'Still certain?'

It was not a good picture, but with all the clever computer manipulation, it was at least clear. Adam nodded and again ran his finger over the picture. The huge nose, broken in a fight in prison in 2000, and then again in a scuffle with the police two years later, was unmistakable.

Gerhard Skrøder came from an apparently good home and was a notorious thief. His father was a top executive in a large public organisation and his mother was an MP for the Socialist Left Party. Gerhard's sister was a corporate lawyer, and his younger brother had just been selected for the national athletics team. Gerhard himself had been sprinting from the police since he was thirteen, but generally lost the race.

The Norwegian Cash Service, or NOKAS, robbery in Stavanger the year before was the biggest armed robbery in Norwegian history, and cost one policeman his life. Never before had so many resources been poured into one case, and they got results. The court case started after Christmas. Gerhard Skrøder had been in the spotlight for some time, but then fell out of it again towards the end of the winter. But as the NOKAS investigation turned the whole armed robbery scene upside down, his name popped up in other, almost equally interesting, connections. When the Munch paintings *The Scream* and *Madonna* were stolen in broad daylight in August 2004, Gerhard Skrøder was in Mauritius with an eighteen-year-old blonde who had no criminal record. And it could be proved. Adam was convinced that the man had played a key role in the planning. And that could not be proved.

'Let me see,' Frank Larsen said and held out his hand for the printout.

He studied it for a long time.

'I choose to believe you,' he said finally, and rubbed his eyes with his knuckles. 'But can you tell me why a guy from the armed robbery league would be involved in a cover-up operation for the kidnapping of the American president?' He looked at Adam with red eyes. 'Can you tell me that, eh? Kidnapping the American president is not exactly what these boys normally get up to, is it? They only think about one thing, those guys, and that's money. And as far as I know, there haven't been any bloody demands yet, not a bloody—'

'You're wrong,' Adam interrupted. 'They don't only think about money. They also think about . . . kudos. But you're probably right about one thing. I don't believe that they've kidnapped the American president. In fact, I don't think that Gerhard Skrøder knows anything about the case. He was just doing a well-paid job, I should imagine. But you can ask him. Those boys . . .' he looked at the picture again, 'they've made choices that mean that we know where they are at any given time. It shouldn't take more than an hour to haul him in.'

He patted his stomach, pulled a face and added: 'And now I *must* have something to eat. Good luck!'

His phone started ringing. He glanced down at the display and then bolted out into the corridor to take the call, without even saying goodbye.

12

The woman was nearly at the lake. She wasn't really dressed for this weather. The sky hung leaden above the water and the waves were being whipped into white horses only a hundred metres from the shore. It had looked so promising in the morning that she had even risked taking her thermal underwear off. Which had been fine on the way out to Ullevålseter, but she now regretted having taken a detour to Øyungen on the way back.

She had parked her small Fiat at Skar; she was still driving, despite her son's desperate attempts to stop her. She had just celebrated her eightieth birthday, and after the party, she had discovered that her car keys were missing from the hook above the hall shelf. She knew that her son meant well, but it still annoyed her that he had done it and that he believed he was a better judge of her health than she was. Fortunately she had an extra set of keys in her jewellery box.

She felt fit as a fiddle, and it was her walks in the forests and hills that kept her that way. She had had a couple of aneurysms, which made her a bit forgetful, but there was nothing wrong with her legs.

She was very cold and desperately needed to pee.

She wasn't shy about going to the loo in the woods, but the thought of pulling down her trousers in the bitter wind made her pick up pace so she wouldn't need to.

But it didn't help. She had to find a suitable spot.

She headed north by the dam and broke a path through the undergrowth and the birch trees that were exploding with catkins and sticky light green leaves. A natural embankment made it difficult to go any further. The old woman gingerly tested a tussock with her boots and then lowered herself down into the ditch behind the embankment, which was about a metre and a half deep. She was just about to undo her trousers when she saw him.

He was lying peacefully asleep. One of his arms was over his face, as if to protect it. The moss he was lying on was thick and soft and the low birch trees almost acted like a duvet.

'Hello,' the woman called, keeping her trousers on. 'Hello there!'

The man didn't respond.

She struggled past a boulder and stepped in some mud. A branch whipped her face. She swallowed a scream, out of consideration for the man under the trees. Finally she managed to fight her way over to him and stood there, gasping.

Her pulse increased. She felt dizzy, and carefully lifted his arm. The eyes that stared at her were brown. They were wide open and there was a fly crawling around in one of them.

She had no idea what she was going to do. She still didn't have a mobile phone, despite her son's constant nagging. It ruined the whole purpose of being outdoors, and could also cause brain tumours.

The man was wearing a dark suit and some good shoes, which were very muddy. The old lady was on the verge of tears. He was so young, no more than forty, she reckoned. His face was so peaceful, with beautiful eyebrows that resembled a bird in flight over his big open eyes. His lips were blue, and for a moment she thought that the right thing to do would be to give him mouth-to-mouth resuscitation. As she pulled back his jacket to get to his heart, something fell out of his inner pocket. It was a kind of wallet, she thought, and picked it up. Then she straightened her back, as if she finally understood that the cold corpse was more than several hours beyond being saved by heart compressions. She still hadn't noticed the bullet hole in the man's temple.

She was suddenly overcome by nausea. Slowly she lifted her right hand. It seemed to be so far away from her, completely out of her control. Fear made her want to run away, back on to the path, to the road through the forest where there were always other people. She put the small black leather wallet in her pocket, automatically, and clambered back over the embankment. Her right leg gave way underneath her; it felt numb, but the old lady managed to struggle through the undergrowth and get back on to the gravel track, thanks to the iron willpower that had kept her so strong and healthy for eighty years and five days.

Then she collapsed and lost consciousness.

13

'There's nothing to discuss,' Johanne said.

'But—'

'Stop. I warned you, Adam. I told you last night and I was sure that you understood how serious I was, but then you apparently didn't care. And that's not why I'm calling.'

'You can't just leave and take the—'

'Adam, don't force me to raise my voice. That will frighten Ragnhild.'

It was a lie and he knew it. He couldn't hear anything that sounded like babbling in the background, and his daughter was never quiet unless she was asleep.

'Have you honestly left me? *For real?* Have you lost your mind?'

'Perhaps a bit.'

He thought he heard the hint of a smile, and breathed easier.

'I'm so disappointed,' Johanne said calmly. 'And absolutely furious with you. But we can talk about that later. Right now, I want you to listen . . .'

'I have a right to know where Ragnhild is.'

'She's with me and she's fine. I cross my heart and promise that I'll phone again later today to talk everything through. And my word is worth slightly more than yours, as we both know. But just listen to me.'

Adam clenched his jaw. He balled his fist and raised it to hit something, but all he could find was the wall. A uniformed police cadet spun round about three metres further down the corridor. Adam lowered his fist, shrugged and forced a smile.

'Is what Wencke Bencke said on the TV true?' Johanne asked.

'No,' Adam groaned. 'Not her again. Please!'

'Just *listen* to me!'

'OK.'

'You're grinding your teeth.'

'What do you want?'

'Is it true that the security cameras show no one going in or out of the President's room? From the time that she went to bed until they discovered that she was missing?'

'I can't answer that.'

'Adam!'

'I'm bound by confidentiality, you know that.'

'Have you gone through the films to see what happened *afterwards*?'

'I haven't gone through anything. I'm Warren's liaison on this case, not an investigator.'

'Are you listening to me?'

'Yes, but I don't have anything to do with—'

'When is a crime scene most chaotic, Adam?'

He bit his thumbnail. Her voice was different now. The wronged, unreasonable tone had almost disappeared. Now he heard the real Johanne, the one that never ceased to fascinate him with her Socratic way of making him see things differently, from another angle from the one he was so used to after thirty years in the force.

'When the crime is discovered,' he said curtly.

'And?'

'In the period immediately after,' he said, uncertainly. 'Before the area is cordoned off and all the tasks are allocated. When everything is just . . . chaos.' He swallowed.

'Exactly,' Johanne replied in a quiet voice.

'Shit,' said Adam.

'The President may not have disappeared during the night. She may have been taken later. Just after seven o'clock, when everybody already thought she was gone.'

'But . . . she wasn't there! The room was empty and there was a note from the kidnappers . . .'

'Wencke Bencke knew about that too. Now the whole of

Norway knows about it. What do you think the function of that note was?'

'To tell—'

'A message like that fools the brain into drawing conclusions,' Johanne interrupted him. She was talking faster now. 'It makes us believe that something has already happened. My guess is that the Secret Service guys looked very quickly around the room when they read it. It's a big suite, Adam. They probably checked the bathroom, and maybe they opened a couple of cupboards. But the note . . . well, the purpose of that was to get them out of there. As quickly as possible. And if things are chaotic at an ordinary crime scene, I can only imagine what it was like at the Hotel Opera yesterday morning. With two national authorities and . . .'

They were both silent.

At last he could hear Ragnhild. Someone was talking to her and she was laughing. He couldn't make out the words and it was difficult to determine the gender of the voice. It sounded coarse and husky, but didn't necessarily sound like a man.

'Adam?'

'I'm still here.'

'You have to get them to watch the tapes from the hour after the alarm was raised. I think it would probably be about fifteen or twenty minutes later.'

He didn't answer.

'Did you hear me?'

'Yes,' he replied. 'Where are you?'

'I'll phone you again this evening. I promise.'

Then she hung up.

Adam stood stock still for a few seconds, staring at the phone. Even his hunger wasn't bothering him any more; he didn't feel anything.

14

Fayed Muffasa was four years older than his brother. He had shorter hair and was better dressed than Al Muffet, who was wearing jeans and a checked flannel hunting shirt, but they were otherwise remarkably similar. Al was about to get into the car to drive his youngest daughter to school when Fayed arrived and climbed out of the hired car with a broad smile.

He's so like me, Al thought as he held out his hand. I always forget how alike we are.

'Welcome,' he said, in a serious voice. 'You're earlier than I'd expected.'

'Doesn't matter,' Fayed said, as if it was he who had been inconvenienced. 'I'll just wait here until you get back. Hi, Louise!' He bent down towards the passenger-side window and looked in.

'My, you've grown!' he shouted and signed to her to wind down the window. 'It is Louise, isn't it?'

She opened the door instead and got out.

'Hi,' she said, shyly.

'How pretty you are!' Fayed exclaimed and opened his arms. 'And what a wonderful place you've got here. Great air!' He took a deep breath, then grinned.

'We're happy here,' Al said. 'Just make . . .'

His keys rattled as he walked back towards the house. He unlocked the door and left it open.

'Sit yourself down,' he said and pointed towards the kitchen. 'Just help yourself to something to eat if you're hungry. There's still coffee in the thermos.'

'Great.' Fayed smiled. 'I've got some reading stuff with me. I'll just find a comfy chair and relax. When will you be back?'

Al glanced at his watch and thought a moment.

'Just under an hour. I'm going to drop Louise off and then I've got something to do quickly in town. About three quarters of an hour, I should think.'

'See you later then,' Fayed said and went in. The netting door slammed shut behind him.

Louise had already got back into the car. Al Muffet drove slowly down the gravel track and then swung out on to the highway.

'He seems nice,' Louise said.

'Sure.'

The road was bad. No one had filled the holes after the long winter's wear. It didn't make any difference to Al Muffet. The uneven surface forced people to lower their speed when they passed. He went over a small hill just a few hundred metres from the house and then stopped.

'Where are you going, Dad?'

'To have a pee,' he said with a fleeting smile, and got out.

He stepped over the ditch by the side of the road and headed back towards the thicket on the brow of the hill. Slowly he made his way through the undergrowth, making sure the whole time that he was in the shadow of the great maple trees by the boulder that balanced on the edge of a small cliff.

Fayed had come back out. He was standing on the path midway between the house and the road, looking around. He dithered before sauntering down to the gate. The flag on the postbox was down, as the postman hadn't been yet. Fayed studied the postbox, which Louise had been allowed to paint the year before. It was bright red, with a picture of a blue galloping horse on both sides.

Fayed straightened up and started to walk back towards the house. He was more focused now and picked up speed. He stopped by the hire car, got in and sat there without starting the engine. He might have been talking on a mobile phone, but it was difficult to say from that distance.

'Dad, are you coming?'

Al was loath to go back.

'Coming,' he mumbled and pushed his way back through the undergrowth. 'I'm just coming.'

He brushed the leaves and twigs off before getting back into the car.

'I'm going to be really late,' Louise complained. 'It's the second time this month and it's all your fault!'

'Yes, yes,' Al Muffet mumbled absently, and put the car in gear.

His brother might just have wanted to stretch his legs. Maybe he wasn't hungry. It was only natural that he might want some fresh air after the long journey. Why then did he get back into the car? Why had he come in the first place, and why on earth had he, for the first time that Al could remember, been so friendly?

'Watch where you're going!'

He turned the wheel sharply to the right and just managed to avoid driving off the road. The car skidded in the opposite direction and he instinctively slammed on the brakes. The back wheel got stuck in the deep ditch. He released the brakes and the car shot forwards, and then came to a stop diagonally across the highway.

'What are you doing?' Louise screamed.

Just a slight paranoia attack, Al Muffet thought to himself. As he tried to start the car again, he said: 'It'll be fine, honey. Don't worry. It'll all be fine.'

15

The American president had no idea what time or day it was any more.

She had tried to focus on the time.

They had taken her watch off and pulled a hood over her head as soon as they got in the car. She hadn't resisted at all, as it had taken her by surprise. It was only when the engine started that she managed to pull herself together and estimated the journey to be just under half an hour. The men didn't say a word in the course of that time, so she had at least been able to count without being distracted. They had tied her hands together in front, not behind her back. So, sitting on her own in the back seat, she could use her fingers to count. Every time she reached sixty, she grabbed hold of the next finger. When ten minutes had passed and she had no fingers left, she scratched herself on the back of her hand with a longish manicured nail. The pain helped her to remember. Three scratches. Thirty minutes. About half an hour.

Oslo was not big. A million inhabitants? More?

The weak red light on the wall by the locked door was the only thing that made it at all possible to see. She kept her eyes fixed on the red light and breathed deeply.

She must have been here for some time now. Had she fallen asleep? She had gone to the toilet in the corner of the room. It wasn't easy to get her trousers down with tied hands, but she had managed. It was worse pulling them up. How many times had she been over to the cardboard box full of newspapers? She tried to remember, to calculate, to get an idea of time.

She must have fallen asleep.

Oslo wasn't big.

Not that big. Not even a million inhabitants.

Sweden was the largest. Stockholm was biggest.

Concentrate. Breathe. Think. You can do it. You know.

Oslo was small.

Half a million? Half a million.

She didn't think she had slept in the car. But afterwards?

Her body felt leaden. It was painful to move. She had been sitting for too long in the same position. She tried carefully to ease her thighs apart. She was astonished to discover that she had soiled herself. The smell wasn't a problem, she couldn't smell anything.

Breathe. Calm. You've been asleep. Concentrate.

She remembered the plane landing.

The town crept up the surrounding hillsides. The fjord forced its way into the heart of the city.

Helen Lardahl Bentley closed her eyes to ward off the red darkness. She tried to recapture her impressions from Air Force One on approach to the airport, just south of Oslo.

North. It was north of the city, she eventually remembered.

It helped to keep her eyes closed.

The forests surrounding the capital were far less wild and frightening than they were made out to be in the family stories that she heard on her grandma's lap. The elderly woman had never been to the old country, but the picture that she painted for her children and grandchildren was vivid enough: Norway was beautiful and frightening, with rugged mountains everywhere.

It wasn't true.

From the window of Air Force One, Helen Bentley had seen a different landscape. It was friendly, with rolling hills and mountains with snow on their north-facing slopes. The trees were starting to parade that luminous green colour that belonged to the time of year.

How big was Oslo?

They couldn't have gone that far.

As far as she had understood, the hotel was in the centre of town. They couldn't have taken her that far in half an hour.

They had turned quite a lot of corners. Maybe they were

necessary manoeuvres, but it might just as easily have been to confuse her. She might still be in the centre.

But she might also be wrong. She might have counted wrong. Had she actually fallen asleep?

She had not slept in the car. She had kept a clear head and counted the seconds. When she twisted her hands, she could feel the three scratches with her fingertip. Three scratches meant thirty minutes.

The hood they had pulled over her head was clammy and smelt strange.

Had she fallen asleep?

Her eyes filled with tears. She opened them wide. Mustn't cry. A tear fell from the corner of her eye and trickled down her nose towards her mouth.

Don't cry.

Think. Open your eyes and think.

'You are the president of America,' she whispered through gritted teeth. 'You are the president of the USA, goddammit!'

It was hard to focus on one thought. Everything was fuzzy. It was as if her brain had got caught in a loop that made no sense, with arbitrary images in an increasingly confusing collage.

Responsibility, she thought, and bit her tongue until it bled. I have responsibility. I have to pull myself together. Fear is an old friend. I am used to fear. I have gone as far as a person can go and I've often been afraid. I have never shown it to anyone, but my enemies have frightened me. Enemies who have threatened me and everything I stand for. I have never let myself be broken. Fear only sharpened my senses. Fear made me clear-sighted and wise.

The blood tasted sweet, like warm iron.

Helen Bentley had plenty of practice in managing fear.

But not panic.

It floored her. Not even the familiar iron claw, which was now clamped round the back of her head, could jolt her from the confused state of paralysed fear that had gripped her since she was taken from the hotel suite. The adrenalin had not made her sharp and clear-sighted, as it normally did in conflict situations or important TV programmes. Quite the opposite. When the man by the side of her bed had whispered his short message, the world stood still and the pain was so overwhelming that he had to help her to her feet.

She had only once before experienced anything like it.

And that was a long time ago, and should have been forgotten.

It should have been forgotten. I should have forgotten it by now.

She was crying now, sobbing silently. Her tears were salty and mixed with the blood from her bitten tongue. The light by the door seemed to be getting brighter and there were threatening shadows everywhere. Even when she squeezed her eyes shut, she felt the red, dangerous dark closing in on her.

I must think. I have to think clearly.

Had she fallen asleep?

The experience of losing count of time confused her more than she might have imagined. For a moment she felt like she had been away for days, but then she reined in her rambling thoughts and made another attempt to reason.

Listen. Listen for sounds.

She opened her ears and senses. Nothing. It was silent.

At the late supper last night, the Norwegian prime minister had told her that the national-day celebrations would be loud. That the whole city would be out.

'This is the children's day,' he had told her.

Trying to reconstruct an actual event was something solid. Something to focus her thoughts on, so that they didn't detach and swirl around like leaves in the wind. She wanted to remember. She opened her eyes and stared straight at the red lamp.

The Prime Minister had stammered, and used bullet points.

'We don't parade our military forces,' he said with a thick accent, 'as other nations do. We show the world our children.'

She hadn't heard any happy children's shouts since she came

to this empty bunker with the horrible red light. No brass bands. Nothing other than complete silence.

She couldn't get rid of her headache. The way she was sitting, with her hands tied in front of her with thin strips of plastic that bit into the skin on her wrists, prevented her from performing her normal ritual. In desperation, she realised that the only thing she could do was to let go of the pain and to hope for salvation.

Warren, she thought, apathetically.

Then she fell asleep, in the middle of the worst attack she had ever experienced.

16

Tom Patrick O'Reilly stood on the corner of Madison Avenue and East 67th Street and longed to be home. It had been a tiring flight, as he hadn't been able to sleep. He had sat on his own from Riyadh to Rome. It felt like being transported by a robot. Only when they landed in Rome did the pilot come out of the cockpit and greet him with a nod, before opening the doors. He had exactly twenty minutes until his next departure on a scheduled flight to Newark. Tom O'Reilly was sure that he wouldn't manage it. But a woman in uniform had suddenly appeared – he had no idea where from – and miraculously rushed him through all the security checks.

The trip from Riyadh to New York had taken exactly fourteen hours, and the time difference made him feel confused and unwell. He never got used to it. His body felt heavier than normal and he couldn't remember the last time his knee hurt so much. He had tried, without success, to cancel a couple of meetings that were scheduled in New York that afternoon.

He just wanted to go home.

The last meal with Abdallah had been eaten in silence. The food was delicious, as always. Abdallah had smiled his inscrutable smile as he ate slowly and systematically from one side of his plate to the other. His family were, as usual, not present. It was just them, Abdallah and Tom, and a silence that seemed to dominate. The servants disappeared too, once the fruit had been served. The candles had burnt down and the only light came from the big terracotta lamps on the walls. Abdallah had eventually got up and left him with nothing more than a quiet good night. In the morning, Tom had been woken by a servant and collected by a limousine. When he got into the car, the palace seemed to be totally deserted.

He had not looked back, and now Tom O'Reilly was standing on a corner on Upper East Side, clutching an envelope in his hand. The unfamiliar uncertainty made him anxious, almost frightened. The terrifying eagle on the postbox looked as if it was about to attack. He put down his small suitcase.

He could, of course, open the letter.

He tried to look around without drawing attention. The pavement was teeming with people. Car horns hooted in irritation. An old woman with a lapdog on her arm bumped into him as she passed. She was wearing sunglasses, despite the grey skies and the drizzle in the air. On the other side of the street, he noticed three youths talking animatedly. Tom thought they looked at him. Their lips were moving, but it wasn't possible to hear what they were saying above the noise of the city. A girl smiled at him when he met her eyes; she was pushing a pram and was lightly dressed for the cool weather. A man stopped just beside him. He looked at his watch and opened his newspaper.

Don't be paranoid, Tom reassured himself, and stroked his chin. They're just normal people. They're not watching you. They're Americans. Just ordinary Americans and I am in my own country. This is my country and I'm safe here. Don't be paranoid.

He could open the envelope.

He could throw it away.

Maybe he should go to the police.

With what? If the letter was illegal, he would be investigated and confronted with the fact that he had actually brought it into the country. If it was OK and Abdallah had been telling the truth, he would have betrayed the man who had looked after him for so many years.

He slowly opened the outer envelope. He pulled out the one inside, with the back facing up. The letter was not sealed, only glued down in the usual way. There was no sender's address. He froze as he was about the turn the envelope over to see who the addressee was.

What he didn't know wouldn't harm him.

He could still throw the envelope away. There was a rubbish bin only a few metres along the street. He could throw the letter away, go to his meetings and forget the whole thing.

But he would never be able to forget it, because he knew that Abdallah would never forget him.

He resolutely dropped the letter into the blue postbox, then he picked up his suitcase and started to walk. As he passed the rubbish bin, he scrunched up the outer envelope with no name on it and dropped it into the bin.

There was nothing wrong with posting a letter.

It was not a crime to do a friend a favour. Tom straightened his shoulders and took a deep breath. He would try to wrap up the meetings as quickly as possible and catch the early-evening flight to Chicago. He wanted to get home to Judith and the kids. He had done absolutely nothing wrong.

He was just terribly tired.

He stopped at the pedestrian crossing and waited for the green man.

Three taxis were hooting furiously, quarrelling about the inside lane on Madison Avenue. A dog barked loudly and wheels screeched on the asphalt. A little girl howled in protest when her mother pulled her by the arm to stand beside Tom. She gave him an apologetic smile. He smiled back, full of understanding, and took a couple of steps out into the road.

When the police reached the scene only a few minutes later, the witnesses all told different stories. The mother with the little girl was almost hysterical and not of much help when it came to establishing what had actually happened when the big middle-aged man was mowed down by the green Taurus. She just hugged her daughter tight and cried. The man in the Taurus was at breaking point too, and could only sob something about 'suddenly' and 'crossed on the red man'. Some of the pedestrians just shrugged their shoulders and mumbled that they hadn't seen anything, while they sneaked looks at their watches and rushed off as soon as the police let them go.

However, it seemed that two witnesses were absolutely certain. One of them, a man in his forties, had been standing on the same side of the street as Tom O'Reilly. He could have sworn that the man had staggered and, without waiting for the green man, had just tumbled into the road. A sudden turn, thought the witness, and nodded sagely. He was more than willing to give his name and address to the overwhelmed policewoman, he said as he glanced over at the body lying motionless in the middle of the road.

'Is he dead?' he asked quietly, and was given a nod in confirmation.

The other witness, a younger man in a suit and tie, had been standing on the other side of 67th Street. He gave a description of events that was remarkably similar to the first man. The policewoman also noted his personal details and was relieved to be able to reassure the distraught driver that it all appeared to be a terrible accident. The driver started to breathe more evenly and some hours later, thanks to the clarity of the witnesses, was a free man again.

Not much more than an hour after Tom O'Reilly had died, the place had been cleared. His body was swiftly identified and driven away. Traffic flowed as before. The remains of blood on the asphalt did make the odd passer-by wonder for a moment, but a shower around six in the evening washed the road clean of the final remains of the tragedy.

17

'Who did you get the idea from?'

The policeman who was sitting in front of the monitor in the gym at the police HQ and who had spent more than a day and a half going through footage that showed nothing other than an empty corridor stared at Adam Stubo with scepticism.

'It's not logical,' he added in an aggressive tone. 'There can't be anyone who would think that something interesting was recorded after the woman disappeared.'

'Yes,' replied Bastesen, Chief of Police. 'It is completely logical, and it's a huge blunder on our part that we didn't think of it. But what's done is done. So now let's see what you can show us.'

Warren Scifford had eventually returned. It had taken Adam half an hour to get hold of him. The American didn't answer his mobile phone and no one picked up the phone at the embassy. When he did show up, he just smiled and shrugged without giving any explanation as to where he'd been. He took off his coat on his way into the gym, where the air was now unbearable.

'Fill me in,' he said, grabbing an empty chair, which he pulled into the table and sat down on.

The policeman's fingers leapt over the keyboard. The screen flickered grey, before the picture was clear. They had seen this part of the video many times before: two Secret Service agents walking towards the door of the presidential suite. One of them knocked on the door.

The digital clock on the top left-hand corner of the screen showed 07:18:23.

The agents stood there for a few seconds before one of them tried the door.

'Strange that the door was open,' muttered the policeman, fingers ready at the keyboard.

No one said anything.

The men went in and disappeared from the scope of the camera.

'Just let the film run,' Adam said quickly, and noted the time. 07:19:02.

07:19:58.

The two mean came tearing out.

'That's where we've stopped,' the policeman said, exasperated. 'That's where I stopped and went back to twenty past twelve.'

'Fifty-six seconds,' Adam said. 'They were in her room for fifty-six seconds before they came running out and raised the alarm.'

'Under a minute to cover more than a hundred square metres,' Bastesen mused and rubbed his chin. 'That's not much of a search.'

'Would you please speak English,' Warren requested without taking his eyes from the screen.

'Sorry,' Adam said. 'As you can see, they can't have done a very thorough search. They saw the apparently empty suite, read the note and that's about it. Hang on. Look, look there!'

He bent down towards the screen and pointed. The policeman at the keyboard had fast-forwarded to a frame where a movement could be seen at the bottom of the screen.

'A . . . a chambermaid?'

Warren squinted.

'Chamber boy,' Adam corrected. 'If there is such a thing.'

The cleaner was a relatively young man. He was wearing a practical uniform and pushing a large trolley in front of him. It had shelves of shampoo bottles and other small items and a deep, apparently empty basket in front for dirty laundry. The man paused a moment before opening the door to the suite and going in, pushing the trolley in front of him.

'07:23:41.' Adam read the numbers slowly. 'Do we have an overview of what was happening elsewhere at that time? In the rest of the hotel?'

'Not a complete one, no,' Bastesen said. 'But I can safely say that it was generally . . . chaotic. The most important thing is that no one was watching the CCTV screens. There was a full alarm and we had problems with—'

'Not even your people?' Adam cut in, looking at Warren.

The American didn't answer. His eyes were glued to the screen. The clock showed 07:25:32 when the cleaner came out again. He struggled to get the trolley over the threshold. The wheels were pressing down against it and the front of the trolley was stuck for a few seconds before he finally managed to push it out into the corridor.

The basket was full. A sheet or a large towel lay on top; one of the corners was hanging over the edge. The trolley approached the camera and the man's face was clearly visible.

'Does he work there?' Adam asked quietly. 'I mean, really work there. Is he an employee?'

Bastesen nodded. 'We've got people on their way to pick him up now,' he whispered. 'But that man there . . .' He pointed to the man who was behind the young Pakistani cleaner; a sturdy figure dressed in a dark suit with dark shoes. His hair was thick and short, and he had a hand pressed against the Pakistani boy's back, as if to hurry him along. He was carrying something that resembled a small, foldable ladder. 'We don't know anything about him for the moment. But it's only twenty minutes since we saw this for the first time, so the work . . .'

Adam wasn't listening. He was staring at Warren Scifford. The American's face was grey, and he had a thin layer of sweat on his forehead. He was biting his knuckles and still had not said a word.

'Is something wrong?' Adam asked.

'Shit,' Warren responded in anger, and then got up abruptly, almost tipping the chair over. He pulled his coat from the chair, hesitated for a moment and then repeated, loud enough for everyone in the room to hear, 'Shit! Shit!'

He grabbed Adam hard by the arm. The sweat had made the curls in his fringe stick to his forehead.

'I have to see the hotel room immediately. Now.'

He stormed over towards the door. Adam exchanged looks with the Chief of Police before shrugging and jogging after the American.

'He didn't say who it was who gave him the idea,' the policeman by the computer said sulkily. 'You know, to check the footage from later. Did you catch who that bloody genius was?'

The woman at the neighbouring table shrugged.

'Now, at least, I've definitely earned a rest,' the man said, and went in search of something that might resemble a bed.

18

Helen Lardahl Bentley woke up from a heavy sleep. She had no idea how long she had been out cold, but she remembered she had been sitting on the flimsy chair by the wall when the attack started. When she tried to sit up, she noticed that her right arm and shoulder had been hurt. A large bump on her temple made it difficult to open her eye.

The fall should have woken her. Maybe she had lost consciousness when she hit the floor. She must have been out of it for a long time. She couldn't get up. Her body wouldn't listen to her. She had to remember to breathe.

Her mind was spinning. It was impossible to focus on anything. She caught a glimpse of her daughter as a child, a little fair-haired three-year-old, the most beautiful one of all – and then she vanished. Billie was sucked into the light on the wall, which was like a deep red hole, and Helen Bentley remembered her grandma's funeral, and the rose she had laid on the coffin; it was red, and dead, and the light was so bright that it hurt her eyes.

Breathe. Out. In.

The room was far too silent. Abnormally still. She tried to scream. All she managed was a whimper, and it was muffled, as if there was a huge pillow in the room. There was no echo from the walls.

She had to breathe. She had to breathe properly.

Time went into a vortex. She thought she could see numbers and clock faces all over the room, and she closed her eyes against the shower of arrows.

'I want to get up,' she shouted in a hoarse voice, and finally managed to haul herself up into a sitting position.

The leg of the chair dug into her back.

'I do solemnly swear,' she said and crossed her right leg over the left, 'that I will faithfully execute . . .'

She twisted round. It felt as if her thigh muscles were about to explode when she finally managed to get up on to her knees. She leant her head against the wall for support, and vaguely registered that it was soft. She leaned her shoulder into the wall too, and with great effort got to her feet.

'. . . the office of the President of the United States.'

She had to take a quick step to the side to avoid falling. The plastic strips had cut even deeper into her wrists. She suddenly felt light-headed, as if her skull had been emptied of everything other than the echo of her heartbeat. As she was only a few centimetres from the wall, she stayed upright.

There was only one door in the room. On the opposite wall. She had to cross the floor.

Warren had betrayed her.

She had to find out why, but her head was empty; it was impossible to think, and she had to cross the floor. The door was locked. She remembered that now. She had tried it earlier. The padded walls swallowed what little sound she managed to make, and it was impossible to open the door. But still, it was the only hope she had, because behind the door was the possibility of something else, someone else, and she had to get out of the soundless box that was about to be the death of her.

With extreme care, she put one foot in front of the other and started to cross the dark, heaving floor.

19

After a while, Adam Stubo started to understand why Warren Scifford had been given the nickname 'The Chief'.

He didn't have much in common with Geronimo. His cheekbones were high, his eyes were deep set, his nose was small and his facial hair was profuse, so that he already had a visible grey shadow. The man had been clean-shaven in the morning. His steel-grey hair fell in soft curls and the fringe was slightly too long.

'No,' Warren Scifford said and stopped outside the door of the Hotel Opera's presidential suite. 'I don't know who the man in the CCTV footage was.'

His face was blank and his look direct, without giving away anything. There was nothing to express indignation at being asked the question, no fake or real surprise at what Adam was intimating.

'It just seemed that way,' Adam insisted, playing with the key. 'It definitely looked like you knew him.'

'Then I gave the wrong impression,' Warren said, without so much as blinking. 'Shall we go in?'

There had been nothing reminiscent of native Indians about the American's outburst in the gym hall, but now he had obviously pulled himself together. He went into the suite and stood in the middle of the room, with his hands in his pockets. He stood there for a long time.

'So we're assuming that she was in the dirty laundry basket on the way out,' he eventually summarised; he seemed to be talking to himself. 'Which would mean that she was hidden away somewhere when the two agents came in at seven o'clock.'

'Or had hidden herself away,' Adam said.

'What?'

'She might have been hidden away,' Adam explained. 'But equally she might have hidden herself. One is more passive than the other.'

Warren wandered over to the window and stood there with his back to Adam. He leaned his shoulder nonchalantly against the window frame, as if he was admiring the view of the Oslo Fjord.

'So you think that she might be involved in this herself in some way?' he said suddenly, without turning. 'That the President of the United States of America might orchestrate her own disappearance in a foreign country. I see.'

'I didn't say that,' Adam replied. 'I simply suggested that there could be many explanations. That all possibilities must be kept open in an investigation like this.'

'That can be ruled out,' Warren said calmly. 'Helen would never put her country in a situation like this. Never.'

'Helen?' Adam repeated, astonished. 'Do you know her that well?'

'Yes.'

Adam waited for him to explain. But he didn't. Instead, he started to walk around the large suite, still with a saunter, still with his hands in his pockets. It was difficult to know what he was looking for, but his eyes darted here, there and everywhere.

Adam sneaked a look at his watch. It was twenty past five. He wanted to go home. He wanted to ring Johanne and find out what was going on, and not least, where she was. If he could get away soon, he might still have a chance of persuading her to come home with Ragnhild before bedtime.

'I think we can assume that the agents only checked the room superficially before they ran out to raise the alarm,' Adam said, in an attempt to encourage the American to be more communicative. 'And there are lots of possible hiding places. The cupboards over there, for example. Have the men been questioned, by the way? Have they been asked what they did in here?'

Warren stopped in front of the double doors of the wardrobe, which were light oak. He didn't open them.

'This really is a beautifully designed room,' he said. 'I love the way Scandinavians use wood. And the view . . .' He threw out his arm and moved over to the window again. 'It's magnificent. Apart from that building site down there. What's that going to be?'

'The opera house,' Adam said, and took a few steps towards him. 'Hence the name of the hotel. But listen, Warren, all this secrecy is not helping anyone. I understand that the case may have implications for the US that we might not, or cannot, understand. But—'

'We will tell you what you need to know. Don't worry.'

'Cut the crap,' Adam hissed.

Warren spun round. He flashed a smile, as if Adam's outburst amused him.

'Don't underestimate us,' Adam said, his cheeks flushed with unfamiliar rage. 'You'd be making a mistake. Don't underestimate me. You should know better.'

Warren shrugged and opened his mouth to say something.

'You knew that man in the film,' Adam snarled. 'None of us who were there are in any doubt. And you don't need to be a detective with nearly thirty years' experience to realise that he must have been in the room all night. It's not the President's hiding place that you're looking for. She could have been anywhere. Under the bed, in the wardrobe.' Adam pointed around the room. 'For that matter, she could have hidden herself behind the curtains. And considering the *terrible* . . .' A fine shower of spray fell on to Warren's face. He didn't move a muscle, and Adam took a step closer as he drew breath, and then continued: '. . . what an *appalling* job those special agents of yours did when they searched the room, the woman could have been hanging from the lampshade without being discovered!'

'They were scared,' Warren said.

'Who was?'

'The agents. They haven't said so themselves, of course. But that's what happened. Frightened people don't do a good job.'

'Frightened? *Frightened*? You're standing here saying that the world's best security agents . . . that your Gurkha boys were *frightened*!'

Warren finally took a step back. His indifferent expression had been replaced by something that resembled scepticism. Adam interpreted it as arrogance.

'This is not like you,' the American said.

'You don't know me.'

'I know your reputation. Why do you think I asked for you, in particular, to be my liaison?'

'I have in fact wondered about that,' Adam said, calmer now.

'The Gurkhas are soldiers. Secret Service agents aren't.'

'Whatever,' Adam muttered.

'But you're right. I do want to find out where the man in the suit might have hidden.'

'Then in heaven's name let's look!'

Warren shrugged again and pointed to the adjoining room. Adam nodded and walked towards the open door. He stood for a moment and waited for Warren to go in first. The American had stopped in the middle of the floor. He was staring at a point on the ceiling.

'The ventilation system has been checked,' Adam said impatiently. 'A metal grate two metres further in means that it wouldn't be possible to get any further. And it hasn't been tampered with.'

'But what about this vent here?' Warren asked, his voice getting higher as he leant his head back. 'There are visible marks on the screw heads. Can you see?'

'Of course there are marks,' Adam said, standing by the door to the office of the suite. 'The police have taken it out to see if the ventilation pipes were used as an escape.'

'But now we know better,' Warren said and pulled a chair over. 'Now we're not looking for an escape, but rather a hiding place. Isn't that so?'

He climbed up on to the chair, carefully placed a foot on each arm and pulled out a Swiss Army knife from his jacket pocket.

'Doesn't the Secret Service use dogs?' Adam asked.

'Yes, of course.'

Warren had teased out a tiny screwdriver from the red knife.

'Wouldn't the dogs have reacted to the smell of a person in the ceiling?'

'Madam President is allergic to dogs.' Warren groaned as he started to unscrew the four screws that held the perforated metal grate in place on the ceiling. 'The Secret Service use sniffer dogs well in advance of her arrival, so there's enough time to vacuum afterwards. Can you give me a hand, please?'

He undid the last screw in the metal grate. It was square, and about half a metre across. He just managed to catch it when it suddenly came loose.

'Here.' He passed it to Adam. 'I assume that fingerprints and the like were secured a long time ago.'

Adam nodded. Warren hopped down on to the floor with remarkable grace.

'I need something higher than this to stand on,' he said and looked around. 'I would rather not touch anything up there.'

'Look,' Adam said quietly; he held the metal grate up to his eyes and squinted. 'Look, Warren.'

The American leant towards him; their heads almost touched. Warren looked over the top of his glasses.

'Glue? Tape?'

He folded the screwdriver back into the army knife and pulled out an awl. With great care he pricked at the almost transparent, apparently sticky mass. It could hardly be more than a millimetre wide and perhaps half a centimetre long.

'Be careful,' Adam warned him. 'I'll get it sent over for analysis.'

'Glue,' Warren stated and straightened his glasses. 'Perhaps the remains of double-sided tape.'

Adam looked instinctively at the ceiling, where an edging of enamelled metal framed the opening. The light in the room made it impossible to see any details in the shaft. The reflection of the table lamp showed that the actual ventilation pipe was matt aluminium. But he was more interested in two tiny specks on the white frame than in the space inside.

'We definitely need something to stand on,' Warren said, and went over to the door into the other room. 'Maybe we can . . .' The rest was swallowed in a mumble.

'I'll call for some people,' Adam said. 'This is the responsibility of Oslo Police and I . . .'

Warren didn't answer.

Adam followed him into the smaller room. A large black desk was positioned at an angle in the middle of the room. The surface was empty apart from a beautiful flower arrangement and a leather folder, which Adam assumed contained writing paper. In front of the glass doors out on to the terrace was a chaise longue with exquisite silk cushions in shades of pink and red. They matched the curtains and a feature wall with Japanese-inspired, patterned wallpaper.

On the opposite wall, behind a sitting area, was a robust bookshelf in solid wood, which must have been about one and a half metres tall. The American tried to tip it.

'It's free-standing,' he said, emptying the shelves of ten or so books and a glass bowl. 'Can you give me a hand?'

'This is not our job,' Adam said and pulled out his mobile phone.

'Give me a hand,' Warren said. 'I just want to look, not touch.'

'No, I'm going to get people over here now.'

'Adam,' Warren exclaimed in exasperation, throwing out his arms, 'you said it yourself. This suite has been gone over with a fine-toothed comb, and all the evidence has been secured. But they still . . . someone has overlooked a small detail. You and I are both experienced policemen. We won't damage anything. I just want to have a look. OK? Then these people of yours can come over and do their job.'

'They're not my people,' Adam muttered.

Warren smiled and started to pull at the bookshelf. Adam

hesitated for a little while longer before reluctantly taking hold of the other end. Together they managed to get the bookshelf into the main room and position it right under the open shaft.

'Will you hold it steady?'

Adam nodded and Warren tested with one foot on the second lowest shelf. It held him, so with his right hand on Adam's shoulder, he carried on climbing to the top. He had to twist his neck in order to study the small specks Adam had noticed.

'Glue here too,' he mumbled without touching it. 'Looks like the same stuff that was on the grate.'

He stuck his head up into the shaft.

'Plenty of room,' he confirmed. His voice sounded hollow and muffled, due to the reverberation within the metal walls. 'It would be perfectly possible for . . .'

Adam couldn't make out the rest.

'What did you say?'

Warren lowered his head down from the opening in the ceiling.

'Just as I thought,' he said. 'It's big enough for a grown man. And these friends of yours . . .' He bent his knees and dropped to the floor. 'I hope that they secured any evidence in the shaft before they crawled in to check the grates.'

'I'm sure they did.'

'But they overlooked this,' said Warren and once again bent down over the loose grate.

'We don't know that for certain.'

'Would there still be traces there if they'd discovered it? Wouldn't the whole grate have been taken in for investigation?'

Adam didn't answer.

'And this,' Warren continued and pointed with his penknife to a spot in the middle of the grate. 'Do you see? All the scratches?'

Adam studied the nearly invisible stripes in the white metal. Someone had scraped against the enamel without breaking it.

'Genius in its simplicity,' he said quietly.

'Quite,' said Warren.

'Someone has unfastened the grate, pulled a stay tied to string or rope through the middle hole, attached double-sided tape to the edge of the grate . . .'

'And climbed in,' concluded Warren. 'It was simply a matter of pulling the grate up to close it. Then there he was. That explains why he was carrying a small ladder.' He pointed at the ceiling with his thumb. 'All he had to do was crawl in when—'

'But how the hell did he manage to get in in the first place?' Adam cut in. 'Can you explain to me how anyone managed to get into the suite where the US president was staying, set up all this . . .' he pointed at the ceiling and then at the loose grate that was lying on the table, 'get comfy in the air vent, then creep out and take the President away with him, and *get away with it*?'

He coughed before continuing, his voice low and exasperated. 'And all that in a hotel room that was minutely examined only a few hours before the President retired. How is it possible? How is that at all possible?'

'There are lots of loose ends here,' Warren said, with his hand on the Norwegian's shoulder.

Adam moved almost imperceptibly, and Warren lifted his hand.

'We have to find out when the CCTV cameras were turned on,' he said swiftly. 'And if they were ever turned off. We must establish when the room was last examined before Madam President came back from the meal. We must—'

'Not we,' Adam corrected and pulled out his mobile phone again. 'I should have called ages ago. That is the investigators' job. Not yours. Not mine.'

He held Warren's gaze as he waited for an answer at the other end. The American was as expressionless as he had been when they came into the suite half an hour ago. When Adam made contact, he turned away and walked slowly towards the windows facing the fjord, talking in a low voice.

Warren Scifford sank down into a chair. He stared at the floor. His arms hung limply by his sides, as if he didn't really know what to do with them. His suit didn't look so elegant any more. It was crumpled and his tie knot was loose.

'Is anything wrong?' Adam asked. He had finished his conversation and turned round without warning.

Warren quickly straightened his tie and stood up. The surprise in his face vanished so swiftly that Adam wasn't sure if he had seen correctly.

'Everything,' Warren laughed. 'Everything's wrong at the moment. Shall we go?'

'No. I'll wait here for my colleagues to come. It shouldn't be long.'

'Then,' Warren started, lightly brushing the right sleeve of his jacket, 'I hope that you won't mind if I go.'

'Not at all,' Adam said. 'Just ring me when you need me.'

He wanted to ask Warren where he was going, but something stopped him. If the American wanted to play that game, he would let him have all the secrets he liked.

Adam had other things to think about.

20

'I've got other things to take care of,' he said and switched his phone from his right to his left hand as he got into the passenger seat of a uniformed Oslo Police car. 'I've been at work since half past seven this morning, and now I'm going home.'

'You're the best,' the voice at the other end said. 'You're the best, Adam, and this is the closest we've come to anything concrete.'

'No.'

Adam Stubo was completely calm when he put his hand over the mouthpiece for a moment and whispered to the driver: 'Haugesvei 4, please. Off Maridalsveien, just before you get to Nydalen.'

'Hello,' the voice on the other end called.

'I'm still here. I'm on my way home. You've given me the job of liaison, and I'm trying to do it to the best of my ability. It's unprofessional, quite frankly, to then suddenly pull me into—'

'Not at all. On the contrary, it is very professional,' the Chief of Police, Bastesen, retorted. 'This case demands that we use only the best people in the country at all times. Regardless of shifts, rank and overtime.'

'But—'

'We have of course cleared it with your bosses. You can take this as an order. Come immediately.'

Adam closed his eyes and let out a long breath. He opened them again when the driver braked suddenly at the roundabout by Oslo City. A young lad in a clapped-out Golf jumped in too fast in front of them.

'Change of plan,' Adam said, exhausted, and closed the

conversation. 'Drive me to the police HQ. Some people obviously think that today has not been long enough.'

There was a loud rumble. Adam patted his stomach and smiled apologetically to the driver.

'And please stop at a petrol station,' he added. 'I have to eat something, a hotdog or three.'

21

Abdallah al-Rahman was hungry, but he still had a couple of things to do before he could have his evening meal. First he wanted to see his youngest son.

Rashid was fast asleep, with a soft horse under his arm. The boy had eventually been allowed to watch the film he had gone on about so much, and was now lying on his back with his legs wide open, his face the picture of peace. He had kicked off his blanket some time ago. His jet-black hair was getting too long. His curls lay like rivers of oil against the white silk.

Abdallah sank down on his knees and spread the blanket carefully over the boy again. He kissed him on the forehead and adjusted the horse so it would be more comfortable.

They had watched *Die Hard* with Bruce Willis.

The nearly twenty-year-old American film was Rashid's favourite. None of his older brothers could understand why. For them, *Die Hard* was incredibly old-fashioned, with hopelessly out-of-date special effects and a hero who wasn't even tough. But for six-year-old Rashid, the action scenes were perfect: cartoon-like and unreal and therefore not frightening. Another bonus was that in 1988, terrorists were Eastern European. They hadn't yet become Arabs.

Abdallah looked up at the old film poster hanging above Rashid's bed. The night light, which the boy was still allowed to keep on because he was scared of the dark, cast a reddish glow over Bruce Willis' bruised face. It was partially covered by Nakatomi Plaza, an explosive tower of fire. The actor's mouth was open, almost aghast, and his eyes were fixed on the unthinkable: a terrorist attack on a skyscraper.

Abdallah got up to leave. He stood for a while in the doorway. Bruce Willis' mouth was a gaping black hole in the semi-dark.

Abdallah thought he could see a yellowish-red reflection of the massive explosion in his eyes; a nascent fury.

That's how they reacted, he thought to himself. Just like that. Thirteen years after the film was made. Shock and disbelief, helplessness and fear. And then came the anger, when American society realised that the unthinkable was now reality.

The terrorist attack on the 11th of September 2001 had been the work of madmen. Abdallah had seen that immediately. He got a distraught phone call from one of his contacts in Europe and managed to turn on the television in time to see United Airlines Flight 175 crashing into the South Tower. The North Tower was already in flames. It was just after four in the afternoon in Riyadh, and Abdallah had not been able to sit down.

For two hours he stood in front of the TV screen. When he finally pulled himself away from the news to answer some of the telephone messages that had been streaming in, he realised that the attack on the World Trade Center would be as fatal for the Arabic world as the attack on Pearl Harbor had been for the Japanese.

Abdallah closed the door to his son's room. There was more to do before he could eat. He started to walk towards the part of the palace where his offices were, towards the east wing, where the morning sun was allowed to stream in at the start of the working day, before it got too hot.

The building was now quiet and dark. The few employees that he felt it was necessary to have out here lived in a small complex he had had built two kilometres closer to Riyadh. Only the private servants stayed in the palace after office hours. And even they had their sleeping quarters some distance from the main buildings, in the low sand-coloured houses by the gate.

Abdallah crossed the square between the two wings. The night was clear, and as always, he took time to stop by the carp pond and look at the stars. The palace was situated far enough from the city lights for the sky to look like it had been perforated by millions of white dots; some were small and sparkling, others big shining stars. He sat down on one of the low benches and felt the evening breeze against his cheeks.

Abdallah was a pragmatist when it came to religion. His family upheld the Muslim traditions, and he made sure that his sons received instruction in the Koran, as well as a rigorous academic training. He believed in the Prophet's word; he had done his *hajj* and paid *zakah* with pride. But for him the relationship between himself and Allah was personal. He said his prayers five times a day, but not if time was short. Which it was more and more frequently, but he didn't let it bother him. Abdallah al-Rahman was convinced that Allah, to the extent that He was bothered by such things, would have the greatest understanding of the importance of taking care of his affairs, over and above following the *salah* rules down to a T.

And he was strongly opposed to mixing politics and religion. To worship Allah as the only God and acknowledge the prophet Mohammad as His messenger was a spiritual matter. Politics, on the other hand – and therefore business – was not about the spirit, but about reality. In Abdallah's opinion, the split between politics and religion was not only necessary from the point of view of politics. It was equally important, if not more so, to protect what was pure and sublime about faith from the cynical, often brutal, processes required by politics.

He was a cynic when it came to business, with no other god than himself.

When al-Qaeda launched its devastating attack on the US on the 11th of September 2001, he was just as horrified as most of the world's six billion inhabitants.

He was appalled by the attack.

Abdallah al-Rahman saw himself as a warrior. His contempt for the US was just as potent as a terrorist's hate for that country. And killing was a means that Abdallah accepted, and at times used. But it was to be used with precision, and only when necessary.

Arbitrary violence was always evil. He had in fact known

several of those who died in Manhattan. Three of them were on his pay roll. Without knowing it, of course. Most of his American companies were owned by holding companies that in turn were affiliated with international conglomerates, which effectively concealed the actual ownership. Via the usual routes, Abdallah made sure that the families of those killed would not suffer financially. They were Americans, all of them, and they had no idea that the generous cheques they received from the deceaseds' employers actually came from a man who was from the same country as Osama bin Laden.

Arbitrary violence was not only evil; it was also inconceivably stupid.

Abdallah had problems understanding why such an intelligent and well-educated man had become involved in such banal terrorism.

Abdallah knew the al-Qaeda leader well. They were about the same age and were both born in Riyadh. They moved in the same circles when they were young; a group of rich men's sons who mixed with the innumerable princes of the house of Saud. Abdallah liked Osama. He was a friendly boy, gentle and attentive, and far less flashy than a lot of the other boys, who wallowed in their wealth and did little to look after their family fortunes that welled up in the country's vast desert. Osama was academically gifted and bright and the two boys had often ended up in a corner having quiet discussions about philosophy and politics, religion and history.

When Abdallah's brother died and his carefree life as the younger son was over, he lost contact with Osama. But that was probably a good thing. The man who was later to become a terrorist leader experienced a political-religious awakening towards the end of the 1970s, a process that was speeded up when the Soviet Union decided to invade Afghanistan.

They had gone their separate ways and had not seen each other since.

Abdallah got up from the bench. He stretched his arms up

towards the stars and felt his muscles being fully extended. The cool evening breeze was soothing.

He wandered slowly over to the east wing.

He believed that al-Qaeda's attack on the US was driven by pure hate, which always made him puzzle at his childhood friend's lack of insight into the Western psyche.

Abdallah knew the limitations of hate. During his convalescence in Switzerland, following his brother's death, he had come to understand that hate was an emotion he must never indulge in. Already then, as a sixteen-year-old, he recognised that rationality was a warrior's most important tool, and that reason was irreconcilable with hate.

Hate only reproduced itself.

The destruction of three buildings and four planes, and the deaths of around three thousand people had unleashed a hate and fear so great that the people accepted gross misconduct on the part of their authorities.

In Abdallah's view, the American people had willingly compromised their constitution in the hope that they would not be attacked again. They accepted tapping and arbitrary arrests, raids and surveillance to a degree that would have been unthinkable a hundred years earlier.

The Americans had closed ranks, Abdallah mused, in the way that people always close ranks against an external enemy.

He opened the big, beautiful carved door to his office. The lamp on his desk was on, and bathed the many carpets that lay on the floor in a golden light. There was a faint humming from the computer and a fragrant smell of cinnamon made him open a cupboard by the window. Here he found a newly made pot of tea, ready on a stand. The last servant always made sure that this was done before leaving the office wing so that Abdallah could complete his evening duties in peace. He poured himself a glass.

This time they would not close ranks.

The thought made him smile. He drank half a glass of tea before sitting down at the computer. It took him a matter of seconds to pull up the ColonelCars' website. There he read that it was with great sadness that the management had to announce the death of the company's CEO, Tom Patrick O'Reilly, in a tragic accident. The management expressed their deepest sympathies to the director's family and reassured their clients that their extensive international operations would continue to be run in the spirit of the deceased, and that 2005 already looked set to be a record year.

Abdallah had his confirmation and logged out.

He would never again think of his old university friend Tom O'Reilly.

22

The man who had just collected his dead mother's personal belongings from the hospital locked the door behind him and went into his sitting room. For a moment he stood there, at a loss, staring down at the anonymous bag that contained his mother's clothes and rucksack. He was still holding it in his hand and didn't quite know what to do.

The doctor had taken time to talk to him. He had comforted him by saying that it had been quick and his mother would hardly have known that anything was wrong before she collapsed. She had been found by another walker, he told him, but unfortunately the old woman had died before she got to hospital. The doctor's smile was warm and open and he said something to the effect that he hoped he would die in much the same way, in the forest one May day, as a healthy eighty-year-old with an alert mind.

Eighty years and five days, thought the son, and wiped his eyes with the back of his hand. No one could complain about getting to that age.

He put the bag down on the dining table. In a way it seemed undignified to unpack it. He tried to win over his reluctance to go through his mother's belongings; it felt like breaking his childhood rule number one: don't poke your nose in other people's business.

The rucksack lay on top. He opened it gingerly. A tin lunch box was the first thing he saw. He took it out. The lid had once sported a picture of the Geiranger Fjord in brilliant sunshine, and an old-fashioned luxury steamship. Now all that remained of it was some dirty blue water and grey sky. He had given her a new bright red plastic lunch box a couple of years ago. She immediately went and exchanged it for a hand whisk, as there was no point in replacing a perfectly usable lunch box.

He emptied the rest of the contents of the rucksack on to the table, and smiled at the thought of his mother's grim face every time he tried to force something new on her. A worn map of Nordmarka. A compass that certainly didn't point north; the red arrow wavered back and forth as if it had drunk some of the alcohol it lay in.

Under the rucksack was her walking jacket. He lifted it up and held it to his cheek. The smell of the old woman and the forest brought tears to his eyes again. He held the jacket out and carefully brushed away the leaves and twigs that were caught on one of the arms.

Something fell out of the pocket.

He folded the jacket and put it down beside the contents of the rucksack. Then he bent down to pick up whatever it was that had fallen to the floor.

A wallet?

It was made of leather, and was quite small. But it was unexpectedly heavy. He opened it and caught himself laughing out loud.

He mustn't laugh, so he gulped and sniffed and opened his eyes wide to stop the tears.

But he couldn't stop laughing and had problems breathing.

His obstinate eighty-year-old mother had met her death with a Secret Service ID card in her pocket.

The wallet could be opened like a small book. The right side was adorned with a gold-coloured metal badge with an eagle on it, spreading its wings over a shield with a star in the middle. It reminded him of the sheriff's badge he'd got from his father for Christmas when he was eight, and now he was no longer laughing.

On the left-hand side, in a plastic pocket, was an ID card. It belonged to a man called Jeffrey William Hunter. A good-looking man, judging by the photo. He had short, thick hair and a serious expression in his big eyes.

The middle-aged man, who had just lost his only remaining

parent, was a taxi driver. His shift had long since started, but his car stood idle outside. He had not sent a message to say that he couldn't work. In fact, he had thought that driving around in town would be just as good as sitting here at home, alone with his grief. Now he was no longer so sure. He examined the painstakingly made badge. He could not for the life of him fathom why his mother was in possession of something like that. The only answer that he could come up with was that she had found it in the forest. Someone must have lost it there.

There were plenty of Secret Service agents in town right now. He had seen them himself, around Akershus Fort, when there was that official dinner there the other night.

He studied the unknown man's face again.

It was so serious that it almost looked sad.

The taxi driver suddenly stood up. He left his mother's belongings lying on the table and grabbed his keys from the hook just inside the front door.

A Secret Service badge was not something you could send in the post. It might be important. He would drive straight to the police.

Now.

23

'You are truly unbelievable,' Adam Stubo said.

Gerhard Skrøder was lying more than sitting in his chair. His legs were wide apart and his head was laid back, his eyes fixed on something on the ceiling. The dark bags under his eyes were in stark contrast to his white skin, and made his nose seem even larger. The man whose nickname was the Chancellor had not touched the coffee or the bottle of mineral water that Adam Stubo had given him.

'I wonder,' the detective chief inspector continued, pulling his ear, 'whether you boys actually realise how idiotic that advice actually is. Don't tip your chair!'

The legs of the chair crashed to the floor.

'What advice?' the man asked reluctantly. He crossed his arms over his chest and scowled at the floor. The two had not had any eye contact yet.

'The rubbish that your lawyers feed you about keeping your mouth shut when you're being questioned by the police. Can't you see how stupid it is?'

'It's worked before.' The man laughed and shrugged without sitting up in the chair. 'And in any case, I haven't done anyhing wrong. It's not illegal to drive around in Norway.'

'There you go!' Adam chuckled. For the first time he glimpsed something that looked like interest in Gerhard Skrøder's eyes.

'What the fuck do you mean?' Skrøder asked and grabbed the bottle of water. He was looking straight at Adam Stubo now.

'You always keep your mouth shut. And then we know you're guilty. But that's just a red rag to a bull, you see. We don't get anything for free from you boys, so we're even more focused on making sure that we do. And you see . . .' he leant over the old, worn table that separated them, 'in cases like this, where you actually think you've done nothing illegal, you can't help yourself. Not in the long run. Let's see, it took . . .' he looked up at the clock, 'twenty-three minutes before you were tempted to speak. Don't you realise that we broke that stupid code of yours years ago? A person who is innocent always talks. A person who talks is often guilty. A person who is silent is always guilty. I know what strategy I would have chosen, put it that way.'

Gerhard Skrøder ran a dirty index finger down the ridge of his nose. The nail was black and bitten to the quick. He started tipping his chair again, backwards and forwards. He was more uneasy now, and pulled his cap down over his eyes. Adam reached over for a pad of A4 paper, picked up a felt tip and started to scribble something down without saying a word.

Gerhard Skrøder had not been difficult to find. He had been enjoying himself with a whore from Lithuania, in a tenement in Grünerløkka. The flat was one of many in the extensive police register of places where criminals hung out. The patrol that had been sent out to find him hit bull's eye on the third attempt. Only a few hours after he had been identified by Adam on a grainy CCTV recording from a twenty-four-hour petrol station, he was in a cell. He had stewed there for an hour or two and had sworn out loud at the sight of Adam Stubo, when he came to collect him.

Since then, he had said nothing. Until now.

Silence was obviously harder to deal with than all Adam's questions and accusations and references to photographic evidence. Gerhard Skrøder chewed at the remains of his thumbnail. One of his thighs was shaking. He coughed and opened the bottle of water. Adam carried on drawing, a psychedelic pattern of blood-red stripes and stars.

'I'll wait for my lawyer, that's for sure,' Gerhard said eventually and sat up in the chair. 'And I have the right to know what you're accusing me of doing. I was just driving around with a couple of people in the car. Since when's that been illegal, eh?'

Adam took his time putting the top back on the felt tip and then put it down. He still did not say a word.

218

'And what the fuck has happened to Ove Rønbeck?' Gerhard complained, obviously having thrown his original strategy overboard. 'You're not allowed to talk to me without my lawyer being present, you know!'

'Yes, yes,' Adam said. 'I am. I can, for example, ask you whether you would like a fresh coffee. You haven't even touched that one and it'll be cold by now.'

Gerhard gave a sullen shake of the head.

'And I can do you another favour.' Adam stood up and walked along beside the table for a couple of steps, then sat down on the edge, half turned away from Gerhard.

'What's that?' muttered the arrestee into his bottle.

'Are you happy for me to do you a favour before your lawyer gets here?'

'Fuck it, Stubo! What the hell are you talking about?'

Adam sniffed and wiped his nose on his shirt sleeve. It was unexpectedly cold in the room. The air-conditioning must have been put on the wrong setting. Perhaps it had been done on purpose, to expel the heat of so many officers working round the clock in the building. Even now, at half past seven in the evening, when the corridors were normally pretty deserted, with rows and rows of closed rooms, you could hear doors slamming and footsteps, voices and the jangling of keys; as much noise as on a busy Friday morning in June.

His jacket was hanging over the chair. He slipped down from the table and grabbed it. As he put it on, he smiled and said in a friendly tone: 'I have never liked you, Gerhard.'

The man picked at a scab and didn't answer.

'And perhaps that's why,' Adam continued, straightening his jacket, 'for once, I'm quite happy that you're keeping your mouth shut.'

Gerhard played with his cap and opened his mouth to say something. He changed his mind a little too late and the word mutated into a strange grunt before he clenched his teeth. He slouched back in the chair again and vigorously scratched his crotch.

'Very happy.' Adam nodded in emphasis. He was standing with his back to the arrestee now, as if he was speaking to an imaginary third person. 'Because I don't like you. And because you're behaving in the way that you are, I can just release you.'

He spun round and made an inviting gesture towards the closed door.

'I can let you go,' he said. 'Because the people out there use completely different methods from the ones that I'm allowed to use. Completely different.'

He laughed, as if the thought of letting Gerhard Skrøder go pleased him greatly.

'What d'you mean?'

'I think I've made up my mind,' Adam said, again as if he was talking to someone else. 'Then I don't have to put up with all this nonsense. I can go home. Call it a day.' He patted down his jacket, as if to check that he had his wallet and keys with him before leaving. 'And then I'll never have to see you again. One crook fewer for the police to waste resources on.'

'*What the fuck are you talking about?*'

Gerhard slammed his fist down on the table.

'You said we should wait for your lawyer.' Adam smiled. 'So you can sit here and do just that. Only alone. I'll make sure that his job is simple. You'll be released when the paperwork is done. A very good evening to you, Gerhard.'

He walked over to the door, unlocked it and was about to open it.

'Wait. *Wait!*'

Adam paused with his hand on the door handle.

'What is it?'

'Who are you talking about? Who is it who . . . What the hell are you talking about?'

'Gerhard, come on . . . they call you the Chancellor, don't they? I would have thought you'd have some idea about international relations with a name like that.'

'Fuck, I . . .'

A thin layer of sweat had appeared on his pallid face, and finally Gerhard pulled off his cap. His hair was flat and greasy, and a matted lock fell down over his eyes. He tried to blow it away.

'D'you mean the Americans?' he asked.

'Bingo,' Adam grinned. 'Good luck.'

He pressed down the door handle.

'Wait. Wait a moment, Stubo! The Americans don't bloody well have any authority to—'

Adam burst out laughing. He threw back his head and roared. The bare walls in the sterile room made the laughter sound sharp and hard.

'Americans? Authority? The Americans!'

He was laughing so hard that he could scarcely speak. He let go of the door handle and clutched his stomach, shook his head and hiccuped.

The arrestee sat watching, with his mouth open. He had a long history with the police and had lost count of the number of times he had been questioned by some idiot pig or other. But he had never experienced anything like this before. His pulse started racing. He could hear the blood pounding in his ears, and his throat tightened. He saw red specks in front of his eyes. He twisted his cap in his hands. When Adam Stubo had to put his hand against the wall to stop himself from collapsing with laughter, Gerhard Skrøder frantically rummaged in his pocket for his inhaler. It was the only thing he had been allowed to keep when he was searched and his belongings were confiscated. He put it to his mouth. His hands were shaking.

'It's a long time since I've enjoyed myself so much,' Adam gasped and wiped his eyes.

'But what could the Americans do to me?' Gerhard Skrøder asked in a feeble voice, high as that of a pubescent boy. 'We're in Norway . . .'

He tried to stuff the inhaler back in his pocket, but missed. It fell on the floor and he bent down to pick it up. When he

221

straightened up, Adam Stubo was standing in front of him, fists firmly planted on the table, with his face only ten centimetres from Gerhard's. His paunch and his unusually broad shoulders made the policeman look like a fair-haired gorilla, and there was not even a hint of humour in his pale blue eyes.

'You think you're king of the world,' Adam snarled. 'You think you're a star out there. You con yourself into believing that you're one of the big boys, because you move on the periphery of the Russian mafia. You think you can look after yourself. You think that you're hard enough to deal with hardboiled Albanian criminals and other Balkan bastards. Forget it! It's now . . . *It's now . . .*' He raised a finger and stuck it up right under Skrøder's nose. His voice was much louder. 'It's now that you'll discover that you're small fry. If you for one moment believe that the Americans will sit still and watch us release a shit like you, you are so *fucking* wrong. Every day, several times a day, we inform them about where we are in the investigation. They know that you're here right now. They know what you've done, and they will—'

'But I haven't done *anything*,' Gerhard Skrøder protested. He was wheezing and obviously found it difficult to speak. 'I . . . only . . .'

'Breathe deeply,' Adam said briskly. 'Take more of your medicine.'

He pulled back a touch and lowered his finger.

'I want to know everything,' he said while the arrestee inhaled from the round blue receptacle. 'I want to know who gave you the job. When, where and how. I want to know how much you got paid, where the money is now, who else you've talked to in connection with the job. I want names and descriptions. Everything.'

'They won't send me to Guantomo?' gasped Gerhard.

'Guantánamo,' Adam corrected him and had to bite his lip hard to stop himself laughing, and this time it would be real. 'Who knows? Who knows these days? They've lost their president, Gerhard. And in practice, they view you as a . . . terrorist.'

Adam could have sworn that Gerhard's pupils dilated. For a moment he thought that his arrestee had stopped breathing. But then he gulped and gasped in deep breaths of air. He wiped his forehead again and again with the back of his hand, as if he thought some fateful word was written there in big letters.

'Terrorist,' Adam repeated and smacked his lips. 'Not a particularly nice label to have in the US.'

'I'll talk,' Gerhard stuttered. 'I'll tell you everything. But then I can stay here. I can stay here, can't I? With you lot?'

'Of course,' Adam said in a friendly voice and slapped him on the shoulder. 'We look after our own, you know. As long as they cooperate. We'll take a break now, though.'

The clock on the wall said that it was thirty-nine minutes to eight.

'Until eight,' he said and smiled again. 'I'm sure your lawyer will be here by then, so we can talk without any fuss. OK?'

'Fine,' mumbled Gerhard Skrøder, who was breathing easier now. 'Fine. But I'll be kept here, won't I? At the station?'

Adam nodded, opened the door and left the room.

He shut the door slowly behind him.

'What happened?' asked Bastesen, who was leaning against the wall, reading a file that he closed quickly when Adam appeared. 'Same old routine? He said nothing?'

'Yep,' Adam replied. 'But he's ready to sing now. We'll hear it all at eight o'clock.'

Bastesen chuckled and punched the air in a gesture of victory.

'You're the best, Adam. You really are the best.'

'Apparently I am,' Adam muttered. 'At acting, at least. But now this Oscar winner needs some food.'

And as he disappeared down the corridor to find something to eat, he didn't hear the ripple of applause as the news spread that Gerhard Skrøder had cracked.

Johanne still hadn't phoned.

24

The woman now hobbling down the long corridor in the cellar, swearing and muttering under her breath, jangling her keys to keep ghosts at bay, had once been Oslo's oldest lady of the night. She was called Hairymary back then, and had miraculously managed to keep herself alive for more than half a century.

'May all the good forces that be protect me,' she muttered, dragging her bad leg behind her. She had to go right to the bottom of the endless corridor. 'And all that is devilry be gone. Damn and doggy-do.'

From the moment that she was born on the back of a truck in war-torn Finnmark, one night in January 1945, Hairymary had defied Fate's frequent and repeated attempts to break her. She had no parents, and had never settled with any of the foster families she was forced into. After a couple of years in a children's home, she ran away to Oslo to fend for herself. She was twelve years old. With no education, the literacy of a six-year-old and an appearance that would frighten most, her career was a given. She had borne four children – a hazard of the job – and they had all been taken from her at birth.

But at the turn of the century, fortune had smiled on Hairymary for the first time.

She met Hanne Wilhelmsen.

Hairymary had been the key witness in a murder case, and for reasons that neither of them could later explain, she moved in with the detective inspector. She had not left the flat since. She started to use her real name and became a hard-working housekeeper and cook. And she wanted only three things in return: methadone, a clean bed and a pouch of tobacco every week. Nothing more, nothing less – until Nefis and Hanne had a daughter. Mary then stubbed out her last cigarette and demanded to have a stock of business cards instead of tobacco. They were gold cardboard, with napped edges, and they said:

Mary Olsen, Governess

She had chosen the font herself. No telephone number, no address. She didn't need them either, as she never went out and never had visitors. The pile of business cards lay on her dressing table, and every evening she would pick up the top one, kiss it lightly and then close her eyes with the card pressed to her heart and say her evening prayer: 'Thank you, God in Heaven. Thank you for Hanne and Nefis and my little princess, Ida. Someone has use for me. Thank you for that. Good night, God.'

Then she would sleep soundly for eight hours, always.

Mary was almost at the right storeroom now. She had the key ready.

'Load of rubbish, eh,' she told herself. 'You're an old bag, frightened of a stupid cellar, eh! Pathetic!'

She swung her thin arm out, as if to brush away her fear.

'Now just you get into that storeroom,' she said in a shrill voice. 'And get out those duvets and things for Johanne. There's nothing dangerous in there, is there, eh? Jesus and Joseph, Mary! You've seen worse things in your life than what you might see in there.'

She finally found the keyhole.

'Has to be posh,' Mary said and opened the door. 'Couldn't be just one of them ordinary storerooms here in the West End, could it! Oh no . . .'

She fumbled for the light switch.

'Here they've got to have real rooms with proper doors and walls and things. None of that chicken wire and padlocks stuff here, no.'

The storeroom was no more than twenty metres square. It was rectangular, with shelves from floor to ceiling along one of the long walls. They were full of cardboard boxes, suitcases and multicoloured storage boxes from IKEA. Everything was carefully labelled. It was Mary who had systemised it all. Letters were not her strong point, whereas she always saw sense in numbers and logic. As she generally got confused by the alphabet, things were stored according to importance. The boxes of tinned food, jams and dry foodstuffs were by the door – in case of a nuclear war. Then came the winter clothes, packed away in boxes with big ventilation holes. Little Ida's baby clothes were in a pink box with a teddy bear drawn on the top that smelt of lavender when Mary opened the lid and fingered the soft textiles.

'Mary's wee girl, eh. My little princess.'

She was whispering now. The smell of Ida's outgrown clothes made her feel safe. She shuffled across the floor and stopped by the far wall, where Nefis' skis were secured beside Ida's sledge.

DUVAY FOR GESTS.

She took down the large box and opened the lid. The duvet was rolled up and tied with two red cords. Mary stuck it under her arm, put the lid back on the box and pushed back in place. Then she shuffled back to the door.

'There now,' she said, relieved. 'Now we can go back up to the shelter of our warm nest.'

She was about to lock the door when she thought she heard a noise.

A rush of adrenalin made her hold her breath.

Nothing.

There it was again. A muffled bang or thump. In the distance, but she could hear it clearly now. Mary dropped the duvet and folded her hands in fright.

'In the name of Our Father . . . Baby Jesus . . .' she gabbled.

There it was again.

Tucked far away at the back of Mary's mind were the remnants of the life she had led for nearly fifty-five years before her luck had turned and all was bright and rosy. As a skinny, ugly waif, she had survived against the odds because she was smart. The young, sharp-tongued Mary had coped with the Oslo streets that she walked in the sixties because she was canny. The old whore, Hairymary, had endured a life of humiliation and drugs for one reason, and one reason alone: she would not be broken.

Now she was so frightened that she thought her heart would come undone at the seams. The room was spinning. More than anything, she just wanted to sit down and let the Ghost get her, let the Devil take her, just as she, deep in her heart, believed she deserved.

'No way. Not yet.'

She swallowed and gritted her teeth. Then she heard the noise again.

It sounded like someone was trying to knock on a door but couldn't quite manage it. It was weak, with no rhythm, and there was nothing aggressive about it.

Mary picked the duvet up from the cement floor.

'Just when I'd found happiness,' she said to herself. 'No one's going to come here and frighten the life out of an old bag like me.'

She started to walk back to the stairs.

Thump. Thumpthump.

Mary was certain now. The noise was coming from a door just by where she was standing. It was painted red, unlike all the other standard white doors. A cardboard label was stuck on with faded tape at about head height. It was torn and the writing was almost illegible. At least for Mary.

She thought she could hear a voice, but it was very weak and maybe it was only her imagination.

Strangely enough, she wasn't frightened any more. An angry defiance had banished her fear. This was her house and her cellar. She had chosen this isolated life in Krusesgate so she could keep her old demons at bay, and neither the living nor the dead was going to take that away from her.

Not now, not ever again.

'Hello,' she said loudly and knocked on the door with her thin, bony hand. 'Hey, is there anyone in there?'

Silence. Then she heard something thumping back, and was so surprised that she took a step back.

The voice sounded like it came from miles away. It was impossible to make out the words.

'Fancy that,' Mary muttered. She scratched her chin, then put her ear to the door. 'Got to be the strangest door in town.'

'Unlock it,' she shouted through the door. 'Just turn the lock, that's all!'·

The thumping continued.

Mary peered at the lock. You needed a key to open it, like all the other storerooms. There would be a latch on the inside, so you didn't get locked in. Or lock anyone else in.

The door had to be secured in some way. Mary no longer doubted that there was someone in there. From the recesses of her memory came an experience that she had tried to leave behind in the outside world, a world that she never missed or wanted to be part of ever again.

Being a street prostitute wasn't just about being a whore. It was worse when you were off the streets. Mary closed her eyes to fend off images of bunkers and storerooms, dirty mattresses in alleys and woodsheds, quick blowjobs in dirty cars that stank of tobacco, greasy food and old pigs.

Mary didn't keep count of all the times she had been raped. As she gradually sank lower and lower down the ranks of girls, she was forced from her corner. Punters were taken from her; she was spat on by the imported girls, those bloody Russians, mocked by young boys and abandoned by her peers. They died like flies around her, one by one, and by 1999, Hairymary was the living dead. She took the tricks that no one else wanted, not even the Lithuanian girls who had ruined the market by accepting fifty kroner for a fuck without a condom.

Hairymary remembered a cellar. She remembered a man.

'I bloody well don't want to remember anything,' she screamed, and hammered on the red door. 'I'll get you out, love. Just you wait, Mary'll help you!'

She shuffled back to her own storeroom, opened the door and grabbed the well-equipped tool box that Nefis was constantly adding new tools to, which no one knew how to use.

'I'm coming,' Mary shouted, pulling the tool box up to the red door. 'I'm coming, love!'

Mary Olsen was skin and bones. But she was strong. And now she was furious as well. First she hacked at the door frame with a chisel and threw the broken woodwork on to the floor. Then she grabbed a hammer and swung it at the latch, as if she was settling accounts with her past.

It broke, but the door was still locked.

'Damn,' Mary snarled. She blew her nose on her fingers, then wiped them on her flowery skirt. 'Something stronger's needed here.'

She emptied the toolbox. The sound of metal clattering on the cement floor was deafening. When all was quiet again, she could hear a faint echo from the knocking on the inside of the door.

'I'm coming,' Mary said and took hold of a huge crowbar that had been lying at the bottom of the box.

With incredible strength, she forced the claw in behind the lock. She used a hammer to win a few extra millimetres' leverage. Then she stood with her back to the stairwell, grabbed hold of the crowbar with both hands and pulled.

The woodwork split. But nothing happened.

'And again,' Mary wheezed.

The woodwork collapsed, but the door remained locked.

'Maybe the other way,' Mary said and did the same thing from the other side.

The lock broke. The door buckled. It was hanging at an angle and Mary forced the crowbar into the gap once more. The gap was wider now, so she got a firmer hold.

'And puuull!' she screamed. She was surprised to see an opening of about ten to fifteen centimetres appear.

She dropped the crowbar. The noise when it hit the floor made her ears ring. She took a firm hold of the door and pulled to make the opening bigger.

'There now, there now,' she said to the person sitting on the floor just inside the door, looking at her. 'I know what it's like. Now we'll—'

'Help,' rasped a woman's voice.

A Russian whore, Mary thought and shook her head.

'I'll help you, I will,' she said and bent down to put her arm round the battered woman's waist. 'Men can't just get their way, shouldn't be allowed. This one bad, eh? And you're all tied up and everything. Hang on . . .'

She found a sheath knife in amongst all the tools and cut through the plastic bindings that were tied round the woman's wrists. With great effort, she managed to get her to her feet. The smell of piss and shit was overwhelming. She glanced over at the back of the door. The latch was not there.

'Crafty buggers, men, eh?' she mumbled in a comforting voice and stroked the woman on her bloody cheek. 'Let's get you a nice hot bath, eh, love? Come on now.'

The woman tried to walk, but her legs wouldn't hold her.

'You smell something terrible, girl. Come along with Mary, now.'

'Help,' whispered the woman. 'Help me.'

'There, there. That's what I'm doing. You probably don't understand what I'm saying. But I've been there too, you know, I've been where you are now and . . .'

Mary talked like this all the way to the stairs, where she had to half carry the woman up the five steps to the lift. When it came, Mary smiled and steered her in.

'Hang on to this,' she said, pointing to the steel rail. 'We'll be there in a jiffy now, love. What d'you look like, eh!'

It was only now, in the bright light from the neon tube on the ceiling, that Mary could take a proper look at the woman's face. She had a great bump on one of her temples, bruising over half her face and one of her eyes was closed. The blood had dried and caked on her neck.

'Nice clothes you got there, though,' Mary said, with a hint of suspicion as she touched the red jacket. 'That's not from the Salvation Army, eh?'

The lift doors opened.

'Now you be a good girl and put your arm round Auntie Mary.'

The woman stood without moving, with her mouth open. Her eyes showed no sign of life, and Mary held her gnarled hand up in front of her face and clicked her fingers.

'Hello, you in there? Come on.'

With her left arm round the woman's waist and her right hand under her arm, she managed to pull the woman over to the front door. She didn't dare let go of her to look for the keys, so she rang the doorbell with her elbow instead.

Several seconds passed.

'Help,' groaned the woman.

'There, there,' Mary muttered impatiently and rang the doorbell again.

'Mary,' Johanne said gladly as she opened the door. 'You were down there so long that—'

'I found a whore in the cellar,' Mary replied briskly. 'Think she's Russian or something like that, from round there, but she needs help all the same. Poor thing. Some jerk's taken liberties with her.'

Johanne stood stock still.

'Move out the way, then!'

'Hanne,' Johanne said quietly, without taking her eyes from the woman. 'I think you should come here.'

'Hanne's not the sort to turn away a battered whore,' Mary fumed. 'Now get out the way. Now!'

'Hanne,' Johanne called again, louder this time. '*Come here!*'

The wheelchair appeared at the end of the hall, silhouetted against the glass wall where the trees cast long evening shadows into the flat.

Slowly she rolled towards them, the rubber wheels squeaking ever so slightly on the wooden floor.

'This one needs a bath,' Mary pleaded. 'And something to eat, maybe. Be nice, Hanne, please. You're a kind-hearted soul.'

Hanne Wilhelmsen rolled closer.

'Madam President,' she said and bowed her head before looking up again and holding her breath for a moment. 'Come in, please. Let's see what we can do to help you.'

25

'So, let me just sum up,' Adam said. 'So there's no misunderstandings.'

He ran his fingers through his hair, then turned the chair round before sitting down so his stomach was against the back of it. He was balancing a red felt pen between his index finger and his thumb.

'You were rung by a man you've never met before.'

Gerhard Skrøder nodded.

'And you don't know where he's from or what he's called.'

Gerhard shook his head.

'Nor what he looks like, obviously.'

The arrestee scratched his neck and looked at the table, embarrassed.

'It wasn't exactly a video phone.'

'So.' Adam spoke with exaggerated slowness and put his hands over his face. 'You're sitting here saying that you took a job from a man you have only spoken to on the phone and you don't even know his name. Someone you've never met.'

'It's not that unusual, that.'

Ove Rønbeck, his lawyer, twitched his hand in warning.

'I mean, it's not so strange . . .'

'Yes, I think it is. What did he sound like?'

'Sound like?'

Gerhard wriggled back on his chair like a teenager who'd been caught taking liberties with a reluctant girl.

'What language did he speak?' Adam asked.

'He was Norwegian, I think.'

'I see,' Adam said, and let out a long breath. 'So he spoke Norwegian?'

'No.'

'No? So why did you come to the conclusion that he was Norwegian?'

Rønbeck raised his hand and opened his mouth, but immediately sat back in his chair again when Adam turned to face him.

'You have a right to be here,' he said. 'But don't interrupt. I don't need to remind you how serious this case is for your client. And for once I'm not actually that interested in Gerhard Skrøder. I just want *to know as much as possible about the anonymous man who gave you the job.*'

He screamed this at Gerhard, who pulled back even more. His chair was right up against the wall now, so there was no room to tip it, as he normally did. His eyes were evasive, so Adam leant forward and pulled off his cap.

'Did your mother not teach you that boys should take their hats off indoors?' he asked. 'Why did you think the man was Norwegian?'

'He didn't speak proper English, like. More like . . . with an accent.'

Gerhard was scratching his crotch furiously.

'You should go to the doctor about that,' Adam said. 'Stop it.'

He got up and went over to a cabinet by the door. He picked up the last bottle of mineral water, opened it, and drank half in one go.

'Do you know what?' He suddenly laughed. 'You're so used to lying that you don't know how to tell a story properly, even when you've decided on it yourself. Talk about occupational injury.'

He put the bottle down and sat on the chair again. With his hands folded behind his neck, he leant back and closed his eyes.

'Carry on,' he said calmly. 'As if you were telling a fairytale to a child, if it's at all possible for you to imagine something like that.'

'I've got two nephews,' Gerhard told him curtly. 'I bloody know what kids are like.'

'Good. Excellent. What are they called?'

'Huh?'

'What are your nephews called?' repeated Adam, with his eyes still closed.

'Atle and Oscar.'

'OK, I'll be Atle, and Rønbeck over there can be Oscar. Now tell us what happened when Uncle Gerhard got a paid job from a man he'd never met.'

Gerhard didn't respond. He was poking at a hole in his camouflages.

'Once upon a time,' Adam started. 'Come on. Once upon a time, Uncle Gerhard . . .'

'. . . got a phone call,' said Gerhard.

There was silence.

Adam made a circular movement with his hand.

'. . . from an anonymous number,' Gerhard continued. 'It didn't show up on the display screen. I answered. The man spoke English. But it was as if . . . as if he wasn't English, like. He sounded kind of Norwegian . . . in a way.'

'Uhuh,' encouraged Adam.

'There was something . . . weird about his language, anyway. He said that he had a really easy deal to offer and that there was loads of dosh to be had.'

'Can you remember if he said "dosh" or something else?'

'Money, I think. Yes. Money.'

'And this was on . . .' Adam leafed through his notes, 'the third of May,' he said, and looked askance at Gerhard, who gave a faint nod and continued to pull at the hole in his trousers. 'Tuesday the third of May, in the afternoon. We'll get a printout of your log so we can check the time.'

'But, it's—'

'You can't—'

Rønbeck and his client protested at the same time.

'Take it easy, *take it easy*!' Adam groaned in exasperation. 'Your telephone log is the least of your problems right now. We'll come back to that. Carry on. You're not very good at telling stories. Now concentrate.'

The lawyer and Gerhard exchanged glances. Rønbeck nodded.

'He said that I should keep the sixteenth and seventeenth of May clear,' Gerhard mumbled.

'Keep them clear?'

'Yes. Not make any plans. Stay sober. Be in Oslo. Available, like.'

'And you didn't know the man who rang?'

'No.'

'But you still said that was fine. You would drop the biggest street party of the year because a stranger phoned and asked you to keep the day clear. Well, well.'

'It was the money. It was a lot of bloody money.'

'How much?'

There was a long pause. Gerhard grabbed his cap and almost by reflex was about to put it on when he changed his mind and laid it back on the table. He still didn't say anything. He was staring at the hole in his trousers.

'OK,' Adam said eventually. 'We get the amount later. What more were you told?'

'Nothing. Just that I should wait.'

'For what?'

'A phone call. On the sixteenth of May.'

'And did you get one?'

'Yes.'

'When?'

'In the afternoon. Can't remember exactly. Around four, maybe. Yes, just after four. I was going to meet some mates in Grünerløkka for a beer before the match. Vålerenga versus Fredrikstad at Ullevål. The guy rang just before I went out.'

'What did he say?'

'Nothing really. He just wanted to know what I was up to.'

'What you were up to?'

'My plans for the evening, like. If I'd stick to the arrangement. That I wouldn't drink and all that. Then he said that I had to be home by eleven at the latest. He said it would be worth it. That it would pay well. So I . . .'

He shrugged, and Adam could have sworn that he blushed.

'I had a beer or three with the boys, watched the match and went home. The score was nil–nil, so there wasn't much to celebrate anyway. Was home before eleven. And . . .'

His discomfort was tangible now. He scratched his shoulder under his sweater and rolled his buttocks from side to side on the chair. His right thigh was shaking noticeably and he was blinking continuously.

'Then he rang. About eleven o'clock.'

'What did he say?'

'I've told you a thousand times. How long do we have to carry on with this?'

'You've told me twice before. And I want to hear it for a third time now. What did he say?'

'That I should be up by the clock tower at Oslo Central Station a few hours later. At four a.m. I was to stand there until a man came with a woman and then we would all go over to a car and drive away. The route would be left in the glove compartment. With half the money. And then they all lived happily ever after.'

'Not quite yet,' Adam stated. 'Didn't you think there was something odd about the job?'

'No.'

'You're told to drive around southern Norway with two passengers you don't know, and to make sure that you're noticed by the staff at various petrol stations, but to avoid being seen on the security cameras. You don't have to do anything else, don't need to steal anything – just drive around. And eventually park the car in a wood near Lillehammer and take the train back to Oslo, and then forget the whole thing. And you thought that was all hunky-dory?'

'Yep.'

'Don't "yep" me, Gerhard. Get a grip. Did you know either of the other two? The woman or the other man?'

'No.'

'Were they Norwegian?'

'Don't know.'

'You don't know?'

'No, we didn't speak.'

'For four hours?'

'Yeah. I mean, no. We didn't say anything the whole time.'

'I don't believe you. That's not possible.'

Gerhard leaned forward over the table. 'I swear. I said a word or two to them, but the guy just pointed at the glove compartment. I opened it and there was a note lying there, like the man on the phone had said. Telling me where to drive and things like that. It also said that we shouldn't talk. Fine, I thought. Fuck it, Stubo, I've told you all there is to tell. For Christ's sake, you've got to believe me!'

Adam held his hands over his chest and wet his lips with his tongue. His eyes were trained on Gerhard.

'Where is that note now?'

'It's in the car.'

'And where is the car?'

'Like I've said a thousand times, in Lillehammer. Just by the ski jump, where there's a—'

'It's not there. We've checked.'

Adam pointed at a memorandum that a policeman had come in with ten minutes earlier.

Gerhard shrugged indifferently. 'Someone's taken it then,' he suggested.

'How much did you get for the job?'

Adam had fished out a cigar case from his shirt pocket and was rolling it between his palms. Gerhard remained silent.

'How much did you get?' Adam repeated.

'Doesn't really matter,' Gerhard replied sullenly. 'I've not got the money any more.'

'How much?' Adam persisted.

As Gerhard continued to stare defiantly at the table without any sign of answering, Adam got up. He went over to the window. It was starting to get dark. The window was dirty. The sill was covered in dust and peppered with dead insects.

A small village had mushroomed between the police HQ and the prison. A couple of the foreign television stations had driven their OB trucks on to the grass, and Adam counted eight marquees and sixteen different media logos before giving up. He gave a friendly wave, as if he'd seen someone he knew. He smiled and nodded. Then he turned round, continued to smile, walked round to the arrestee's side of the table, and bent over him. His mouth was so close to Gerhard's ear that the other man pulled away.

Adam started to whisper, fast and furious.

'This is highly irregular,' protested Rønbeck, the lawyer, half standing up in his chair.

'A hundred thousand dollars,' Gerhard said. He was almost shouting. 'I got a hundred thousand dollars!'

Adam patted him on the shoulder.

'A hundred thousand dollars,' he repeated slowly. 'I guess I'm in the wrong business.'

'There was fifty thousand in the glove compartment, and then I got the same amount from the guy when we were done. The man who was in the car with me.'

Even the lawyer had difficulty in hiding his dismay. He slumped back into the chair and gave his jaw a somewhat frantic rub. He looked like he was trying to think of something sensible to say, but couldn't. So he rummaged around in his pockets instead and found a sweet, which he popped in his mouth as if it were a tranquilliser.

'And where's the money now?' Adam asked, his hand still resting on Gerhard's shoulder.

'In Sweden.'

'In Sweden. I see. Where in Sweden?'

'Don't know. I gave it to some guy I owed money.'

'You owed someone one hundred thousand dollars?' Adam asked with exaggerated emphasis. His grip on Gerhard's shoulder was becoming increasingly firm. 'And you have already managed to pay your creditor back. When did you do that?'

'This morning. He turned up at my place. Bloody early, those boys there – the ones from Gothenburg – they're not to be—'

'Hang on a minute,' Adam said and put up his hands in a sudden exasperated movement. 'Stop. You're right, Gerhard.'

The arrestee looked up. He seemed smaller now, dishevelled and obviously tired. His disquiet had translated into a noticeable tremble and his eyes were wet when he asked in a feeble voice: 'Right about what?'

'That we should keep you with us. It seems there's a lot more to unravel. But someone else can do that. You need a rest, and certainly . . .' the clock on the wall showed a quarter past nine, 'I do, too.'

He gathered up his papers and tucked them under his arm. The cigar case had fallen on to the floor. He looked over at it, hesitated, and let it stay there. Gerhard Skrøder got up stiffly, and willingly followed the police officer who had been called, down to his cell.

'Who pays a hundred thousand dollars for a job like that?' Rønbeck asked in awe as he packed his things. He seemed to be talking to himself.

'Someone who has unlimited resources and who wants to be one hundred per cent sure that the job is done,' Adam replied. 'Someone who has so much capital that he doesn't need to worry about how much things cost.'

'Frightening,' Rønbeck said. His face was tense and his mouth looked like the slot in a piggy bank.

But Adam Stubo didn't respond. He had taken out his mobile to see if there were any missed calls.

There were none.

26

'Should you or I phone the police?' Johanne whispered, holding up her mobile phone.

'Neither of us,' Hanne Wilhelmsen said quietly. 'Not yet.'

The American president was sitting on a bright red sofa with a glass of water in her hand. The smell of excrement, urine and fear was so strong that Mary, without any particular discretion, had opened the sitting room window as far as it would go.

'The lady needs a bath,' she fussed. 'Can't understand how she can just sit there happily with that horrible smell. A president and all, and we have to humiliate her like that.'

'Now calm down,' Hanne said in a firm voice. 'Of course the lady will have a bath. And I'm sure she'll be hungry soon too. Go and make something warm, please. Soup. Don't you think that would be best? A good soup?'

Mary's slippers slapped out of the room and she muttered to herself all the way to the kitchen. Even when she had closed the door, they could still hear short bursts of her barking in amongst the noise of pots and pans being thumped on to the draining board.

'We must ring,' Johanne said again. 'Dear God . . . The whole world is waiting . . .'

'Ten minutes more is neither here nor there,' Hanne said and rolled herself over to the sofa. 'She's been missing for over a day and a half. I actually think that she has the right to decide too. For example, she might not want to be seen in this state. By anyone other than us, I mean . . .'

'Hanne!' Johanne put a hand on the back of the wheelchair to stop her. 'You're the one who was in the police,' she said, indignant but trying to keep her voice down. 'She can't get washed and changed until she's been examined! She a walking wealth of evidence! For all we know, she might—

'I don't give a damn about the police,' Hanne interrupted. 'But I do give a damn about her. And I won't throw away any evidence.'

She looked up. Her eyes were bluer than Johanne remembered ever having seen them. The black ring around the iris made them look too big for such a narrow face. Her determination had wiped away the wrinkles round her mouth and made her appear younger. She didn't look away, but raised her right eyebrow a touch, and Johanne let go of the wheelchair as if it had burnt her. For the first time since they had met, six months ago, Johanne saw a glimpse of the Hanne she had heard stories about but had never experienced herself: the intelligent, cynical, analytical and incredibly headstrong investigator.

'Thank you,' Hanne said in a quiet voice, and carried on over to the sofa.

The President was sitting absolutely still. The glass of water, which she had barely touched, was on the table in front of her. She was sitting with a straight back, her hands on her lap and her eyes fixed on an enormous painting on the wall.

'Who are you?' she asked, unexpectedly, when Hanne approached.

It was the first thing she had said since Mary had shoe-horned her into the flat.

'I'm Hanne Wilhelmsen, Madam President. I'm a retired police officer. And this is Johanne Vik. You can trust her. The woman who found you in the cellar is Mary Olsen, my housekeeper. We only want the best for you, Madam President.'

Joanne didn't know whether she was more surprised by the fact that the President could speak, given the state she was in, or the fact that Hanne had said she was someone to be trusted, or that the language that Hanne had used was so formal. It was as if Hanne felt humbled by meeting the American president, no matter how dishevelled Helen Bentley was.

Johanne didn't really know what to do with herself. It didn't seem right to sit down, but she felt ridiculous standing in the middle of the floor, like an unwelcome eavesdropper on a private conversation. The situation was so absurd that she found it difficult to gather her thoughts.

'We will, of course, contact the appropriate authorities,' Hanne continued in a gentle voice. 'But I thought that you might want to freshen up a bit first. I should have some clothes that will fit you. If you wish, of course. If you would rather—'

'Don't do it,' Helen Bentley cut in, still without moving, still with her eyes focused on the abstract painting on the opposite wall. 'Don't contact anyone. How are my family? My daughter? How . . .'

'Your family are fine,' Hanne Wilhelmsen said, to reassure her. 'According to reports on TV and in the papers, they're under extra protection at a secret location, and given the circumstances, they are fine.'

Johanne stood there, spellbound.

The woman on the sofa was wearing filthy clothes, had a black eye and smelt revolting. An enormous bump on her temple and bloody matted hair made her look like one of the many battered women that Hanne and Johanne had seen so many times before. The President reminded Johanne of something she never thought about, something she never wanted to think about, and for a moment she felt sick.

After nearly ten years' research into violence, she had almost forgotten why she started in the first place. The motivation had always been a deep desire to understand, a genuine need for insight into something she found inexplicable. Even now, after a PhD, two books and at least a dozen academic articles, she felt she was no nearer the truth as to why some men used physical violence on women and children. And when she had chosen to extend her maternity leave, she had disguised the decision with an unconscious lie: that she wanted to look after her family.

She would stay at home for another year for the children's sake.

The truth was that she was at the end of the road. She was caught in an academic dead end and didn't know what to do. She had spent all her adult life trying to understand criminals because she could not accept the consequences of being a victim. She couldn't bear the shame, that loyal companion of violence – neither her own, nor that of others.

But Helen Bentley did not seem to be ashamed, and Johanne couldn't understand it. She had never seen such a proud and upright beaten woman. Her chin was raised and she did not bow her head. Her shoulders were straight as a ruler. She didn't seem to be in the slightest bit embarrassed. Quite the opposite.

When the President's good eye suddenly moved to focus on her, Johanne was startled. Her gaze was strong and direct, and it felt like she had somehow intuited that it was Johanne who wanted to call for help.

'I insist,' the President said. 'I have my reasons for not wanting to be found. Not yet. But I would very much appreciate a bath . . .' she attempted a polite smile, and her upper lip split as she turned to face Hanne again, 'and I wouldn't say no to some clean clothes.'

Hanne nodded. 'I'll sort that out immediately, Madam President. I hope you understand, though, that I do need a reason for not telling anyone that you're here. Strictly speaking, I'm committing a crime by not phoning the police . . .'

Johanne frowned. She couldn't think of a single penal provision against letting battered women be. She said nothing.

'So I will need an explanation.' Hanne smiled, before adding: 'Of some sort, at least.'

The President tried to get up. She stumbled, and Johanne rushed over to stop her from falling but stopped abruptly halfway.

'No thanks, I'm fine.'

Helen Bentley stayed remarkably still as she touched her temple and tried to pull loose a bloody lock of matted hair that had stuck to her skin. The expression of pain vanished as quickly as it had come. She coughed and looked from Hanne to Johanne and back again.

'Am I safe here?'

'Completely.' Hanne nodded. 'You couldn't have ended up anywhere more isolated and still be in the heart of Oslo.'

'Is that where I am then?' the President asked. 'In the middle of Oslo?'

'Yes.'

The President straightened her soiled jacket. For the first time since she'd appeared, there was a twinge of embarrassment round her mouth when she said: 'I will of course make sure that everything that has been damaged is replaced. Both here . . .' she gestured to the dark stains on the sofa, 'and in . . . the cellar?'

'Yes. You were locked in the cellar. In an old sound studio.'

'That explains the walls. They were kind of soft. Could you show me to the bathroom, please, I need to tidy myself up a bit.'

Again a swollen smile swept over her face.

Johanne was confused. She couldn't believe the President's apparent self-control. The contrast between the woman's wretched appearance and her polite, determined tone was too great. Most of all, she wanted to take her by the hand. To hold her tight and wash the blood away from her forehead with a warm cloth. She wanted to help her, but had no idea how to comfort a woman like Helen Lardahl Bentley.

'No one has actually physically abused me,' the President said, as if she could read Johanne's mind. 'I must have been drugged in some way, and my hands were tied together. It's all a bit unclear. But I do know that I fell off a chair. Very hard. And I don't have . . .'

She stopped.

'What day is it?'

'The eighteenth of May,' Hanne told her. 'And it's twenty past nine in the evening.'

'Nearly forty-eight hours,' the President said, as if she was talking to herself. 'I've got quite a lot to do. Can I get access to the Internet here?'

'Yes.' Hanne nodded. 'But as I said earlier, I would be grateful for an explanation as to—'

'Am I assumed dead?'

'No. Nothing is assumed. It's more . . . confusion. In the US, they believe—'

'You have my word . . .' the President said, holding out a slim hand. She staggered slightly and had to step sideways to catch her balance. 'You have my word that it is of the utmost importance that no one is told that I've been found. My word should be more than enough.'

Hanne took hold of her hand. It was freezing.

They looked at each other.

The President stumbled to one side again. It was as if her knee kept buckling. She tried to straighten up after what looked like a comical curtsy, then let go of Hanne's hand and whispered: 'Don't ring anyone. It's essential that no one must know!'

She sank slowly back down into the sofa and fell to one side, like an ancient ragdoll. Her head hit the cushion. She stayed lying like that, with one hand on her hip and the other tucked under her cheek, as if she had suddenly decided to take a nap.

'Here's some soup,' Mary said.

She stopped in the middle of the room with a steaming bowl in her hands.

'Poor thing's exhausted,' she said and turned. 'If anyone else wants some, they'll have to come into the kitchen.'

'We've got to phone,' Johanne said in desperation, squatting down beside the unconscious president. 'We at least need to get a doctor.'

27

The May night had fallen over Oslo.

The clouds were heavy and grey and so low that the top floors of the Hotel Plaza had vanished. It was as if the severe, slim tower had simply evaporated into the sky. The air was chilly, with gusts of warmer wind that promised a better day tomorrow.

Adam Stubo had never really liked spring. He didn't like the changes in the weather, from baking summer sun to a bitter three degrees; from icy rain to swimming weather, turn and turn about and completely unpredictable. It was impossible to dress appropriately. When he went to the office, he wore a sweater against the morning chill, and then was drenched in sweat by lunch. An impulsive barbecue that seemed like a good idea in the morning could turn into a freezing nightmare by dinner.

He thought that spring smelt bad as well. Especially in the centre of town. The mild weather uncovered all the rubbish left from winter, the decay of autumn and turds from innumerable dogs that shouldn't be living in town.

Adam was an autumn person. November was his favourite month. Rain from start to finish, with steadily falling temperatures, which with any luck would bring snow before Advent. November smelt wet and raw and was a predictable, melancholy month that always made him feel happy.

May, on the other hand, was another story.

He sat down on a bench and breathed in deeply. The surface of the water in Middelalderparken, a park with medieval ruins, rippled gently in the breeze. There wasn't a soul around. Even the birds that carried on a volley of calls from dawn until dusk at this time of year had settled for the night. A small cluster of ducks was resting on the bank, with their beaks under their wings. Only the rotund drake waddled happily around, keeping watch over his family.

It was as if the events of the past couple of days had drained not only Oslo of its energy, but the whole of the Western world. Adam had managed to watch the news earlier on in the evening. The streets of New York had never been so deserted. The city that never slept had fallen into a stupor, a state of numb, unresolved waiting. In Washington and Lillesand, in metropolises and small towns, it seemed that everyone saw the disappearance of the President as an omen of something worse to come; something terrible was going to happen, so it was safest to withdraw and stay at home behind locked doors and closed curtains.

He shut his eyes. The constant sound of the city and the odd noisy trailer in the traffic flow on the other side of the water reminded him that he was sitting in the middle of a capital. Otherwise he could have been somewhere completely different. He felt utterly alone in the world.

He had been trying to get hold of Warren Scifford for over an hour. There was no point in going home before they'd spoken. He had left two messages, one on his mobile phone and one at the embassy. They hadn't seen Mr Scifford at the hotel since the early afternoon.

The dead Secret Service agent, Jeffrey William Hunter, was found about an hour after a flustered taxi driver had turned up at a police station with a badge he had found in his dead mother's jacket pocket. As the ambulance service could immediately tell them where the dying woman had been picked up, they just had to spread out and search the area.

The man was found twelve metres from the spot where the woman had collapsed. He was lying in a ditch near the track. A 9mm bullet from a SIG-Sauer P229, which he was holding in his hand, had made a path straight through his skull. The team examining the scene had been puzzled for a while by the fact that his right arm was partially hidden, wedged into a space between two big rocks, which they initially thought would be

248

impossible for a dead man to do. However, a quick and informal reconstruction of the fall had convinced them that it was in fact a case of suicide. The pathologist was of the same opinion, though with the reservation that it would take several days to reach a definite conclusion.

It was nearly half past ten and Adam gave a long yawn. He was tired and yet at the same time awake. On the one hand, he longed to go to bed. His body was heavy and exhausted. On the other, he was overwhelmed by a disquiet that would make it impossible to sleep.

The police HQ had become unbearable. There was no longer any talk of overtime or when the seemingly endless shifts would be over. People hurried around like ants in a heap. More and more people arrived at the huge curved building, and no one seemed to leave. The corridors were crawling with people. All the offices were in use. Some cleaning cupboards were even being used as temporary accommodation for contracted office staff.

It felt like the building was besieged. The village on the grassy slope down towards Grønlandsleiret was expanding steadily. A couple of Swedish TV companies had chosen to set up camp on the other side of the HQ building. They had blocked Åkebergveien for a while with two buses. They had then been moved to Borggata, just by Grønland church, but the side road was so narrow that the police cars couldn't get out of the car park if the buses stayed where they were. The Swedes had been arguing with the duty officers for three quarters of an hour when Adam suddenly decided he couldn't take any more. He had to get some air.

He had been stuffing himself with food at every opportunity since the afternoon. Before he went out, he helped himself greedily to a barely warm pizza from Pepe's. There were flat pizza boxes everywhere. In the course of two days, Oslo Police had become the fast-food chain's largest customer ever.

He still felt hungry.

He patted his stomach. It was a long time since he had been able to call himself simply large. Without really knowing when it happened, in much the same way that his hair was now thinner, Adam had become fat. His stomach hung heavily over his belt, which he loosened as soon as he thought no one could see. He had pushed the reminder from the police doctor to one side with the excuse that he was too busy. He didn't dare to go. In silence he thanked the fact that routines were so poor that he wouldn't be sent another reminder until next year. Sometimes, when he woke up at night because he needed the toilet, he could feel the cholesterol sticking to his arteries like some horrible, life-threatening slime. He thought he noticed double beats and felt pains in his heart and left arm, and for the first time in his life he was kept awake at night worrying about his health.

When morning finally came, he realised with some relief that it was all imagination, and sat down to a hearty fried breakfast, as always. He was a large man and he needed real food. He would start exercising again. When he had more time.

His phone rang.

'Johanne,' he whispered, and dropped the phone.

The display fell face down, and he didn't check it when he picked it up again as quickly as possible. 'Hello.'

'Hello. It's Warren.'

'Oh, hi. I've been trying to get hold of you.'

'That's why I'm calling.'

'You were lying about the man on the CCTV tape.'

'Was I?'

'Yes. You knew who he was. The man in the suit was a Secret Service agent. You lied. And we don't like that.'

'I can understand that.'

'We've found him. Jeffrey Hunter.'

There wasn't a sound on the other end of the phone. Adam kept his eyes on the drake. It waggled its tail feathers a few times before settling down on a big tuft of grass a couple of metres away from its flock, as if it was a watch tower. The light was reflected in its jet-black eyes. Adam tried to pull his coat tighter around him, but it was too small. He let Warren take the time he needed.

'Shit,' the American said, eventually.

'You can say that. The man's dead. Suicide, we assume. But I guess you knew that.'

Again there was silence.

The drake continued to keep an eye on Adam. It quacked quietly and repeatedly, as if it just wanted to let him know that it was still watching.

'I think it would be best if we could have a meeting,' Warren suggested, all of a sudden.

'It's nearly eleven o'clock.'

'There's no end to days like today.'

Now it was Adam's turn not to say anything.

'A meeting in ten minutes,' Warren insisted. 'Salhus, you and me. No one else.'

'I don't know how many times I have to explain to you that this is a police investigation,' Adam said in exasperation. 'The Chief of Police or one of his people has to be there too.'

'If you say so,' Warren said crisply. Adam could just imagine him shrugging his shoulders with indifferent arrogance.

'Shall we say quarter past eleven, then?'

'Come to Police HQ. I'll be there in ten minutes. Then we can see if the Chief of Police is about, and whether Peter Salhus is available.'

'They should be,' Warren said and hung up.

Adam sat there and stared at the phone. The display panel went dark after a few seconds. He felt a peculiar rage. His stomach was acid and painful. He was ravenous and furious. For a start, it was he who had every reason to be angry with Warren, but the American had still managed in some way to manipulate the situation so that Adam was inferior. It seemed that Warren believed absolutely that he was not dependent on anyone, just like his country, and therefore had no reason to be ashamed of being caught lying outright.

Adam's phone rang again.

He swallowed when he saw Johanne's name flashing in blue on the display. He let it ring four times. His eardrums were ringing; he could feel his blood pressure rising. He tried to keep his breathing even and pushed the green icon.

'Hi,' he said in a quiet voice. 'You're calling late.'

'Hi,' she said, equally softly. 'How are you?'

'OK, I guess. Exhausted, of course, but then we all are.'

'Where are you?'

'Where are *you*?'

'Adam,' she said in a small voice. 'I'm really sorry about this morning. I was just so hurt and sad and angry and—'

'It's all right. The most important thing is that I know where you are. And when you're coming home. I can come and collect you in . . . an hour or so. Maybe two.'

'No, you can't.'

'I'll—'

'It's eleven o'clock already, Adam. You know what happens when you wake Ragnhild in the middle of the night.'

Adam pressed his thumb against one eye and his index finger against the other. He said nothing. Red circles and spots danced around in the empty blackness behind his eyelids. He felt heavier than ever, as if the surplus fat in his body had turned to lead. The bench hurt his back and his right leg was about to fall asleep.

'Please just let me know where you are,' he said.

'I simply can't do that.'

'Ragnhild is my daughter. It's my right and my duty to know where she is. At all times.'

'Adam—'

'No! I might not be able to force you to come home, Johanne, and you're right, it would be stupid to wake Ragnhild in the middle of the night, but . . . I want to know where you are!'

The drake woke up and flapped its wings. A couple of the other ducks joined in.

'Something has happened,' Johanne said. 'Something that—'

252

'Are you both OK?'

'Yes,' she answered swiftly and clearly. 'We're both fine. But I can't tell you where I am, no matter how much I might want to. OK?'

'No.'

'Adam—'

'It's out of the question, Johanne. You and I are not like that. We don't just disappear with the children and refuse to tell the other where we are. That's just not us.'

She was silent on the other end.

'If I say where I am,' she said eventually, 'can you promise to believe me and not try to come and find me before I say you can?'

'To tell you the truth, I'm getting a bit fed up with all these promises you keep asking me to make,' he said, trying to keep his pulse slow. 'Adult life is not like that! Shit happens and things change. You can't just make a promise and . . .'

He stopped when he realised that Johanne was crying. Her quiet sniffs made scratching noises on the phone and he felt an icy finger run down his spine.

'Are you sure there's nothing wrong?' he asked, holding his breath.

'Something has happened,' she sobbed. 'But I've promised not to say anything. It's nothing to do with Ragnhild or me, so you can . . .'

She was overcome with tears. Adam tried to get up from the bench, but his right leg had now gone to sleep. He pulled a face, supported himself on the back of the bench and got up after a fashion so he could shake some life into his dead leg.

'My love,' he said gently. 'I promise. I promise I won't come to find you until you say I can, and I promise I won't ask any more questions. But where are you?'

'I'm at Hanne Wilhelmsen's,' she said and sobbed. 'In Krusesgate. I don't know the number, but I'm sure you can find out.'

'What . . . what the hell are you doing with—'

'You promised, Adam. You promised not to—'

'OK, OK,' he said quickly. 'That's fine.'

'Night night, then.'

'Good night.'

'Bye.'

'Bye.'

'Love you.'

'Mmm.'

He stood with the phone against his ear for a long time once she had hung up. There was a light drizzle in the air. His leg was still buzzing with pins and needles. The duck family had set off for a swim; they didn't dare to have him nearby any more.

Why do I always let myself be taken in? he asked himself, and started to hobble towards the ruins of Maria Church, over the wet, newly cut grass. Why is it always me who has to back down? Always! For everyone!

28

'Here? This door here?

DI Silje Sørensen stared at the terrified thirty-year-old and tried to hide her irritation.

'Are you certain that it was this door?'

He nodded frantically.

She could, of course, understand the man's fear. He was originally from Pakistan, but was a Norwegian citizen now. All his papers were in order, as far as he was concerned. But that was not the case for the young Pakistani woman whom he had recently married. She had been deported from Norway as a teenager for having stayed illegally in the country. A year later she was arrested at Gardermoen, carrying false papers and a neat little consignment of heroin in her luggage. She had pleaded that she had been forced to do it by the dealers, who would now kill her, and unbelievably she got away with simply being deported again, this time for ever. However, it didn't stop her father from getting her married to a second cousin with a Norwegian passport. She had been smuggled back into Norway via Svinesund early one morning a few weeks ago, in a trailer from Spain, hidden behind four pallets of tomato juice.

Ali Khurram must really love her, Silje Sørensen thought to herself as she examined the door that he had pointed out to her. On the other hand, his extreme fear regarding his wife's fate might also be connected to what his father-law-might do. Even though he lived in Karachi, nearly six thousand kilometres from Oslo, he had already managed to push two lawyers on DI Sørensen. Surprisingly, they had both been very understanding. They could see why a man who had smuggled the American president out of a hotel room in a dirty laundry basket might be asked for an explanation. They had nodded gravely when they were given some insight into the investigation, having been strictly reminded of their duty of confidentiality. One of the lawyers, who himself was of Pakistani origin, had then had a brief and whispered conversation with Ali Khurram in Urdu. The chat was so effective that Khurram had dried his tears and said he was happy to show them where in the cellar he had left the cleaning trolley.

Silje Sørensen looked at the architect's drawings again. The enormous sheets were difficult to handle. The constable she had with her tried to hold one end, but the stiff paper buckled rebelliously in between them.

'It's not shown here,' the constable said, trying to fold away any parts of the drawings that were not relevant.

'We are in the right corridor, aren't we?'

Silje looked around. The neon light on the ceiling was bright and unpleasant. The long corridor ended at a door in the west wall, behind which were some stairs that led up to ground level, two storeys above.

'There are two basement levels,' said a middle-aged man, who was nervously biting his puny moustache. 'This is the lower level. So . . . yes, we are in the right corridor.'

He was the technical operations manager for the hotel and looked like he was about to crap himself. His legs were trembling nonstop and he couldn't leave his moustache alone.

'But it's not shown on the drawings,' Silje said, looking at the door with suspicion, as if it had been installed there in contravention of all laws and regulations.

'Which drawings do you actually have?' the operations manager asked, and tried to find a date.

'What do you mean?' the policeman said, making another attempt to fold the big sheets.

'He said he was from the Secret Service when he rang my mobile number,' whimpered Ali Khurram. 'I couldn't know that . . . He showed me his ID and everything! Like the ones you see on TV, with a photo, and stars and . . . He told me earlier

256

on in the day that I had to come up as soon as he called. Immediately, he said! He was from the Secret Service and all that! I wasn't to know that—'

'You should have let us know when you realised what had happened,' Silje said frostily and turned away from him. 'You should have raised the alarm immediately. Have you figured it out?' she asked the operations manager.

'Yes, but my wife . . .' Ali Khurram continued. 'I was terrified because of . . . What's going to happen to my wife? Is she going to have to leave now? Can't she . . .'

'Let's not go over this again now,' Silje said and raised a hand. 'You've been explaining yourself for several hours now. The situation won't change, either for you or your wife, just because you keep going on about it. Stand over there. And keep quiet.'

She pointed firmly at a point on the floor a few metres away from the door. Ali Khurram slunk down the corridor. He had his hands in front of his face and was mumbling in Urdu. The uniformed policeman followed him.

'You've got the wrong drawings,' the operations manager said finally. 'These are the originals. From when the hotel was built, I mean. It was finished in 2001. This door wasn't there then.'

He smiled, which was presumably an attempt to charm her, as if the door was no longer anything to worry about, now that the mystery of the incorrect drawings had been cleared up.

'The wrong drawings,' Silje Sørensen repeated, in a flat voice.

'Yes,' the operations manager said keenly. 'Or, well . . . actually, this door isn't shown on any of the drawings. We were ordered to make a door from here into the car park, in connection with the building of the opera, you know, with explosions and the like, just in case anything should happen . . .'

'Which car park?' Silje Sørensen asked, exasperated.

'That one,' the operations manager said and pointed at the wall.

'That one? *That one?*'

Silje Sørensen was a rarity: a very rich policewoman. She did what she could to hide her greatest weakness, which was her arrogance, the result of a sheltered childhood and inherited wealth. But she was having great difficulty now.

The operations manager was an idiot.

His jacket was tasteless. Burgundy and badly fitted. His trousers were shiny on the knees. His moustache was ridiculous. His nose was narrow and crooked and reminded her of a beak. And he was crawling to her. Despite the seriousness of the situation, he was smiling all the time. Silje Sørensen felt an almost physical disgust for the man, and when he put his hand on her arm in a gesture of camaraderie, she shrugged it off.

'*That one,*' she repeated, trying to control her temper. 'That's a little imprecise, isn't it? What do you mean?'

'The car park for Central Station,' he explained. 'There's no exit there from the hotel. You have to go round. So if the guests—'

'You just said that this door goes through to there,' she interrupted and swallowed.

'Yes.' He smiled. 'It does! But it's not used. We were ordered to make it when they were building the opera, in connection with the excavations.'

'You've already said that.' She ran her hand over the rather coarsely fitted door frame. 'Why is there no handle?'

'As I said, the intention was never to use the door. We were just ordered to make an entrance into the car park. We've taken the handle off for security reasons. And as far as I know, it was never added to any drawings.'

He scratched his neck and bent down. Silje could not understand how a door could be used as an emergency exit in the event of an explosion or similar if it couldn't be opened. But she couldn't face going into any more detail. Instead she held out her hand for the loose door handle that the operations manager

258

had pulled from a voluminous bag with the hotel's logo on the side of it.

'The key,' she demanded and put the handle in place.

The operations manager obeyed. It only took a couple of seconds to unlock the door. She was careful not to leave any fingerprints. Forensics were already on their way to see if there was still any technical evidence there. She opened the door. The dark smell of parked cars and old exhaust hit them. Silje Sørensen just stood in the doorway and did not go into the car park.

'The exit's over there, isn't it?' She pointed right, towards the east.

'Yes. And I might add . . .' He was smiling even more now, and his nervousness seemed to ease as he continued: 'It was the Secret Service themselves who inspected this area. Everything was in perfect order. They even got their own handle and key. For the door and for the lift. They did a very impressive job. They inspected the hotel from top to bottom, several days before the President arrived.'

'Who did you say got the key and a handle?' Silje asked him, without turning round.

'The Secret Service.'

'Who in the Secret Service?'

'I . . . um . . . who . . .' The operations manager laughed nervously. 'The place was crawling with them. Obviously I didn't get to know all their names.'

Silje Sørensen finally turned around. She closed the heavy door, pulled the handle out again and put it in her bag, along with the key. From a side pocket she produced a sheet of paper, which she then held up for the operations manager to see.

'Was it him?'

The man squinted and pushed his face out to get a closer look at the paper, without moving his body. He looked like a vulture.

'That's the one! Names escape me, but I never forget a face. Hazard of the job, I guess. In the hotel business—'

'Are you absolutely certain?'

'Yes.' The operations manager laughed again. 'I remember him well. Really nice guy. He was down here a couple of times, in fact.'

'On his own?'

The man had to think about it. 'Um . . . yes . . .' He drew it out. 'There were so many of them. But I'm almost certain that he covered this part of the basement himself. I was with him, of course. I personally—'

'That's fine,' Silje said and put the photograph of Jeffrey Hunter back in her bag. 'Did anyone come down here afterwards?'

'What do you mean by afterwards? After the President had disappeared?'

'Yes.'

'No,' the operations manager said, and then added: 'In the hours immediately after the alarm had been raised, the whole building was searched from top to bottom. Of course, I can't be sure, as I was in the office with the police, checking everything with the drawings . . .' he waved at the papers that were sticking up out of Silje's bag, 'and giving orders about this and that. In any case, the basement was cordoned off.'

'Cordoned off? The basement?'

'Yes, of course.' He smiled meaningfully. 'For security reasons . . .'

The phrase sounded like a mantra, something he said hundreds of times a day and which had therefore lost all meaning. 'The lower basement was closed off well before the President arrived. As I understood it, the Secret Service wanted to . . . minimise all risk. They closed off parts of the west wing too. And sections of the seventh and eighth floor. What they call minimal risk, or . . . minimising risk . . .' He desperately tried to remember the new English phrase he had learnt. 'Minimalise the risk area,' he said happily in Norwegian in the end. 'Quite normal. In those circles. Very sensible.'

260

'So the police might actually never have come down here,' Silje said slowly. 'In the hours after the President had been kidnapped, I mean.'

'No . . .'

Again he seemed to be unsure about what she actually wanted to hear. He stared at her intently without finding the answer.

'Well, the whole floor was closed off. Locked. You can only take the lift down here if you have a key. I'm sure you understand that we don't want guests wandering around down here. Technical equipment and . . . Yes, you understand. Like I said, we had given keys to the Secret Service, but no one else had them. Apart from me, and those of my employees who—'

'Were these drawings used when the building was searched?' Silje Sørensen asked and grabbed the papers from her bag.

'No. Those are the original drawings. We used the most recent ones, which include the presidential suite. But the drawings of the basement are just the same, so that the floor plan you have . . .' he pointed at it, 'is identical. The basement. In both versions.'

'And none of the drawings include this door?' Silje asked again, as if it was hard to believe.

'We cooperated fully with the police,' the operations manager assured her. 'We worked closely and well with them, both before and after the kidnapping.'

Oh my God, Silje thought to herself and swallowed. There were too many of us. Far too many cooks and an incredible mess. The basement was closed off and locked. According to the drawings, there's no door here. They were looking for an escape route and everything was chaotic. We didn't find the door because we weren't looking for it.

'Could I go home now?' Ali Khurram asked, still standing close to the wall, several metres away. 'Can I not go now?'

'People like you never cease to amaze me,' Silje Sørensen said savagely, without taking her eyes from the desperate man.

'Don't you understand anything? Do you really think that you can break the law as you please and then be allowed to go home to your wife as if nothing had happened? Do you really believe that?'

She took a step towards him. Ali Khurram said nothing. Instead he looked up at the constable. The tall policeman was called Khalid Mushtak, and had graduated from police college a couple of years earlier with the best marks in his year. His eyes narrowed and his Adam's apple gave away the fact that he had swallowed, but he said nothing.

'When I said people like you,' Silje corrected herself swiftly, puncturing the air with great big speech marks, 'I didn't mean people like you in that sense. I meant . . . I meant people who haven't learnt to understand our system. Who don't understand how . . .'

She stopped abruptly. The constant buzz of the colossal unprotected ventilation system that ran along the ceiling was the only thing to be heard. The operations manager had finally stopped smiling. Ali Khurram wasn't snivelling any more. Khalid Mushtak stared at the policewoman, but didn't say a word.

'I apologise,' Silje Sørensen said eventually. 'I'm sorry. That was a very stupid thing to say.'

She held her hand out to the policeman.

He didn't accept.

'It isn't me you should be apologising to,' he said in a neutral tone, and put handcuffs on the arrestee. 'It's this guy here. But you'll have plenty of opportunity to do that. My guess is that he'll be detained for some time.'

The smile he gave her as he snapped the handcuffs shut was neither cold nor scornful; it was sympathetic.

Silje Sørensen could not remember the last time she had felt like such a complete fool. But it was even worse that there was an emergency exit from the Hotel Opera that no one had known about, other than a Secret Service agent who had now taken his own life.

Presumably out of shame, she thought as she felt herself blushing.

Worst of all was the fact that it had taken a day and a half to find it.

'A bloody door,' muttered the woman who never swore.

She went up the stairs behind Khalid Mushtak's broad back.

'It took us forty hours to find a damn door. God knows what else we haven't found yet!'

29

'A door. They found a door.'

Warren Scifford passed his hand over his eyes. His hair looked wet, as if he'd just washed it. He had changed out of his suit into jeans and a wide dark blue sweatshirt, with YALE written in big letters across the chest. His boots looked like they were made from real snakeskin. The outfit made him look older than he did in a suit. The fact that his skin was starting to loosen on his neck was more obvious in a baggy sweatshirt. His suntanned complexion no longer gave a healthy, sporty impression. On the contrary, there was something forced about his appearance in such youthful clothes that somehow highlighted the fact that his skin was unnaturally tanned for the time of year. He had one leg crossed over the other and might have looked like he was about to fall asleep, had it not been for the toe of the upper boot that was tapping nervously. Again he was lying more than sitting in the chair, with his elbows resting on the arms.

'A door that we can confirm was checked by the Secret Service,' Adam Stubo said. 'By Jeffrey Hunter. When did you discover that he'd disappeared?'

Warren Scifford took his time straightening up. Only now did Adam notice that he had cut himself badly and the blood was seeping through a plaster just by his left ear. The smell of aftershave was a hint too strong.

'He called in sick,' the American said eventually.

'When?'

'On the morning of the sixteenth of May.'

'So he was here before the President came to Norway?'

'Yes. He was the person in charge of securing the hotel. He came here on the thirteenth.'

The Chief of Police, Bastesen, stirred his coffee. He watched the whirlpool in his cup with fascination.

'I thought those guys were completely incorruptible,' he mumbled in Norwegian. 'No wonder we haven't got anywhere.'

'Pardon me?' Warren Scifford snapped, obviously irritated.

'So he called in sick,' Adam interjected quickly. 'It must have been something pretty serious, eh? For the person in charge of security at the hotel to call in sick twelve hours before the President arrives – can't happen very often. I would assume that—'

'The Secret Service had enough people,' Warren interrupted. 'And anyway, everything was on schedule. The hotel had been examined, plans had been made, parts of the area were cordoned off, a system had been set up. The Secret Service is never sloppy. They've got back-up for pretty much everything, no matter how unlikely it may seem.'

'Well, I'm afraid it has to be said that they've been sloppy here,' Adam said. 'When one of their own special agents is involved in the disappearance of the elected president of the United States.'

The room was silent. The Director General of PST, Peter Salhus, unscrewed the lid of his Coke bottle. Terje Bastesen had finally put down his coffee cup.

'We're taking this very seriously indeed,' he said after a while, and tried to catch the American's eye. 'You must have realised fairly early on that one of your own people was involved. The fact that you didn't—'

'No,' Warren exclaimed sharply. 'We were not . . .'

He stopped. Again he passed his hand over his eyes. It almost seemed that he wanted to hide them on purpose.

'The Secret Service was not aware that Jeffrey Hunter had disappeared until late in the day yesterday,' he said, after a pause that was so prolonged a secretary had had time to come in with yet another lukewarm pizza and a case of mineral water. 'They had other things to think about. And yes, his illness did seem to be serious. A slipped disc. The guy couldn't move. They tried pumping him full of painkillers in the morning of the sixteenth of May, but all he managed to do was lie in bed, dozing.'

'Or so he said.'

Warren looked at Adam, and gave a hint of a nod. 'Yes, that's what he said.'

'Was he examined by a doctor?'

'No. Our people are medically trained. A slipped disc is a slipped disc, and there isn't much to be done about it, except rest or have it operated on. And if that was going to happen, it would have to be after the President's visit.'

'An X-ray would have shown the truth.'

Warren didn't bother to answer. Instead he leant over towards the pizza, wrinkled his nose ever so slightly and did not help himself.

'And as far as the FBI are concerned,' he said, taking a bottle of water instead, 'we were not aware of anything until you showed me that film this afternoon. We have, of course, made our own investigations since. Compared them with what the Secret Service has found out . . .'

Warren got up and went over to the window. They were in the Chief of Police's office on the sixth floor of the Police HQ, and had a fantastic view of the grey May night. The lights from the media village on the grass outside the window were stronger now, and continued to grow in number. It was only an hour or so now until the darkest time of night, but the grass was bathed in artificial light. The trees along the road to the prison were like a wall against the dark on the other side of the park.

He drank some water, but said nothing.

'Could it be something as simple as money?' Peter Salhus asked quietly. 'Money for his family?'

'If only it was that simple,' Warren said to his own reflection in the window. 'It was the children. And now there's a desperate widow sitting somewhere in a residential area between Baltimore and Washington DC who realises that she and her husband have

266

done something terrible. They've got three children. The youngest is autistic, but given the circumstances he's doing OK. He goes to a special school. It's expensive and Jeffrey Hunter presumably had to watch every penny to make it possible. But he had never accepted black money. There is nothing to indicate that. However, the boy has been kidnapped twice in the past two months. Each time he reappeared again before a full alarm was raised, but he was gone long enough for the parents to panic. The message was clear: do what you're asked to do in Oslo, or the boy will disappear for good.'

Peter Salhus was genuinely shocked when he asked: 'But would an experienced Secret Service agent let himself be blackmailed in that way? Couldn't he just make sure that his family was put under protection? A government agent, if anyone, must surely be able to withstand such a threat.'

Warren was still standing with his back to them. His voice was flat, as if he nearly couldn't bear to get involved in the story.

'The boy was taken from his school the first time, which should, in practice, be impossible. Public and especially private schools, like this one, are hysterical when it comes to the safety of their pupils. But someone managed to do it. The boy was then sent into hiding with an old school friend of his mother's in California. Here he was given home tutoring, and no one, not even his brother and sister, knew where he was. But he disappeared from there too, one afternoon. He was only gone for four hours, and neither the school friend nor anyone else could explain how it had happened. But the message was crystal clear.'

With a short burst of dry laughter, Warren finally turned around and went back to his chair.

'They would find the boy, no matter what. Jeffrey Hunter felt like he had no choice. But obviously the betrayal was too much to live with. The shame. He realised full well that sooner or later someone would discover that he was involved; that someone at some point would think about checking the CCTV footage from the time after the kidnapping.'

'So he wandered the streets of Oslo until it was late enough to take a bus up to the forest,' Bastesen summarised. 'And then he walked into the forest for a while, hid himself in a ditch and killed himself with his own government-issue weapon. Poor man, he can't have been in a good way, walking up towards Skar, knowing that he only had a few more minutes to live. That he would never—'

Adam felt a slight flush rising in his cheeks as a result of the Chief of Police's clumsy speech, and quickly interrupted. 'Could Jeffrey Hunter's suicide be an explanation for why we haven't heard anything from the kidnappers? After all, they said in the note that was left in the suite that they would be in touch.'

'I doubt it,' Warren said. 'Particularly as Jeffrey Hunter was nothing more than a cog, really. There is absolutely no indication whatsoever that he was involved in anything other than getting the President out of the hotel.'

'I'm afraid I have to contradict you a bit there,' Adam said. 'I don't see how the information about the President's clothes can have come from anywhere other than inside.'

'What do you mean? Clothes?'

'The two cars that were driving around . . .' Adam lifted two fingers, and then interrupted himself. 'We've found the driver of the second car, by the way. We're getting just as little out of him as we are from Gerhard Skrøder. Same sort of lowlife good-for-nothing, same methods, same incredible fee.'

'But the clothes,' Warren repeated. 'What about them?'

'The red jacket, the elegant blue trousers. White silk blouse. The national colours of the States and Norway. Whoever is behind the kidnapping must have known what she was going to wear. The lookalikes had the same clothes on. Not exactly the same, but they looked similar enough to make the decoy successful. We lost a lot of valuable time and effort chasing shadows.'

Adam took a deep breath, hesitated and then continued: 'I take it as given that Madam President has both a hairdresser and a dresser with her when she travels. What have they got to say?'

Warren Scifford was obviously having problems. His poker face, which normally made it possible for him to lie without blinking, had disintegrated into a dejected, tired expression. His mouth seemed narrower and Adam could see the muscles in his face tensing.

'I'm actually quite impressed by the way you consistently manage to underestimate us,' Adam said in a low voice. 'Don't you think that we considered that problem a long time ago? Don't you realise that we have long feared that it might be an inside job? Don't you understand that you, by playing Mr Secret, have poured petrol on the flames?'

'The President's clothes are recorded on a computer,' Warren said.

'Which anyone has access to?'

'No. But her secretary has an overview. And she has a very good relationship with Jeffrey Hunter. They are . . . were good friends. They had talked about the . . . national day that you celebrate here at an information lunch in early May. We have of course questioned the secretary and she can't for the life of her remember who brought up the topic. But anyway, they talked about the fact that the President had bought lots of new clothes for her first overseas visit. Including a jacket that she was going to wear on the Norwegian national day in exactly the same shade of red as the Norwegian flag. Someone had told her that you are quite . . . sensitive about things like that.'

A fleeting smile crossed his face, but no one responded.

'And you are a hundred per cent certain that no one else from your people is involved? That Jeffrey Hunter was operating alone?'

'As certain as it's possible to be,' Warren Scifford said. 'But with all due respect, I have to say that I don't like the direction this meeting has taken at all. I'm not here to be lectured by you. I'm here to give you the information you need to find President Bentley. And to hear how far you've got with the investigation.'

There was a hint of irony in his voice as he straightened his back. Terje Bastesen cleared his throat and put down the coffee cup that seemed to be a permanent fixture in his hand. He was about to say something when Adam pipped him to the post.

'Don't even go there,' he said.

His voice was friendly, but his eyes narrowed enough to make Warren blink.

'You know everything from our side,' Adam said. 'We give you the information as soon as we can get hold of you. Which has proved to be difficult at times, by the way. We have two thousand people . . .' he stopped, as if he had only just grasped the huge number, 'working on this case, from the police organisations alone. In addition, there are the people from the ministries, the directorates and, to a certain extent, the mili—'

'We have a total of sixty-two thousand Americans,' Warren interrupted without raising his voice, 'who at this moment are trying to establish who kidnapped the President. In addition—'

'This is not a competition!'

Everyone looked at Peter Salhus. He had stood up. Adam and Warren exchanged looks like two boys who had been caught quarrelling in the playground by the headmaster.

'There can be absolutely no doubt that this is a top-priority investigation in both countries,' Salhus said. His voice was even deeper than normal. 'And I'm quite sure that the Americans are looking at the possibilities of a bigger conspiracy and context. The CIA, FBI and NSA have adopted quite a new . . . let's say attitude to exchanging information and intelligence over the past twenty-four hours. It is counterproductive to say the least, but doesn't prevent us from seeing the direction in which you're working. We also have our sources, which I'm sure you know about. And it is, of course, only a matter of time before journalists in the US get wind of the methods you are using.'

Warren didn't blink.

'And that will be your problem,' Salhus said and shrugged. 'My interpretation of the data we've received, which I've compared with the information that cannot be kept out of the public domain . . .'

He bent down and pulled a document from a file lying on the floor by the chair he had just got up from.

'Very limited air traffic,' he read. 'Complete stop of air traffic from certain countries, most of them Muslim. Extensive reductions in staff in public offices. Schools have been closed until further notice.' He waved the paper around before putting it back in the file. 'And I could go on. The sum of it all is obvious. You expect further attacks. Attacks with far greater consequences than stealing the American president.'

Warren Scifford opened his mouth and raised his hand.

'Spare us your protests,' the Norwegian director of intelligence said. His bass voice trembled with suppressed anger. 'I will only repeat what Stubo here just said. Do not underestimate us.'

His great index finger was only centimetres from the American's nose.

'What you have to remember, what you *have to remember* . . .'

Warren wrinkled his brow and pulled his head back. Salhus just came closer. His finger was shaking.

'. . . is that it is us, the Norwegian police, who have a chance of solving this case. *The actual case*. It is us, and us alone, who are able to map out the actual event, how the American president was taken from her hotel room in Oslo . . . how on earth that could even happen in the first place. D'you understand?'

Warren sat completely still.

'So you can carry on trying to place the event in a bigger context, without any interference from us. *Do you understand?*'

The man gave an almost imperceptible nod.

Salhus took a deep breath, lowered his hand and continued. 'What I find incredible is that not only are you refusing to help us, but you are in fact sabotaging our investigation by not giving us information like, for example, the fact that a Secret Service agent has mysteriously disappeared.'

He was standing right in front of the American.

'If an old lady out for a walk in the forest had not wandered off

271

the track into the ditch, and then collapsed unconscious a few metres away, we would have had no idea that . . .'

Peter Salhus coughed and paused, as if he really had to stop himself flying into a rage.

'I have, together with the Chief of Police, Mr Bastesen here, the Minister of Justice and the Foreign Minister, sent a formal complaint to your government,' he continued, without sitting down. 'And it was copied to the Secret Service and the FBI.'

'I'm afraid that my government, the FBI and the Secret Service have more serious things to worry about at the moment than a complaint,' Warren said, without any expression. 'But please . . . be my guest! I can't stop you from corresponding with others if you have the time for that sort of thing.'

He got up suddenly and grabbed the military-green sports jacket that was hanging over the arm of the chair.

'I'm basically done here,' he said with a smile. 'I've got what I came for. And you've got something out of it too. A satisfactory meeting, in other words.'

The three other men in the room were so astonished by this sudden closure that they couldn't think of anything to say. Warren Scifford had to put his hand on Salhus' arm to move him out of the way.

'And by the way,' the American said, turning around once he had crossed the room; the others still could think of nothing sensible to say. 'You're wrong about who's going to solve this case. *The actual case*, as you called it. As if a kidnapping can be detached from the motives, planning, consequences and context.'

He was smiling broadly with his mouth, but his eyes were anything but friendly.

'The party that finds the President,' he added, 'is the one that will be able to solve the case. *The whole case*. And I unfortunately doubt that it will be you. *That* worries . . .' he stared straight at Salhus, 'my government, the FBI and the Secret Service. But good luck, to be sure. And good night.'

The door slammed behind him, a bit too loudly.

30

'We've found the President,' whispered Johanne Vik. 'It's in . . .'

She didn't know what to say and felt the urge to giggle. But as that would be about as inappropriate as laughing at a funeral, she pulled herself together. And started to cry again instead. She felt totally exhausted, and the absurdity of the situation was in no way diminished by the fact that Hanne stood resolutely by her decision not to raise the alarm. Johanne had tried everything: reason and common sense, begging, threats. Nothing helped.

'A woman like Helen Bentley knows best herself,' Hanne said softly, and carefully laid a blanket over the President. 'Can you give me a hand, please?'

Helen Bentley's breathing was heavy and even. Hanne held two fingers flat on her wrist and looked at her watch. She moved her mouth as she counted silently, until she gently put the President's hand back on her hip.

'Good steady pulse,' she whispered. 'In fact, I don't think she's unconscious. I think she's just asleep. Conked out. Completely exhausted, mentally and physically.'

She rolled her chair into the next room as quietly as possible. On the way out, she turned to the voice-operated light switch: 'Dark!'

The lights dimmed slowly until they switched off. Johanne followed Hanne out and closed the door behind them. This sitting room was smaller. A huge gas fire with brushed-steel surrounds was on full blaze and filled the room with flickering shadows. Johanne sat down on a deep chaise longue and leant her head back on the soft headrest.

'Helen Bentley doesn't have any immediate need for a doctor,' Hanne said and positioned her chair by the chaise longue. 'But we should give her a little shake once an hour, just in case. She might have a bit of concussion. I'll take the first shift. When does Ragnhild start to stir normally?'

'Around six,' Johanne said and yawned.

'I'll definitely take the first shift then. That way you can get at least a couple of hours' sleep.'

'Good, thank you.'

But Johanne didn't get up. She stared into the flames dancing on the artificial logs. They almost seemed to hypnotise her: a beautiful airy blue base that rose into a yellowy-orange flame.

'You know what,' she said and caught a whiff of Hanne's perfume. 'I don't think I've ever met anyone quite like this.'

'Like me?' Hanne smiled and looked at her.

'Like you, yes, as well. But I was actually thinking about Helen Bentley. I remember the campaign so well. I mean, I normally manage to keep up with things pretty well . . .'

'Pretty well!' Hanne Wilhelmsen exclaimed with a laugh. 'You're obsessed with American politics! I thought my fascination with that country was bad, but you're even worse. Do you . . .'

She cocked her head. She seemed to be evaluating whether her question would cross the important boundary between being friendly and friendship.

'It would be nice, a glass of wine, wouldn't it?' she asked all the same, and then regretted it. 'Sorry, that was stupid. It's a bit late really. Forget it.'

'It would be lovely,' yawned Johanne. 'Yes please!'

Hanne rolled her wheelchair over to a cupboard that was built into the wall. She opened it by pressing the door gently, and without hesitating took out a bottle of red wine with a label that made Johanne's mouth fall open.

'Don't open that one,' she said quickly. 'We're only going to have a glass!'

'Wine is Nefis' thing. I'm sure it would make her happy to know that I'd helped myself to something good.'

She opened the bottle, put it between her legs, grabbed two wine glasses, which she carefully placed in her lap, closed the door and then rolled back. She poured a generous glass for them both.

'It was a miracle really that she was elected,' Johanne said, and took a sip. 'Fantastic! The wine, that is.' She lifted her glass in a discreet salute and took another sip.

'What was it that made her win?' Hanne asked. 'How did she manage it? When absolutely all the commentators felt that it was too early for a woman in the White House?'

Johanne smiled. 'The X-factor, largely.'

'The X-factor?'

'The inexplicable. The sum of virtues that can't actually be pointed out. She had everything. If anyone was going to have a chance as a woman, it was her. And only her.'

'What about Hillary Clinton?'

Johanne licked her lips and swallowed the wine she had resting on her tongue.

'I think this is the best wine I've ever tasted,' she said and stared into the glass. 'It was too early for Hillary. She realised that herself as well. But she can follow. Later. She's in good health and I think the time might be ripe for her when she's around seventy. But that's not for a while yet. The advantage with Hillary is that everyone knows all her shit already. Her whole life was turned inside out on her way to becoming the First Lady. Not to mention her years in the White House. Her dirty laundry was hung out long ago. And we need a bit of distance from it now.'

'But Helen Bentley's life was also put under the microscope,' Hanne said, trying to straighten herself up in her chair. 'They were after her like bloodhounds.'

'Of course. The point is that they didn't find anything. Nothing of any importance. She had the sense to admit that she hadn't exactly lived like a nun when she was at university. And she did that before anyone had the chance to ask. And she said it with a big smile. She even winked at Larry King, live. Knocked that one on the head. Genius.'

When she held the wine glass up to the fire, she saw a shifting range of colour in the wine, from an intense, deep red to a light brick red around the edges.

'Helen Bentley even did one tour in Vietnam,' Johanne said and had to smile again. 'In 1972, when she was twenty-two. And she was smart enough not to say anything about it until some muttonhead, or perhaps I should say hawk, pointed out early on in the nomination process that the US was in fact at war with Iraq – and that the commander-in-chief had to have experience of war. Which is absolute nonsense! Look at Bush! Ran around for a while in an air force uniform when he was young, but never set foot nor wing out of the US. But you know . . .'

The wine was making her feel light-headed.

'Helen Bentley turned it around completely. Went on TV and said, with a serious face, that she had never made a point of her twelve months in 'Nam out of respect for the veterans who had suffered serious physical and mental injury, as all she had done was basically sit behind a typewriter. She had not been forced to go to war, but had volunteered because she felt it was her duty. She came back, she said, as a wiser, more mature woman, and with the firm belief that the war had been a fatal mistake. And the same was true of the war in Iraq, which she had initially supported, but which had now developed into a nightmare, so that the country had to make every effort to find an honourable and responsible way in which to withdraw. As quickly as possible.'

She quickly put her hand over her glass when Hanne wanted to pour her more wine.

'No thank you. It's delicious, but I have to go to bed soon.'

Hanne didn't protest and put the cork back in the bottle.

'Do you remember sitting here watching the swearing-in ceremony together?' she said. 'And that we talked about how incredibly good they must be at planning their lives. Do you remember?'

'Yes,' Johanne replied. 'I was, well . . . more engrossed, shall we say, than you were.'

'That's only because you're not as cynical as I am. You still allow yourself to be impressed.'

'It's impossible not to be,' Johanne said. 'Whereas Hillary Clinton struggles with her image of being hard, uncompromising and wilful, I would—'

'I see she's trying hard to change that.'

'Yes, definitely. But it'll take time. Helen Bentley has something . . .' She cocked her head and tucked her hair behind her ear. Only now did she notice that her glasses were dirty with Ragnhild's sticky fingerprints. She took them off and cleaned them with her shirtsleeve.

'. . . indefinable,' she said after a while. 'The X-factor. Warm, beautiful and feminine, and yet at the same time, strong, as she has shown in her career and the fact that she volunteered for Vietnam. I'm sure she's hard as nails and has lots of enemies. But she treats them . . . differently.'

She popped her glasses back on her nose and looked at Hanne.

'Do you know what I mean?'

'Yes.' Hanne nodded. 'She's good at fooling people, in other words. She even gets bitter enemies to believe she's treating them with real respect. But I wonder what it is about her.'

'What it is about her? What do you mean?'

'Oh come on.' Hanne smiled. 'You don't think she's as shiny and pure as she makes out.'

'But she has . . . If there was anything, surely someone would have discovered it. American journalists are the best at . . . they're the meanest in the world.'

For the first time in their short nascent friendship, Hanne seemed to be strangely happy. It was as if having the kidnapped American president asleep on her couch had jolted her out of her impenetrable armour of friendly indifference. The whole world was holding its breath in growing fear of what might have happened to Helen Lardahl Bentley. Hanne Wilhelmsen obviously enjoyed keeping them in suspense. Johanne didn't know how to interpret that. Or whether she liked it.

'Don't be silly.' Hanne laughed and leant over to nudge her. 'There isn't a single person, not one person in the whole world, who doesn't have something they're ashamed of. Something they're frightened that other people might find out. The higher up the ladder you are, the more dangerous even the most minor transgression in the past can be. I'm sure that our friend in there has something.'

'I'm going to go to bed,' Johanne said. 'Are you going to stay up?'

'Yes,' Hanne said. 'Until you wake up, that is. I'm sure I'll doze a bit in the chair, but I've got plenty to read.'

'Until Ragnhild wakes up,' Johanne corrected her, and yawned again as she padded out in her borrowed slippers to get some water from the kitchen.

She turned in the doorway.

'Hanne,' she said quietly.

'Yes?'

Hanne didn't turn the chair. She stayed where she was, staring at the dancing flames. She had poured herself some more wine and lifted her glass.

'Why are you so set against telling anyone that she's here?'

Hanne put down her glass. She slowly turned the wheelchair to face Johanne. The room lay in darkness, except for the fire and what little light remained of the May night that stubbornly pressed itself against the window. Her face looked even thinner in the dark shadows and her eyes had disappeared.

'Because I promised her,' she said. 'Don't you remember? I gave her my hand. Then she fainted. And you should always keep a promise. Don't you agree?'

Johanne smiled. 'Yes,' she said. 'On that, we agree.'

31

It was exactly six o'clock in the evening on the east coast of the United States.

Al Muffet had let his youngest daughter, Louise, make dinner. They had to celebrate the arrival of her uncle, she said. After the death of Al's mother, they had had practically no contact with his family, so Louise had insisted. Al closed his eyes in a silent prayer to the kitchen gods when he saw her opening the cupboard for more and more delicacies.

There went the foie gras.

And now she was taking out the last jar of Russian caviar. He had been given a case by a very happy family after he had relieved their puppy of constipation.

'Louise,' he said in a cautious voice. 'You don't need to use everything we've got. Just hold your horses a bit now.'

The girl looked up with an injured pout.

'You might not think there's any reason to get excited about family, Dad, but I think it's worth celebrating. And who are we going to give these things to if you won't let my uncle have them? My uncle, Dad! My own flesh-and-blood uncle.'

Al puffed out his cheeks and let the air out slowly.

'Remember that he's a Muslim,' he muttered. 'Don't use anything with pork in it.'

'What about you, then? You love spare ribs! Shame on you.'

He loved it when she laughed. She had her mother's laugh, the only thing that was left of her when Al Muffet closed his eyes and tried to recreate a picture of his wife, without seeing the thin shadow she had become in the final months of her life. He never managed. Her face had been erased. The only thing he could remember was the smell of the perfume he had given her when they got engaged, and that she had worn ever since. And her laughter. Melodious and clear as bells. Louise had inherited it, and sometimes he caught himself telling a joke just so he could close his eyes and listen.

'What's going on out here?' Fayed asked from the doorway. 'Are you the cook in the family?'

He went over to the counter and ruffled Louise's hair. She smiled, then picked up an aubergine, which she started to cut with a practised hand.

I'm never allowed to ruffle her hair, Al Muffet sulked to himself. You don't treat a teenager like that, Fayed. And certainly not one you barely know.

'Great girls you've got,' Fayed said, putting down a bottle of wine on the coarse oak table in the middle of the room. 'I think this one'll be good. Where are Sheryl and Catherine?'

'Sheryl's twenty,' Al muttered. 'She left home last year.'

'Oh,' Fayed said lightly, and had to take a quick sidestep to regain his balance as he opened a drawer. 'Do you have a bottle opener?'

Al thought he caught a whiff of alcohol already. When Fayed turned to face him, Al could have sworn that his brother's eyes were glazed and his mouth was sagging.

'Do you drink?' he asked. 'I thought—'

'Hardly ever,' Fayed cut in and coughed, as if he was trying to pull himself together. 'But on a day like today . . .'

He burst out laughing again and nudged his niece.

'I can see that you're preparing a celebration,' he said. 'And I agree with you. I've got some presents for you girls. We could open them after dinner. It really is so good to see you all!'

'Well, strictly speaking, you've only seen two of us so far,' Al said and pulled open a drawer. 'But Catherine will be here soon. I said that dinner was around half past six. She had a match this afternoon. It should be over by now.'

The corkscrew was caught in a whisk. He eventually managed to separate the two utensils, and handed the corkscrew to his brother.

'What are you saying?' Fayed joked as he took it. 'My niece is playing in a match and you don't even tell me? We could have gone to watch! My children aren't interested in anything like that.' He shook his head and pulled an unhappy face. 'None of them. None of them has a competitive spirit.'

Louise smiled in embarrassment.

Fayed opened the bottle and looked around for glasses. Al opened a cupboard and took out a glass and put it on the table.

'Are you not going to have any?' Fayed asked, astonished.

'It's Wednesday. I have to get up early tomorrow.'

'Just a glass,' Fayed pleaded. 'Heavens above, you can manage a glass! Are you not pleased to see me?'

Al took a deep breath, then he got out another glass and put it down beside the first one.

'Only so much,' he said and indicated a couple of centimetres from the bottom. 'Stop.'

Fayed poured himself a generous amount and then raised his glass.

'Cheers!' he said. 'To the Muffasa family getting together again!'

'We're called Muffet,' Louise said in a small voice, without looking at her uncle.

'Muffet. Muffasa. Same thing!'

He took a drink.

You're drunk, Al Muffet caught himself thinking in surprise. You, who was always the religious one, who I've never seen take even one beer with the boys! You turn up like a jack-in-the-box without having been in touch for three years, and then you get drunk on something I haven't even given you.'

'Food's ready,' Louise said.

She seemed to be shy, which she wasn't normally. It was as if she had suddenly realised that her uncle wasn't quite as he should be. When he leant towards her to stroke her back, she pulled away with an embarrassed smile.

'Please sit down,' she said and pointed to the dining room.

'Aren't we going to wait for Catherine?' Al asked. He nodded reassuringly at his daughter. 'She'll be here soon.'

'I'm back,' came a shout as the door slammed. 'We won! I had a home run!'

Fayed took his glass with him into the sitting room.

'Catherine,' he said affectionately and stopped to fully appreciate his niece.

The fifteen-year-old stopped in her tracks. She looked suspiciously at the man who was incredibly like her father, except his eyes were glazed and difficult to read. He also had a moustache, which she didn't like, a big moustache with pointy ends that curled down to his mouth and hid his upper lip.

'Hi,' she said quietly.

'I told you that Uncle Fayed was maybe going to drop by today,' Al said with forced cheer. 'And here he is! Come on, let's sit down. Louise has made dinner, so let's see how she's done.'

Catherine smiled cautiously.

'I'll just put my things in my room and wash my hands,' she said and bounded up the stairs in four strides.

Louise came in from the kitchen with two plates in her hands, and two more balanced on her lower arms.

'Wow, look at that,' Fayed said. 'A real professional!'

They sat down. Catherine came bounding down the stairs again, just as fast as she had gone up. She had short hair, a pretty, square face and broad shoulders.

'So, you play softball?' Fayed asked unnecessarily, and popped a piece of foie gras in his mouth. 'Your father played baseball. Back in the day. That was a long time ago, wasn't it, Ali?'

No one had called their father Ali since their grandmother died. The girls exchanged looks and Louise stifled a giggle with her hand. Al Muffet mumbled something inaudible that was supposed to put a stop to all this talk of his miserable career in athletics.

Fayed emptied his glass. Louise was just about to get up to fetch the bottle from the kitchen when her father stopped her with a hand on her leg.

'Uncle Fayed's had enough wine,' he said mildly. 'Here, have some refreshing, cold water.'

He poured a large glass and pushed it over to his brother, who was sitting on the opposite side of the table.

'I think I'll have a little bit more wine.' Fayed smiled. He didn't touch the water.

'I don't think so,' Al said, giving him a fierce look.

Something was very wrong. Fayed might of course have changed a lot in the years since they last saw each other and started drinking. But it seemed unlikely. And he didn't seem to be able to handle alcohol very well either. Even though he obviously had had something before he came into the kitchen, the one generous glass of wine had made him noticeably more drunk. Fayed was clearly not used to alcohol. And Al couldn't understand why he was drinking now.

'No,' Fayed said loudly, breaking the embarrassing deadlock. 'You're absolutely right. No more wine for me. Very good in small quantities, daaangerous in more.'

When he said *dangerous*, he wagged his finger wildly at his nieces, who were sitting at either end of the table.

'How's the family?' Al asked, with his mouth full.

'How's the family . . . well.' Fayed had started to eat again. He chewed slowly, as if he had to concentrate on making sure his teeth ground the food. 'Well, I assume. Yes. If you can say that things were going well for anyone in this country. With our ethnic background, I mean.'

Al was immediately on his guard. He put down his knife and fork and rested his elbows on the table as he leant forward.

'We haven't got any problems,' he said and smiled at the girls.

'I wasn't really talking about people like you,' Fayed said. He wasn't slurring his words quite so much any more.

Al wanted to object, but not when the girls were sitting there. He asked if everyone had finished with their starter, and cleared away the dishes. Louise followed him out into the kitchen.

'Is he ill?' she whispered. 'He's kind of weird. So . . . inpre-dictable, in a way.'

'Unpredictable,' her father corrected in a hushed voice. 'He always has been. But don't judge him too harshly, Louise. He hasn't had it as easy as we have.'

Fayed has never got over nine/eleven, he thought. He was on his way up the career ladder, in a demanding, well-paid job. But that all came to a standstill after the catastrophe and he only just managed to hold on to his middle-management position. Fayed is a bitter man, Louise, and you are too young to be exposed to the bitterness.

'He's a good guy really.' He smiled at his daughter. 'And as you said, he's your flesh-and-blood uncle.'

They went back into the dining room, each carrying a plate of delicious caviar and home-grown shallots.

'. . . and they have never managed to do anything about the injustice. And never will do either.' Fayed shook his head and rubbed his temple with a finger.

'What are you talking about?' Al asked.

'The blacks,' Fayed replied.

'Afro-Americans,' Al said. 'You mean Afro-Americans.'

'Call them what you like. They let themselves be exploited. It's in their genes, you know. They will never manage to redeem themselves.'

'We don't allow that kind of talk in this house,' Al said calmly and put a plate down in front of their guest. 'I suggest we change the subject.'

'It's genetic,' Fayed continued, unabashed. 'Slaves had to be hard-working and strong without being able to think too much. If there were any intelligent ones among them back there in Africa, they were allowed to go free. The genetic material that was transported over the ocean makes them unsuitable for anything other than sport. And crime. But we're different. We don't need to put up with that shit.'

Crash!

Al Muffet thumped his plate down on the table so hard that it broke.

'That's enough,' he hissed. 'No one, not even my brother, has my permission to say such rubbish. Not here, not anywhere. Do you understand? *Do you understand?*'

The two girls sat still as statues, only their eyes moving to and fro between their uncle and their father. Even Freddy, the little terrier, who was tethered out in the yard and normally barked his way through every meal he wasn't allowed to join, was quiet.

'Perhaps we should eat,' Louise said after a while. Her voice was higher than normal. 'Dad, you can have mine. I don't really like caviar. And by the way, I think that Condoleezza Rice and Colin Powell are very smart. Even if I don't agree with them. You see, I'm a Democrat.'

The twelve-year-old smiled carefully. Neither of the men replied.

'Here,' she said, and passed her plate to her father.

'You're right,' Fayed said eventually. He shrugged something that resembled an apology. 'Let's change the subject.'

That proved to be difficult. For a long time they concentrated on eating, without anyone saying anything. If Al had looked over at his daughter, he would have seen that Louise had teardrops shivering on her eyelashes and a trembling lower lip. Catherine, on the other hand, seemed to be highly interested by the situation. She continued to stare at her uncle, as if she couldn't quite understand what he was doing there.

'You're very alike,' she said suddenly. 'If you ignore the moustache, that is.'

The two men finally had to look up from their food.

'We've been told that ever since we were boys,' replied her father, taking a piece of bread to mop up the remains of his caviar. 'Despite the age difference.'

'Even Mother got confused sometimes,' Fayed said.

Al looked at him with suspicion.

'Mother? She never confused us. You were four years older than me, Fayed!'

'When she died,' Fayed said. There was an undertone to his voice that Al had never heard before and couldn't interpret. 'In fact, she thought I was you. Presumably because she loved you more. That's what she would have wanted. Her favourite son to be sitting there talking to her in her final moments of lucidity. But you . . . didn't make it in time.'

His smile was ambiguous.

Al Muffet put down his knife and fork. The room was starting to spin. He felt the blood leave his head and adrenalin being pumped into every muscle, every nerve in his body. The palms of his hands were glued to the table. He had to hold on so he didn't fall off his chair.

'I see,' he said without expression, trying not to alarm the girls, who were staring at him as if he had suddenly put on a red clown's nose. 'She thought—'

'You're acting weird, Dad! What's wrong?'

Louise stretched her slim girl's hand over the table and put it on her father's large hand.

'I'm . . . It's fine. Everything's fine.'

He pulled a face that was supposed to be a reassuring smile, but he realised he would have to follow it up with an explanation.

'I just suddenly got a pain in my stomach,' he said. 'Maybe the caviar didn't agree with me. It'll pass.'

Fayed was looking at him. His eyes seemed even darker than usual. It was as if he had a supernatural ability to pull them back into his head, or push his forehead out to make his face more threatening, more frightening. Al remembered that his brother had looked at him like this, in exactly the same way, when they were little and Fayed had done something wrong and was lying through his front teeth, while their father embarked on one of his tirades that became more and more frequent and passionate over the years.

And he realised, without understanding why, the significance

286

of the fact that his mother had confused her two sons on her deathbed.

But what he couldn't for the life of him comprehend was why his brother had chosen to come here now, three years later, completely out of the blue, and then to behave like a stranger and disrupt the routine, happy life that Al Muffet had built up with his daughters in a north-eastern corner of the US.

'I think I have to lie down for a moment. Just for a while.'

Something's wrong, he thought as he went upstairs. Something is very wrong and I have to pull myself together.

Ali Shaeed Muffasa, you have to think!

32

A bdallah al-Rahman was woken by his own laughter.

As a rule, he slept heavily for seven hours, from eleven at night until six in the morning. But on the odd occasion, a feeling of unease woke him up. A stressful feeling of not having trained enough. Sometimes life was too hectic, even for a man who had learnt to delegate as much as possible over the last ten years. He owned a total of three hundred companies of varying sizes all over the world and they all required different kinds of follow-up from him personally. Most of them were run by people who didn't even know he existed, in the same way that he had long ago recognised the expediency of concealing the lion's share of his companies with the assistance of an army of lawyers, most of whom were American or British, who lived on the Cayman Islands and had impressive, luxurious offices and anorexic wives whom he almost couldn't be bothered to greet.

Naturally, at times there was too much to do. Abdallah al-Rahman was nearly fifty and needed two hours' hard training every day to keep himself in the shape he felt a man like him should be in; another benefit was heavy, effective sleep. When he didn't train, his nights were restless. But fortunately, that was very seldom.

He had never been woken by his own laughter.

He sat up in bed, astonished.

He slept alone.

His wife, who was thirteen years younger and the mother of all his sons, had her own suite elsewhere in the palace. He visited her frequently, most often in the early morning, when the chill of the night still hung in the walls and made her bed even more inviting.

But he always slept alone.

The digital characters on the clock by his bed showed 03:00.

Precisely.

He propped himself up on his pillows and rubbed his eyes. Midnight in Norway, he thought to himself. They would just be starting the day that would be Thursday the 19th May.

The day before the day.

He sat completely still and tried to remember the dream that had woken him. It was impossible. He couldn't remember anything. But he was in a remarkably good mood.

One thing was that everything had gone as it should. Not only had the abduction been carried out according to plan, but it was obvious that the finer details had also worked. It had cost him money, a lot of money, but that didn't bother him in the slightest. It was a higher price to pay that so many in the system had to be burnt. But that didn't really matter either.

That was the way it had to be. It was the nature of the game that the hand-picked and well-groomed objects could only be used once. Some of them were far more valuable than others, of course. Most of them, like those he had hired in Norway, were just petty criminals. Hired and paid for a job just around the corner, then no need to think about it any more. Others it had taken years to hone and prepare.

Some, like Tom O'Reilly, he had looked after personally.

But they were all *dispensable*.

He remembered a joke that a braying, rosy-cheeked Swiss man had once told during a business meeting in Houston. They were sitting in the top storey of a skyscraper when a window-cleaner was lowered down in front of the vast panorama windows in a gondola. The corpulent businessman from Geneva had said something about how it would have been better to use one-off Mexicans. The other participants had looked at him askance. He had burst out laughing and described the queue of Mexicans on the roof, each with a cloth in his hand. They would throw themselves over the edge one by one and would each clean a stripe, the end result being you were done with both the window and the Mexicans.

No one laughed. They should have, being Americans. They didn't find the joke in the slightest bit funny, and the Swiss man was embarrassed for about half an hour.

If you were going to use people, it would have to be to greater use than window-cleaning, Abdallah had thought.

He got up. The carpet – the fantastic carpet that his mother had knotted for him and that was the only possession he had that he would never, under any circumstances, sell – felt soft under his bare feet. He stood there for a few moments, digging his toes into the plump, cool silk. The play of colours was wonderful, even in a nearly dark room. The glow from his clock and a narrow slit of subdued light from the window was enough to make the golden tones change as he slowly crossed the carpet on his way to the enormous plasma screen. The remote control was on a small hand-made gold-chased metal table.

When he had turned the TV on, he opened a fridge and took out a bottle of mineral water. Then he lay back down on the bed, well supported by a sea of cushions.

He felt excited, almost happy.

The goddess of good fortune always smiled on the victor, Abdallah thought as he opened the bottle of water. He could never, for example, have anticipated that Warren Scifford would be sent to Norway. He had initially seen it as a serious disadvantage, but now it seemed to be the best thing that could have happened. It had proved far easier to break into a Norwegian hotel room than to get into the FBI chief's flat in Washington DC. It had, of course, not been strictly necessary to give back the watch, once the redheaded escort girl had found out what she had been amply paid to discover.

But it was a neat detail.

Just as the sound studio in the West End of Oslo was. It had taken a long time to find it, but it was perfect. An abandoned and isolated cellar storeroom, in an area where people barely registered what their neighbours were up to, as long as they didn't stick their necks out and had enough money to be one of them.

The best thing would, of course, have been for Jeffrey Hunter to kill the President before he locked her in the storeroom. But Abdallah hadn't even considered it. It had been necessary to take some tough measures to get the Secret Service agent to assist in the kidnapping of a person he had dedicated his life to protecting, so it would have been completely impossible to get him to kill his own president.

And what was possible was best, in Abdallah's view. The sound studio appeared to have been the right choice. Driving far out into the countryside would have been risky; the more time it took before the President was locked away, the more risky it was for the project.

Everything had gone smoothly.

CNN were still running round-the-clock news programmes about the kidnapping and its consequences, interrupted only by a bulletin at the top of every hour with other headlines, which basically interested nobody. Right now, they were talking about the New York Stock Exchange, which had plummeted in the past couple of days. Even though most analysts believed that the sharp drop was an ultra-nervous reaction to an acute crisis and the market would not continue to fall so dramatically, everyone was gravely concerned. Particularly as oil prices had taken an equally sharp upturn. Rumours were buzzing in political circles of a hyperfast cool-down in the already tense relationship between the US and the most important oil-producing countries in the Middle East. You didn't need to be particularly politically informed to realise that the American government was primarily focusing its attention in its investigation of the kidnapping on Arab countries. Persistent claims, coupled with a particular focus on Saudi Arabia and Iran, had resulted in hectic activity for the countries' diplomats. Three days ago, before Helen Bentley had disappeared, the price of oil per barrel had been forty-seven dollars. An elderly gentleman with a hooked nose and the title of professor gave the TV presenter a glowering look and declared: 'Seventy-five dollars within a few days. That's my prediction. A hundred in a couple of weeks if this doesn't cool down.'

Abdallah drank some more water. He spilt a bit and some of the ice-cold liquid ran down his naked chest. He shivered and his smile widened.

A much younger man back in the studio tried nervously to point out that Norway was also an oil nation and that the extremely wealthy small country on the periphery of Europe could therefore potentially earn billions from the disappearance of the President.

The embarrassed silence that ensued in the studio did nothing to diminish Abdallah's good mood. A senior adviser to the Federal Reserve then gave the whippersnapper a thirty-second lecture. It was true that Norway stood to gain from a higher oil price, in isolation, but the Norwegian economy was so integrated and dependent on the global economy that the fall on the New York Stock Exchange, which had of course spilled over into stock exchanges the world over, was also catastrophic for them.

The young man gave a forced smile and checked his notes.

These are the true American values, Abdallah thought. Consumption. We're getting closer now.

Having spent sixteen years in the West – six in the UK and ten in the US – he was still astounded when he heard otherwise educated people talking about American values as if they really believed that they were about family, peace and democracy. This had been a central theme during the election campaign the year before. The debate on values was Bush's only ticket to re-election. The electorate had already begun to tire of war and was more open to a president who would get them out of Iraq with their collective dignity intact, so George W. Bush tried to make the bloody, unsuccessful and apparently endless war in Iraq into a question of values. The fact that more and more young American boys were being sent home in coffins covered by the flag was the price they had to pay to preserve the American Ideal.

In Bush's rhetoric, the continued fight for peace, freedom and democracy in a country that most Americans didn't care two hoots about, and that was more than ten thousand kilometres away from the closest domestic shore, had become a fight to protect key American values.

For a long time, people had believed him. For too long, they started to realise when Helen Lardahl Bentley came sailing into the election campaign and offered a better alternative. The fact that it would prove far harder than Candidate Bentley anticipated to withdraw from the hell that Iraq had become for the Americans was another matter. The US still had full forces present in the country, but Bentley had now been elected.

Abdallah stretched on the bed. He picked up the remote control and turned the volume down a bit. The programme switched over to the CNN team in Oslo, who looked like they'd set up camp in some kind of garden in front of a low, Eastern European-looking building.

He closed his eyes and cast his mind back.

Abdallah could still remember the fateful conversation as if it had been yesterday.

It was during his time at Stanford. He was at a party and as usual was standing on the fringes, with a bottle of mineral water, watching the noisy, laughing, dancing, drinking Americans through half-shut eyes. Four boys, who were sitting at a table groaning with half-full and empty beer bottles had called him over. He dithered a bit before sauntering over.

'Abdallah,' one of them laughed. 'You're so bloody smart. And not from here. Sit down, man! Have a beer!'

'No thank you,' Abdallah had replied.

'Listen,' the boy continued. 'Danny here, who's a bloody communist by the way, if you ask me . . .'

The others howled with laughter. Danny ran his fingers through his long, messy hair and then smiled as he raised his beer bottle in a sloppy salute.

'He says that all this talk about American values is bullshit. He says we don't give a damn about peace, the family, democracy, the right to defend ourselves with weapons . . .'

His memory blanked on the basic key values, and he paused for a moment while he waved his beer bottle around.

'Whatever. The point that Danny-boy wants to make is that . . .' The boy hiccuped, and Abdallah remembered wanting to leave. He just wanted to get away. He didn't belong there, so he was never really included in anything on American soil.

'He says that we Americans basically have only three needs,' the boy slurred, and tugged at the sleeve of Abdallah's jacket. 'And they are the right to drive a car wherever we want, whenever we want and cheaply.'

The others laughed so loudly and made such a noise that more people started to come over to see what was going on.

'And then there is the right to shop wherever we want, whenever we want and cheaply.'

Two of the boys were now lying on the floor clutching their stomachs, rolling around with laughter. Someone had turned the music down a notch or two, and a small crowd had gathered round to find out what it was that was making the second-year students laugh so much.

'And the third thing is,' the boy shouted, getting the others to say it with him, '*to watch TV whenever we want, to watch whatever we want, and cheaply.*'

More people laughed. Someone turned the music up even louder. Danny got up and gave a deep and exaggerated bow, holding his right arm over his stomach and making a gallant sweeping gesture with his left arm, the beer bottle still in his hand.

'What d'you reckon, Abdallah? Is that what we're like?'

But Abdallah was no longer there. He had slipped away unnoticed, between the giggling, drinking girls who eyed his body with curiosity and made him go home long before he had planned to.

That was back in 1979 and he had never forgotten it.

Danny had been absolutely right.

Abdallah was hungry. He never ate at night, as it was not good for the digestion. But now he felt that he would need something in his stomach if he was going to get any more sleep. He picked up a phone that was built into the bed frame. After two rings, he heard a sleepy voice on the other end. He gave his order in a quiet voice and then put the phone down.

He leant back again in the bed with his hands folded behind his neck.

Danny-boy: a long-haired, unkempt, sharp Stanford student who had seen reality so clearly that, without knowing it, he had given Abdallah a recipe that he would use more than quarter of a century later.

Abdallah al-Rahman knew all about military history. As he had had no choice but to take on responsibility for his father's business empire very early on, the possibility of a military career was lost. He had always dreamt of being a soldier, particularly as a boy. For a period he had studied and read about all the old generals; the art of Chinese warfare, in particular, fascinated him. And the greatest strategist of them all was Sun Zi.

A beautifully bound copy of the 2,500-year-old book, *The Art of War*, always lay by his bed.

He picked it up now and leafed through the pages. He himself had commissioned a new Arabic translation, and the book he held in his hand was one of only three copies that he had had made. He owned them all.

It is best to keep the enemy's state intact, he read. *To crush it is the next best thing. For to win one hundred victories in one hundred battles is not the acme of skill. To subdue the enemy without fighting is the acme of skill.*

He stroked the thick hand-made paper. Then he closed the book and laid it carefully back in its usual place.

Osama, his old childhood friend, only wanted destruction. Bin Laden believed that he had won on the 11th of September, but Abdallah knew better. The catastrophe on Manhattan was a massive defeat, but it did not destroy the US; it only changed the country.

For the worse.

Abdallah had bitter experience of that. Over two billion dollars of his assets had immediately been frozen in American banks. It had taken him several years and vast sums of money to free up most of the capital, but the effect of a complete, sustained stop in some of his most dynamic companies had been disastrous.

But he had pulled through. His business dynasty was complex. He had lots of legs to stand on. The losses in the US were to some extent offset by the rise in oil prices and successful investments elsewhere in the world

Abdallah was a patient man, and business was his greatest priority after his sons. The months went by. The American economy could not exclude Arab interests for ever. It wouldn't survive. In the years immediately after 2001, he had to some extent extracted himself from the US market, but then a couple of years ago he had felt that the time was right to invest again. And this time, the investment was bigger and bolder and more important than ever.

Helen Bentley was his chance. Even though he had never trusted a Western person before, he had seen a strength in her eyes, something different, a glimmer of integrity that he chose to trust. It looked like she was heading for a victory in November 2004 and she seemed to be rational. The fact that she was a woman never worried him. On the contrary, when he left his meeting with her, he felt a reluctant admiration for this strong, sharp woman.

She betrayed him only a week before the election, because she saw that it was necessary if she was going to win.

The art of war was to crush the enemy without fighting.

To fight the US in the traditional sense was futile. But Abdallah had realised that the Americans really only had one enemy: themselves.

If you deprive the average American of his car, shopping and

TV, you take away his joy in life, he thought to himself, and turned off the TV screen. For a moment he saw a picture of Danny at Stanford again, with his crooked smile and a bottle of beer in his hand: an American with insight.

If you take the joys of life away from an American, he gets angry. And this anger starts at the grass roots, with the individual, with those who struggle to survive; the person who works fifty hours a week and still can't afford to have dreams other than those that are fed to him from the TV screen.

With this thought, Abdallah closed his eyes.

They won't close ranks this time. They won't direct their rage at the enemy, at someone out there, *someone who isn't like us and who wants to hurt us.*

They will snap and fight upwards. They will turn against their own. They will turn their aggression on the people who are responsible for everything, for the system, for ensuring that things work, that cars can drive and that there are still dreams to cling on to in their otherwise miserable existence.

But there is chaos at the top. The commander-in-chief is missing and her soldiers are running around like headless chickens, with no direction, in the vacuum that is created when a leader is neither alive nor dead but has just vanished.

A confusing blow to the head. Then a fatal blow to the body. Elementary and effective.

Abdallah looked up. The servant came in silently, carrying a tray. He put the fruit, cheese, bread and a large carafe of juice down by the bed. Then he disappeared again, giving a faint nod at the door. He had not said a word and Abdallah did not thank him.

Only one and a half days to go.

Thursday 19 May 2005

1

At first, when Helen Lardahl Bentley opened her eyes, she had no idea where she was.

She was lying in an uncomfortable position. Her right hand was squashed under her cheek and had gone to sleep. She sat up gingerly. Her body felt stiff and she tried to shake some life into her arm. She had to close her eyes to fight a sudden bout of dizziness, and then she remembered what had happened.

The dizziness passed. Her head still felt strange and light, but when she carefully stretched her arms and legs, she realised that she was not seriously injured. Even the wound on her temple felt better. She ran her fingertips over the bump and could feel that it was smaller than when she had fallen asleep.

Fallen asleep.

The last thing she remembered was that she had taken the woman in the wheelchair by the hand. She had promised . . .

Did I fall asleep on my feet? Did I faint?

It was only now that she realised she was still as dirty. The stench immediately became unbearable. Using her left hand as a support against the back of the sofa, she slowly levered herself up. She had to get washed.

'Good morning, Madam President,' a female voice said quietly from the doorway.

'Good morning,' Helen Bentley replied in surprise.

'I was just out in the kitchen making some coffee.'

'Have you . . . did you sit up all night?'

'Yes.' The woman in the wheelchair smiled. 'Thought you might have concussion, so I woke you up a couple of times during the night. You were pretty groggy. Would you like some?'

She held out a steaming cup.

Madam President waved it away with her free hand.

'I want to shower,' she said. 'And if I'm not . . .' She seemed confused for a moment, and ran her hand over her eyes. 'If I'm not mistaken, you offered me some clean clothes.'

'Of course. Can you manage by yourself, or should I wake Mary?'

'Mary?' mumbled the President. 'That was the . . . house-keeper?'

'Yes, that's right. And my name is Hanne Wilhelmsen. You've probably forgotten. You can call me Hanne.'

'Hannah,' the President repeated.

'Near enough.'

Helen Bentley took a few tentative steps. Her knees were shaking, but her legs held up. She looked askance at the other woman.

'Where am I going?'

'Follow me,' was Hanne Wilhelmsen's friendly reply as she rolled towards the door.

'Have you . . .'

The President stopped and followed. The dawn light outside told her that it must still be very early. But she had already been there quite some time. Several hours at least. The woman in the wheelchair had obviously kept her promise. She hadn't let anyone know. Helen Bentley could still do what she had to before raising the alarm. It was still possible to work the whole thing out, but to do that, no one must know she was still alive.

'What's the time?' she asked as Hanne Wilhelmsen opened the bathroom door. 'How long have I . . .'

She had to lean against the door frame for support.

'Quarter past four,' Hanne replied. 'You've been asleep for about six hours. I'm sure that's not enough.'

'It's a lot more than I usually get,' the President said and managed a smile.

The bathroom was impressive. A double-width sunken bath dominated the room. It was almost a small pool. The President could make out something that looked like a radio and something

302

that was definitely a small TV screen in the unusually spacious shower cabinet beside the bath. The floor was covered in oriental-patterned mosaics, and an enormous mirror with an elaborate gilded wooden frame hung above the two marble sinks.

Helen Bentley thought she remembered the woman saying that she was a retired policewoman. There certainly wasn't much in this flat that had been bought on a policeman's salary. Unless this was the only country in the world that paid its police what they were actually worth.

'Make yourself at home,' Hanne Wilhelmsen said. 'There are towels in the cupboard over there. I'll put some clothes outside the door, so you can get them when you're ready. Just take the time you need.'

She rolled her chair out of the bathroom again and shut the door.

It took Madam President a while to get undressed. Her muscles were still tender and sore. For a moment she was unsure what to do with the soiled clothes, before she noticed that Hanne had put a folded bin liner by one of the sinks.

What a strange woman, thought the President. 'But weren't there two of them? Three, with the housekeeper.'

She was naked now. She stuffed the clothes into the bin liner and tied it carefully. What she really wanted was a bath, but a shower was probably more sensible, given how dirty she was.

The warm water poured from a showerhead that was about the size of a dinner plate. Helen Bentley groaned, partly from pleasure and partly from the pain that coursed through her body as she leant her head back so the water would wash over her face.

There *was* another woman there last night. Helen Bentley remembered it clearly now. Someone who wanted to tell the police. The two women had spoken together in Norwegian, and she hadn't been able to make out anything, other than a word that sounded like *police*. The woman in the wheelchair must have won the argument.

The shower was helping.

It was like purification in every sense. She turned the tap on full. The pressure increased noticeably. The jets of water felt like arrows massaging her skin. She gasped. Filled her mouth with water so she could hardly breathe, then spat it out, let everything run over her. She scrubbed herself thoroughly with a hemp glove that felt coarse and comforting on her hand. Her skin went red. Bright red from the hot water and flaming red from the hemp glove. Her cuts stung intensely when the water hit them.

She had stood exactly like this that late autumn evening in 1984, the evening she had never shared with anyone and that therefore no one must know about.

She had showered for nearly forty minutes when she got home. It was midnight. She remembered that clearly. She had scrubbed herself with a loofah until she bled, as if it were possible to scrape a visual impression off your skin. Make it vanish for ever. The hot water had run out, but she'd stayed in the freezing cascades until Christopher had come in and asked with some concern if she was going to get Billie ready for bed.

It had been raining outside. The rain had poured from the skies in deafening sheets that hammered on the tarmac, on the car, on the roofs and trees and the playground over the road from the house, where a swing swung backwards and forwards on the gusts of wind, and a woman had been standing waiting.

She wanted Billie back.

Helen's daughter had been born to another woman. But all the papers were in order.

She remembered screaming, *All the papers are in order*, and she remembered pulling her purse from her bag and waving it in front of the other woman's pale, determined face: *How much do you want? How much do I need to pay you not to do this to me?*

It wasn't about the money, Billie's biological mother said.

She knew that the papers were valid, she said, but they said nothing about Billie's father. And he had come back now.

She said that with a slight smile, a vaguely triumphant expression, as if she had won a competition and couldn't help boasting about it.

Father! Father! You never said anything about the father! You said you weren't sure, and that in any case, the guy was gone, over the hills, an irresponsible slob, and you wouldn't want Billie to be exposed to him. You said you wanted what was best for Billie, and that was for her to come and live with us, with Christopher and me, and that all the papers were in order. You even signed them! You signed, and Billie has her own room now, a room with pink wallpaper and a white crib with a mobile that she can reach out and touch, which makes her smile.

The father wanted to look after both of them, the woman said. She had to shout in the howling storm. He wanted to look after Billie and Billie's real mother. Biological fathers had rights too. She was stupid not to have given his name when Billie was born, because then all this could have been avoided. She apologised. But that was the situation now. Her boyfriend was out of prison and had come back to her. Things had changed. Surely being a lawyer, Helen Bentley would understand that.

She unfortunately had to have Billie back now.

Madam President laid her palms against the tiles.

She couldn't bear to remember. For over twenty years she had tried to suppress the memory of her panic as she turned away from the woman and ran towards the car on the other side of the road. She wanted to get the diamond necklace that her father had given her earlier that evening. They had been celebrating Billie, and her father's face had been flushed and sweaty, and he had laughed and laughed about his little granddaughter, while everyone exclaimed how beautiful she was, how cute, little Billie Lardahl Bentley.

The necklace was still in the glove compartment, and maybe Helen could use the diamonds and a credit card to buy her child again.

Two credit cards. Three. Take them all!

305

But while she was fumbling with the car key and trying to hold back the tears and panic that were threatening to overwhelm her, she heard the loud thump. A frightening, solid sound that made her turn in time to see a body in a red raincoat sail through the air. Then she heard another thud through the rain as the woman hit the tarmac.

A small sports car spun off round the corner. Helen Bentley didn't even register the colour. All was quiet.

Helen no longer heard the rain. She didn't hear anything. Slowly and mechanically she walked across the road. When she was a few metres from the red-coated woman she stopped.

She was lying in such a peculiar position. So twisted and unnatural, and even in the poor light from the street lamp, Helen could see the blood pouring from a wound on her head. It mixed with the rainwater and became a dark river that twisted its way to the gutter. The woman's eyes were wide open and her mouth was moving.

'*Help me.*'

Helen Lardahl Bentley took a couple of steps back.

Then she turned and ran to the car, pulled open the door, jumped in and drove off. She drove home, and stood in the shower for forty minutes, scrubbing herself with a loofah until she bled.

They never heard any more from Billie's biological mother. And almost exactly twenty years later, on a November night in 2004, Helen Lardahl Bentley was pronounced the winner of the presidential election in the US. Her daughter stood with her on the podium, a tall, blonde young woman who had never made her parents anything but proud.

Madam President pulled off the hemp glove, took down a bottle of shampoo and soaped her hair. It made her eyes sting. But it felt good. It broke up the image of the injured woman lying on the wet tarmac, with her head covered in blood and muck.

Jeffrey Hunter had shown her a letter when he woke her in the hotel room, silently and far too early. She was confused and he had put his finger on her lips in a disconcertingly intimate manner.

They knew about the child, it said. They would expose her secret. She had to go with Jeffrey. The Trojan Horse was operative and they would disclose her secret and destroy her.

The letter was signed by Warren Scifford.

Helen Bentley mentally grabbed the name and clung on to it. She clenched her teeth and let the water fall on her face.

Warren Scifford.

She wasn't going to think about the woman in the red raincoat. She had to think about Warren. And him alone. She had to focus. She rotated slowly in the shower and let the water pummel her aching back. She lowered her head and breathed in deeply. In and out.

Verus amicus rara avis.

A true friend is a rare bird.

That was what had convinced her. Only Warren knew about the inscription on the back of the watch that she had given him after the election. He was an old, good friend and had contacted her before the final televised debate with George W. Bush. The opinion polls had been in favour of the presiding president for several days prior to the debate. She was still in the lead, but the Texan was catching up. His security rhetoric was starting to hit home with the public. He presented himself as a man of action, balanced with the experience and insight needed by a country at war and in crisis. He represented continuity. You knew what you were getting, which was hardly true of Helen Bentley, inexperienced in foreign affairs as she was.

'You have to let go of Arabian Port Management,' Warren had said and taken her by the hands.

All her advisers, internal and external, had told her the same. They had all insisted. They had ranted and pleaded: the time wasn't right. Later perhaps, when there was more water under the bridge after 9/11. But not now.

She refused to back down. The Dubai-based, Saudi-owned

operations company was sound and efficient, and had run ports all over the world, from Okinawa to London. The two companies, one of them British, that had until now managed some of the biggest ports in the States, were interested in selling. Arabian Port Management wanted to buy them both. One would give them the operation of New York, New Jersey, Baltimore, New Orleans, Miami and Philadelphia; the other covered Charleston, Savannah, Houston and Mobile. In other words, the Arabic company would have considerable control over all the most important ports on the east coast and in the Gulf.

Helen Lardahl Bentley thought that it was a good idea.

For a start, it was the best company, by far the most profitable and the one with most expertise. The sale would also play a significant role in normalising relations with powers in the Middle East that it was in the interests of the US to be on good terms with. In addition, it would help to rebuild respect for good Arab-Americans, which was perhaps the important thing for Helen Bentley.

She felt they had suffered enough, and stubbornly stuck to her guns. She had had meetings with the top management of the Arabic company, and even though she wasn't stupid enough to promise anything, she had clearly signalled her goodwill. She was particularly pleased that the company, despite any uncertainty regarding approval of the sale, had already invested heavily on American soil, in order to be as primed as possible for a future takeover.

Warren had spoken quietly. He hadn't let go of her hands. He looked straight into her eyes when he said: 'I support your intention. Wholeheartedly. But you will never achieve it if you ruin your chances now. You have to launch a counterattack, Helen. You have to hit back at Bush where he least expects it. I've spent years analysing the man. I know him as well as anyone can, without actually meeting him. He also wants this sale to be concluded! It's just he's experienced enough not to make it public yet. He knows that it will trigger an emotional response that's not to be played with. You have to expose him. You have to catch him out. Now listen, this is what you should do . . .'

Finally she felt clean.

Her skin was stinging and the bathroom was full of warm steam. She stepped out of the shower cabinet and grabbed a towel. When she had wrapped it round her body, she took a smaller towel and wound it round her head. With her left hand, she rubbed a clear circle in the condensation on the mirror.

The blood on her face was gone. The bump was still obvious, but her eye had opened again. Her wrists were in fact the worst. The small strips of plastic had cut so far into her skin that there were deep open wounds in several places. She would have to ask for some disinfectant, and hopefully they would have some proper bandages.

She had followed Warren's advice. Albeit with considerable doubt.

In reply to the presenter's question on how she viewed the security threat in connection with the sale of key American infra-structure, she had looked straight into the camera and given an impassioned and inspiring forty-five-second call for people to fraternise with 'our Arab friends', and then talked about the importance of nurturing a fundamental American value and right, that of equality, no matter where in the world your ancestors hailed from, and which religion they practised.

Then she had stopped to draw breath. A glance over at the presiding president made her realise that Warren had been absolutely right. President Bush was smiling the smile of a victor. He shrugged in that peculiar way of his, with his hands leading from his body. He was sure of what was coming.

He got something completely different.

But, Helen Bentley continued calmly, it was a very different matter when it came to infrastructure. She was of the view that nothing should be sold to anyone who was not American, or at least a close ally. She said that the ultimate goal had to be that everything, from the highways and airports to ports, customs stations, border checkpoints and railways, should always and for ever be owned, operated and managed by American interests.

For the purposes of national security.

And finally, she added with a fleeting smile, that it would of course take a long time and require great political will to achieve this. Not least as President George Bush himself had said he was warmly in favour of selling to Arab interests, in an internal document that she then held up to the camera for a few seconds before putting it back on the lectern and gesturing to the presenter that she was finished.

Helen Lardahl Bentley won the debate by eleven percentage points. A week later, she became 'Madam President', thus fulfilling a dream she had had for more than ten years. Warren Scifford was appointed as the head of the newly established BSC Unit shortly after.

The position was not a reward.

The watch was.

And he had abused it. He had tricked her with her own declaration of eternal friendship.

Verus amicus rara avis. It had proved to be truer than she thought.

She went over to the door and opened it carefully. There was a folded pile of clothes just outside as promised. As quickly as her aching body would allow, she bent down, snatched up the pile and closed the door again. Then she locked it.

The underwear was completely new. The labels were still attached. She noted this kind gesture, before putting the bra and panties on. The jeans also looked new and were a perfect fit. When she put on the pale pink cashmere V-necked sweater, she felt the fibres scratching at the cuts on her wrists.

She stood looking at herself in the mirror. The ventilation fan had dispensed with most of the steam and the bathroom was already a few degrees cooler than when she'd got out of the shower five minutes ago. From force of habit, she considered for a moment putting on some make-up. There was an open lacquered

Japanese box by the sink, full of cosmetics. But she decided against it. Her lips were still swollen and the cut on her lower lip would look ridiculous if she was to put lipstick on.

Many years ago, during Bill Clinton's first term in office, Hillary Rodham Clinton had invited Helen Bentley to lunch. It was the first time that they had met in more personal circumstances, and Helen remembered that she had been extremely nervous. It was only a few weeks since she had taken her seat in the Senate, and she had had more than enough on her plate, learning about all the customs and etiquette that a young and insignificant senator had to know in order to survive more than a few hours on Capitol Hill. Lunch with the First Lady was a dream. Hillary had been just as personable, attentive and interested as her supporters said she was. The arrogant, cool and calculating person that her enemies made her out to be was not in evidence. She did, of course, want something, just as everyone in Washington always wanted something. But on the whole, Helen Bentley got the impression that Hillary Rodham Clinton wished her well. She wanted her to feel comfortable and confident in her new environment. And if, in addition, Senator Bentley would be willing to read through a document about a health reform that would benefit middle America, she would make the First Lady very happy indeed.

Helen Bentley remembered it well.

They got up after the meal. Hillary Clinton looked discreetly at her watch, gave Helen a formal peck on the cheek and shook her hand.

'One more thing,' she said, still holding her hand. 'You can't trust anyone in this world. Except one person, your husband. As long as he is your husband, he's the only person who will always want the best for you. The only one you can trust. Never forget that.'

Helen had never forgotten it.

On the 19th of August 1998, Bill Clinton admitted that he had betrayed not only the entire world, but also his wife. A couple of

311

weeks later, Helen bumped into Hillary Clinton in a corridor in the West Wing, following a meeting at the White House. The First Lady had just come back from Martha's Vineyard, where the presidential family had sought refuge from the storm. She had stopped and taken Helen by the hand, just as she had during their first meeting, many years before.

'I'm sorry, Hillary. I'm truly sorry for you and Chelsea.'

Mrs Clinton said nothing. Her eyes were red. Her mouth trembled. She managed to smile, nodded and let go of Helen's hand before moving on, proud, straight-backed, meeting the eye of anyone who dared to look.

Helen Lardahl Bentley had never forgotten the advice of the President's wife, but she had not followed it. Helen couldn't live without trusting someone. Nor could she have set course for the country's top position without a handful of loyal staff, whom she trusted implicitly. An exclusive group of good friends who wished her well.

Warren Scifford had been one of them.

That was what she had always believed. But he was lying. He had betrayed her, and the lie was bigger than him.

Because he couldn't know what he claimed in the letter the Trojans knew. No one knew. Not even Christopher. It was her secret, her burden, and she had carried it alone for more than twenty years.

It was totally incomprehensible, and it was only the panic, the paralysing, overwhelming fear that engulfed her when Jeffrey Hunter showed her the letter that had prevented her from seeing that.

Warren was lying. Something was very wrong.

No one could know.

Her teeth felt like they were covered in fur and she had a bad taste in her mouth. She looked timidly around the bathroom. There, she saw it by the mirror. Hanne Wilhelmsen had put out a glass for her, with a new toothbrush and a half-used tube of toothpaste in it. She struggled with the obstinate packaging and

312

cut herself on the plastic before managing to extract the tooth-brush.

President Bentley bared her teeth at the mirror.

'You bastard!' she whispered. 'May you burn in hell, Warren Scifford! That's the only place for people like you!'

2

Warren Scifford felt awful.

In the half-dark he fumbled around for his mobile phone, which was playing a mechanical version of something that was supposed to sound like a cockerel. The noise would not stop. He sat up in bed, confused. He had forgotten to close the blackout curtains again before going to bed, and the grey light behind the thin curtains gave him no idea of what time it was.

The cockerel got louder and Warren swore passionately as he searched around on the bedside table. Finally he caught sight of the mobile phone. The display said it was 05:07. It must have fallen on the floor in the course of his three hours of restless sleep. He couldn't imagine how he had managed to set the alarm so wrong. He had meant to set it for five past seven.

He missed a few times before he finally managed to turn the alarm off. He sank back into the bed. He closed his eyes, but knew immediately that there was no point. His thoughts were crashing and colliding and creating chaos, so it would be impossible to sleep. He stood up, resigned, padded into the shower and stood under the water for the next fifteen minutes. If he wasn't rested, he could at least scrub himself into some sort of waking state.

He dried himself and pulled on his boxer shorts and a T-shirt.

It didn't take him long to rig up the portable office. He left the ceiling lamp switched off and closed the blackout curtains. The table lamps gave sufficient light to work. When everything was set up, he filled the kettle and stood leaning against the bookshelf, waiting for it to boil. For a moment he considered coffee. But the powder looked old and tasteless, so he took a tea bag and dropped it into the cup instead, then filled it with boiling water.

No new emails.

He tried to work his way back. It was around two in the morning when he went to bed. That would be around eight in the evening in Washington DC. So now it would eleven o'clock back home. Everyone was working flat out. No one had sent him anything for more than four hours.

He tried to reassure himself that it was because they thought he was asleep.

It didn't work. The fact that he was being frozen out was becoming increasingly apparent. The more time that passed without the President being found, the more Warren Scifford's role was diminishing. Even though he was still the contact person for the local police, it was obvious that operations at the embassy on Drammensveien had increased in scope and content without him being fully informed. The operative investigators the FBI had sent to Norway some hours after he had arrived were the kings of the castle. They stayed at the embassy. They were linked to communications technology that made his little office, with his selection of mobile phones and encrypted PC, look like a pathetic delivery to a technical museum.

They didn't give a damn about the Norwegian police.

Some of them did still come to the meetings he tried to set up several times a day in an attempt to coordinate the American effort with anything that the Norwegian police might have discovered regarding clues, evidence and theories. When he informed them that the body of Jeffrey Hunter had been found, he was given something that might at least resemble attention. As far as he could understand from the ambassador, a minor diplomatic tussle had ensued regarding the man's earthly remains. The Norwegians wanted to keep him for further examination. But the US authorities simply refused.

'I don't give a damn,' whispered Warren Scifford and gave his face a good rub.

He had warned Ambassador Wells.

'They're going to hit the roof when they realise what you're up to,' he'd said in exasperation when they met at the embassy

315

the day before. 'OK, they might have a US-friendly government, but I realise that this is a country where opposition can be strong. They might be stubborn, as you warned me, but they're not stupid. We simply can't —'

The ambassador had interrupted him with an ice-cold stare and a voice that made Warren hold his tongue. '*I* am the one who knows this country, Warren. I am the US ambassador to Norway. I have three meetings a day with the Norwegian foreign minister. The government of this country is constantly informed of what we are doing. *Everything that we are doing.*'

It was a complete lie and they both knew it.

Warren took a sip of the tea. It didn't taste of much, but at least it was warm. The room was too. Far too warm. He went over to a box on the wall to see if he could turn down the temperature. He had never managed to get the hang of the whole Celsius system. The switch was turned to twenty-five degrees, and that was certainly too hot. Maybe fifteen would be better. He held his hand up to the vent in the wall. The air cooled immediately.

He hesitated for a moment, and then turned his computer off. There were two files on the desk. One was as thick as a book. The other contained no more than twenty pages. He took both of them and lay back down on the bed, bolstered by the pillows and cushions at the head of the bed.

He looked through the classified report on the intelligence situation first. It was more than two hundred pages long and he had not received it in a coded email, as he should have done according to various agreements and routines. He had discovered, by accident, that it existed when he overheard some snippets of conversation in the headquarters at the embassy, and had had to argue his way to a copy. Conrad Victory, the sixty-year-old special agent who was in charge of operations at the embassy, thought that Warren didn't need the document. And in situations like this they operated with a strict 'need-to-know' policy, which Warren, given his experience, should understand.

316

His role was to be the liaison between the Norwegian and American police. He had himself complained how difficult it was to resist the pressure the Norwegians put on him with regard to American information and intelligence. The less he knew, the less Oslo Police would interfere.

But Warren didn't give in. When nothing else worked, he resorted to highlighting his close personal relationship with the President. Between the lines, of course. It worked. Finally.

He had fallen into bed at two in the morning and had not really had a chance to look at the document until now.

It was frightening reading.

In the intense search for the President's kidnappers, it was becoming increasingly clear that her disappearance would be followed by a major terrorist attack. But neither the FBI nor the CIA, nor any of the other numerous organisations that fell under the umbrella of Homeland Security, was willing to use the name that Warren Scifford's BSC Unit had given to such a potential attack: *The Trojan Horse*.

They didn't dare to call it anything yet.

The problem was that no one knew what or who would be the target of any such attack. The intelligence was extensive, in terms of the amount of reports, tips, and theories, and speculation was overwhelming. But the information was fragmented, confusing and to a large extent contradictory.

It could be an Islamist conspiracy.

It *presumably* was an Islamist conspiracy.

It *had* to be the Muslims.

The reports indicated that the authorities had a full overview of all other potential criminals, attackers and relevant terrorist groups – to the extent that anyone could ever have a full overview. And as far as twisted, fanatical American citizens were concerned, they were always a latent threat, as the bomber Timothy McVeigh had shown when the Gulf veteran killed 168 people in Oklahoma City in 1995. The problem was that there were no indications of abnormal activity in any of the many ultra-reactionary groups in the US. They were still under comprehensive surveillance, even post-9/11, when most of the attention was now focused in another direction. There was nothing to indicate that extreme animal-rights or environmental activists had taken the step from illegal, bothersome protests to real terrorist attacks. There were fanatical religious groups all over the States, but as a rule they were really only a threat to themselves. And there was nothing extraordinary to report from their ranks either.

And kidnapping an American president from a hotel room in Norway was light years away from what any known American group would have the ability to orchestrate.

It had to be an Islamist conspiracy.

Warren straightened his glasses.

The tangible angst in the report was fascinating. In all his thirty years in the FBI, Warren Scifford had never read a professional analysis that was so permeated by impending catastrophe. It was as if the truth had finally dawned on the entire Homeland Security system: someone had managed the impossible. The unthinkable. Someone had stolen the American commander-in-chief, and it was hard to imagine that those responsible had any limits as to what they might do.

The fear was focused on an attack targeting various unidentified installations on American soil. It was based on a number of reports and events, but the reports were insubstantial and the events ambiguous.

The most worrying and confusing factor was all the tips.

The American authorities were constantly receiving such communications, and more often than not there was no substance to them. House-owners who wished unpleasant visits from uniformed police on their neighbours could come up with the most fantastic claims about what was going on on the other side of the fence. Suspicious visits, strange sounds at night, abnormal behaviour and something that could only be dynamite in the garage. Or maybe even a bomb. Property sharks found it both convenient and effective to get help from the FBI in evicting troublesome tenants. There were no limits to what people claimed they had seen. Arabs going in and out at all times of day and night, conversations in foreign languages and the transport of boxes that contained God only knows what. Even teenagers might decide to report a classmate as a terrorist, simply because the guy had shown disrespect in trying it on with a girl he should have kept his hands off.

This time the tips seemed more like warnings.

The FBI's field offices had received an unusual number of anonymous messages in the past few days. Some were phoned in, others came in emails. But the content was exactly the same, and they all claimed basically that something was going to happen, something that would make 9/11 pale into insignificance. Most of them said that the US was a weak nation that couldn't even look after its president. They only had themselves to blame for leaving their ranks open. This time the attack would not be targeted on a specific area. This time the whole of the US would suffer, in the same way the US had caused suffering throughout the world.

It was payback time.

The most alarming thing was that the phone calls could not be traced.

It was incomprehensible.

The many organisations associated with Homeland Security had a technological advantage that they thought was absolute, and that made it possible to trace any phone call to or from American soil. Generally it took no more than a minute to identify a sender's PC. In the shadow of the wide-ranging powers of attorney that George W. Bush had passed since 2001, the National Security Agency had gained what they believed to be almost total control of telephonic and electronic communication. The organisation saw no problem in the fact that they exceeded these powers of attorney in their efforts to be effective. They had a job to do. They had to ensure national security. The few who had the opportunity to discover these transgressions and the possibility to do anything about them chose to turn a blind eye.

The enemy was powerful and dangerous.

The US had to be protected at all costs.

These sinister messages, however, could not be traced. Not to the right place, at all events. The cutting-edge technology found the sender's IP address or telephone number almost instantly, but when they were then investigated, the information appeared to be wrong. One call, where a deep man's voice accused the American authorities of being arrogant and warned them not to harass decent citizens who had done nothing wrong other than having a Palestinian father, had apparently been made from the telephone of a seventy-year-old lady in Lake Placid, New York. At the time that one of the FBI's offices in Manhattan received the call, the frail old woman was having a tea party with four equally charming friends. None of them had touched the phone and a log from the local telephone company showed the widow was telling the truth: no one had used the phone at that time.

The tea had cooled. Warren took a sip. He glasses steamed up for a moment, as if someone had breathed on them.

He turned to the more technical section of the report. He couldn't understand much of it, and wasn't particularly interested in the details. He wanted to read the conclusion, which he found on page 173: it was entirely possible to manipulate addressees in the way that had been done.

Slightly unnecessary conclusion, Warren said to himself. They've already documented more than a hundred and thirty cases of the phenomenon.

He adjusted one of the pillows behind his head to make it more comfortable.

Manipulation of this sort required substantial resources.

Yeah, yeah, he thought. No one ever thought it was the work of a poor man.

And presumably a telecommunications satellite. Or access to capacity on one. Rented or stolen.

A satellite? A bloody spaceship?

Warren was starting to feel cold; fifteen degrees was obviously not warm enough. He got up again to reset the switch in the box on the wall. This time he turned it to twenty degrees and then climbed back into bed and continued reading.

Satellites of this type were located in stationary orbits about forty thousand kilometres from the surface of the earth. Since all the telephone calls and electronic messages were linked to phones and computers on the east coast of the States, the actions were compatible with the use of an Arabic satellite.

An Arabic satellite would not be able to penetrate further into the country than that.

But it could reach the east coast.

Tracking, Warren thought impatiently and leafed quickly through the pages. With all the billions of dollars and powers of attorney and technology that we have, what about the tracking and reconstruction of the phone calls and messages?

Warren Scifford was a profiler.

He respected technique. In the course of his work tracking down serial killers and sadistic, sexually motivated murderers, he had over the years developed a deep respect for forensic pathologists and their magic, using chemistry, physics, electronics and technology. On occasion, he even sneaked a peak at an episode of *CSI*, in deep awe of the profession.

But this was beyond him. He could set up a PC and learn a few codes, but generally he was happy to let others look after the technology.

His area of competence was the soul.

He couldn't understand this.

He carried on reading.

The messages stopped suddenly at 9.14 a.m., Eastern Time. At the exact time that the FBI went to investigate the first address they had traced. According to NSA's log, someone had phoned the FBI headquarters in Quantico from a small house on the outskirts of the Everglades in Florida, with a chilling message that the USA was heading for a fall.

An old man with poor eyesight and terrible hearing lived in

the house. His telephone wasn't even connected. It lay covered in dust in the cellar, but his subscription was still live as his son in Miami paid all his father's regular bills. Obviously without checking what they were for. Presumably he hadn't visited the old man in years.

The messages had stopped at exactly the same time.

And none had been received since.

The report finished by saying that work was ongoing to analyse the voices and the language used, but nothing of any value to the investigation could be said yet about the recordings of the threats or the sixty or so emails with similar content. The voices were scrambled and distorted, so expectations were not high. The only thing that could be said with any certainty was that all the callers were men. For obvious reasons it was more difficult to establish the sex of the originators of the electronic messages.

End of report.

Warren was hungry.

He went to the minibar, took out a bar of chocolate and opened a bottle of Coke. Neither of them tasted any good, but did help to increase his blood sugar. The slight headache that he got when he didn't have enough sleep disappeared.

He went back to bed. The thick document fell to the floor. According to instructions, it was to be destroyed immediately. But that could wait. He picked up the thinner file and held it at arm's length for a few seconds. Then he lowered his arm on to the duvet.

The slim report was a masterpiece.

The problem was that no one seemed to be particularly interested in reading it, and even less so in responding to it.

Warren knew it almost off by heart, even though he had only read through the paper twice. The report had been prepared by the BSC Unit at home in DC and he had contributed as much as he could from this godforsaken place they called Norway.

Warren longed to go home. He closed his eyes.

He had started to feel old more and more frequently. Not just older, but old. He was tired and had bitten off more than he could chew with this new job. He wanted to go back to Quantico, to Virginia, to his family. To Kathleen, who had put up with him and his countless, deeply hurtful infidelities over the years. To his grown-up children, who had all settled near their childhood home. To his own house and garden. He wanted to go home, and felt a great pressure under his ribs that did not disappear even though he swallowed several times.

The thin report was a profile.

As always, they had started their work by analysing the actions and events. The BSC Unit worked along timelines and in depth, putting the events in context, analysing the causes and effects and studying the costs and complexity. Every detail in the sequence of events was set against alternative solutions, because that was the only way in which they could come close to capturing the motives and attitudes of the people who were behind the kidnapping of Madam President.

The picture that slowly emerged over the twenty pages worried Warren and his loyal colleagues in the BSC Unit just as much as the thick report scared the life out of the rest of the FBI.

They thought they would establish the profile of an organisation. A group of people, a terrorist cell. Possibly a small unit, an army fighting a holy war against Satan's bulwark, the US.

Instead they saw the profile of a man.

One man.

Obviously he could not be acting alone. Everything that had happened since the BSC Unit saw the first vague signs of the Trojan Horse more than six weeks ago indicated that a disconcerting number of people were involved.

The problem was that they didn't seem to belong together. In any way. Instead of developing a more detailed description of a terrorist organisation, the BSC Unit had outlined a single individual who used people the way that others used tools, and showed the same lack of loyalty or other human emotion to his helpers that anyone else would to a toolbox.

Nothing was done to look after or help the various actors afterwards. Once they had played their role, done their bit, there was no protection. Gerhard Skrøder had been thrown to the wolves, as had the Pakistani cleaner and all the rest of the pieces in this complex jigsaw puzzle.

Which must mean that they didn't know who they were working for.

Warren yawned, shook his head briskly and opened his eyes wide to force back the tears. His hand, which was still holding the report, felt heavy as lead. He pulled himself together, lifted it up and caste his eyes over the front page.

The title was modestly placed at the top of the page in the same font size as the rest of the document, only it was in bold: **The Guilty. A profile of the abductor**.

Warren wasn't sure whether he liked the name they had chosen. On the other hand, it was neutral, with no ethnic or national connotations. Again he tried to make himself more comfortable, and then started to read:

I.i. The Abduction.

As usual, their starting point was the key event.

The actual kidnapping of the President gave the BSC Unit strong characteristics in terms of the perpetrator's profile. Ever since he had been woken in his flat in Washington DC at some ungodly hour by an emotional agent who told him that the President had apparently been kidnapped in Norway, Warren Scifford had been thoroughly perplexed. On the flight to Europe, he had constantly been expecting, and in some absurd way hoping, that he would arrive to be told that Madam President had been found dead.

He had already dismissed the possibility that she would be found alive.

The key question was: why kidnapping? Why not kill Helen Bentley instead? By all accounts, it was far easier to carry out an assassination, and therefore far less risky. Being the commander-in-chief of the US was definitely a high-risk job, due to the simple fact that it was impossible to fully protect any individual from sudden fatal attacks by other people, unless that individual was kept in isolation.

The kidnapping had to have a purpose, its own value. And this had to be something to do with what could be gained by keeping the US in suspense, rather than letting the American people gather in shared shock and grief over their murdered president.

The obvious effect of the disappearance was that the country was now more vulnerable to attack.

Just the thought made Warren's skin crawl.

He turned to the next page before taking a swig of Coke. He still had a feeling in his stomach that he couldn't define, and wondered for a moment whether he should order some food to see if that would help. The clock on his mobile phone showed three minutes to six, so he abandoned that idea. Breakfast would be served in an hour.

The use of Secret Service agent Jeffrey Hunter was as genius as it was simple. Even though it might in theory be possible to kidnap the President without the help of an insider, he could imagine no way in which it would be possible to carry it out in practice. The fact that the Guilty had an apparatus in the States that could abduct an autistic boy, twice, in order to frighten a professional security agent into cooperation was one of the elements that made the profile increasingly clear. And even more overwhelming.

The phone rang.

The sound gave Warren such a surprise that the Coke bottle that was wedged between his thighs fell over. He cursed, managed to catch the bottle of sticky dark fluid and grabbed the phone.

'Hello,' he grunted, drying his free hand on the duvet cover.

'Warren?' a distant voice said.

'Yes.'

'It's Colin.'

'Oh, hi, Colin. You sound very far away.'

'I have to be quick.'

'Sounds like you're whispering. Speak up!'

'Dammit, Warren, listen to me. We're not exactly in people's good books at the moment.'

'No, I noticed that here, too.'

Colin Wolf and Warren Scifford had worked together for nearly ten years. Warren's first choice when he was putting together the BSC Unit was his peer. Colin was old school. His name might be Wolf, but he looked like a bear and he was thorough, calm and compliant. His voice was higher than normal and the delay on the line made him stressed.

'They won't listen to us,' Colin said. 'They've made up their minds.'

'About what?' Warren asked, even though he knew the answer.

'That there's some Islamist organisation or other behind it all. And they're back on the al-Qaeda track again. Al-Qaeda! They're no more involved in this case than the IRA. Or the Scouts, for that matter. And now they've seen red. That's why I'm calling.'

'What's happened?'

'They've discovered an account.'

'An account?'

'Jeffrey Hunter. Transferred money to his wife.'

Warren swallowed. The brown stain on his groin was disgusting. He pulled the duvet over it with his sticky hand.

'Hello?'

'Yes, I'm still here,' Warren said. 'Well I'll be damned.'

'Quite. It's all too good to be true.'

'What do you mean?'

'Listen, but I have to be quick. I want you to know. The amount was two hundred thousand dollars. The money was of course filtered through the usual channels so there is no identity, but we've managed to trace it back to the sender all the same. It only took the boys over in Pennsylvania Avenue five hours.'

'And who did they find?'

'Are you sitting down?'

'I'm lying in bed.'

'The cousin of the Saudi oil minister. He lives in Iran.'

'Shit.'

'You can say that again.'

Warren picked up the BSC Unit report again. The papers stuck to his hand. That wasn't right. That couldn't be right. *They* were right: Colin and Warren and the rest of the small, marginalised group of profilers who no one would listen to.

'That just can't be right,' he said pensively. 'The Guilty would never have done anything in such an amateur way that the money could be traced.'

'What?'

'That can't be right!'

'No, that's why I'm calling! It's too simple, Warren. But what about if we turn the whole thing on its head?'

'What? I can't hear, there's . . .'

'Turn the whole thing on its head,' Colin shouted. 'Let's suppose that the trail to Saudi Arabia was laid *on purpose*. If we're right, and the intention was that the money would be found and traced . . .'

Then everything falls into place, thought Warren, aghast. That's the way the Guilty works. He wants this to happen. He wants chaos, he creates crises, he's . . .

'Don't you see? Do you agree?'

Colin's voice was so distant.

Warren wasn't listening properly.

'It won't take long before this leaks,' Colin said, as the connection deteriorated. 'Have you been watching the stock exchange?'

'Vaguely.'

'When the link between Saudi Arabia and Iran becomes known . . .'

Oil prices, Warren realised. They'll rocket, like never before in history.

'. . . dramatic fall in the Dow Jones, and it's so bloody sharp and . . .'

'Hello,' Warren shouted.

'Hi. Are you still there? I'll have to stop, Warren. I have to run because . . .'

The crackling was unbearable. Warren held the receiver out a few centimetres from his ear. Suddenly Colin came back. The connection was crystal clear for the first time.

'They're talking about a hundred dollars a barrel,' he said grimly. 'Before the end of next week. That's what he wants. It fits, Warren. It all fits. I have to go. Call me.'

The connection was cut.

Warren got up from the bed. He had to shower again. With his legs wide apart, so that his sticky thighs wouldn't touch, he waddled over to his suitcase.

He still hadn't unpacked properly.

'The Guilty is a man with enormous capital and a sound understanding of the West,' he parroted from the report. 'He has well-above-average intelligence, incredible patience and a unique ability to plan and think long term. He has built up an impressive international and extremely complex network of helpers, presumably through the use of threats, capital and costly cultivation. There is every reason to believe that few of these people know who he is. If any.'

Warren couldn't find any clean boxer shorts. He checked and double-checked the side pockets of the suitcase. His fingers touched something heavy. He waited a moment before fishing the object out of the narrow opening.

His watch.

Verus amicus rara avis.

He'd thought that he'd lost it for good. It had bothered him more than he liked to admit. He liked the watch and was proud to have received it from Madam President. He never took it off.

Except when he had sex.

Sex and time did not go together, so he always took it off.

Deep down, he was afraid that the watch had been stolen by

328

the woman with red hair. He couldn't remember what she was called any more, even though it was only a week since they'd met. In a bar. She worked in advertising, he seemed to remember. Or maybe it was film.

Whatever, he said to himself and slipped the watch on to his wrist.

There were no clean boxer shorts in his suitcase.

He would just have to make do without.

'It is unlikely that he is American,' Warren imagined a voice saying, as if the profile document was being played on a tape recorder in his head. 'If he is a Muslim, he is more secular than he is fanatical. He presumably lives in the Middle East, but he also has places to stay in Europe.'

It was now thirty-three minutes past six and Warren Scifford no longer felt in the slightest bit tired.

3

As he approached the guest room, Al Muffet looked down over the banister to the grandfather clock in the hall below. It was thirty-three minutes past midnight. He was sure he'd read somewhere that people slept most deeply between three and five in the morning. As his brother had been rather drunk that evening, Al reckoned he would already be sound asleep.

He didn't have the patience to wait any longer.

He took care to avoid the floorboards that creaked. He was barefoot and regretted not having put on a pair of socks. The soles of his feet were moist and made a gentle sucking sound on the wooden floor. Whereas Fayed was unlikely to be disturbed by it, the girls, Louise in particular, were very light sleepers. They had been ever since their mother died at ten past three one November night.

Fortunately he had managed to pull himself together during the evening meal, when Fayed's comment about his mother's death had knocked him sideways for a moment or two. After a quick trip to the bathroom, where he splashed his face and hands with ice-cold water, he had been able to go back down to his brother and daughters and continue the meal with some composure. He sent the girls to bed at ten, with great protest, and was relieved when Fayed announced half an hour later that he too wanted to go to bed.

Al Muffet went up to the door behind which his brother was sleeping.

His mother had never confused her two sons.

The age difference was one reason. But Ali and Fayed had such different personalities. Al Muffet knew that his mother felt that he was much more like her, a friendly person, open to most things and most people.

Fayed was the black sheep. He was smarter than his brother at school, and in fact was one of the brightest in the whole school. But he was hopeless with his hands. His father realised early on that there was no point in forcing him to help with the odd bit of work in the garage. Little Ali, on the other hand, knew the principles behind a car engine by the time he was eight. He passed his driving test when he was sixteen, and built his own car from old parts that his father had let him have.

His brother's sullen, suspicious nature was physically visible from an early age. He viewed the world from the corner of his eye and his furtive attitude made people doubt that he was ever really listening. He also had a slightly sideways walk, as if he was always expecting to be attacked and wanted to be ready to throw a punch, better first than last.

Their faces were, however, remarkably similar. But their mother had still never mistaken one for the other. She would never have done that, Al Muffet thought as he carefully turned the door handle.

If she had really done that, because she was only minutes away from death and could neither see nor think clearly, it could be disastrous.

The room was silent and dark. It took a few seconds for Al's eyes to adjust.

He could see the outline of the bed against the wall. Fayed was lying on his stomach with one leg hanging over the edge of the bed and his left hand under his head. He was snoring quietly and regularly.

Al pulled a torch from his breast pocket. Before he turned it on, he checked that his brother's suitcase was on the low chest of drawers by the door to the smallest bathroom in the house.

He shaded the beam with his hands. A small stripe of light fell on the floor, which helped Al to get to the suitcase without stumbling over anything.

It was locked.

He tried again. The code lock would not open.

Fayed gave a loud snort and turned in the bed. Al froze. He didn't even dare to turn off the torch. He stood for several minutes listening to his brother's breathing, which became slow and rhythmical again.

It was on ordinary medium-sized black Samsonite suitcase.

A normal code lock, Al reckoned, and rolled the numbers to his brother's birthday. A normal lock might have the most normal code of all.

Click.

He did the same on the lock to the left. Now he could open the suitcase. He did it slowly and without a sound. It had clothes in it. Two sweaters on top, a pair of trousers, several pairs of underpants and three pairs of socks. Everything was carefully folded. Al put his hand down under the clothes and lifted them out.

At the bottom of the suitcase lay eight mobile phones, a laptop and a diary.

No one needs eight mobile phones, Al thought, unless they sell them for a living. He felt his pulse quicken. All the telephones were switched off. For a moment he was tempted to take the laptop away with him for closer investigation. He quickly dismissed that thought. It was probably full of codes that he wouldn't be able to work out, and the risk that his brother might wake up before he managed to put the computer back was too great.

It was a black leather diary, with a strap and press stud which doubled up as a pen loop for an exclusive ballpoint pen. Al held the torch in his mouth, with the beam on the diary, and opened it.

It was an ordinary Filofax. The pages on the left-hand side were divided into the first three days of the week and the remaining four days were on the right-hand page. Sunday was given least room, and as far as Al could see, his brother never had any appointments on Sundays.

He turned the pages back and forth. The appointments didn't tell him anything other than that his brother was a busy man. He knew that already.

In a moment of inspiration, he turned to the year planner, with only one line per day. Personally, he kept these at the back of his diary, but his brother obviously found it more useful to have them at the front. Fayed had kept the last five years' planners. Special days and anniversaries were carefully marked. In 2003, Fayed's family had spent the 4th of July on Sandy Hook. Labor Day 2004 was celebrated at Cape Cod with someone called the Collies.

The 11th of September 2001 was marked with a black star.

Al realised that he was sweating, even though the room was chilly. His brother was still sleeping heavily. His fingers shook as he turned to the date that his mother died. When he saw what his brother had written there, he was finally certain.

His eyes rested on the writing for a few moments. Then he closed the diary and put it back in its place. His hands were steadier now and nimble. He closed the suitcase and the locks.

Just as quietly as he'd come, he tiptoed back to the door. He stood there looking at the sleeping body, as he had so many times in his childhood, watching his sleeping brother from his bed at night, when he couldn't sleep. The memories were so vivid. After long, exhausting days in the firing line between his parents and Fayed, Ali would sit up and watch his back as it rose and fell in the other corner of their room. Sometimes he was awake for hours. Sometimes he cried quietly. All he really wanted was to understand his defiant, wronged brother, the surly, wild teenager who always made their father so angry and their mother so desperate.

Standing there by the door of the room where his brother was sleeping, Al Muffet felt as sad now as he had back then. Once upon a time he had liked Fayed. Now he realised there was nothing left between them. He didn't know when it had happened – at what point everything had been lost.

Perhaps it was when their mother died.

He closed the door carefully behind him. He had to think. He had to find out what his brother knew about the kidnapping of Helen Lardahl Bentley.

4

'Anything new?'

Johanne Vik turned towards Helen Lardahl Bentley and smiled at her as she lowered the sound on the TV.

'I've just turned it on. Hanne had to go to bed. Good morning, by the way. You really do look very . . .'

Johanne stopped and blushed, then got up. She brushed the front of her shirt with her hands. The crumbs from Ragnhild's breakfast showered the floor.

'Madam President,' she said, and stopped herself from wanting to curtsy.

'Forget the formalities,' Helen Bentley said briskly. 'This is what one might call an extreme situation. Call me Helen.'

Her lips were no longer as swollen and she managed to smile. She still looked battered, but the shower and clean clothes had worked wonders.

'Is there a bucket and some detergent anywhere?' she asked, looking around. 'I want to try to limit . . . the damage in there.'

With a slim hand, she pointed to the sitting room with the red sofa.

'Oh, that,' Johanne said lightly. 'You can forget that. Mary's already done it. Some of it has to be dry-cleaned, but it's—'

'Mary?' Helen Bentley repeated mechanically. 'The housekeeper.'

Johanne nodded. The President came closer.

'And you are? I'm sorry, last night I wasn't quite . . .'

'Johanne. Vik. Johanne Vik.'

'Johanne,' Helen Bentley said, holding out her hand. 'And the little one . . .'

Ragnhild was sitting on the floor with a pan lid, a ladle and a box of Duplo bricks. She was making happy noises.

'My daughter.' Johanne smiled. 'She's called Ragnhild, but we generally call her Agni, because that's what she calls herself.'

The President's hand was dry and warm and Johanne held it just a fraction too long.

'Is this some kind of . . .' Helen Bentley looked like she was afraid of offending someone and hesitated, 'collective?'

'No, no. I don't live here. My daughter and I are just visiting. For a few days.'

'Oh, so you don't live in Oslo?'

'Ye-es. I live . . . This is Hanne Wilhelmsen's flat. And Nefis. Hanne's partner. Life partner, that is. She's Turkish, and has taken Ida, their daughter, with her to Turkey to visit the grandparents. But they're the ones who actually live here. I'm just—'

The President raised a hand and Johanne stopped talking immediately.

'That's fine,' Helen Bentley said. 'I understand. Can I watch the news with you? Do you get CNN here?'

'Would you . . . like any food? I know that Mary's already . . .'

'Are you American?' the President asked, in surprise.

There was something new in her eyes. Up until now she had had a wary, neutral expression, as if she was constantly keeping something back and that way was always on top of the situation. Even yesterday, when Mary had dragged her up from the cellar and she wasn't able to stand upright, there was something strong and proud about her face.

But now there was a glimmer of something that could be fear, and Johanne could not understand why.

'No,' Johanne assured her vigorously. 'I'm Norwegian. Completely Norwegian!'

'But you speak American.'

'I studied in the US. Should I get something for you? Something to eat?'

'Let me guess,' the President said, and the wisp of fear had vanished again. 'Boston.'

She drawled the 'o' out so that it sounded more like an 'a'.

A fleeting smile crossed Johanne's face.

'Well, if there isn't a party here,' Mary muttered as she limped in from the hall with a loaded tray in her hands. 'Not even seven o'clock yet and we're in full swing. Doesn't say anything in my papers about night shifts, you know.'

The President stared at Mary with fascination as she put the tray down on the coffee table.

'Coffee,' said the housekeeper, pointing. 'Pancakes. Eggs. Bacon. Milk. Orange juice. Help yourself.'

She put her hand over her mouth and whispered to Johanne: 'I've seen the thing about pancakes on TV. They always eat pancakes for breakfast. Strange people.'

She shook her head, stroked Ragnhild's hair and pottered back out into the kitchen.

'Is this for you or me?' the President asked and sat down by the food. 'Actually looks like there's enough for three here.'

'Please eat,' Johanne said. 'She'll be offended if everything's not gone when she comes back.'

The President picked up a knife and fork. It seemed she was unsure about how to tackle the robust breakfast. She prodded a pancake that was rolled up with masses of jam and sour cream. Sugar had been sprinkled on the top.

'What's this?' she asked quietly. 'Some kind of crêpe Suzette?'

'They're Norwegian pancakes,' Johanne whispered. 'Mary thinks it's the same kind that Americans eat for breakfast.'

'Mmm. It's good. Really. But very sweet. Who's that?'

Helen Bentley nodded towards the TV screen, where a news programme from the day before was being repeated. NRK and TV2 were still broadcasting special news programmes round the clock. At around one in the morning, they turned the pile around and showed the evening's newscasts in repeat until the first real news at half past seven.

Wencke Bencke was in the studio again. She was having an animated discussion with a retired policeman. He had set himself

336

up as an expert on criminal cases, following a not entirely successful career as a private detective. Both of them had been ferried between the major stations in recent days and they always produced the goods.

They couldn't stand one another.

'She's a . . . writer, in fact.' Johanne grabbed the remote control. 'I'll find CNN,' she mumbled.

The President froze. 'Wait! *Wait!*'

Johanne stopped in surprise and sat there with the remote control in her hand. She looked from the President to the TV screen and back. Helen Bentley sat with her mouth open and her head cocked, deep in concentration.

'Did that lady just say Warren Scifford?' the President whispered.

'What?' Johanne turned up the volume and started to listen.

'. . . and there is absolutely no reason to accuse the FBI of using illegal means,' Wencke Bencke said. 'As I said, I have personally met the man heading the FBI agents who are now working with the Norwegian police, Warren Scifford. He has . . .'

'There,' the President whispered. 'What's she saying?'

'Working with? *Working with?* If Miss Crime Writer here . . .' the retired policeman spat this out as if it was sour milk, 'had any idea of what's happening in this country at the moment, where a foreign police force is just doing as it pleases . . .'

'What are they saying?' the President asked in a sharp tone. 'What are they talking about?'

'They're arguing,' Johanne whispered, trying to listen at the same time.

'About what?'

'Hang on.' Johanne lifted a hand.

'*And I must . . .*'

The presenter had to fight to be heard. 'I'm afraid that's all we have time for, as we are, in fact, already on overtime. I'm sure that this discussion will continue over the coming days and weeks. Good night.'

The titles rolled, the jingle played. The President was still holding her fork with a piece of pancake on it that was dripping jam on to the table. She didn't seem to notice.

'That woman was talking about Warren Scifford,' she repeated, transfixed.

Johanne took one of the serviettes and wiped the table in front of the President.

'Yes,' she said quietly. 'I didn't catch much of the discussion, but they seemed to disagree about how much the FBI . . . They were arguing about . . . well, about whether the FBI is taking liberties on Norwegian soil, as far as I could make out. It has actually been . . . quite a topic in the last twenty-four hours.'

'But . . . *is Warren here*? In Norway?'

Johanne's hand stopped in mid-air. The President was no longer either controlled or majestic. She stared at her.

'Yes . . .'

Johanne didn't know what to do, so she picked up Ragnhild and sat her on her knee. The little girl squirmed and wriggled, but her mother did not let go.

'No,' Ragnhild howled. 'Mummy! Agni down!'

'Do you know him?' Johanne asked, largely because she couldn't think of anything else to say. 'Personally, I mean . . .'

The President didn't answer. She took a couple of deep breaths, before starting to eat again. Slowly and methodically, as if it hurt to chew, she finished off half a pancake and some bacon. Johanne couldn't keep Ragnhild on her knee. She slipped back down to her toys again. Helen Bentley took a long drink of juice, and then poured some milk into her coffee.

'I thought I knew him,' she said and took a sip of coffee.

Her voice was remarkably calm, given that she just seemed to have been in shock. Johanne thought she heard a slight tremor in her voice as Helen Bentley carefully patted down her hair and continued. 'I seem to remember that I could use the Internet. I need a computer, of course. It's time I started to tidy up this miserable affair.'

338

Johanne swallowed. She swallowed again. She opened her mouth to say something, but no sound came out. She noticed that the President was looking at her. Gently she put her hand on Johanne's arm.

'I knew him too, once,' Johanne whispered. 'I thought I knew Warren Scifford too.'

Perhaps it was because Helen Bentley was a stranger. Perhaps it was the knowledge that this woman did not belong here, in Johanne's life, in Oslo or Norway, that made her speak. Madam President would be going home. Today, tomorrow or sometime soon at least. They would never meet again. In a year or two from now, the President would barely remember who Johanne Vik was. Perhaps it was the enormous social, physical and geographical distance between them that made Johanne, finally, after thirteen years of silence, tell the story of how Warren had betrayed her so spectacularly and she had lost the child they were expecting.

When she had finished her story, Helen Bentley had resolved any doubts she might have had. Carefully she pulled Johanne to her. Held her and stroked her back. And when she finally stopped crying, she got up and quietly asked if she could use a computer.

5

It was Abdallah al-Rahman himself who had come up with the name *The Trojan Horse*.

The thought had amused him enormously. Choosing a name was not, strictly speaking, necessary, but it had made it far easier to trick Madam President into leaving her hotel room. In the weeks after it had been announced that the President was to visit Norway in the middle of May, he had applied guerrilla tactics to American intelligence.

Quick in. Quick out.

He had planted information that was fragmentary and insignificant. But it did intimate that something was going to happen, and by carefully using phrases like 'from within', 'unexpected internal attack' and then the mention of a 'horse' in a memo that the CIA found on a corpse that floated ashore in Italy, he had them exactly where he wanted them.

When the information reached Warren Scifford and his men, they took the bait and it became the Trojan Horse, just as he wanted.

Abdallah was back in the office after having gone for a ride. Morning in the desert was one of the most beautiful things he knew. The horse had really gone through its paces, and afterwards he and the mare had bathed in the pond under the palm trees, by the stable. The animal was old, one of the oldest he had, and it felt good to know that she was still fast, supple and lively.

The day had started well. He had already finished his regular business. Answered all his emails, had a telephone conference. Read a board report that told him nothing of any interest. As early morning changed to mid-morning, he noticed his concentration flagging. He told reception that he was not to be disturbed and logged out of his computer.

CNN news was playing, without sound, on a plasma screen on one of the walls.

On the opposite wall was an enormous map of the US.

A large number of coloured pinheads were spread out over the country. He sauntered over to the map and zigzagged between them with his finger. He stopped at Los Angeles.

That was perhaps Eric Ariyoshi, Abdallah al-Rahman mused, and gave the pinhead a slight caress. Eric was a Sansei, third-generation American-Japanese. He was nearly forty-five and had no family. His wife left him four weeks after they married, when he lost his job in 1983, and since then he had lived with his parents. But Eric Ariyoshi had not let himself go under. He did odd jobs wherever he could until, at the age of thirty, he finished evening classes and became a qualified cable engineer.

But the real change came when his father died.

The old man had been detained on the west coast during the Second World War. He was only a boy at the time. Together with his parents and two younger sisters, he had spent three years in a prisoner-of-war camp. Only a handful of the detainees had actually done anything wrong. Most had been good Americans since they were born. His mother, Eric's grandmother, died before they were released in 1945. Eric's father never got over it. When he grew up, he settled on the outskirts of Los Angeles and ran a small flower shop that only just managed to keep him, his wife and their three children alive. And he filed a suit against the American state. It was a long case, which became very expensive.

When Eric's father died in 1994, it was discovered that all he had left behind was crippling debt. The small house that his son had used all his income on for the past fifteen years was still registered in his father's name. The bank repossessed the house, and Eric once again had to start from scratch. The suit that his father had filed against the American state for unjust internment never came to anything. The only thing that old Daniel Ariyoshi had got from sticking to the rules and listening to increasingly expensive lawyers was a life of bitterness that ended in ruin.

It said in the report that it had been easy to persuade Eric.

Naturally he wanted money, lots of money, given how poor he was. But he had also earned it.

Abdallah's finger moved on, from pinhead to pinhead.

Unlike Osama bin Laden, he didn't want to use suicide bombers and fanatics to attack a US that they hated and had never understood.

Instead he had built up a silent army of Americans. Of dissatisfied, betrayed, repressed, conned Americans, ordinary people who belonged to that country. Many of them had been born there, all of them lived there and the country was theirs. They were American citizens, but the US had never repaid them with anything other than betrayal and defeat.

'The spring of our discontent,' Abdallah whispered.

His finger stopped by a green pinhead outside Tucson, Arizona. It might represent Jorge Gonzales, whose youngest son had been killed by the sheriff's assistant during a bank raid. The boy was only six years old, and just happened to be cycling past. The sheriff made a short statement to the local press saying that his excellent assistant had been certain that the boy was one of the robbers. And that everything had happened very fast.

Little Antonio only measured four foot two, and had been six metres from the policeman when he was shot. He was sitting on a green boy's bike, wearing a slightly too big T-shirt with Spiderman on the back.

No one was punished for the incident.

No one was even charged.

The father, who had worked at Wal-Mart since he came to the country of his dreams from Mexico as a thirteen-year-old, never got over his son's death and the lack of respect shown by the people who should have protected him and his family. When he was offered a sum of money that would allow him to move back to his homeland as a wealthy man in return for doing something that wasn't at all frightening, he grabbed the chance with both hands.

And so it continued.

Each pinhead represented yet another fate, another life. Abdallah had, of course, never met any of them. They had no idea who he was, and never would do either. And the thirty or so men who had worked for him since 2002, finding and recruiting this army of broken dreams, equally had no idea where the orders and money came from.

A red reflection from the plasma screen made Abdallah turn round.

The picture showed a fire.

He went back to his desk and turned up the volume.

'... *in this barn outside Fargo. This is the second time in less than twelve hours that illegal petrol stores have caused fires in the area. The local authorities claim that ...*'

The Americans had started hoarding.

Abdallah sat down, put his feet up on the huge desk and grabbed a bottle of water.

With petrol prices rising by the hour, and disconcerting news stories about increasingly agitated diplomatic rhetoric in the Middle East, people were rushing out to get fuel. It was still night in the US, but the pictures showed queues of irascible drivers with cars full of barrels and buckets and plastic containers. One reporter who was standing in the way when a pick-up finally made it to the pumps had to jump to one side to avoid being mowed down.

'They can't deny us the right to buy petrol,' a grossly over-weight farmer shouted into the camera. 'When the authorities can't guarantee reasonable prices, we've got the right to take matters into our own hands.'

'What are you going to do now?' asked the interviewer while the camera zoomed in on two men fighting over a jerrycan.

'First I'm going to fill all of these,' the farmer shouted and waved his hand at one of five oil barrels on the back of his truck. 'And then I'm going to empty them into my new silo. And I'm going to carry on doing that all night and tomorrow morning and for as long as there's a darned drop left in the state . . .'

The sound stopped and the reporter stared into the camera, confused. The producer quickly cut back to the studio.

Abdallah drank the water. He emptied the bottle and then looked over at the map with all the pins in it, all his soldiers.

They had nothing to do with oil and petrol.

A large number of them worked in cable TV.

Many of them were employed by Sears or Wal-Mart.

The rest were computer people: young hackers who could be persuaded to do anything for a little money, and more experienced programmers. Some of them had lost their jobs because they were deemed to be too old. There was no place in the industry for good, loyal workers who had learnt about computers back in the day when you used punch cards and who had had to work their socks off to keep up with developments.

But the most beautiful thing of all, thought Abdallah as he reached for the photograph of his dead brother, Rashid, was that none of the pinheads knew about the others. The role that each and every one of them would play was, in itself, small. A minor detail, an offence that was worth the risk, given the payment that would follow.

But combined, the impact would be fatal.

An extraordinary number of headends – installations where cable TV signals were received and distributed to subscribers – would be affected; the generally unmanned stations had proved to be an easier target than Abdallah had imagined. Signal amplifiers and cables would be sabotaged to such an extent that it would take weeks, maybe even months, to correct it.

In the meantime, the anger would grow.

And things would get worse when the security systems and cash registers in the largest supermarket chains ceased to function. The attack on the supermarkets would be carried out in stages, with lightning attacks in selected areas, followed up by new incidents in other areas, unpredictable and strategically unreadable, like any good guerrilla warfare.

The whole invisible army of Americans, spread over the entire continent, unaware of each other's existence, knew exactly what to do when the signal was given.

And it would happen tomorrow.

It had taken Abdallah more than a week to work out the final strategy. He had sat here in this office, with long lists of recruits in front of him. For seven days he had moved them round on the map, estimated, calculated and evaluated the impact and maximum effect. When he had finally written it all down on paper, all that was left to do was to call Tom O'Reilly to Riyadh.

And William Smith. And David Coach.

He had summoned the three couriers. They had been in the palace at the same time, without knowing about the others. They had each been sent back to Europe in a separate plane, at thirty-minute intervals. Abdallah smiled at the thought, and lightly stroked the picture of his brother.

He could never be certain of anything in this world, but by burning three of his safest bridges, he could be fairly sure that at least one of the letters would reach an American postbox.

He had used three couriers, and all three had died just after they had posted the letters that all said the same thing. The envelopes were addressed to the same person and the contents would be meaningless to anyone other than the receiver, if they should by any chance fall into the wrong hands.

And that was the weakest link in his plan: they all had the same addressee.

Like every good general, Abdallah knew his strengths and his weaknesses. His greatest strengths were his patience, his capital and the fact that he was invisible. But the latter was also his most vulnerable point. He was dependent on operating at many levels, using straw men and electronic detours, through covert manoeuvres and, occasionally, false identities.

Abdallah al-Rahman was a respected businessman. Most of his operations were legitimate, and he used the best brokers in Europe and the US. He was swathed by a mysterious inaccessibility, but nothing and no one had ever blemished his reputation as an unmitigated capitalist, investor and stock-market speculator.

And that was the way he wanted things to stay.

But he needed one ally. One person who knew.

Operation Trojan Horse was too complicated for everything to be controlled from a distance. There were to be no traces that could lead back to anything that might involve Abdallah, so he had not been to the States for more than ten months.

At the end of June 2004, he'd had his meeting with the Democrats' presidential candidate. She had been positive. She was impressed by Arabian Port Management. He could tell. The meeting had run on for half an hour longer than planned because she wanted to know more. On the flight home to Saudi Arabia, he had for the first time since his brother's death thought that it perhaps wouldn't be necessary to implement the project after all. The thirty years of planning, positioning and developing a network of sleeping agents all over the US might in fact go to waste. He had leant his head against the window of his private jet and looked out at the clouds below, which were an intense pink colour in the last rays of the sun they were flying away from. He had told himself that it didn't matter, that life was full of investments that gave nothing back. Taking over the majority of America's ports would make it all worth it.

She had as good as promised him the contract.

Then she had just dropped him, so she would win.

All the letters would go to one recipient, a man who would then set into action Abdallah's detailed plans. Nothing must go wrong, and Abdallah had to take the risk of making direct contact. He trusted his helper. They had known each other for a long time. It bothered him sometimes that this last remaining, fragile link between him and the US would have to be eliminated as soon as Trojan Horse had been implemented.

Abdallah rubbed the glass in the frame carefully with his shirtsleeve, then put the photograph of Rashid back down on the desk.

He did trust Fayed Muffasa, but on the other hand, he hated having to rely on another living soul.

6

'Well, isn't this a Kodak moment?'

President Helen Bentley was sitting with Ragnhild on her knee. The little girl was asleep. Her blonde head had flopped back, her mouth was wide open and you could see her eyes moving from side to side behind her paper-thin eyelids. At regular intervals she produced little grunts.

'There was certainly no need for you to . . .' Johanne stretched out her arms to pick up the child.

'Just let her be.' Helen Bentley smiled. 'I need a break.'

She had been sitting in front of the computer screen for three hours. The situation was serious, to put it mildly. Far worse than she had imagined. The fear of what might happen when the New York Stock Exchange opened in a few hours' time was enormous, and it seemed that the media had been more concerned about the economy than politics over the past twenty-four hours. As if it was possible to make such a differentiation, Helen Bentley thought to herself. All the TV stations and Internet papers were still reporting regularly from Oslo to keep the public updated on the President's disappearance. But it still seemed that Helen Bentley and her fate had actually been pushed out on to the periphery of people's consciousness. The focus was now on essential things, like oil and petrol and work. The tumult in more than a few places was close to rioting and the first two suicides on Wall Street were now a fact. The Saudi Arabian and Iranian governments were united in their fury. Her own Secretary of State had had to reassure the world several times that rumours of a link between the two countries and the kidnapping of the President were unfounded.

The words from his speech the night before were still hanging in the air and the conflict was escalating.

348

She had for a brief moment surfed public pages on the Internet. But she knew that sooner or later she would have to access websites that would make alarm bells ring in the White House, so she would wait to do that until it was absolutely necessary. The temptation to set up a Hotmail address and send a reassuring message to Christopher's private inbox was almost overwhelming at times. But thankfully she had had the willpower to withstand it.

There was still far too much that she didn't understand.

The fact that Warren had double-crossed her was in itself unbelievable. But her life experience had taught her that people took the most incredible gambles sometimes. And if God's ways were mysterious, they could in no way compete with those of mortal beings.

It was the bit about the child that she couldn't work out.

The letter that Jeffrey Hunter had shown her early that morning, which now felt like a lifetime ago, had said that they knew. That the Trojans knew about the child. Or something to that effect. She couldn't for the life of her remember the exact wording. As she read the letter, an image of her daughter's biological mother had flashed in front of her: the red-coated figure in the rain with eyes wide open, the plea for help that was never answered.

Little Ragnhild tried to turn.

She was a beautiful child. Fair, wispy hair and white teeth behind wet red lips. Her eyelashes were long and beautifully curved.

She looked like Billie.

Helen Bentley smiled and made the child more comfortable. This really was a strange place. It was so quiet here. In the distance, she could hear the roar of the world from which she had hidden. There were five people in here, and they chose not to speak.

The odd housekeeper was sitting by the window, crocheting. Every now and then she smacked her lips noisily and looked out at the enormous oak tree. Then she seemed to talk herself round again in a silent mumble, and focused on her bright pink handiwork.

The child's mother was a fascinating woman. When she told the story about Warren, it felt like she had never told it to anyone else before, which gave Helen a feeling of shared destiny. Paradoxically, she thought, since her secret was about her own betrayal, whereas Johanne had very definitely been betrayed.

Us women and our damned secrets, she thought to herself. Why is it like that? Why do we feel ashamed whether we have reason to or not? Where does it come from, that crushing feeling of always carrying the blame?

She couldn't work out the woman in the wheelchair at all.

Right now, she was sitting on the other side of the kitchen table, with a paper on her knees and a cup of coffee in her hand. But she didn't seem to be reading the paper. It was still open at the same place that it had been about quarter of an hour ago.

Helen couldn't work out who belonged to whom in this home. For some reason, it didn't matter. Her strong need to control would normally have made the situation unbearable. But instead she now felt calm, as if the unclear constellations made her own absurd situation more natural somehow.

They hadn't asked her a single question since she woke up at daybreak. Not one.

It was unbelievable.

The child on her lap sat up, drunk with sleep. For a moment she caught the smell of sweet milky breath before the child looked at her suspiciously and said: 'Mummy. Want Mummy.'

The housekeeper was up faster than she dreamed was possible for such a scrawny, lame person.

'You come to your Auntie Mary, darlin'. Let's go look for Ida's toys. Let the ladies sit here in peace.'

Ragnhild laughed and held up her arms.

They must come here quite a lot, Helen Bentley thought. The little girl looked like she adored the old scarecrow. They disappeared into the sitting room. The sound of the child chatting and the woman scolding faded into the background and there was silence. They must have gone into another room.

She turned back to the computer. Somehow she had to find the answers she was looking for. She had to keep searching. She must be able to find what she was looking for somewhere in the chaos of information that swirled around in cyberspace, before she let anyone know where she was and got the world back on its feet.

But she wouldn't find the answer on an ordinary computer. She knew that. There was nothing in the outside world that could help before she logged on to her own website.

She caught herself staring at her hands. The skin was dry and she had broken a nail. Her wedding ring seemed to be too big. It was loose and felt like it would slip off when she caught it between two fingers and turned it. Slowly she raised her head.

The woman in the wheelchair was looking straight at her. She had the most incredible eyes that Helen Bentley had ever seen. They were icy blue, almost bleached of colour, and yet at the same time they gave the impression of being deep and dark. It was impossible to read her face: no questions no demands. Nothing. The woman just sat there looking at her. It made her feel small and she tried to look away, but it wasn't possible.

'They tricked me,' Helen Bentley said in a quiet voice. 'They knew what they had to do to make me panic. To make me go with them, willingly.'

'Do you want to tell me what happened?' the woman asked and started to fold the newspaper carefully.

'I think I have to,' Helen Bentley said, and took as deep a breath as she could. 'I don't have any other choice.'

351

7

'And that's all you have to say?'

The head of intelligence, Peter Salhus, looked dissatisfied and scratched his cropped head. Adam Stubo shrugged and tried to sit as comfortably as he could on the desperately uncomfortable chair. The TV on the filing cabinet was switched on. The volume was turned down and was distorted. Adam had already seen the same clip four times.

'I give up,' he said. 'After that episode last night, it's not been possible to get so much as a peep out of Warren Scifford. I'm almost starting to believe the rumours myself, that the FBI are doing their own thing. Someone in the canteen even said that they had broken into a flat during the night. In Huseby. Or . . . maybe it was a villa.'

'Just rumours,' Peter Salhus muttered and pulled open a drawer. 'They might be arrogant and behaving badly, but they know they can't be complete cowboys. We would have received a full report if it was true.'

'God knows. I just think it's all . . . so frustrating.'

'What? The fact that the Americans are more or less doing as they please on someone else's territory?'

'No. Yes, actually. But . . . Thank you!'

He took the red box that Peter Salhus offered him. With the utmost care, as if he was accepting the most treasured gift, he selected a thick cigar and stared at it for a few seconds before running it under his nose.

'CAO Maduro Number 4,' he said solemnly. 'The Sopranos' favoured cigar. But . . . can we smoke here?'

'Emergency situation,' Salhus said briskly, taking out a cutter and a large box of matches. 'And with all due respect, I don't care.'

Adam laughed and prepared the cigar with a practised hand before lighting up.

'You were about to say something,' Peter Salhus continued and leant back in his chair.

The cigar smoke rose up in soft circles to the ceiling. It was only around mid-morning, but Adam suddenly felt weary, as if he'd had a big meal.

'Everything,' he muttered and blew a smoke ring towards the ceiling.

'What?'

'I'm frustrated about everything. We've got God knows how many men rooting around trying to find out who's kidnapped the President and how they did it, and that just doesn't seem to matter.'

'Of course it matters, it—'

'Have you been watching the box recently?' Adam nodded towards the television. 'It's all power politics, the whole thing.'

'What did you expect? That the case would be just like any other missing-person case?'

'No. But why are we working our backsides off to find losers like Gerhard Skrøder and that Pakistani who shits his pants if we so much as look at him, when the Americans have already decided what happened?'

Salhus looked like he was enjoying himself. Without answering, he put his cigar in his mouth and his feet on the table.

'What I mean is . . .' Adam started, looking around for something to use as an ashtray, 'last night, three men sat for five hours trying to piece together the puzzle to establish when Jeffrey Hunter hid himself away in the ventilation shaft. It was complicated. Lots of loose ends: when was the presidential suite last inspected? When did the sniffers come in? When was it vacuumed afterwards, because the President is allergic to dogs? When were the cameras switched on and off? When did . . . You get the idea. They did finally manage to get it all to fit. But what's the point?'

'The point is that we have a case to solve.'

'But the Americans don't give a damn.'

He looked sceptically at the plastic cup that Salhus was holding out for him, then he shrugged and tipped the ash off into it.

'Oslo Police are hauling in one crook after another,' he continued, 'and they all seem to have been involved in the kidnapping. They've found the second driver. They've even managed to get hold of one of the president lookalikes. None of them can tell us anything about the job other than that it was well paid and they have no idea where the money came from. We'll have the cells full of bloody kidnappers before the night's over!'

Peter Salhus roared with laughter.

'But are they at all interested?' Adam asked rhetorically and leant forward on the desk. 'Does Drammensveien show the slightest bit of interest in what we're doing? No, not at all. They're busy running around doing their own thing, playing cowboys and Indians, while the rest of the world is going to the dogs. I've had it. I give up.'

He took another draw on his cigar.

'You have a reputation for being phlegmatic,' Salhus commented. 'You're supposed to be the calmest man in the NCIS. But I have to say that that all seems to be rather unfounded. What does your wife have to say about it all?'

'My wife? Johanne?'

'Do you have more than one?'

'Why should she have anything to say about it?'

'As far I know, she's got a PhD in criminology and some experience with the FBI,' Salhus said, raising his hands in defence. 'Would have thought she was qualified to have an opinion, if nothing else.'

'It's possible,' Adam said, staring at the cigar ash that had fallen on his trouser leg. 'But I actually don't know what she thinks. I've no idea what she thinks of this case.'

'Well, that's the way it is,' Peter Salhus said lightly, pushing the plastic cup even closer to Adam. 'We've barely been home in the past couple of days, any of us.'

'That's the way it is,' Adam repeated in a monotone and stubbed out his cigar even though there was still quite a lot left, as if the stolen pleasure was too good to be true. 'That's the way it is for us all.'

It was twenty to eleven, and he still hadn't heard a thing from Johanne.

8

Johanne had no idea what time it was. She felt as if she had been transported to a parallel universe. The shock she had felt when Mary appeared with the half-dead President the night before had changed into a feeling of being completely disconnected from the world outside the flat in Krusesgate. She had watched the news, but she hadn't even been out to buy the papers.

The flat was like a fortress. No one came in and no one went out. It was as if Hanne's resolve to honour the President's request not to raise the alarm had created a moat around their existence. Johanne really had to concentrate to remember whether it was morning or evening.

'It has to be something completely different,' she said suddenly. 'You're focusing on the wrong secret.'

She had been silent for a long time. She had quietly listened to the other two women. She had followed their conversation, which was at times eager and at other times hesitant and pensive, for so long without saying anything that Helen Bentley and Hanne Wilhelmsen had almost forgotten she was there.

Hanne raised an eyebrow. Helen Bentley frowned, a puzzled expression that made the eye on the bruised side of her face close.

'What do you mean?' Hanne asked.

'I think you're thinking about the wrong secret.'

'I don't understand,' Helen Bentley said, leaning back and crossing her arms, as if she had been offended in some way. 'I hear what you're saying, but I don't understand.'

Johanne pushed her empty coffee cup to one side and tucked her hair behind her ear. For a moment she sat staring at a mark on the table, with her mouth half open, without breathing, as if she didn't really know where to begin.

'We humans are deluded,' she said finally, and added with a disarming smile, 'We all are, in some way or other. And perhaps especially . . . women.'

She paused to think again. She cocked her head and twisted a lock of hair round her finger. The two other women still looked sceptical, but they were listening. When Johanne started to speak again, her voice was lower than usual.

'You said that you were woken by Jeffrey, who you knew. Obviously you were very tired. Judging by what you've said, you were pretty confused at first. *Very* confused, you said. Which isn't in the slightest bit strange. The situation must have felt very . . . extraordinary.'

Johanne took off her glasses and peered short-sightedly at the room.

'He showed you a letter,' she continued. 'You don't remember the exact contents. What you remember is that you panicked.'

'No,' Helen Bentley said decisively. 'I remember that—'

'Hold on,' Johanne said, raising a hand. 'Please. Hear me out first. That's actually what you said. You keep stressing that you panicked. It's as if you're hopping over a link. It's as if you . . . you're so ashamed that you couldn't deal with the situation that you can't even reconstruct it in your mind.'

She could have sworn that she saw a blush pass over the President's face.

'Helen,' Johanne said, and reached her hand over towards the other woman.

It was the first time she had addressed the President by her first name. Her hand lay palm up, untouched, on the table, so she withdrew it again.

'You are the President of America,' she said in a gentle voice. 'You have literally been in the wars before.'

The hint of a smile crept over Helen Bentley's face.

'To panic in a situation like that,' Johanne continued, drawing breath, 'is not particularly, well, president-like. Not in your view. You're being too harsh on yourself, Helen. You don't need to be.

357

To be honest, it's not very helpful. Even a person like you has weaknesses. Everyone does. The only disaster in this situation was that you thought they had found yours. Why don't we try to go back a bit further? Let's see what happened in the seconds *before* you felt the world tumbling around your ears.'

'I read the letter from Warren,' Helen Bentley said succinctly.

'Yes, and it said something about a child. You don't remember any more than that.'

'Yes, I do. It said that they knew. That the Trojans knew. About the child.'

Johanne polished her glasses with a serviette. There was obviously some grease on them, because when she put her them on again, she saw the world through a veiled filter.

'Helen,' she tried again, 'I appreciate that you can't tell us what all this Trojan stuff is about. I also respect the fact that you want to keep your secret about the child to yourself, the secret that you thought they knew about and that made you . . . well, panic. But could it . . . might there . . .'

She hesitated and pulled a face.

'You're getting yourself in a tangle now,' Hanne said.

'Yes.'

Johanne looked at the President. 'Could it be that you automatically thought about your secret?' She was talking quickly now so that she wouldn't lose her thread. 'You thought about that one because it's the worst. The most shameful.'

'I'm really not following you here,' Helen Bentley said.

Johanne got up and went over to the sink. She put a drop of washing-up liquid on her glasses and let the hot water run while she rubbed the lenses with her thumb.

'I have a daughter who's nearly eleven,' she said, drying her glasses meticulously. 'She's mentally handicapped, but we don't know what it is. She's my . . . she's my Achilles heel. I feel that I never understand her well enough. That I'm not good enough for her, good enough *with* her. She makes me so incredibly vulnerable. She makes me so . . . deluded. If I overhear a conversation about poor parenting or neglect, I automatically think that they're talking about me. If I see a TV programme about some miracle cure for autism in the US, I feel like I'm a bad mother because I haven't looked for anything like that. The programme becomes an accusation against me personally, and I lie awake at night and feel terrible.'

Both Helen Bentley and Hanne were smiling now. Johanne sat down at the table again.

'There you go,' she said, returning their smiles. 'You recognise yourselves in that. That's what we're like, all of us. To a greater or lesser extent. And basically, Helen, I think that you thought of your secret because it's *your* Achilles heel. But that's not what the letter was referring to. It was something else. Another secret, maybe. Or another child.'

'Another child,' the President repeated, nonplussed.

'Yes. You insist that no one, absolutely no one, can know about . . . about this incident in the distant past. Not even your husband. So then it's logical that . . .'

Johanne leant forward over the table.

'Hanne, you were a detective for many years. Isn't it reasonable to assume that when something is impossible . . . well . . . it is in fact impossible! And then you have to look for another explanation.'

'The abortion!' Helen Bentley exclaimed.

The angel that passed through the room took its time. Helen Bentley stared into space. Her mouth was open and her frown was deep. She didn't seem to be in anyway frightened or ashamed, or, for that matter, embarrassed.

She was concentrating, hard.

'You've had an abortion,' Johanne said eventually, very slowly, after what felt like minutes of silence. 'That's never come out. Not that I'm aware of. And I keep my eyes and ears open, to be honest.'

There was a light chiming sound. Someone was ringing the front door bell.

'What should we do?' Johanne whispered.

Helen Bentley froze.

'Wait,' Hanne said. 'Mary, you open the door. It'll be fine.'

All three held their breath, partly due to the suspense and partly because they wanted to hear the conversation between Mary and whoever it was who had rung the bell. None of them could make out the words.

About half a minute later the door closed. A second later, Mary was in the kitchen, holding Ragnhild on her hip.

'Who was it?' Hanne asked.

'One of the neighbours.' Mary sniffed and picked up a glass of water from the worktop.

'And what did one of the neighbours want?'

'To tell us our storeroom was open. Bugger. Forgot to go back down last night. Lordy, couldn't just drop the lady for something as mosaic as locking the storeroom, could I?'

'And what did you say to the neighbour?'

'Thanks for the information. And when he started going on about one of the doors down there having been busted, and did I know anything about it, I told him to mind his own business. That's all.'

Then she put down her glass and disappeared.

'What? What was all that about?' Helen Bentley asked eagerly.

'Nothing,' Hanne said, waving her hand. 'Just something about a cellar door being open. Forget it.'

'There *was* another secret,' Johanne pressed.

'I've never thought of it as a secret,' Helen Bentley said in a calm voice. The idea seemed to surprise her. 'Just something that was no one else's business. It was a long time ago. Summer 1971. When I was twenty-one, a student. It was long before I met Christopher. He knows about it, of course. So it's not really a . . . secret. Not in the truest sense.'

'But an abortion . . .' Johanne ran her finger across the table and repeated: 'An abortion! Wouldn't that have been disastrous for your campaign if it got out? And couldn't it still make life very uncomfortable for you? The abortion issue creates a great and virulent divide in the States, to put it mildly . . .'

'I actually don't think it does,' Helen Bentley said firmly. 'And in any case, I've always been prepared for it. Everyone knows that I'm pro-choice. It's true that my position did almost cost me the election . . .'

'That's the understatement of the day,' Johanne said. 'Bush did what he could to knock you on that one.'

'Yes, it's true. But it all turned out well, mainly because I managed to win lots of votes from women who are . . . how should I put it, less fortunate. Surveys show that in fact I had support from an impressive number of women who weren't even registered as voters before. And I made a point of the fact that I'm strongly against late abortions, which made it more palatable for even the anti-abortionists. But I was always quite clear that there was a possibility that my own abortion would become public knowledge. It was a risk I had to take. I'm not ashamed of it. I was far too young to have a child. I was in my second year at college. I didn't love the father. The abortion was carried out legally; I was seven weeks pregnant and I went to New York. I was and am a supporter of a woman's right to have an abortion within the first trimester, and can stand up for what I did.'

She took a deep breath, and Johanne noticed a tiny tremble in Helen Bentley's voice as she continued.

'But I paid a high price. It made me sterile. As you know, my daughter Billie is adopted. There's no discrepancy here between words and reality, and at the end of the day, that's what counts for us politicians.'

'But I'm sure there are some people who would think it was dynamite,' Johanne said.

'Definitely,' Helen Bentley agreed. 'Plenty, I'm sure. As you said, abortion is something that splits the US in two, and it's an incredibly sensitive issue that will never be resolved. If it did become known that I'd had an abortion, I would certainly have to work for my money. Like I said, I—'

'Who knows about it?'

'Who . . .'

She thought about it, furrowed her brow.

'No one,' she said hesitantly. 'Well, Christopher, of course. I told him before we got married. And my best friend at the time, Karen, she knew. She was fantastic and a great support. She died a year later in a car accident. When I was in Vietnam and . . . I can't imagine that Karen would have told anyone. She was . . .'

'What about the hospital? There must be records somewhere.'

'The hospital burnt down in 1972 or '73. Pro-life activists went a bit far during a demonstration. It was before the technology revolution, so I assume . . .'

'The records aren't there,' Johanne said. 'Your friend's no longer here.'

She ticked them off on her fingers and paused before daring to ask her next question. 'What about the father? Did he know?'

'Yes, of course. He . . .'

She broke off. There was an unfamiliar gentleness about her, a softness to her mouth, and her eyes narrowed, making all her wrinkles disappear. She looked years younger.

'He wanted to get married,' she said. 'He really wanted to have the child. But when he realised that I was serious, he supported me in every way. He came with me to New York.'

She looked up. The tears spilled over. She made no attempt to dry her eyes.

'I didn't love him. I don't even think I was in love. But he was the kindest . . . I think he is the kindest man I have ever met. Thoughtful. Wise. He promised me that he would never tell anyone. I can't imagine that he would ever break his promise. And if he has, he must have changed radically.'

'It does happen,' Johanne whispered.

'Not with him,' Helen Bentley said. 'He was a man of honour, if ever I met one. I'd known him for nearly two years before I got pregnant.'

'It's thirty-four years ago,' Hanne said. 'A lot can happen to a person in that time.'

'Not him,' Helen Bentley repeated and shook her head.

'What was he called?' Hanne asked. 'Can you remember?'

'Ali Shaeed Muffasa,' Helen Bentley said. 'I think he changed his name later. To a more . . . English-sounding one. But to me, he was just Ali, the kindest boy in the world.'

9

At last, it was half past seven in the morning. Luckily it was a Thursday and both girls had to be at school early. Louise was going to play chess before her classes started and Catherine was going to do circuit training. They asked after their uncle, but believed it when their father hinted that he had had a bit too much to drink the night before and was sleeping it off.

The house in Rural Route # 4 in Farmington, Maine, was never quiet. The woodwork creaked. Most of the doors were warped. Some of them were difficult to open, whereas others hung loose in their frames and bumped and slammed in the continual draught from the windows that were not properly insulated. The great maple trees at the back were planted so close to the house that the branches tapped on the roof with the slightest hint of wind. It was as if the house was alive.

Al Muffet didn't need to tiptoe around any more. He knew that no one would turn up before the postman came by on his round. And that wasn't normally until two. After taking the girls to school, Al had dropped by the office. He told his secretary that he wasn't feeling well. Sore throat and slight temperature, so they would unfortunately have to cancel today's appointments. She had looked at him with sad eyes and great sympathy, and told him to get better.

He had picked up what he needed, coughed a goodbye and gone home.

'Are you comfortable?'

Al Muffet looked over at his brother. His arms were fastened to the head of the bed with masking tape around each wrist. His feet were tied together with a rope that was then coiled around one of the posts at the foot of the bed, and tightened into great knots. Al had put a piece of grey sticky tape over his brother's mouth.

'Mmffmm,' his brother said, shaking his head frenetically. The sound was muffled by the face cloth that was held in place by the tape.

Al Muffet opened the curtains and the morning light poured in. The dust in the guest room danced over the worn wooden floor. He smiled and turned towards his brother on the bed.

'You're fine. You barely woke up when I injected a sedative into your butt last night. You were so easy to overpower that I almost didn't recognise you, Fayed. Once upon a time it was you who was the fighter. Not me.'

'Mmmfff!'

There was a wooden chair by the window. It was old and rickety, and the seat had been worn by a century of use. It had come with the house. When Al Muffet bought the house, it had been full of old, beautiful things that had helped the family to settle in faster than could have been hoped.

He pulled the chair over to the bed and sat down.

'This,' he said, calmly, holding a syringe in front of his brother's eyes, which stared back at him, wide with disbelief, 'this is a lot more dangerous than what I gave you last night. This, you see . . .'

He pushed the plunger down slowly until a couple of fine drops came out of the thin needle.

'This is ketobemidone, an effective and strong opioid preparation. Very effective, in fact. And here I've got . . .' he squinted and held the syringe up to the light, 'one hundred and fifty milligrams. In other words, a lethal dose.'

Fayed rolled his eyes and tried unsuccessfully to pull free his hands.

'And this,' Al continued, unperturbed, holding up another syringe from the bag he had put down on the floor beside him, 'is Naloxone, the antidote.'

He put the second syringe down on the bedside table and pushed it out of reach, just to be on the safe side.

'I'm going to undo your gag soon,' he explained and tried to

365

catch his brother's eye. 'But first I'm going to give you some of the morphine. You'll feel the effects very quickly. Your blood pressure and pulse will fall. You'll feel ill. You might have problems breathing. After that, it's up to you. You can either answer my questions, or I'll give you more. And so we'll continue. Very simple, isn't it? When you've given me the information I need, I'll give you the antidote. But only then. Do you understand?'

His brother twisted and turned desperately on the bed. There were tears in his eyes. Al noticed that his pyjama bottoms were wet around the crotch.

'And one more thing,' Al said as he injected the needle into his brother's thigh, straight through the fabric of his pyjamas. 'You can scream and shout as much as you like, but it's a waste of time. It's a good mile to the next neighbour. And he's away. It's a weekday, so no one will be out walking. Forget it. There now . . .'

He withdrew the needle and checked how much he had injected. He nodded, satisfied, and put the syringe down with the other one on the bedside table, then pulled the gag off in one go. Fayed tried to spit the face cloth out, but had to retch and turned his head to one side. Al pulled the cloth out with two fingers.

Fayed gasped for air. He sobbed and was obviously trying to say something, but all he managed to do was hawk and retch.

'We haven't got much time now,' Al said. 'So you should answer as fast as you can.'

He licked his lips and paused for thought.

'Is it true that Mother thought you were me before she died?' he asked.

Fayed just managed to nod.

'Did she tell you something that you knew was meant for my ears only?'

His brother had pulled himself together now and was calmer. It was as if he had finally understood that there was no point in trying to break free. He lay completely still for a moment. Only his mouth was moving. It looked like he was trying to produce

366

some moisture after having had the cloth in his mouth for several hours.

'Here,' Al said and held a glass of water to his lips.

Fayed drank. He took several sips. Then he gave a deep cough and spat water, snot, phlegm and loose threads straight into his brother's face.

'Fuck you,' he said hoarsely, and leant his head back.

'Hmm, you're not being very sensible here,' Al said and dried his face with his sleeve.

Fayed said nothing. He seemed to be thinking, assessing what he needed to do to negotiate a deal.

'We'll try again,' Al said. 'Did Mother say something to you about my life because she thought you were me?'

Fayed still didn't answer. But at least he lay still. The morphine had started to work. His pupils suddenly dilated visibly. Al went over to the chest of drawers by the bathroom door, opened the coded suitcase and pulled Fayed's Filofax from under the clothes. He turned to the year planner for 2002 and pulled it out with a tug.

'Here,' he said and went back over to the bed. 'Here's the date Mother died. And what have you written there, Fayed? On the day Mother died, when you were sitting with her?' He held the page up for his brother, who turned his head away.

'June 1971, New York, is what you've written. What does that date mean to you? Did Mother tell you? Was Mother talking about that day when you were sitting with her?'

Still no answer.

'You know what,' Al said in a muted voice as he waved the calendar around. 'Dying from a morphine overdose is not as pleasant as people might think. Can you feel your lungs struggling? Can you feel that it's harder to breathe?'

His brother snarled and tried to tense his body like a bridge, but didn't have the power.

'Mother was the only one who knew,' Al said. 'But she didn't judge me, Fayed. Ever. It was hard for her to accept my secret, but she never used it against me. Mother was my soulmate. She could have been yours too, if you'd behaved differently. You could at least have tried to be part of the family. Instead you did what you could not to belong.'

'I never did belong,' Fayed wheezed. 'You made sure of that.'

He was pale now. He lay completely still and closed his eyes.

'Me? Me? It was me who . . .'

He resolutely took the syringe of morphine and injected another ten milligrams into Fayed's thigh muscle.

'We haven't got time for this. What's going to happen, Fayed? Why are you here? Why have you come to see me after all these years, and *what the hell have you used the information about Helen's abortion for?*'

It had started to look as if Fayed was really frightened. He tried to gasp for breath, but his muscles wouldn't obey. A white froth appeared on his lips, as if he didn't even have the capacity to swallow his own spit.

'Help me,' he said. 'You have to help me. I can't . . .'

'Answer my questions.'

'Help me. I can't . . . Everything . . . according to plan.'

'Plan? What plan? Fayed, what plan are you talking about?'

He was about to die. It was obvious. Al felt hot. He noticed that his hands were shaking as he grabbed the syringe with Naloxone and got it ready.

'Fayed,' he said and put his free hand under his brother's chin so he could force him to look at him. 'You really are in trouble now. I have the antidote here. Just tell me one thing. One thing! Why did you come here? Why did you come to me?'

'The letters,' Fayed mumbled.

His eyes looked completely dead now.

'The letters are coming here. If anything goes wrong . . .'

He stopped breathing. Al gave him a good thump on the chest. Fayed's lungs made another attempt to defy death.

'I'll pull you down with me,' he said. 'You were the one they loved.'

Al grabbed a knife from his bag and cut the tape that bound Fayed's right arm to the headboard. He had injected the morphine straight into Fayed's muscle, but now he needed a vein. He slowly emptied the antidote into a blue vein in his brother's lower arm. Then quickly, so he wouldn't lose heart again, he taped his arm back to the headboard. He got up and took a few steps. Now he couldn't hold back the tears.

'Fucking hell! *Fucking hell!* All I ever wanted in my life was peace and quiet. No quarrelling! No fuss! I found this little backwater where everything was going well for me and the girls, and then you have to come and . . .'

He was sobbing now. He wasn't used to crying. He didn't know what to do with his arms. They were just hanging at his sides. His shoulders were shaking.

'What letters are you talking about, Fayed? What have you done? *Fayed, what have you done?*'

Suddenly he stormed across the floor and bent down over his brother. He put his hands to his cheeks. Fayed's moustache, the great big ridiculous moustache that he had recently grown, tickled his skin as he stroked his brother's face, again and again.

'What have you done this time?' he whispered.

But his brother didn't answer, because he was dead.

10

It was just gone two o'clock when Helen Bentley came back into the kitchen. She looked awful. Six hours' sleep and a long shower had worked wonders for her in the morning, but now she was deathly pale. Her eyes were glazed and she had moon-shaped bags under her eyes. She sank heavily down on to a chair, and greedily took the coffee that Johanne offered her.

'The New York Stock Exchange opens in an hour and a half.' She sighed and drank some coffee. 'It's going to be a black Thursday, perhaps the worst since the thirties.'

'Have you found anything out?' Johanne asked tentatively.

'I've got some kind of overview. It's clear that our friends in Saudi Arabia were not so friendly after all. There are persistent rumours that they're behind it, together with Iran. Without anyone in my administration admitting anything, of course.'

She forced a smile. Her lips were nearly as pale as the rest of her face.

'Which means that Warren must've sold out to the Arabs,' Johanne said, still speaking quietly.

The President nodded and put a hand over her eyes. She sat like this for a few moments, before suddenly looking up and saying: 'I just can't work out how all this fits together without logging on to my secured pages in the White House. I'll have to use my own code. And even then there will still be a lot that I can't access as I need other equipment. But I have to find out if Warren has been burnt. I have to find out how much my people know about all this before making any sound. If they don't know anything about his—'

'He's in full swing here in Norway,' Johanne said. 'I would have known if anything had happened to him. If he'd been arrested or anything like that, I mean.'

She paused for a moment, and looked over at her mobile. 'Or at least, I think I would.'

'But that doesn't necessarily mean anything,' the President said. 'If they know that he's involved, they may just as easily feel that it's expedient to keep him on his toes. But if they *don't* know . . .' she took a deep breath, 'then it might be dangerous to have him running around freely when I raise the alarm. I have to get into my pages. I just have to do it.'

'It'll only take them a few seconds to discover you,' Johanne said, with some scepticism. 'They'll see the IP address and find out that the computer is here. And then Armageddon will break loose.'

'Yes. Could it . . . No. I don't need a long time, really. Just a couple of hours, I hope.'

The door to the sitting room opened and Hanne Wilhelmsen rolled in.

'An hour's nap here and there,' she said and yawned. 'It actually makes you feel quite rested. Have you managed to make any headway?'

She looked at Helen Bentley.

'A fair bit. But now I've got a problem. I have to access my secured pages, but if I use your computer, that will immediately tell them that I'm alive, and not only that, where I am.'

Hanne sniffed and wiped her nose with her finger.

'A problem, hmm. What should we do?'

'My computer,' Johanne said, surprised at herself, and raised her finger. 'What about using that?'

'Your computer?'

'Do you have a computer? Here?'

The other two looked warily at her.

'It's in the car,' Johanne said eagerly. 'And it's registered with the University of Oslo. They would, of course, also be able to trace the IP address there, but it would take longer to . . . They would have to contact the university first, then they would have to find out who the laptop had been lent to, and then they would

371

have to establish where I was. And in fact . . .' she looked guiltily at her mobile phone again, 'Adam is the only one who knows,' she finished, subdued. 'And he doesn't really know either.'

'Do you know,' the President said. 'I think that's a good idea. I don't need more than a couple of hours. And that is presumably the amount of time we can buy by using another computer.'

Hanne was the only one who was still sceptical.

'I don't know a lot about IP addresses and things like that,' she said. 'But is either of you absolutely certain that this will work? That it's not the line itself that's traced?'

Johanne and Helen Bentley exchanged looks.

'I'm not certain,' the President said. 'I simply have to take that chance. Could you get it?'

'Of course,' Johanne said and got up. 'I'll only be five minutes.'

As the front door closed, Helen Bentley sat down on the chair beside Hanne's wheelchair. She seemed to be struggling to find the right words. Hanne looked at her with an expressionless face, as if she had all the time in the world.

'Hannah. Do you . . . You said you were a retired policewoman. Do you have a gun in the house?'

Hanne rolled away from the table.

'A gun? What do you want—'

'Shhh,' the President said. There was a hint of authority in her voice that made Hanne stiffen. 'Please. I'd rather Johanne didn't know about this. I wouldn't like my one-year-old to be in the same flat as a loaded gun. Of course, I don't think it will be necessary to use it. But you must remember that—'

'Do you know why I'm sitting here? Has the thought never occurred to you? I'm sitting in this bloody wheelchair because I was shot. My spine was destroyed by a bullet. I don't exactly have a good relationship with guns.'

'Hannah! *Hannah! Listen to me!*'

Hanne tightened her lips and looked straight at Helen Bentley.

'I am normally one of the world's best-guarded people,' the President almost whispered, as if she was frightened that Johanne might already be back. 'I have heavily armed bodyguards with me everywhere, all the time. That's not for no reason, Hannah. It is absolutely necessary. The moment that it's known that I'm here in this flat, I will be completely defenceless. Until the right people get here, and then I'll be protected by them again. But until then, I have to be able to defend myself. I know you'll understand, if you just think about it.'

Hanne was the first one to look away.

'I do have a gun,' she said eventually. 'And ammunition. I never had those heavy steel cupboards removed, and they . . . Are you any good?'

The President gave a shy smile.

'My teachers might say otherwise. But I can handle a gun. I'm the commander-in-chief, remember?'

Hanne was still staring at the table without expression.

'One more thing,' Helen Bentley said, and laid her hand on Hanne's arm. 'I think it's best if you all leave. Leave the flat, in case something happens.'

Hanne lifted her head and stared at the President with a look of exaggerated disbelief. Then she started to laugh. She threw her head back and roared with laughter.

'Good luck,' she hiccuped. 'I will *not* be budged. And as for Mary, she lives with a radius of about thirty metres. You will never, and I repeat *never*, get her to leave this flat. I occasionally manage to convince her to go down into the cellar, but you won't be able to do that. And as for—'

'Here you go,' Johanne said, out of breath. 'It's full summer outside, by the way!'

She put her laptop down on the kitchen table. With practised hands, she plugged in the external mouse, laid down a mat, put the plug in a socket and turned on the machine.

'*Voilà!*' she said and logged on. 'There you go, Madam President. A computer that it will take time to trace!'

She was so excited that she didn't notice Hanne's worried face as she reversed out from the table, turned round and rolled off into the flat. The rubber wheels squeaked on the parquet floor. The sound vanished when a door was shut, somewhere deep in the heart of the enormous flat.

11

The young man who was sitting in front of a monitor in a tiny office close to the Situation Room in the White House noticed that the characters and numbers were starting to dance on the screen. He closed his eyes hard, shook his head and tried again. It was still difficult to focus on one row, one column. He gave his neck a massage. The stringent smell of old sweat rose up from his armpits and made him drop his arms in shame and hope that no one would come in.

This wasn't what he had gone to university for. When he got a job at the White House, two years after qualifying as a computer engineer and having worked in the commercial sector, he couldn't believe his luck. Now, five months on, he was already bored. He had demonstrated his abilities in the small computer company that had headhunted him after graduation, and had thought that it was his indisputable talents as a programmer that had made the Bentley administration poach him.

But now, nearly six months later, he felt he had been little more than a runner.

And he had been sitting in a stuffy room with no windows, sweating and stinking, for twenty-three hours, staring at codes that flickered on the screen. He had been asked to create some kind of order in the chaos. It was important that he kept focused.

He pressed his fingers against his eyes.

He was so exhausted that he was no longer sleepy. It was as if his brain had just stopped. It didn't want to do any more. He felt like his own hard disk had logged out and left the rest of his body to fend for itself. His hands felt numb and a stabbing pain in his lower back had been bothering him for hours.

He breathed out slowly, and opened his eyes as wide as he could to try to get some moisture. He should really get something more to drink, but it was another quarter of an hour before he could take a break. He must try to have a shower.

There. There was something there.

Something.

He blinked and his fingers moved like lightning across the keyboard. The screen froze. He lifted a reluctant hand and ran his index finger along a row from left to right, before he started to hammer on the keyboard again.

Another screen came up.

It couldn't be true.

It *was* true, and he was the one who had seen it. He had discovered before anyone else, and suddenly he didn't regret switching jobs any more. Once again his fingers moved busily over the keyboard. Then he pressed Print, grabbed the phone and waited in suspense for the next screen.

'She's alive,' he whispered, forgetting to breathe. 'She's fucking alive!'

12

'This is the most beautiful place in the whole of Oslo,' Adam Stubo said, and pointed to a simple bench by the water. 'I think we could both do with a bit of air.'

Summer had ambushed the city. The temperature had risen by nearly ten degrees in the course of twenty-four hours. The sun blasted the sky in an explosion of white light. The leaves on the trees along the banks of the Aker River seemed to have turned a darker shade of green in that time alone, and there was so much pollen in the air that Adam's eyes started to run as soon as they got out of the car.

'Is this a park?' Warren Scifford asked without any real interest. 'A big park?'

'No. This is the edge of the city. Or the start of the forest, whichever way you want to look at it. This is where the two meet, trees and houses. Lovely, isn't it? Sit yourself down.'

Warren looked at the dirty bench with suspicion. Adam produced a hanky and wiped away the remains of the national-day celebrations. A patch of hardened chocolate ice cream, a stripe of ketchup and something he'd rather not guess at.

'There. Sit down.'

He took two enormous rolls and two cans of Diet Coke out of a plastic bag.

'Have to think about my weight,' he said, putting it all down on the bench between them. 'I actually prefer regular Coke. *The real thing.* But you know . . .'

He patted his stomach. Warren said nothing. He didn't touch the food. Instead he sat watching three Canada geese. A small dog, which was half the size of the largest bird, was being chased around on the grassy bank down by the water. It seemed to be enjoying itself. Every time the biggest goose chased it away with

377

a snapping beak, the swift little beast spun round and zigzagged its way back.

'Don't you want any?' Adam asked with his mouth full.

Warren still didn't say anything.

'Listen,' Adam said and swallowed. 'I've been given the job of following you around. It's becoming more and more obvious that you're not particularly keen on telling me anything at all. Or perhaps I should say us. Keeping us informed. So can't we just . . .' he took another big bite of his roll, 'enjoy ourselves instead?'

The words disappeared in the food.

The dog had got bored, and no longer cared about the hissing geese. Instead it was scurrying around on the bank with its nose on the ground, heading towards Maridalsvannet.

Adam continued eating in silence. Warren turned his face to the sun, rested his left foot on his right knee and closed his eyes against the bright light.

'What's up?' Adam asked when he'd finished his roll and eaten half of Warren's.

He crumpled up the plastic wrappers and put them in the bag, then opened one of the cans and took a drink. 'What's up with you?' he repeated and tried to swallow a burp.

Warren still didn't move.

'As you like,' Adam said, taking out a pair of sunglasses from his breast pocket.

'There's a monster out there,' Warren said, without changing position.

'There are lots of them.' Adam nodded. 'Far too many, if you ask me.'

'There's one that wants to break us.'

'Uhum . . .'

'He's already started. The problem is that I don't know how he intends to continue. And there's no one who'll listen to me.'

Adam tried to find a more comfortable position on the wooden bench. For a moment he put his foot on his knee, like Warren.

But his stomach protested against being squashed, and he put his foot down again.

'I'm sitting here,' he said. 'My ears are open.'

Finally, Warren smiled. He shaded his eyes with his hand and looked around.

'It really is beautiful here,' he said quietly. 'How's Johanne?'

'Well . . . she's very well.'

Adam rummaged around in the plastic bag and produced a bar of chocolate. He opened it and offered it to Warren.

'No thanks. With my hand on my heart, I can say that she was the best, brightest student I ever had.'

Adam looked at the chocolate. Then he wrapped the paper around it again and put it back in the bag.

'Johanne's very well,' he repeated. 'We had a daughter last winter. A healthy, lovely little girl. And other than that, I think we should change the subject, Warren.'

'Is it that bad? Is she still . . .?'

Adam took off his sunglasses.

'Yes, it's that bad. I don't want to talk to you about Johanne. It would be fundamentally disloyal. And in any case, I just don't want to. OK?'

'Of course.'

The American bowed slightly and opened his hands.

'My greatest weakness,' he said with a tight-lipped smile. 'Women.'

Adam didn't know what to say to that. He started to wonder whether the outing had been a good idea. An hour earlier, when Warren had appeared at Peter Salhus' office without warning and without really having anything to tell, Adam had thought that a break in their usual routine might help them to get talking again.

But he certainly did not want to talk about Johanne.

'You know,' Warren continued. 'Sometimes when I lie awake at night and sweat, thinking about the mistakes I've made in my life, it strikes me that they are all related to women. And now I find myself in a situation where, if President Bentley is not

379

found alive, my career is over. A woman holds my destiny in her hands.'

He gave a demonstrative sigh.

'Women. I don't understand them. They are irresistible and incomprehensible.'

Adam realised he was grinding his teeth. He concentrated on not doing it. It was almost impossible, and he stroked his cheek with his hand to try to relax it.

'You don't agree,' Warren laughed.

'No.' Adam sat up abruptly. 'No,' he repeated. 'I find very, very few of them irresistible. Most of them are very easy to understand. Not always, not all the time, but generally. But . . .' he threw open his arms and looked completely the other way, 'that also means that you have to see them as equals.'

'*Touché*,' Warren said and gave the sun a broad smile. 'Very politically correct. Very . . . Scandinavian.'

A ringtone interrupted the sound of birdsong and running water. Adam felt all his pockets to locate his phone.

'Hello,' he barked, when he finally found it.

'Adam?'

'Yes.'

'It's Peter.'

'Sorry?'

'Peter Salhus.'

'Oh, right. Hello.'

Adam was about to get up and move away from the bench when he suddenly remembered that Warren didn't speak Norwegian.

'Anything new?' he asked.

'Yes. But between you and me, Adam. Can I have your word?'

'Of course. What is it?'

'Without going into any details, I have to admit that we have . . . Well, we've got a fairly good idea about what's going on at the American embassy. Let's put it that way.'

Pause.

They're tapping them, Adam thought to himself and grabbed

380

the half-empty can of Coke. They've tapped an allied embassy on Norwegian soil. What the hell . . .

'They think the President is alive, Adam.'

Adam's pulse increased a hint. He coughed and tried to keep a straight face. Just to be on the safe side, he turned away from Warren.

'And where is she?'

'Well, that's the whole point. They believe that the President has accessed websites that she needs a code to get into. Either it's her, or someone else has managed to get her to give them the codes. And even if the latter is true, it would still mean that she's alive.'

'But . . . I don't quite . . .'

'They've traced her to your wife's IP address. But luckily they don't know that yet.'

'Joh—'

He stopped. He didn't want to say her name when Warren might hear.

'They traced an IP address to a computer that belongs to the university. Now they're arguing with the management up there to find out who uses the machine. We think we managed to delay them a bit, but not for that long. But I thought . . . I'll get Bastesen to send a patrol car out to your house, just in case. If there's any truth in these rumours that the FBI has taken the law into their own hands, you know. And if I was you, I'd go home.'

'Yes . . . Of course. Thank you.'

He finished the conversation, without it crossing his mind that the patrol car should be sent somewhere else. Johanne wasn't at home. She and Ragnhild were somewhere in Frogner. At an address he didn't know.

He stood up in a rush.

'I have to go,' he said and started to walk.

He left the plastic bag and unopened can of Coke on the bench behind him. Warren stared at the rubbish in surprise before running after Adam.

'What is it?' he asked when he caught up with him.

'I'll drop you off in town, OK? There something I have to sort out.'

His heavy body quivered as he started to run towards the car. Just as he was getting in, Warren's phone rang. His answers were brief: yes and no. After about a minute and a half, he hung up. When Adam took his eyes off the road for a second and looked at the American, he got a shock. Warren was ashen, his mouth was open and it looked like his eyes were about to disappear into his skull.

'They think they've found the President,' he said in a flat voice and put his mobile phone back in his breast pocket.

Adam changed gear and pulled out on to the main road.

'Circumstances might indicate that she's with Johanne,' Warren continued in the same flat voice. 'Are we on our way back to your house?'

Shit, Adam thought in desperation. How have they managed to do that already? Couldn't you have delayed them any longer?

'I'll drop you off in town,' he said. 'You can make your own way from there.'

With one hand on the wheel, driving up Maridalsveien at full speed, he tried to call Salhus back. The phone just rang and rang until an answering machine came on.

'Peter, it's Adam,' he barked. 'Call me straight away. Immediately, d'you hear?'

The best thing would probably be to take the ring road to Smestad. Snaking down through town at this time of day would take for ever. He swung the car on to the roundabout over Ring 3 and accelerated westwards.

'Listen,' Warren said quietly. 'I'll let you in on a secret.'

'About time you started to tell me something,' Adam muttered, but he was barely listening.

'I'm at loggerheads with my own people. And it's about to blow.'

'D'you know what, I'm sure you can talk to someone about that, just not me.'

He switched lanes to overtake a lorry and nearly collided with a small Fiat that got in the way. He swore angrily, swerved round the Fiat and accelerated again.

'If you're on your way to Johanne now,' Warren tried, 'then you should take me with you. It's a very dangerous situation, to put it mildly, and I—'

'You won't be coming.'

'Adam! *Adam!*'

Adam slammed on the brakes. Warren, who hadn't put his seatbelt on, was thrown on to the dashboard. He just had time to put his arms out in front of him. Adam let the car roll on to the hard shoulder just by the toll booths below Rikshospitalet.

'What?' he roared at the American. 'What the fuck do you want?'

'You can't go alone. I'm warning you. For your own sake.'

'Get out. Get out of the car. Now.'

'Now? Here? On the motorway?'

'Yes.'

'You don't mean it, Adam. Now listen—'

'Get out!'

'Listen to me!'

There was a hint of desperation in his voice. Adam tried to breathe regularly. He gripped the wheel with both hands. All he wanted to do was punch the American.

'Like I just said in the park. I'm an idiot when it comes to women. I've done so many . . .' He held his breath for a long time. When he started to talk again, it all came out in a rush. 'But do you doubt my abilities as an FBI agent? Do you think incompetence would have got me where I am today? Do you really believe that it's wise for you to go alone into a situation about which you know nothing, rather than taking an agent with thirty years' experience with you to back you up? And what's more, I've got a gun.'

Adam bit his lip. He exchanged a brief look with Warren, put the car into first gear and pulled out into the road again. He rang

Johanne's number. She didn't answer. The answerphone didn't kick in.

'Fuck,' he said through clenched teeth and rang 1881. 'Fucking bastard hell.'

'Excuse me,' said a voice on the other end. 'What did you say?'

'An address in Oslo, please. Hanne Wilhelmsen. Krusesgate, what number?'

The woman replied curtly after a few seconds.

As they took the exit from the ring road to Smestad, he called another number. This time it was the central switchboard.

He had no intention of going into a dangerous situation alone.

But nor did he have any intention of taking with him a foreign national, whom he now knew he disliked.

Intensely.

13

Helen Lardahl Bentley was more confused after she had read the secured pages than she had been before. There was so much that didn't make sense. The BSC Unit had obviously been pushed to one side. That might, of course, be because they had realised what Warren was up to. The heads of the FBI might think that it was wise not to confront him with it, yet at the same time they wanted to marginalise his potential to manipulate the investigation. But she still couldn't work out why the profile that Warren and his men had developed was being so discredited by the rest of the system. The document seemed to be incredibly thorough. It correlated with everything they had initially feared when the first vague suggestions about the Trojan Horse had reached the FBI only six weeks ago.

The profile frightened her more than anything else she found.

But there was something that wasn't right.

On the one hand, it seemed that everyone agreed that an attack on the US was imminent. On the other hand, none of the powerful organisations under the Homeland Security umbrella had found anything that would indicate links to existing or known organisations. It was as if they were clutching at straws. Jeffrey Hunter's money could be traced to the cousin of the Saudi Arabian oil minister and to a consultancy firm he owned in Iran, but that was that. She couldn't see that anyone had got any further, and she turned hot and cold when it started to dawn on her just how hard the American government, led by her own vice president, had hit out at the two Arab countries. Without decoding equipment, she couldn't get in to the pages where the actual correspondence was saved, but she had started to comprehend the scale of the catastrophe towards which her country was headed.

She was sitting in an office at the far end of the flat.

When the doorbell rang, she only just heard it. It rang again. She listened. It rang a third time. Quietly she got up and picked up the gun that Hanne had found and loaded for her. She left the gun locked, put it inside her waistband, and pulled her sweater down over it.

Something was terribly wrong.

14

Warren Scifford and Adam Stubo were standing outside the door to Hanne Wilhelmsen's flat in Krusesgate, arguing at the tops of their voices.

'We'll wait,' Adam said, furious. 'A patrol car will be here any second!'

Warren pulled his arm out of the Norwegian's firm grip.

'It's *my* president,' he hissed back. 'It is *my* responsibility to find out if *my country's* top leader is behind that door. *My life depends on it, Adam!* She is the only one who believes me! No way am I waiting for a gang of trigger-happy uniformed—'

'Hello,' said a hoarse voice. 'Who's that?'

The door opened ten centimetres or so. At about face height there was a taut steel safety chain, and an old woman stared out at them with wild, wide-open eyes.

'Don't open it,' Adam said immediately. 'Please, woman, please close the door now!'

Warren kicked the door. The woman jumped back with a stream of oaths. The chain was still intact. Adam grabbed hold of Warren's jacket, but it slipped out of his hand and he lost his balance. He made a desperate attempt to grab Warren's trouser leg, but the older man was much fitter. When he pulled his leg loose, he also planted a powerful foot right in Adam's groin, which made the Norwegian collapse and black out. The old woman inside stopped her carry-on when another kick to the door made the chain come loose. The door flew open and hit the woman, who was thrown backwards and landed on a shoe rack.

Warren stormed in with his gun in his hand. He stopped by the first door and pulled himself in to the wall before shouting: 'Helen! Helen! Madam President, are you there?'

No one answered. With his gun raised, he moved on and went into the next room.

It was a large sitting room. There was a woman in a wheelchair sitting by the window. She didn't move and her face was expressionless. However, he did notice that she was looking at a door at the back of the big room. There was another woman sitting on the sofa, with her back to him and a child on her lap. She pulled the child tightly to her and looked terrified.

The child wailed.

'Warren.'

Madam President came in.

'Thank God,' Warren said and took two steps closer as he put his gun back in its holster. 'Thank God you're alive!'

'Stay where you are.'

'What?'

He stopped instantly when she pulled out a gun and pointed it at him.

'Madam President,' he whispered. 'It's me! Warren!'

'You betrayed me. You betrayed America.'

'Me? I haven't—'

'How did you find out about the abortion, Warren? How could you use that against me, you who—'

'Helen . . .'

He tried to move closer, but quickly stepped back when she raised the gun again and said: 'I was tricked to leave the hotel by a letter.'

'I swear . . . I don't know what you're talking about!'

'Hands above your head, Warren.'

'I—'

'Put your hands above your head!'

He reluctantly put his hands in the air.

'*Verus amicus rara avis*,' Helen Bentley said. 'That's how the letter was signed. No one else knows about the inscription. Only you and me, Warren. Just us.'

'*I lost the watch! It was . . . stolen! I . . .*'

The child was screaming like it was possessed.

'Joanna,' the President said. 'Take your daughter with you and go into Hannah's office. Now.'

Johanne got up and ran across the room. She didn't even look in the man's direction.

'If your watch was stolen, Warren, what is that you're wearing on your left arm?'

She cocked the gun.

In slow motion, as if to avoid provoking a reaction, he turned his head to look. His sweater had slid down his arms when he raised his hands. He was wearing a watch around his wrist, an Omega Oyster with diamonds for numbers and an inscription on the back.

'It's . . . You see . . . I thought it was . . .'

He let his hands fall.

'Don't,' the President warned him. 'Lift them up again.'

He looked at her. His arms were hanging loosely by his sides. His palms were open and he started to lift them towards her in a peremptory, pleading gesture.

Madam President fired.

The bang made Hanne Wilhelmsen jump. The echo thundered in her ears and she felt her hearing vanish into a drawn-out whistling sound for a few seconds. Warren Scifford lay motionless on his back on the floor, with his face up. She rolled over to him and put her finger on his pulse. Then she sat up and shook her head.

Warren smiled and raised his eyebrow, as if he had thought of something amusing at the moment of death, an irony that no one else could share.

Adam Stubo stood in the doorway. He was holding his balls and his face was white. When he saw the dead body, he groaned and stumbled forward.

'Who are you?' the President asked calmly; she was still standing in the middle of the room with the gun in her hand.

'He's a good guy,' Hanne said, quick as a flash. 'Police. Johanne's husband. Don't . . .'

The President raised her gun and handed it to Adam by the butt.

'Then it's best that you look after this. And if it's not too much bother, I'd like to phone my embassy now.'

The noise of sirens grew in the distance.

And got louder and louder.

15

Al Muffet carried his dead brother down into the cellar and put the body in an old chest that had presumably been in the house since it was built. It wasn't long enough. Al had to put Fayed in sideways, bending his knees and neck, like a foetus. Having to pull and struggle with the body repulsed him, but he finally managed to force the lid down again. His brother's suitcase was at the back of the cupboard under the stairs. Neither Fayed nor his belongings would be staying there for very long. The most important thing was to remove all traces before the girls came home from school. His daughters did not need to see their dead uncle. Nor their father being arrested. He had to send them away. He could make the excuse of an unexpected conference or an important meeting out of town, and arrange for them to stay with their dead mother's sister in Boston. They were too young to stay at home on their own.

Then he would ring the police.

But first he had to make sure that the girls had somewhere to stay.

The biggest problem was the car that Fayed had hired. It took Al a long time to find the keys. They were under the bed. Maybe they had been lying on the bedside table, and had been knocked off when he was trying to get Fayed to tell what he knew about the disappearance of President Bentley.

Al Muffet sat on the steps outside his picturesque New England house with his face in his hands.

What have I done? What if I made a mistake? What if this is all due to an arbitrary and fatal misunderstanding? Why didn't you say anything, Fayed? Couldn't you just have answered me before it was too late?

He could drive the car into the old, dilapidated barn. The girls had no reason to go there; as far as he knew, no wild cats had had any kittens recently. Only kittens could tempt Louise into the barn, which was full of spiders and webs that normally scared the life out of her.

He wasn't even able to cry. An icy claw was hooked somewhere just inside his breast bone, which made it difficult to think and impossible to speak.

But who would he speak to anyway? he thought, emotionally drained. Who could help him now?

He tried to straighten his back and take a deep breath.

The flag on the postbox had been raised.

Fayed had talked about a letter.

Letters.

He could barely manage to stand up. He should move the car, remove all traces of Fayed Muffasa, and then pull himself together so he could welcome his daughters home from school. It was three o'clock, and certainly Louise was going to be home early.

His legs could only just carry him as he walked down the drive. He looked around. There was no sign of human life anywhere, except the hum of a motor saw somewhere far in the distance.

He opened the postbox. Two bills and three identical envelopes.

Fayed Muffasa, c/o Al Muffet.

Then the address. Three identical, thickish envelopes that had been sent to Fayed, at Al's address.

His mobile phone rang. He put the letters back in the postbox and stared at the display. Unknown number. No one had phoned him during this horrible day. He didn't want to speak to anyone. He wasn't sure that he even had a voice any more. He put the phone back into his breast pocket, took the letters from the postbox and started to walk slowly back towards the house.

The person who was calling didn't give up.

He stopped when he got to the steps and sat down.

He had to galvanise his energy to move the damned car.

The telephone kept ringing and ringing. He couldn't bear the noise any more; the high, shrill tone made him shiver. He pressed the button with the green phone.

'Hello,' he said. His voice was barely there. 'Hello?'

'Ali? Ali Shaeed?'

He said nothing.

'Ali, it's me. Helen Lardahl.'

'Helen,' he whispered. 'How did . . .'

He hadn't watched TV. He hadn't listened to the radio. He hadn't been near his computer. All he had done all day was despair over his dead brother and try to work out what kind of a life his girls would have after this.

Finally, he started to cry.

'Ali, listen to me. I'm on a plane, crossing the Atlantic. That's why the connection is bad.'

'I didn't let you down,' he shouted. 'I promised you I would never tell anyone, and I haven't broken that promise.'

'I believe you,' she said calmly. 'But you realise that we're going to have to investigate this. And the first thing I want you to do is—'

'It was my brother,' he said. 'My brother spoke to my mother on her deathbed, and . . .'

He stopped and held his breath. He could hear the hum of an engine in the distance. A cloud of dust rose behind the hillock with maple trees. A dull, rotating noise made him turn to the west. A helicopter was circling over the trees. The pilot was obviously looking for a place to land.

'Listen to me,' Helen Bentley said. 'Listen to me!'

'Yes,' Al Muffet said and stood up. 'I'm listening.'

'The FBI are coming. Don't be frightened. OK? They got their orders directly from me. They're coming to talk to you. Tell them everything. If you're not involved in this, everything will be fine. I promise you.'

A black car swung into the drive and drove slowly up towards the house.

393

'Don't be frightened, Ali. Just tell them what there is to tell.'

The phone was cut off.

The car stopped. Two dark-suited men got out. One smiled and held out his hand as he approached.

'Al Muffet, I presume!'

Al took his hand, which was warm and firm.

'I hear that you're a friend of Madam President,' the agent said and did not let go of his hand. 'And a friend of the President's is a friend of mine. Shall we go inside?'

'I think,' Al Muffet said, and swallowed, 'I think that you should take care of these.'

He handed him the three envelopes. The man looked at them without giving anything away, and then took them by the corner between his fingers and indicated to his colleague to find a plastic bag.

'Fayed Muffasa,' he read quickly, his head cocked. Then he looked up. 'Who's that?'

'My brother. He's in a chest in the cellar. I killed him.'

The FBI agent looked at him, long and hard.

'I think it's best we go in,' he said and patted Al Muffet on the shoulder. 'Seems there's a lot to sort out.'

The helicopter had landed and all was quiet again.

16

There was only one hour left of Thursday the 19th of May 2005. The intense summer heat had lasted the whole day, leaving a balmy, still evening in its wake. Johanne had opened all the windows in the sitting room. She had had a bath with Ragnhild, who was exhausted and had fallen asleep happily as soon as she was put down in her own familiar bed. Johanne felt almost as euphoric as the one-year-old. Coming home felt like purification. Just walking through the front door had almost made her cry with relief. They had been held by the PST for so long that Adam had eventually called Peter Salhus and threatened to rip up the pile of confidentiality papers they had signed if they weren't allowed to go home immediately.

'I think we can forget the idea of any more children,' Adam said, as he padded, flat-footed, over the floor, dressed in only a pair of wide pyjama bottoms, which had been cut open at the groin, just in case. 'I don't think I've ever experienced anything so painful in all my life.'

'You should try giving birth.' Johanne smiled and patted the place next to her on the sofa. 'The doctor said you'd be OK. See if it's comfortable to sit down here.'

'. . . *proved to be a conspiracy in America's own ranks. At a press conference at Gardermoen, President Bentley stated . . .*'

The TV had been on since they got home.

'They don't know for certain yet,' Johanne said. 'That there are only Americans involved, I mean.'

'That's the truth they want us to know. The most convenient truth right now. It's the truth that will allow oil prices to fall, in other words.'

Adam lowered himself down on to the sofa as carefully as he could, and sat with his legs wide open.

'. . . *following a dramatic shoot-out in Krusesgate in Oslo, where the American FBI agent Warren Scifford . . .*'

The picture they showed must have been his passport photograph. He looked like a criminal, with a surly expression and half-closed eyes.

'. . . *was shot and killed by a Norwegian intelligence officer who has not been named. Sources at the American embassy in Norway have said that the plot involved only a very small number of people, and that all of these are now being questioned by the authorities.*'

'The most impressive thing, really, is that they managed to cook up this story so quickly,' Johanne said. 'Especially the fact that the President wasn't kidnapped at all, but had "disappeared" in order to help uncover the planned assassination. Do they have scenarios like that ready, just in case?'

'Maybe. But I doubt it. We'll witness a masterful smokescreen over the next few days. And if they don't have the stories there already, they certainly have experts in the field. They'll put something together and tighten all the nuts and bolts, so that in the end they have a story that most people will be happy with. And then the conspiracy theories will follow. This will be a feast for the paranoid. But no one listens to them. And so the world will continue to limp on, until it's no longer possible to know what's true and what's false, and no one is that bothered any more. It's easiest that way. For everyone. Bloody hell, that hurts!'

He winced.

'. . . *expected that President Bentley, who will arrive back in the States in a few hours, will offer an unconditional apology to Saudi Arabia and Iran. The American people have been informed that she will give a speech tomorrow morning at . . .*'

'Turn it off,' Adam said and put his arm round Johanne.

He kissed her on the temple.

'We've heard enough. It's all just stories and lies anyway. I can't be bothered.'

She picked up the remote control. There was quiet in the room. She snuggled in to him and gently stroked his hairy arms.

They sat like this for a long time, and she breathed in Adam's smell and was happy that summer had finally made an appearance.

'Johanne,' Adam said quietly. She was nearly asleep.

'What?'

'I want to know what Warren did to you.'

She didn't answer. But she didn't pull away either, as she always had done before, at the slightest mention of the hornets' nest that had hung between them since they met on a warm spring day almost exactly five years ago. She didn't hold her breath, or turn away. He couldn't see her face, but he didn't feel that she had closed up and was pursing her lips tight, as she normally did.

'I think it's time,' he said and put his mouth to her ear. 'It's high time, Johanne.'

She took a deep breath.

'I was only twenty-three, and we were in DC to . . .'

It was three in the morning by the time they went to bed.

The new day had just started to peek over the trees to the east, and Adam would never know that he wasn't the first to share Johanne's painful secret.

It didn't matter, she thought.

The first was the President of the United States of America, and they would never meet her again.

Friday 20 May 2005

When the news that President Bentley was still alive had made its way round the world on Thursday evening, European time, Abdallah al-Rahman had stopped all his usual activities and locked himself away in his office in the east wing.

It was now nearly six in the morning. He didn't feel particularly tired, despite having been awake all night. He had tried to take a nap several times, on the low divan in front of the plasma screen, but a growing unease had kept him awake.

The President was about to land at an unspecified military base in the US. The CNN reporters were all talking over each other in their eagerness to guess where it was. The US Air Force photographers and cameramen who sent the images to TV channels all over the world, were extremely careful to avoid showing any of the surroundings or buildings that might indicate where the President was to touch American soil again.

It wasn't over yet.

Without turning off the television, Abdallah sat down in front of his computer.

He typed in a number of search words, for the sixth time in six hours. Several thousand hits came up on the screen, so he narrowed down the search, which meant that he only got a few hundred. He was uncertain, but then he added yet another word in the search field.

Five articles.

He scrolled quickly through four of them. Nothing of interest there.

The fifth told him that the Trojan Horse attack would never take place.

He realised that after scanning only the first few lines, but forced himself to read the whole article three times before logging out and turning off the computer.

He went back to the divan, lay down and closed his eyes.

The FBI had swooped on a small town in Maine, with helicopters and lots of men. Local reporters had made a speculative link between the operation and the Helen Bentley case, and within the hour, the place was surrounded by journalists from all over the state. However, the local police soon assured people that the incident was in no way related. They had been working with the FBI for some time now, trying to catch a gang who were trapping endangered birds for sale on the black market. A local vet had been very helpful to the investigation. Unfortunately, one of the gang had been killed during the raid, but the police now had everything under control. The article included a photograph of the vet, who was so like Fayed that only the moustache would distinguish them.

Fayed had let him down.

Fayed was supposed to launch the attack, following the instructions in the coded letters that Abdallah had had to sacrifice three couriers to send.

Fayed was dead and Madam President was back in place.

Abdallah al-Rahman opened his eyes and got up from the divan. He started methodically to pull the pins out of the map. He sorted them by colour. They could be used again later.

There was a knock on the door.

He was surprised, given what time it was. But he opened the door. His youngest son was standing outside, dressed in his riding clothes. He was inconsolable.

'Father,' Rashid cried. 'I was going to go with the others for a morning ride. But then I fell off and the others just rode on. They say I'm too little, and . . .'

The boy sobbed and showed his father a graze above his elbow.

'There, there,' Abdallah said, and hunkered down in front of his son. 'You'll just have to try again, that's all. You'll never

402

manage to do anything if you don't try and try again. I'll come with you. Let's go for a ride together.

'Yes, but . . . I'm bleeding, Daddy!'

'Rashid,' Abdallah said, blowing on the wound. 'We don't give up just because we've had a minor defeat. It hurts for a while, but then we try again. Until we succeed. Do you understand?'

The boy nodded and dried his tears.

Abdallah took his son by the hand. As he was about to shut the door behind them, his eyes fell on the big map of America. The odd coloured pinhead could still be seen, stuck in at an angle, in a webbed pattern with no system or structure.

He stood there, wondering about dates. 2010, he thought to himself. By then I'll be strong enough to try again. By 2010.

'What did you say, Father?'

'Nothing. Come, let's go.'

He had already decided.

Author's note

I have taken liberties with several public figures in this book, putting words into their mouths. I have made every effort to do this with the utmost respect, and hope that I have succeeded.

I have also taken liberties in relation to a specific building in Oslo, Thon Hotel Opera, which is called Hotel Opera in my book. I needed to use the hotel's location in order to tell the story, and have been true to reality with regard to the building's exterior and location. Inside, however, the hotel in this book is entirely the product of my own imagination. The same is true of the hotel employees who feature in the book.

Anne Holt
Larvik, June 2006

PUNISHMENT
Anne Holt

A serial killer is on the loose – a killer of the worst kind. Abducting children and murdering them in an undetectable way that confounds the police, he then returns the child's body to the mother with a desperately cruel note:

'You got what you deserved'.

It is a perplexing and terrible case, and Police Superintendent Adam Stubo is the unlucky man in charge of finding the killer. In desperation he recruits legal researcher Johanne Vik, a woman with an extensive knowledge and understanding of criminal history. So far the killer has abducted three children, but one child has not yet been returned to her mother. Is there a chance she is still alive . . .?

This suspenseful and sophisticated crime novel
is the first in a new series and has already been
a huge bestseller in Europe.

'A thoughtful, tense novel . . . This is the first of a new series.
I look forward to the subsequent ones'
Peter Guttridge, *Observer*

978-0-7515-3714-7

THE FINAL MURDER
Anne Holt

A talk-show star is found killed in her home, her tongue removed and left on her desk, cleaved in two. And when a second body, that of a right-wing party leader, is found crucified to the bedroom wall, Superintendent Adam Stubo is pulled from leave to lead the investigation. Is there a celebrity-slaying serial killer on the loose?

Adam's partner, Johanne Vik, agrees to help with the case but begins to see a pattern, one that traces back to her FBI days. If she's right, the pattern will end in the murder of the investigating officer . . . Adam.

'Anne Holt is the latest crime writer to reveal how truly dark it gets in Scandinavia' Val McDermid

978-0-7515-3715-4

Other bestselling titles available by mail

☐ Punishment   Anne Holt   £6.99

☐ The Final Murder   Anne Holt   £7.99

The prices shown above are correct at time of going to press. However, the publishers reserve the right to increase prices on covers from those previously advertised, without further notice.

―――――――――― sphere ――――――――――

Please allow for postage and packing: **Free UK delivery.**
Europe: add 25% of retail price; Rest of World: 45% of retail price.

To order any of the above or any other Sphere titles, please call our credit card orderline or fill in this coupon and send/fax it to:

Sphere, PO Box 121, Kettering, Northants NN14 4ZQ
Fax: 01832 733076   Tel: 01832 737526
Email: aspenhouse@FSBDial.co.uk

☐ I enclose a UK bank cheque made payable to Sphere for £ . . . .
☐ Please charge £ . . . . . . to my Visa/Delta/Maestro

Expiry Date ☐☐☐☐   Maestro Issue No. ☐☐

NAME (BLOCK LETTERS please) . . . .

ADDRESS . . . .

. . . .

. . . .

Postcode . . . . Telephone . . . .

Signature . . . .

Please allow 28 days for delivery within the UK. Offer subject to price and availability.